For Luca, Alessia and Leo McCormick
For those who came before
and those who will come after.

Contents

Introduction – The Promised Land - Escape from Lithuania

There was an almost irresistible surge of emigrants from Lithuania to the promised lands of America, and Britain in the latter part of the nineteenth century. Whether their adoptive countries came up to their expectations is a moot point. How could the city slums of London or the meat-packing factories of Chicago possibly compare with the unpolluted and beautiful environment of the Lithuanian countryside? The main considerations which drove them however were economic, and the powerful need to achieve for their children more than would have been possible at home in a country wanting in wealth and justice.

It is the year 1812 and a French army marches through Europe to attack Russia. In Lithuania, a Russian province, the people try to remain on the sidelines but the peasant Kadišius family is dragged into it. As the story unfolds revealing the everyday lives of succeeding generations we understand what it meant to live in this beautiful but poor, little known country occupied by an alien power.

Years later the peasants are still under the Russian yoke. Poverty, cruel persecution of the Jews and the attempted erasure of Lithuanian culture forces an Exodus from the country of Biblical proportions towards the West. It is a decision not easy for the migrants but one which many have been forced to take. In 1894 Elzbièta, a farm girl, and her sister Juoza, are seeking something better. They set out on their eventful journey through life, by road, train and ship. Arriving in England, the country which has offered them sanctuary, Elzbièta is appalled to discover the teeming slums of London's Stepney, where she is destined to live. The culture shock is great as she quietly battles to retain her identity huddled together with others of her kind in the Lithuanian ghetto. She and her family's trials, throughout the years, are mirrored by world events. They fight against the odds armed with intelligence, humanity, honesty, and a religious faith which is sometimes not without its contradictions. The family progresses despite many setbacks. Between them they make a huge difference to the lives of others. In wartime and peace they are involved in major events as were their Lithuanian ancestors. This story is about the striving of the human soul for something better.

Zillah Moody 2016

In 1763 Internal chaos in Lithuania reached its height. The various national parties appealed for aid alternately to Prussia and Russia, who then partitioned the defenceless country. In 1793 there was a second and in 1795 a third partition of both Poland and Lithuania. The Lithuanian provinces of Kaunas, Vilnius and Gardinas were attributed to Russia. Suvalki was attached to Prussia, who in 1815 ceded it to Russia. Such was the end of Lithuania. This ancient land which in the past had subdued the power of the Teutonic Knights and repulsed the Tartar invasion was sold into bondage like so much merchandise. Nothing remained of her proud traditions. The "Lietuvos Vytis" (Lithuanian Knight), symbol of a glorious past, was relegated together with the Polish Eagle to the dustheap. From that moment the Black Eagle of Russia spread its sombre wings over Lithuania.

In 1795 the greater part of the country was attributed to Russia and it is one of history's ironies that subjugation of the Lithuanian people should have coincided with the French revolution and the fall of the Bastille. The Lithuanians were expelled from office and replaced by a horde of Russian functionaries.

In 1831 a rebellion broke out in Lithuania which was suppressed with ruthless brutality. In 1861 the Russian government decoyed the Lithuanian peasantry by the official abolition of serfdom so that they took little part in the insurrection of 1863.

The Russian General Muraviev then set out to devastate the land. He only asked for forty years to obliterate the Lithuanian national character. In 1864 the name of Lithuania was effaced from the map of the world. All Lithuanians became subjects of the Russian North-Western Provinces.. Kalmucks and Tartars were let loose on the land to put down all manifestations of national sentiment.

By 1894 all remaining hope was quashed. To be eligible for employment on the railways, in the post offices, even to repair the roads one had to be Russian.

Worse still, Russian tyranny extended to the intellectual and spiritual life of the people. The university of Vilnius was closed down and its contents scattered among cities in Russia. With it were suppressed eighteen higher schools run by Jesuits, Basilians and others. Only three large seminaries were left in Lithuania, at Vilnius, Varniai and in Seinei. In the incomplete educational establishment that remained, the Russian language reigned as master. Roman Catholicism was replaced by the Russian Orthodox state religion. Private schools were strictly prohibited. On the other hand a school was founded in every district which had a substantial population. Well-to-do peasants sometimes engaged instructors who went from place to place to teach the children but the school system was notoriously inadequate. Many children could not travel the distances separating their homes from the schools particularly in bad weather, and the task of education fell on the family.

The Russian schools were unsuccessful, since the families and the clergy secretly opposed their influence. The Russian teacher was merely the representative of a foreign bureaucracy speaking a language incomprehensible to the children and evoking no echo in their hearts.

The only schools worthy of the name were the parochial schools in which the Lithuanian clergy taught the children in their mother tongue. But these were closed in 1832 and thereafter the people had to make do with books smuggled in from outside printed in Lithuanian. The family, the hearth of life, had to replace the schools. In many cases the clergy took advantage of religious instruction to foster a patriotic feeling among the children. As soon as the Russians got wind of this they subjected the clergy to a pitiless persecution which reaped a lavish crop of martyrs.

But the most ruthless blow to Lithuanian intellectual life was dealt by the infamous manifesto of 1863 which banished the native language from the schools altogether. The speech which every Lithuanian had learnt at his mother's knee was branded a crime and the Lithuanian child was forced to learn an alien tongue. From that moment on the popular schools were deserted. Only those seeking to curry favour sent their children to them. The Lithuanian was now not even allowed to pray in his own language. Religious instruction now had to be imparted in the privacy of the home. The sculptor Petras Rimša left a touching symbol of a mother at a spinning wheel, at the same time teaching her child.

In 1863 Muraviev banned the use of the Latin alphabet and circulated a Lithuanian grammar in Russian characters. Nothing more could be printed in Lithuanian characters. The country was inundated with Russian writings to replace the forbidden Lithuanian books. Thus the world was confronted with an almost unprecedented spectacle, that of a nation of three million souls dwelling on the soil of their ancestors, yet deprived of the right to use their mother tongue. The soft musical sounds of the native idiom might not be pronounced save behind carefully closed doors with the bolts drawn.

Lithuanian books crossed the frontier as contraband on dark nights. Russian police spies were posted at the portals of churches to seize the prayer-books of the worshippers. In return Lithuanian books printed in Russian characters were gratuitously offered but scornfully rejected by the people.

In less that two years Muraviev had sent 128 persons to the gallows; 972 Lithuanians were condemned to penal servitude and 1,427 exiled to Siberia.

In all some 9,361 persons fell victim to the fury of Russification not to mention the thousands of others who also suffered in some form or another from Russian persecution. Confusion in the administration of justice accompanied the Russian domination. In 1848 Tsar Nicholas I abolished the Lithuanian constitution which had been formed in 1529. In the course of time it had been supplemented and revised. It would have been quite possible to adapt this constitution but the Russian occupants preferred simply to rescind it. The administration of justice became very complicated. In Suvalki which Napoleon had united with the Duchy of Warsaw the Code Napoléon was in force. Elsewhere Russian law prevailed. When serfdom was officially abolished in 1861 no legislation was passed for the new free men. Each commune administered justice as it saw fit. The judges were Russians, who understood hardly anything of the language of the country and were accessible to every kind of corruption. The Suvalki government, which for a time had been attached to Poland, was deprived of jury trial. The inhabitants of the country were not equal in the eyes of the law, whilst the use of Russian, which many of the litigants did not understand, frequently operated to the detriment of the accused. In this manner the Russians provoked hopeless confusion in the sphere of justice. Disorder resulted from the conflicting Russian law, the Code Napoléon and common law. But the Russian government wished to have all Lithuanian law abolished. It was indifferent to what sort of legislation took its place provided that it was not Lithuanian.

In the wake of the loss of liberty and the mother tongue came the turn of agrarian wealth. The insurrections of 1831 and 1863 provided the Russians with the pretext for expelling many Lithuanians from their small patch of ground. If a single peasant revolted, the entire village was punished and the inhabitants set out on their long and weary march to Siberia.

After their suppression the wealth of the monasteries reverted to the State. Inadequate compensation was assigned to those who had depended upon them and had lost their livings, parish priests, professors and teachers.

An edict of 1865 forbade the Lithuanian aristocracy to acquire landed property. In order to weaken the Catholic nobility they were allowed only to rent land and then only under a lease of not more than twelve years. The same measure was applied in 1894 to Protestants and also to Russians who had married Catholic women.

The peasant who wished to acquire land was obliged to present a certificate of patriotism which was granted to those with whose political attitude the central authorities were satisfied.

In 1870 it was decided that no Lithuanian peasant might receive more than 60 hectares (about 150 acres) of land. A decree of 1889 prohibited the cession of landed property to political and religious chiefs of Lithuania.

In 1892 a new law forbade the acquisition of land by all peasants who had opposed the closing of the churches and the destruction of the latter by dynamite. All these decrees had a terrible effect upon the country. The peasant would no longer attach himself to his strip of ground since he didn't know at what moment his produce might be confiscated by the Russian chinovniks. In these circumstances immense territories fell out of cultivation and the peasants migrated in thousands. Lithuania became a land accursed, and accursed was he whose misfortune it was to dwell therein, since the Russian overlords regarded him as little more than a criminal and an outcast.

The iron hand of Russia may have been able to bend but it could not break the national spirit of the people. All along the frontiers Lithuanian magazines cropped up. Little by little these printed invocations penetrated into the soul of the people and set up vibrations by no means welcome to the Russians. The Russian police agents were everywhere, even in stables and cattle sheds in the hope of finding this prohibited literature. They set up a vigilant watch at the frontiers.

Although they intercepted thousands of illicit publications a highly organised contraband system was able to distribute a large number among the people who read and re-read them surreptitiously. Thousand of journals, prayer books and other pamphlets sent by secret press associations crossed the frontier despite all the law could do to prevent it. Many of these publications were not printed but written by hand and they circulated until they became illegible.

To mock the Russian Government, notoriously stupid, as well as brutal, the larger part of them, printed abroad, bore the name of Vilnius on their title pages, together with the date 1863, the last year of freedom for the Lithuanian press. Posters sprung up overnight and in 1892 many were distributed in broad daylight. The struggle on both sides grew more and more embittered.

In 1904 Russia capitulated, the interdict against Lithuanian printing was removed.

Shortly afterwards the Russian revolution extended to Lithuania but the struggle was not violent thanks to the concessions made by the government on the question of the national language.

Adapted from, Lithuania Past and Present, by E.J.Harrison, 1922

Lithuanian surnames

Lithuanians within families can be distinguished by varying surname forms.

Father / husband	Married woman or widow	Unmarried woman
Paulauskas	Paulauskienė	Paulauskaitė
Bimbirys	Bimbirienė	Bimbirytė
Adamkus	Adamkienė	Adamkutė
Kulėšius	Kulėšienė	Kulėšiūtė
Kadišius	Kadišienė	Kadišiūtė
Kurtinaitis	Kurtinaitienė	Kurtinaitė

Upon arrival abroad these additional endings were usually dropped.

Examples: Mr Kurtinaitis — Mrs Kurtinaitis — Miss Kurtinaitis
              Mr Kadišius   — Mrs Kadišius —— Miss Kadišius

Pronunciation

The Lithuanian   č   is pronounced like **ch** in church.
                  š ————————— **sh** in shall.
                  ž ————————— **z** in azure.
                  j ————————— **y** in you
                  ė ————————— **e** in parqu<u>et</u>
                  ū ————————— **u** in d<u>u</u>ke

Lithuanian terms and diminutives within families.

mama	–	mum	marti	– daughter-in-law
mumija	–	mummy	žentas	– son-in-law
tėtis	–	dad	sūnelis	– sonny
tėvelis	–	daddy	brolis	– brother
senelis	–	grandfather	sesuo	– sister
senis	–	grandad	brolis teisės	– brother-in-law
senelė	–	grandmother	sesuo teisės	– sister-in-law
močiutė	–	granny	labas rytas	– good morning
tevas	–	father	prašom	– please
motina	–	mother	ačiū	– thank you
teta	–	aunt	kazokai	– cossack
tetulė	–	auntie	Rusijos	– Russian
dėdė	–	uncle	Rusai	– Russians
sūnus	–	son	Lenkija	– Poland
dukra	–	daughter	Lenkijos žmonės	– Polish people
pusbrolis	–	cousin	bažnyčia	– church
pusbroliai	–	cousins	katedra	– cathedral

Chapter 1

Cossack – 1813

The bitingly cold harsh bleakness of the barren new year accompanied the disorganised retreat of Napoleon's bedraggled, defeated army westward from Moscow through Eastern Europe in its desperate attempt to reach home. What had started with the crossing of the river Nemunas into Russian territory the previous summer, heralding invasion of Russia, had ended in ignominious failure. The whole of the north-western provinces including Lithuania were now in the grip of one of the most furious winters in living memory sweeping through from the Siberian Arctic Circle borne on piercing winds which turned the snowflakes into flurrying, sharp needles of ice. Important events had been decided in the course of these two momentous seasons involving the destiny of many nations. Thousands upon thousands of individual crises, matters of life and death were unfolding daily, the results of a gross miscalculation. Most were anonymous, never to be recorded for posterity only to be suffered to the inevitable bitter end, the awful legacy of a doomed enterprise.

The peasant Kadišius family, in common with the other serfs who peopled this landscape, now cursed the foreign army which had despoiled them of their crops and animals the summer before. Their survival this year would depend upon how well they could eke out whatever they had managed to hide from the French. They had contended with upheaval imposed upon them by the visitation of these foreign soldiers who had marched amongst them. But now it was over they settled back into the servitude and complacency of their mundane existences. The struggle for food and warmth was paramount in this seasonally barren, snow covered Lithuania. The odd, desperate, lone person was out with traps and snares using all their inherited country skills and the guile of the Lithuanian serf in order to pit their wits against nature in this the harshest of winters. Others, more elderly, infirm or wretched, remained snowbound huddled in their farms and hovels, in a struggle for survival on the little they had managed to lay up the summer before. Some would never see another spring. Such had been the effect of war, the ravaging of the territory that the advancing horde had passed through. Events had only added to the misery of the already fragile balance which existed in their communities between good years and bad, adequacy and famine, life and death, in this impoverished land.

But shortly after the turn of the year one particular Russian hunter would be descending upon that family who would affect them for ever, in a meeting which they may well have preferred to avoid.

The Cossack was relentless, terrifying in his determination. He came from the Ukraine from the right bank of the River Dnieper but he knew this country. He had travelled it many times. He knew the landscape he knew the people, he knew everything there was to know about hunting. Since the age of three he had been doing it. When they had first presented him with a bow, an arrow, a cartridge, a bullet and a gun he had been trained in the outdoor pursuits of fighting, riding and hunting. At the age of eight, by which time he had been taught to fish, and to ride unsupervised in public, he had been singled out for future command. He had risen to the rank of captain in a Ukrainian Cossack battalion of the Russian army and he was proud to be in the service of His Imperial Majesty Tsar Aleksander the First and engaged in the defence of the Holy Motherland.

His dedication to his homeland was deep and powerful and so heavily ingrained into his being that he wore a small stitched cloth sachet attached to a leather lace around his neck, next to his body. It contained a pinch of his native Ukrainian soil.

It was in the depths of winter as he approached Sejny in Poland, to the north west of his native land following the faint tracks of his quarry. He noticed that the marks in the snow and ice had skirted the town and were now receding into the distance, moving away from it. He doggedly continued. They disappeared for a time at the edge of a frozen river and after traversing it and casting about on the opposite bank he picked up the trail again. Further still to his right was the beginning of a pine forest all sheathed in white, a mass of towering shimmering stalagmites. It was late in the afternoon and the light was starting to diminish. He eased over towards the trees through thick snow, heading for their shelter. It was time to think about making camp for the night. It wasn't going to snow again but the huge freeze was continuing. He would carry on with the hunt in the morning.

This was becoming the coldest winter he had ever experienced and he knew that the elements should always be taken seriously. Weather lore had been drilled into him almost from birth, to hold nature in the greatest respect, because one oversight could lead to death.

Behind him on a halter was his packhorse, a medium sized shaggy, hardy thing little more than a pony but very strong and ideally suited to these harsh conditions. It was almost a duplicate of the one he was riding. Sometimes he interchanged them to give each one a break. Both horses were shod with iron crampon winter shoes.

They had been bred over centuries from those small fast creatures which had swept the Mongols across the vast Russian steppes in their fearsome quest for new lands and territories in the west during the middle ages. Both this man and the horses were descendants of that same stock. All of them gave prodigiously, almost it seemed, out of proportion, for the amount they consumed.

The horse at the back was saddled with a light wooden contraption made from pine and birch with many compartments. Kyril Tymoshenko's field equipment was stowed here. It was all mostly designed for lightness. He had a waxed canvas sheet carefully rolled and a long pole and two shorter ones, which had a cruck at one end. These were to provide him with shelter wherever he stopped. Another contained kindling and a tinder box and was equally waterproofed in a folded envelope once again wrapped in waxed cloth. He carried with him a supply of dried meat, a small sack of oats for the horses, some light tools and a flintlock smoothbore musket, also wrapped up, together with cartridges and gun cleaning equipment. A tripod and small metal pot completed the stores plus one or two other bits and pieces, some tea and some personal items.

On the top of the wooden saddle was a wide, open box like structure and on it sat a huge long haired hound called Yuri. It was the dog which had kept him on track when in places it had seemed the trail was running cold. All Captain Tymoshenko had to do was lift the dog down and it would cast about on the snow and ice until it picked up the scent again whereupon it took no second bidding when he told it to hop back up onto its perch again. Even the horses were quite used to this. Behind his own sheepskin covered saddle he carried a rolled up sleeping bag of the same material tucked into a waterproof outer case. He himself was dressed, in addition to undergarments and stockings, in a pair of voluminous cotton trousers and a long thigh length tunic made of white flax gathered at the waist with a leather belt and a waistcoat of mink fur. Attached in a sheath to the belt was a knife. Covering everything was a long bearskin double breasted coat dyed grey on the smooth outside. The coat had epaulettes with his badges of rank emblazoned upon them secured with brass buttons. The greatcoat had a central slash at the back to accommodate the rump of a horse, and knee length boots with the fur turned inwards, heavily heeled in thick tanned and seasoned cowhide, a rowelled spur on the back of each one and soled with hobnailed thick leather.

On his head he wore a knitted wool-lined and stuffed sheepskin hat with a soft brim which was sometimes turned up forming a thick headband but on this occasion it was pulled down against the cold at the sides and back. His face and neck was muffled in a long flaxen scarf and he wore snow goggles carved from flat bone with a few slits cut out of it in front of each eye. His sabre hung down on two leather straps from an outer belt and the front of his saddle had a pair of holsters containing loaded pistols under buckled leather flaps, one on either side. He had heard of the heavy hunting pike which they had used in centuries past to kill boar but he preferred his straight shafted ash lance with its deadly long sharp blade. As far as he was concerned it was easier to pull out after the kill. He took out his map, unfolded it and raised his goggles. He knew he was somewhere near the border between Russian Lithuania and Poland. The town he had skirted he realised was Sejny or Seinei in Lithuanian. To the north-west of that he noticed was Smolany or Smalenai. The borders were always changing, it was an old map. The names were shown in several languages.

With his lance held in travelling fashion at a shallow angle, so that it wouldn't snag, attached to the horses harness, with his shoulder length greasy black hair and his filthy beard and moustaches he made a formidable figure, a one man, single-minded professional fighting and hunting machine. He was slowly but surely overhauling his prey. Tomorrow, he estimated, all being well, he would catch up with it.

Chapter 2

A Tale from the Past – 1840

Jurgis Itzhak Kadišius had taken to his bed. He had been feeling progressively worse over the past few months and he had lost some weight. He felt so tired these days and his face had begun to betray a peculiar yellow pallor which somehow showed through from under his normally weathered complexion. It had started one morning about three months earlier. He had woken up at daybreak and hadn't felt quite right. As days passed he became progressively worse and his feeling of lethargy was now accompanied by some discomfort and occasionally pain somewhere inside his body high up in his midriff slightly to the right. He really felt quite ill.

Now that he had reluctantly been compelled to remain in bed his wife Veronika was rightly worried. There was not much she could do. They couldn't afford a doctor but she did have a wide knowledge of all sorts of remedies for grievous ills. Most local people made do for themselves as they had been wont to do from time immemorial. It wasn't surprising, as they were knowledgeable, resourceful people. No one else would help these peasants if they didn't look after themselves.

She suspected that the problem might lie with his liver. She knew that no matter how badly off they were there had always seemed to be enough credit to get liquor, and frequently he also distilled it himself from grain or potatoes in special metal containers he had got hold of from somewhere. She had never interfered with that. She thought that having a little hobby would do him no harm. Occasionally he sold some of it. The odd person would arrive with an empty wickerwork-covered stone jar complete with stopper, and leave with it full. She never turned her nose up at the little bit of extra money this produced. Of course it was inevitable that he would be sampling his own concoction at every opportunity. She wondered if that was the cause of his sickness or, if it wasn't, then perhaps it was something to do with his diet. They did tend to eat lots of fat and puddings, starch and suety things but this heavy diet was necessary during those short cold days of autumn and the long winter months. Such sources of energy were essential in that part of the world in those conditions. She thought that perhaps in later life these foods could maybe have an adverse effect on people who were no longer active in burning it off. She nursed him and attended to all his needs, and brought him hot drinks and soup, when he felt like eating. The medicine she made from the bark of the willow helped to ease the pain and she kept him clean and tidy, propped up in bed with pillows. If he was too weak to get out of bed she helped him with the china chamber pot and emptied it. Sometimes he would feel sick and she would bring him a bowl and then clear it away afterwards. She had committed to him years ago and she wasn't about to ease off now, just when he needed her more than ever. Her dour competence, the way she took everything in her stride was so typical of her, the same as most self-reliant, confident women the world over. She had always been the same.

Many years before, when Veronika had been in Smalenai one day early on in her marriage, she had witnessed some terrible goings on when a French foraging party had burst into the village commandeering food left, right and centre. Although the people knew there was something big happening and there were rumours of a huge French army moving eastwards further to the north nevertheless it was still a shock to see them in these circumstances.

This party of around twenty soldiers armed to the teeth, overconfident to the point of arrogance, had stolen wagons and horses and loaded them up with thatch torn from people's rooftops as animal fodder. When they had commandeered all the food they could carry they found some sacks of peas which had been hastily hidden by a few of the villagers, who evidently must have had some warning of their arrival, and they just threw them into the river. They manhandled some of the peasants and stomped around in their houses as if they owned them, taking whatever took their fancy although it wasn't much and afterwards they laughed their heads off while the peasants stood around helpless. They didn't find all of the hidden food though but they did trample around in the unripe corn pulling up whatever they could to add to the fodder. It was a bullying chaotic shambles and they carried out their actions with no thought for the rest of the army which would be following on behind as they outstripped their own supply column.

One of the soldiers, a younger man, who seemed to be in charge, noticed her watching them and after mounting his steed and consulting another soldier also mounted alongside him, they both cantered over towards her looking powerful and overbearing. The young officer gazed down at her sternly and asked in French and very broken Polish why she was looking at him. His companion alongside was a much older man, a Polish Lancer from another of the French regiments who interjected now and then with translation in a terse gruff

8

voice. She squinted upwards towards the officer and straight into the summer sun just behind his shoulder, him seated high up in the saddle. The light glittered off the highly polished Shako, brim covering his eyes, and glinted on his brass accoutrements and the horse's harness and his sabre. His three little plaited pigtails were neatly tied up at the ends. He was every inch a splendid cavalryman, but the timbre of his voice gave him away. In truth he was only a lad in a man's trappings and she addressed him as she would any of her own younger brothers. In a slightly scolding tone she asked him in Polish, "What would your mother say if she could see what her brave son was up to?" He looked questioningly at the Lancer who spoke a few words. He turned back to look down on her and seemed to be in some confusion and hesitated. He half understood the tone of her voice and realised he was being told off. The Lancer faltered with embarrassment and struggled for a moment to re-translate her comment. The Frenchman seemed at first affronted then abashed by this spirited reply. He reined his mount around and galloped away followed by his comrade. Shortly afterwards he gave some orders and they all moved out still carrying what they had seized. Veronika knew exactly what to do in any situation.

"What harm would he do me anyway?" she always said afterwards, "He was only a bit of a boy!"

Jurgis had struggled for the best part of his adult life to work and feed his wife and children as well as having to pay taxes to his local overlord which could also be in kind, – a proportion of whatever they grew or raised. It was only after that relentless debt was settled month after month that there was barely enough left over from their land to feed themselves. At those times they really suffered. There had been bad harvests and famines forcing them to improvise with whatever mushrooms or acorns or plants and lichens they could find, and game they could snare or catch in the forest. Fishing was another source of food down on the lake. He thanked God for the chickens. They

were a gift from above, low maintenance, and they laid eggs, repro-
duced themselves and afterwards they could be killed and eaten. But
food still had to be found for them. Even they had to eat. In some
years the harvest was slightly better than others and Jurgis could lay
up barely enough oats, peas, grain, vegetables and fodder to see them
through and there might be enough grain to feed the hens. Then
they would keep as many as they could, collecting the eggs for sale
to a Jew in town who gave them a price on market day. He bought
dozens of eggs from many different farmers and sent them in large
quantities into Seinei where he made a profit on them. Life became
slightly more easy as the children had grown up and moved on. Now
only Jonas was left at home, and the boy's mother and Jurgis were
very proud of him. He had learned a trade and was in demand as a
carpenter and he was so good at it that he could work for people at his
own discretion. He had built things in wood at the manor, repaired
carriages and was generally well thought of. Jurgis often basked in the
reflected glory. He was the apple of their eye, and the mainstay on the
farm who kept everything running these days.

There was always something Jurgis had wanted to tell Jonas and
indeed the others, some bits and pieces of family folklore he had intended to pass on but he had never had the time to do so. When he
did mention anything, them being so young, their attention span was
short, as easily distracted they rushed off to do something else. Now
deep inside he felt that he had almost left it too late.

He was the only person still alive who knew the full story. He felt
they ought to be aware of their heritage but he didn't quite know why.

He thought back many, many years to a morning in early January.
The weather once again had been devilishly cold. That winter the
first dusting of snow had arrived on November the sixth.

He remembered the snow beginning to fall on his wife's birthday.
She was a year younger than he was.

From that day the weather had got rapidly worse all the way up to

Christmas and beyond into the New Year. It never let up as the cold wind blew steadily from the east.

On that particular January day he had risen as usual at dawn to relieve himself into the night bucket and then he put his face outside the door to look at the weather. He sensed immediately that something was not right. Quickly going back inside and dressing in a panic, he started to go out again. "What's wrong?" asked Veronika, looking concerned and bleary eyed as she pulled on her long skirt. She checked to see if her two younger children were alright but they were sleeping soundly, one at each end of a low cot. The other older ones, huddled sleeping around the warmth of the oven. The dog was going this way and that under their feet alternately yelping and crying quietly as their panic communicated itself to him. The children stirred. His sister Marija also appeared, looking worried.

"I don't know what, but something's happened."

He took up his axe from the porch and opened the door as the dog almost knocked him over in its eagerness to get out. Jurgis skirted the house following the dog and approached the rear of the ramshackle building. Then he realised there was no sound coming from the sty. Normally they would be able to hear squealing or grunting as the pig optimistically expected to be fed when it heard movement from the house first thing in the morning. The dog was barking by now running backwards and forwards sniffing the ground from side to side.

Jurgis approached the door of the sty and found it was open.

There were signs of a struggle but it had been an unequal one and the pig was gone. The mess around the sty told the full story even before they spotted the wolf's paw prints in the snow. Normally the wolves from the forest kept away from the farmstead but the extreme conditions and lack of food had forced this one to take a chance. It must have waited until the early hours as no one had heard anything. The sty was a long way from the house, downwind and the pig's squeals had been borne away. The howling wind must have carried its terrified protests in the opposite direction.

"How did the wolf know he wouldn't be heard?" Jurgis thought. But at the same time he knew just how intuitive wolves could be, such intelligent creatures. They had more sense than his old dog which had just slept by the oven all through the night as far as he knew.

The dog wasn't much good for anything any more except eating and sleeping. As a guard dog he had lost his edge. Juozas wasn't particularly sentimental when it came to farm animals. Because things was so hard, everything had to have a use or a value otherwise it became a waste of food resources. In this instance however he was mindful of the useful service the dog had given in the past and he was content to treat it now as a pet – providing it didn't eat too much! His grandmother had been the same, spending much of her day dozing by the fire too, occasionally waking up to tell Jurgis stories or potter about, but then she had died when he was still a boy. But his mother Magdalena Cernauskas was fully competent and would certainly put her shoulder to the wheel and step forward with a positive contribution whenever it was necessary.

Still the dog had worked hard in its time and he couldn't really lay the blame at its door. No, it was his own fault. Why hadn't he seen about getting a new young dog? They couldn't afford the loss of the pig. It was next year's food. Nevertheless he still swung a boot in the dog's direction but missed, as the animal was still not so old that he couldn't react quickly enough to dodge it.

He had known full well that a wolf had been prowling about. He had seen the paw prints two days ago just inside the forest, which began about fifty metres behind the house, but he had done nothing. He had also seen the flock of ravens circling above. They often followed wolves knowing that they would pick up carrion from their kills sooner or later. This worked both ways and wolves were very much aware that where there were ravens there was also food.

They found the pig's carcase a few paces in from the forest's edge. They only had to follow the drag marks in the snow. It was just a young pig which is why the wolf had been able to pull it this far.

This most legendary and fearsome predator had ripped open the pig's belly and had feasted on the organs inside. Sure enough, as they approached, two or three ravens fluttered lazily upwards cawing in protest as their pickings, which were already beginning to freeze, were abruptly denied them temporarily. There was no sign of the wolf.

Jurgis raised himself slightly and took a sip of the infusion of Salix bark from the wooden cup which stood on the floor beside the bed.

"Can you go and call Jonas and bring him to me?"

Veronika did as he had asked, and found their son, the mainstay on the farm now, round at the back brushing down their old horse. He left off from what he was doing and came to the house straight away while his mother hauled her weary body down to the well to break the ice on the surface of the water again, a job which had to be done over and over, day by day throughout the winter.

Entering the one main room, Jonas went over to the corner near the oven where his father's bed was situated and pulled up a stool.

"How are you feeling Tėtis?" he asked.

"Quite a bit better Sūnus" the elderly man lied.

"How's the horse"

"Old and tired!" replied his son, "He's almost had it."

"Like me then," Jurgis muttered.

"Don't say that Tėvelis," he replied, addressing his father more affectionately. "You'll be up and about in no time and back on the booze again and back to your usual self, just like normal."

"Well! Maybe, God willing. – I've been thinking,"

"What about?"

"About things that happened a long time ago during the war of 1812 when Mama and I had been married for a while but before you were born. Some things happened which taught me a lot about life and people"

"Go on Tėtis," his son entreated, intrigued.

Jurgis then started to tell him about the day the pig was taken by

13

the wolf. He reached the part about finding it dead with the best bits missing as he realised with despair what it would mean to them all.

"So what happened?"

"I was younger then and full of energy and I decided to go after the wolf and see if I could trap it or kill it."

"But honestly Tėtis, what chance did you have of doing that"?

"Every chance I thought, and I had to do something. I figured out it was a lone wolf. It didn't seem to belong to a pack. The nearest pack we heard that winter was miles away, faintly in the distance. You could just barely hear them howling when the wind was in the right direction and then most of the time you couldn't, so I guessed this animal wasn't part of a pack.

He'd probably lost the leadership in a fight with another younger wolf perhaps and had been driven out. That was what I assumed anyway. But I couldn't take the chance that he wouldn't be back again. Wolves can't get enough of a good thing."

"Yes they can be quite a problem. Do you remember Tėtis when I was about ten and you took me into town and some came out of the woods and followed us for a while out on the main road after dark on the way back, and we could see their eyes gleaming? Then two of them closed in on the cart, chasing us, and they leapt up at the horse but you soon shouted and clapped and fired your pistol and scared them off. I can admit now I was terrified, what with all those fairy stories Mumija and Močiutė used to tell me about wolves. Lucky it was summer and maybe they weren't particularly hungry. I suppose they were just following their instincts."

"Well anyway," his father continued.

"I went back and geared myself up and got those two bear traps we still have. At that time the horse was young and strong, only three years old, so I saddled him up and stowed the gear behind the saddle and in the saddle bags and set off. I wrapped myself up warm, took my axe and told Mumija, Močiutė and your Auntie Marija, not to leave the house and to keep an eye on the children. I reckoned that although the wolf may have eaten his fill he would be back for the rest of it sooner or later so I set one of the traps under the snow, near the remains of the pig, and fixed it by its chain to a tree.

It took some strength to open the thing up and set it, even with the aid of the axe handle, as you know yourself. I don't think I would be strong enough to do it now. I thought I would see if I could follow the tracks and perhaps set the other one up somewhere along the way and maybe double up on the chances of trapping the wolf. I wasn't intending to be away that long. I know I'm a farmer not a tracker but the ground was covered in snow."

"So did you catch it then?"

"Well, I carried on following its tracks along that old overgrown road which leads inside. You might remember that path which leads into the depths of the forest. I don't think you and I ever did follow it too far when you were a child. It must go on for miles. Nobody ever goes there. I believe it's a very old, even an ancient, route. But I did stop to set the other trap in the middle of the path. I used the length of chain again to fix it to a tree and then covered it up with some branches I pulled from a spruce and then I disguised the whole thing with a sprinkling of snow. The wolf seemed intent on where it was going. It twisted and turned and seemed to be following an older trail. The forest was very gloomy and quiet in there once I was out of sight of the edge. It was a bit like walking in a lofty ice cavern. The tops of the pines had trapped a lot of the snow above before it had a chance to reach the ground and it was in a state of suspended animation. The eerie silence was only broken sometimes by a soft plop, as a lump of it dislodged itself and fell to the forest floor. Whatever our wolf had caught wind of must have been somewhere up ahead.

Then after a while I noticed with a shock that another set of prints came in from one side and mostly blocked out the first in fact there were so many tracks I was confused but I carried on. I saw the marks of at least two horses and, at one point, boots and some smaller paw prints and then just the horses again."

"Who was it Tétis?" said Jonas eagerly, his appetite now thoroughly whetted by this tale.

"I reckoned, judging by a faint scent on the wind that wafted back towards me from ahead, that it was a couple of men on horseback who had been on the road for some time. The smell was such and the tracks so fresh that I thought that I must be hard behind whoever it was. This continued for about a mile or so and then the most recent tracks took a turn off to the right and disappeared and the air became fresher. I could see the wolf's trail again and decided to follow it just a little further. I was beginning to think I had come far enough and had almost decided to give up and turn round when I heard the sound of a click behind me. Coming up behind was a huge man riding a horse and leading another. He was obviously a fighting man as he was carrying a long spear and a musket which was pointing straight at me."

"'Tovarich?'" "he half asked, half stated in Russian."

"'Tovarich!'" "I shouted back confidently, being as definite as I possibly could.

I asked him if he was going far. He said he had come a long way but that he hoped he wouldn't be going much further. He asked me who I was and I told him. He asked me what my business was. I mentioned the wolf. He must have been reassured because he lowered his gun.

He told me he was also hunting vermin and suggested we do it together. I was a little afraid so I agreed and we continued along the way. As he pulled up alongside me the stink became apparent again. He told me that he had been on the trail of this creature and others like it for weeks until he realised that he was being followed himself which was why he had doubled back and come up behind me and had taken me by surprise.

"'How did you know I was there'" I asked him.

"'Let's just say I can sniff people out, I have finely tuned field skills coupled with acute intuition,'" he answered with a smirk, waiting for me to smile. I thought that coming from him it was strange. His personal sense of smell couldn't have been that good. But seeing my puzzled look he went on, "'Actually it was the dog who first alerted me, he kept looking back with his ears pricked up. But now I see you are unarmed and harmless, perhaps we can ride on and together we can catch this animal. I could do with some company.'"

The tone of this request sounded very much like an order and so we continued on our way.

I asked him where he was from and he told me he was a Cossack officer from the Ukraine.

"'Is there a big bounty on wolves then that you hunt them so far afield?'" I asked him. He roared with laughter leaned across and punched me hard on the shoulder with the heel of his hand."

"'Holy Mother Russia. By all the Saints. No indeed!'" he laughed, "'I'm not hunting wolves, nor bears, nor wild boar. I'm hunting men, and when I catch them I am going to kill them!'"

"He continued to chuckle and laugh to himself shaking his head as we rode along and I was filled with a feeling of the utmost dread and foreboding at how any God-fearing human being could be so matter of fact about such an inhuman prospect."

Chapter 3

The Quarry – 1813

"Later in the day we came upon a bundle of rags which had been discarded and which were lying close up against a fallen log.

As we approached it, a huge grey shape which had been nosing and pawing at the bundle turned towards us with its lips drawn back in a snarl with its ears cocked forward and its tail upright. The Cossack immediately spurred his horse into action and grasped his lance. As he did so the wolf, startled, jumped away growling and flattening its ears and made off into the undergrowth.

The Cossack came back and rejoined me as I got down to examine the bundle. I saw on closer inspection that it wasn't just old rags but a man and he was frozen solid. Upon closer examination his cloth-wrapped hands were just visible tucked under his cloak where he must have been trying to keep them warm, and his eyes, what I could see of them, were open. What amazed me was the almost complete absence of a beard. He was barely more than a lad but a smart one no doubt to have come thus far. His feet though seemed to be in a mess, wrapped up in sacking and rags as they were.

The Cossack just uttered a snort of disappointment prodding the corpse with the tip of his spear as if somehow he thought the Frenchman, for that was what he seemed to be, was only feigning death. He dismounted and rooted round in the man's stiffened clothes and pockets and with a cry of triumph came up with a fob watch. He looked at it and then up towards a chink of sky where the weak sun was faintly gleaming through the snow-heavy forest canopy then peered at the dial again. He shook it a couple of times but it was frozen, then with a curse he put it inside his own coat somewhere.

"'How low can you get?'" I thought to myself. He looked up the trail and shouted out that there was another one. Then with a sharp cry to his horse he urged it on into a trot continuing up the path following a fainter track which continued further. Left to my own devices, I looked back again at the body. I could just see his dirty blue threadbare tunic with the remaining buttons which seemed to be brass with a number embossed upon them, under a woman's fur stole and cloak, which the wolf must have loosened as he mauled the body about. On his head he was wearing a French military shako, wrapped in its oilskin cover, strapped under the chin and stuffed with bits of evergreen foliage which poked out around his face. The whole lot was held in place by a scarf tied up under his chin. This man you could see was in a terrible state before he froze to death. I think this must have been a merciful release. Scattered nearby I found his satchel and a musket wrapped up in waterproof. I noticed that he had a pistol tucked in his belt right round the back. You know me Jonas, I hate to see anything wasted, it wasn't really a personal effect, not like a watch, so I took it from him, having to prise it away where it was held fast by the build up of frost, and put it in my pocket under my coat. As I looked round on the other side of the log I noticed that a makeshift shelter had been made up against it with pine branches and there were signs that two people had rested there. There were the remains of a fire with some burned pine cones, so these fugitives must have had kindling and tinder. It just seemed to me that they had been fairly resourceful to have survived for as long as they had in this wilderness on foot. I reckoned that they must have had help along the way.

We all knew in Smalenai from the news read out at Mass every Sunday that the French had miscalculated and their whole enterprise had turned into disaster. We were sorry in a way because we had been hoping that, if he had been successful, Napoleon would have freed us from the burdens of foreign tyranny and serfdom. There was always someone bossing us about. If it wasn't the Poles it was the Russians. If it wasn't the Russians it was the Poles. If it wasn't them it was our lord of the manor. We were let down though by their attitude when they raided the village. Although I don't suppose that Napoleon ordered them to behave like that, he ought to have known. It was an eye-opener."

"So what did you do with the rest of the stuff?"

"The satchel I tied over the saddle pommel."

"Is that the old black leather thing with the brass eagle on the front hanging in the horse's shed?"

"Yes, that's the one"

"The one which used to have all the cartridges in it?"

Jurgis seemed to lose his train of thought wincing as a pang went through his body. Jonas wondered if it was his illness or if it had been prompted by these painful memories.

"I saw the Russian coming back, I thought that he seemed like a man possessed, I couldn't understand what was eating him or where his motivation was coming from. He just seemed obsessed with finding the second fugitive."

"I showed the Russian the makeshift shelter and the remains of the fire and he seemed thoughtful and then muttered that he thought the remaining Frenchman was probably still fairly operational as an adversary."

"I asked him why he thought this one had died.

"'Who knows?'" "he said." "Either they had a difference of opinion or he left the shelter for some other reason of necessity and then made the cardinal mistake of allowing himself to fall asleep.'" "He told me that this was one of the basic rules of survival in these conditions, not to fall asleep outdoors in the cold, death often follows. This was what he thought may have happened, in all balance of probability."

"By this time it was beginning to get dark and the Cossack said it would be better if we made use of the shelter until morning rather than setting up another one. So I was forced to spend the night with this man who had been on the road for months. Not an experience I would care to repeat in a hurry."

"He produced all this stuff from nowhere and before too long had lit a fire and boiled up some snow in a little pot and we were drinking tea from little wooden cups and chewing on dried meat. He was actually quite generous, even though he slurped away at his tea and smacked his lips as he chewed, the slobber trickling down into his already dirty beard"

"'Tovarich, I am captain Kyril Tymoshenko, one of Tsar Aleksander's loyal Cossacks. What is your real name ?'"

"When I told him he seemed more amenable.

"'Ah, you're not named after a saint then.'"

"'Well, I *am* named after a saint. My mother told me it means earth-worker or farmer. It's similar to your Giorgi – who killed a dragon,'" "I added with a smug look."

"'A fine reply Mister Jurgis, I see now that even though you are only a farm worker you are not silly.'"

"I think he was taken by my spirited response."

"The Cossack then asked me about my way of life and my family at home and the farm and how we lived. Then after a pause he seemed to make up his mind about something – about me maybe."

"'Listen!'" "he said," "'This Frenchman we're going after, I think he could be more of a problem than I thought. I might need your help. Where's that musket you found?'" I reached round and picked it up and unwrapped it. The covering had thawed in the heat thrown out by the fire. The firearm itself wasn't frozen.

"'Have you ever used a gun like this before'"

"I said that I hadn't, I'd never used a gun at all."

"'Alright I'll show you,'" he said

"He took the gun and looked down the barrel from the breech end after pulling back the hammer which caught on a latch of some sort with a satisfying click. It contained a piece of flint held in a vice padded with a piece of thin leather. He then let the hammer down slowly and peered into it. He said, "'It's already loaded. Our fugitive must know we're here so if he hears this go off it doesn't much matter.'"

"He got up and moved outside and downwind about twenty metres pointed the gun up into the air and discharged it. I heard the bang outside but apart from the horses starting slightly and the dog's ears pricking up there was no other effect. The Cossack returned quickly to the bivouac. "'It's cold out there!'"

"He settled down again."

"'At least we know definitely it's not loaded now. Actually this gun is quite clean, normally they get all furred up inside the barrel after a dozen shots but I think these chaps kept their weapons up to scratch.'"

"He took a cartridge from his own pack."

"'These will do,' he said. "I use a French musket anyway. All these bullets are slightly too small. It's deliberate because the powder residue builds up inside the barrel. But it means it is not accurate, you will have to wait until he is within about 10 metres of you before you fire. In here, in this little waxed paper package is a measured charge of gunpowder and a lead ball. What you do is this. You open the pan here, then you bite the end off this cartridge which contains the ball and gunpowder. It's only waxed paper so it's quite easy. Keep the lead ball in your mouth. You pour a small amount of powder into the pan and then close it. Then stand the rifle on its butt and remove the ramrod from its housing, here. You pull it right out because you are going to use it to push the rest of the powder, the ball and the remains of the paper cartridge, plus the piece you first bit off, in that order, down the barrel from the muzzle end and ram it hard right to the other end. Then return the ramrod to the housing alongside the barrel again so it doesn't get lost. You are now in charge of a lethal weapon so gently hold the hammer and take up the strain while you pull the trigger to release it to a safe position. Point it away from people while you are doing this – just in case. But make sure the hammer doesn't strike the frizzen. The last thing you want at this stage is a spark. That is – unless you want to kill someone! If you should get a misfire just recock the hammer and try again but don't hang about'"

"I then asked why he was so resolutely determined, so dead set on killing this fugitive."

"'He has violated our sacred land by coming here uninvited. He has killed our men in battle, raped our women, stolen our food, murdered old men and children and looted all our towns and cities along the way. No retribution would be too great for him.'"

"'You mean this one man had done all that? He must be the arch-villain of all time! How do you know that?'"

"'To me he represents them all. When word gets back to France from all quarters about how we have punished them they will never try to invade us again.'"

"'I doubt they will ever try to invade you ever again after what they have been through. Would you, if the situation was reversed? This man you are so determined to kill is obviously just a lad. They all are from what I have heard. He's somebody's son. Bonaparte has already used up and destroyed most of the youth of Europe. Now he's scraped the barrel sending these kids to firm up what was left of existing regiments. I heard that the majority of this army are conscripts except for their Old Guard and the staff officers, and these are not officers, – are they?'"

"'Not sure, but you could be right in that respect, the dead one was not an officer, didn't seem like one. Conscripts they may well be but the fact is they should have refused to fight'"

"'What? and be shot? With all due respect Captain you are not being realistic. You have won, you've driven them out, how far do you want to take it? I know you Cossacks have a reputation which you must feel you have to live up to, but in the name of God and the Holy Mother can't you ease off with this obsession?'"

I felt I had gone too far with him and that he would be angry but it seemed he was enjoying the debate.

"'They must pay for their crimes'"

"'But do you really know who started it and who should be held to account?'"

"'No and I don't much care.'"

"'Supposing it was your son then in that situation? Do you have children?'"

"'Yes, I do have a son who is only twelve yet but he wouldn't go marching into someone else's land without good cause.'"

"'Who knows what is good cause and what isn't? These people are barely a couple of years older than your own boy, but the result of this, if you succeed, will be more suffering in a land far away from here.'"

"'I appeal to you as a father to let this drop. God will think all the more of you for it.'"

This argument went on and on bouncing this way and that. In the end I don't know if I bored him into submission or what, but he went a bit quiet.

You know Jonas, for the first time I saw what I took to be doubt in his eyes – I hoped it was. Whether it was directed towards his own intentions or whether he just didn't trust me to back him up if needed I wasn't quite sure at the time."

Jurgis continued the story as Jonas listened.

"He gave me back the gun telling me to wrap it up again and put it somewhere safe. He must have been tired out by the discussion plus the exertions of the day, because Kyril, – we were now on first name terms – unrolled his sleeping bag and climbed inside then seemed to lapse into a fitful slumber leaning against the log in the warmth thrown out by the burning pine cones. The horses had their nosebags, blankets and hobbles on and stood nearby.

I took the opportunity to have a look at the pistol under my coat and saw it worked in the same way as the musket, so I practised on that and when I had loaded it with a cartridge from the satchel I put it back again out of sight. I began to reflect on the disturbing thought that he was expecting me to help him kill someone if necessary. That nagging doubt kept me awake for quite a while, as did thoughts of the family wondering what had happened to me, as my stomach churned away. Also the cold didn't help. I had no sleeping bag, but I managed well enough in my thick coat."

"I felt as if I was the prisoner of this Cossack. I think his dog sensed my disquiet. I believed I had convinced the dog with my arguments. He at least didn't talk back. He just sat there looking up at me before he too slumped, yawning, eyes shut with his nose resting upon his paws. I liked that dog. I yawned a few times then myself before I too passed into oblivion."

Chapter 4

The Trap

"At first light we both woke automatically through habit. Me because of years of farming, rising at dawn to start the day's work and he through military routine. Captain Tymoshenko quickly saddled his horses and I did the same with mine. There wasn't much breaking of camp to be done and it was all left as it was as we rode off again following the trail. The tracks of the wolf were now forgotten. They had gone anyway. We came upon a point where another set of prints had come in from the right hand side and followed the first set. It seemed a bit odd. Further along off to the right again we could see a rudimentary shelter and some smoke from a nearly extinguished fire near another makeshift bivouac.

The Cossack waved us on because it was clear no one was at home. Another two hundred paces further on, the second set of tracks veered off to the right again leaving the single ones continuing forward further into the forest.

"'He's a crafty devil this one.'" said the Cossack, "'You know what he's done don't you? He must have realised he was being followed. I bet he doubled back and laid in wait for us until he thought he was safe, that we had stopped for the night. Then he must have rested up himself and moved on again at dawn swinging back onto the route. "'So I reckon he's armed and dangerous and has his wits about him. The main thing he has against him is that he is on foot while we are on horses. He will tire long before we do and we are steadily over-hauling him. What I can't understand though is how he knew he was being followed.'"

"I tell you Jonas, I had to smile to myself . With all the twists and turns of this ancient road we were now upwind of the fugitive and Captain Tymoshenko was the rankest smelling individual I had ever come across. A man like that plus two horses and a dog didn't really have the greatest chance of remaining undetected when the wind was blowing in the wrong direction"

"Dad, surely the Frenchman must have noticed it too."

"Yes I think he must have noticed it on the pure, clean air."

"How could you be so certain about that Dad?"

"Let's not sidetrack. Allow me to continue!"

"Shortly after that the tracks disappeared entirely in a clearing, in a stretch of ice and rock, frozen solid by the wind blowing through a gap in the trees. I knew that if we continued, the forest was pretty impenetrable further out, so I suggested to the Cossack that we give it up and turn back. He thought long and hard and for some reason he seemed to agree, so we began to retrace our steps. By this time the tracks were so many and so jumbled that all we had to do was follow them back the way that we had come. We moved on for perhaps an hour or two until we came back to the first camp. The dead French soldier was still there exactly as we had left him, frozen and slumped. It worried me slightly that he hadn't been touched by wild animals which led me to wonder if the wolf had gone back to the dead pig or

to the house. The Captain was a bit further ahead of me and continued on, giving the little camp a cursory glance as it came into view to satisfy himself that it was as we had left it. As we approached the corpse it suddenly sprang into life and seized a musket which had been concealed under its leg. Raising it in one fluid movement he fired and Captain Tymoshenko fell from his horse backwards. The Frenchman was on his feet by now producing a pistol which he aimed at me. The French soldier pulled the trigger and nothing happened. He re-cocked the pistol and fired again, still there was no shot. The powder must have been damp. Terrified, I threw myself to the ground half winding myself as I did so. In a daze I could just make out a figure lunging at me who hit me on the side of the head with the pistol butt and I lost consciousness.

When I came to, who was lifting me up and pouring vodka between my lips but Tymoshenko. "'I thought you were dead,'" "I managed to mutter."

"'So did I,'" he replied. "'Good job I took the other one's watch. The ball hit it fair and square. Shame really, now I'll never know if it would have worked or not. It never will now but I must admit it knocked the breath out of me. The crafty bugger has taken one of my horses and backtracked and my lance and pistols with it, but I still have my musket and you have yours.

I guess that will eventually take him back towards your house won't it Mr Earthworker?'"

"I was worried now for the safety of your mother and Granny Magdalena, the children and your aunt Marija."

"I bet you were Dad, but obviously they must have survived because I remember Granny Magdalena, and Marija, God rest their souls –

and Mama is still here."

"Yes," replied Jurgis a touch sarcastically.

"Well done you've got it right."

Jonas smiled to himself inwardly. "He's having a good day, he can't be that ill."

"We were so lucky. We hurried back along the road with our two horses, us on foot, when the Captain uttered a yell of triumph. As he groped for his musket and started to raise it I could see ahead the figure of a Frenchman in rags, just like his dead comrade, but with his foot caught in the bear trap. It seemed to have him firmly in its grip across the sole of his left boot because he wasn't making a sound. He just looked at us helplessly. All the things he had been carrying had been scattered out of reach. You could see where he had tried to reach them but the chain was too securely fastened to the tree. I don't know how long he must have been there but he looked all in.

The Cossack walked up to him through the trampled snow and put the muzzle of the rifle to his head. The boy just stared back defiantly. He knew the game was up"

"'Au revoir Monsieur,'" the Cossack muttered.

"I never did find out what it meant but at the time I didn't care, I wasn't going to see that lad shot down in cold blood. I raised the gun I was carrying and pulled it into my shoulder cocking it as I did so."

"'Wait!, He's in my trap. He's my prisoner. Stop or I'll shoot,'" "I said."

"I almost frightened myself by this course of action which I was thoughtlessly embarking upon. The Cossack just looked round at me smiling and winked then turned his attention back to his target. I saw his finger begin to tighten on the trigger. Time seemed to stand still but he didn't squeeze it any further. He was actually hesitating. For an instant I could almost hear the previous night's arguments again, and I jerked at my own musket almost in a reflex action certainly with no real intention to injure anyone. I must have had a rush of blood to the head. Have you ever had those? When you just get into a situation which is almost out of control and you do something which, if you'd had the time to think about it, you may not have done."

"The hammer of the musket shot forward with a crack and the flint hit the frizzen producing sparks and knocking it shut. Then the powder in the pan flashed and ignited the main charge. There was this huge puff of smoke and a loud bang. The musket kicked back and rose up in the air and the Cossack Captain was lying on the ground with a useless right arm and blood everywhere dripping from the bottom of the sleeve, screaming his head off. Juozas, if you have ever seen anyone with a severe injury involving a broken bone and a compound fracture you will know that even the strongest man will give full vent to his agony. He must have fallen on his arm too when he hit the ground. The screaming just went on and on. It frightened me and made me sick to my stomach I can tell you. My first instinct was to help him but my overall intention was more important in my mind. Firstly, it was to survive myself. Tough though he may have been he was in no mood for anything heroic, which was what I had heard. The Cossacks' strength, it was rumoured, lay in surprise attacks, harrying the enemy when they themselves had the advantage. But it seemed that when things weren't going their way they lost a bit of interest, to say the least."

"The first thing I did then was to get out the pistol which I had loaded the night before with one of the cartridges in my pocket, the way Kyril had taught me. I didn't yet know the measure of the Frenchman. All the while the Russian was still in terrible agony rolling around."

"I then got my axe and pushed the handle between the jaws of the trap which was holding the Frenchman. As I had thought, the main force of it had been contained by the width of the thick sole but there was some pain evident on this man's face and I could see that one of the blades had penetrated the softer part of the boot. I reckoned this lad wasn't going very far on foot after that type of injury so I used the axe handle to lever open the trap's jaw as I stood on the other one putting my full weight on it. He carefully lifted out his foot, wincing badly as he did so. I only just got my own foot clear as the trap sprang shut again. Those traps frighten me even now."

"It was fortunate for him his boots were fairly new. I think that was what saved him. Judging by his friend's cloth bound feet this one was lucky. I thought he must have stolen them fairly recently from some person or building along their route."

"Dad, why did you never tell us anything of this before? It's an amazing story. Why did you and Mama, and Granny for that matter, keep it so dark?"

"Well we all thought later, after we sat down and discussed it that the fewer people who got to know about this the less risk there would be of any repercussions."

"But why *would* there be any repercussions?"

"You know yourself Juozas, how people can talk and almost always get it all wrong. We just thought it best they didn't know at all. We were supposed to be helping the Russians, not the French!"

"The Cossack was still suffering badly and the Frenchman or should I say the French boy was still grimacing. The missing horse, with the Captain's gear still loaded on it, was loitering further down the path so I carefully went towards it and after several advances and retreats the horse started to recover from its fear and I managed to catch its bridle and bring it back to the scene. This horse didn't realise the narrow escape it had just had. The boy had been leading it at that point otherwise it would have been the end for it had it stepped into the jaws of the trap first, and not him.

I still had my musket but the pistol was handier and loaded. Both these men were now unarmed but I didn't trust either of them so I kept it very much in evidence. Luckily they weren't in any mood for heroics. They just went along with whatever I told them to do. I motioned with sign language and a bit of Polish for the boy to come over with me to the Cossack and together we helped him up onto a horse where he slumped groaning and cursing under his breath. He had stopped screaming by now and had turned very white under his filthy face and very soon he seemed to be shivering and semi-conscious. Then I got the boy to hop over to the other horse. I removed the carrying frame and its equipment, then lifted his good leg with both hands and he swung his bad foot over the horse's rump and settled on its back. There was no problem with the boy. He clearly realised that I had saved his life. He had heard the altercation between me and the Cossack. I know it was in Russian but he must have got the gist of it and also for Heaven's sake I had just shot the man in his defence. He must have seen me as some kind of divine saviour. I picked up all the discarded weapons and tied them to one of the horses."

"Dad, why have you left it so late to tell me all this?"

"I don't really know Jonas. I have a theory that time passes at different rates for different people depending upon where they are in their lives. Right now, time for me is tearing along. Maybe it's because when you are young you don't have a yardstick to measure its passage by. At the moment I am getting on a bit and I'm ill and I've seen a lot. Who knows what the future holds? This is family lore which you and the others ought to know about. It's part of our family's history. In many ways I regret that I didn't ask my own parents much when I was a child. My dad tried to tell me things but it just went in one ear and out of the other. After he died I regretted it. I suppose that's really why I'm acquainting you with this story before it's too late. Mamija knows quite a lot too."

Jonas sighed, pursing his lips and blowing air out in an exasperated way looking all round and up at the ceiling, not realising that later in life, when he was older and wiser, he would attach great importance to this dialogue and be grateful for it.

Chapter 5

Peasant Charity

"I realised that the Russian was in a bad way and was suffering from shock. The best thing I could do for all of us was to get us back home as fast as I could

"Were they surprised when you arrived back"

"Indeed they were, but once they got over the initial astonishment the three of them fussed around sorting things out with the help of your brothers and sisters – of course you weren't yet born. As they did so, I told them bits and pieces about what had happened. They took it in their stride. They hadn't seen the wolf since, thank God. I was not surprised, wolves are instinctively clever creatures. I reckon he was unimpressed with what he witnessed of human behaviour and never wanted anything more to do with it again." Jurgis said with a painful smile. "It was decided to treat the Russian's injury first. The women did this near the warmth of the oven. They pulled a cot over to it and the Russian slumped onto it. We were all used to the smell of the farmyard but this was too much. We were breathing through our mouths as all this was going on. We managed to get his outer layers off and threw them outside. The stench got worse. The mood was lightened by us making noises of disgust. We got used to it. He was in severe pain but fortunately only half aware of what was happening. After their initial curiosity the children went and played in the corner. Granny gave him a concoction of her own made from poppy seeds which put him out after a while. We then inspected his arm. It was in a state. The ball had smashed the upper arm bone and some splinters were sticking through the other side but they could see the lead ball had not exited. The bulk of his enormous arm had absorbed the impetus of the ball and it was still lodged in there somewhere near the bone. Instead of being straight, the bone was now misaligned and crooked. Granny actually operated on him with a long sharp knife heated in the fire. We all knew that wounds got worse when dirt got in, we learned it by keen observation really. As you know, we have found that whenever we have to do anything with animals such as lancing boils, castrations, removing ticks and so on if we used an implement which has been drenched in boiling water the success rate is a lot higher, infections are a lot less. So we just apply the same procedure to humans. We were completely different to city people in those days, you observed things about life denied to townsfolk"

"What was happening with the Frenchman Tètis?"

"We had found out his name and that of his companion who had died. What we did was, each of us pointed to ourselves and said our name. He cottoned on straight away and his name was Nicolas Deschamps. It wasn't until a lot later that we found out more. We didn't try Lithuanian with him as that would have meant starting from scratch but he already knew some fragments of Polish so we persevered with that. So with introductions having been made all round except for Kyril, as he was unconscious, we got on with sorting out his wound first. Močiutė put the steel long nosed forceps which we had for removing bee stings and wood splinters, into boiling water and left them there for a quarter of an hour so that any dirt would be boiled off them and wouldn't enter his wound. She then probed through the hole in his arm and found the lead ball but there were a lot of grinding sounds which made me nearly pass out myself but the Cossack was oblivious. Then she washed it all with hot water and went in again this time extracting some shards of bone which had splintered. She told me she couldn't get the ball out. If we couldn't, the man would die from lead poisoning. At the same time, luckily for him, we applied our minds to the solution. I hoped the shot had missed the main artery but by the amount of blood maybe at least a vein had been ruptured, it was a very serious wound. I would imagine that in the field, in the heat of battle, the arm would have been amputated."

"You know the pigs nose-ring squeezer? I thought of using that to reach the ball."

This was actually a pincer like implement with a half ring on the end of each arm. The end on each side was formed into a half circle but hollowed on the inside into a groove. An opened-out small brass ring from a bag of them was placed within these grooves on either side and then squeezed into the part of a boar piglet's snout between the nostrils. It was to make them easier to control as they grew up. They had a much larger one with great long handles which they used for bulls.

"I did look at them but the pivot was much too near the working end and I doubted if we would have been able to get the handles far enough apart to open the jaws sufficiently.

The injury which had been seeping blood was beginning to stabilise as nature took over. At first we did think the blood might have been arterial there was so much of it, some in a semi-coagulated state, but we then realised it was too dark for that. I asked her to give me the forceps and before she did so she rinsed the blood off them. I went outside and got a pair of pliers and turned the end of each prong of the forceps inwards and roughed up the inside of each prong a bit and made each point sharper with a file. Once again she boiled the forceps and tried again. It was a difficult manual task to open the forceps apart, wider than the bullet, once they were inside, against the resistance of the muscle around. Between us we did it by sheer brute force and got the prongs around the ball. Lucky lead is softer than steel and the points stuck into it on either side. We got it out. He was very fortunate that the main bone wasn't completely shattered. Mumija said that she thought the ends could be realigned, which was where I came in. I had to get a pair of straps and tie each one around opposite ends of the arm and use them to force the two ends of the bone apart where they had become very slightly overlapped. The sweat was pouring off us by the time we had finished and the patient was yelling before he passed out again, but the arm seemed to be about the right length again, so Mama got the honey from the jar in the cupboard and filled the wound with it and then bandaged it all up which stopped the worst of the bleeding. The honey would get rid of the inflammation, swelling and pain. Then she got three sticks from the firewood bucket spaced them equally round the upper arm and bound them in place, then another one diagonally from shoulder to wrist so that the whole thing was immobilised, – the entire arm. We then made him a sling and tied the bent arm up against his chest so it wouldn't move and to help stabilise the blood flow. I really think your mumija is so clever she could have been a doctor given the opportunity. Most of the time after the bone was re-set the Russian was out cold except when the probing was going on, then he made a few groans and moved a bit but that was all. Where she learned about the poppies I don't know. I assume her mother must have told her. In other countries she might well have been accused of being a witch. We had read in a news sheet something about witchcraft abroad. Once upon a time anyone could

36

be accused of it and hanged. They always seemed to be elderly women for some reason. It used to happen a lot in England and America it said. I'll bet Kyril and Nicolas were thankful it didn't really happen in Lithuania. But I'm digressing – after that we had the unenviable task of washing down his body. We dropped all the underclothes straight onto the fire after cutting them away. The fumes in the house became oppressive for a while. Then we half lifted him off the cot and pulled out the paliasse from under the top half of him. Then we did the other half. After that Granny Magdalena washed him right down with warm water and soap and she didn't bat an eyelid. The water just fell straight through the slats and Marija mopped it up. I think it was a shock, the whole train of events, but she took it in her stride. The last thing we had to do was to dress him up in some new clothes, a bit like a big doll. We found some old things of Grandpa's. He was a big chap, and the clothes fitted. Then we left him in the warm to come round which he did eventually with a lot of shouting at first but it became less violent as he realised where he was. Grandma gave him another weaker dose of her concoction which started to quieten him down again. It seemed that his idea of how a Cossack should be seen by the outside world was also returning to him along with his senses."

"Well what about this Frenchman Dad – Nicolas?"

"Oh he was no problem. He was another hard brought up person and for all his youth he was tough, as he had already proved, and resourceful. His wound was pretty clean and Mumija gave him much the same treatment with the help of Marija with the honey and bandages, but he was still mobile. He had been on the run for a long time too, he was painfully thin and gaunt and he didn't exactly smell of roses but he cleaned himself up in the other room with a bucket of hot water and soap. There was only one bone broken, one of the smaller toes as well as the puncture which was just a flesh wound. It just needed bandaging to hold it in place while it healed. So he sat with it raised most of the time and later hobbled around with the help of Marija, laughing through his watering eyes and his pain as she made fun of his gait"

"So now you had two invalids around the place to look after, as well as doing the milking, feeding the animals, fetching the water, cooking, lighting the fire every morning and everything else, did you? and what happened to the dog?"

"The dog followed us home. Once we gave it a bone it was happy. We decided, just in case, that we had better separate the two patients. So after a couple of days near the oven with the rest of us when Captain Kyril had woken up on the third day and was in a more reasonable state we walked him slowly over to the barn and up the ladder. Although it was still freezing outside at least the howling wind had stopped blowing through every chink. We settled the Russian down on a cot up in the hayloft in the eaves. At least it was warm from the heat which rose off the animals in their stalls, and it was dry and clean up there. His dog followed up the ladder like a cat and lay alongside him in the hay. When it got fed up with that it soon learned to scramble down the rungs again and run outside. We made room for the extra horses alongside the milking cow and our own horse. That was one large horse two smaller ones, one cow and one Russian sharing the quarters, and the dog from time to time."

"It was a pure fluke that when this farm of ours was first conceived they gave more thought to the comfort of the animals than they did to the humans. The stable was bigger than the house, and with a usable loft area. We had to look at our food situation too. To suddenly have two extra mouths to feed was something we could just about cope with if we were careful. We hoped they would soon be gone. "

"So how did you keep all this a secret."

"If and when anyone called, or was even nearby, the dog barked, at least the Russian one did, and you could see right down the track to the gate where it meets the main road, the boy made himself scarce in the barn while they were at the house"

"What did the Cossack think of that arrangement? Not much I would have thought."

"Surprisingly he didn't seem to mind. I think he welcomed the company especially when the lad took him up some of my home brewed vodka. He seemed to prefer it to his own bottle, or perhaps it was because it was free. He also took him back some of his own clothes mended and washed, and new underwear."

"I called Nicolas a boy because he was quite a bit younger than me at the time. It was amazing, that lad harboured no animosity towards the Russian at all even though he'd just escaped death at his hands. Nicolas was a very pleasant young man. We trusted him. He wasn't going to let us down. You could just tell. It was just the way he responded and acted. A genuine boy put into this situation by chance. His misfortune had then turned around completely and fate was now smiling upon him.

I think the Russian began to realise that too, but also that he was in a difficult position with this enemy combatant. He needed the continuous treatment that Mama was giving him until his wound healed and the bone re-grew and knitted together. He would never have been able to mount, let alone control, a horse until then and he knew it. But we were worried at what might happen to us once he regained his strength and remembered who he was supposed to be and what his duty was. We were a little afraid of him and what he might do. We wouldn't be able to control him."

"Nicolas turned out to be a Godsend once his foot healed up after three weeks. We gave him some old clothes and burned the rags he had with him. We sat down with him during that time and went through the essentials of the Polish language at his request. He was about the same age as your aunt Marija and she taught him all sorts of stuff. They got on really well, she always laughing at his silly mistakes, but he never seemed to make the same one more than a couple of times. He learned quickly, – which I suppose was a quality which had kept him alive for so long. He told us he had got the boots from a Frenchman, who had looted them from somewhere. The man exchanged them with Nic for a frozen half-loaf which he had picked up from an upturned cart he had found off the road fifty versts back. The best trade he ever made. The boots even fitted quite well, a bit on the loose side perhaps. He already had some food of his own, some pieces of two cats they had enticed and killed which were semi-frozen in his haversack. The quality of that boot was to save his foot perhaps even his leg. From then on he and his travelling companion had pressed on back the way they had come. The other man was Dutch, an infantryman in the Grand Army whom he had fallen in with after the nightmare of the Berezina bridge crossing."

Nicolas told us all about his conscription and his mother's dismay. She had seen so much upheaval and war since 1789. It never seemed to stop. One régime was exchanged for another. One local French village peasant philosopher who was able to read had pragmatically mentioned that, "Things must change so that everything can remain the same." This ancient adage was as old as the hills. He had read it somewhere in a book. She knew well enough it was all a waste of time, – just a complicated power struggle. But even being aware of that, she also realised that they had been marginally better off since, with the monarchy gone. There was a slightly more equal air about things in some respects but there was still authority, and the drafting of youngsters had to be complied with."

"So off he went then I suppose."

"Yes, he had no choice, but what he went through was unbelievable – a nightmare. He told us all about it. He was conscripted into a cavalry regiment because he was good with horses, his father had two of them and ploughed for other farmers. During the training Nic already had a head start over the rest because of that familiarity with the animals. Once they had been trained in all the aspects of mounted warfare, weaponry, drill and fieldcraft he was posted to an existing regiment where he soon settled in, coached by the old hands who formed its heart. He was also quickly given a temporary commission. So the recruits were being used to bolster regiments which had been depleted in previous battles and campaigns. Nic's regiment for example had been reduced considerably in Spain. Although the lad himself was up to the mark, some of the recruits were less so.

Once they were on the march, it was glorious at first until it was well under way and they began to realise just how far it was they were expected to ride in the oppressive heat and that they were outstripping their supplies. It was all too ambitious and not only that but unwieldy, he said. It was the biggest such enterprise ever undertaken. As is often the case, the rank and file had a better idea of what was going on than the generals did. Orders were issued and the high command went off expecting them to be carried out, never checking, and of course many couldn't be complied with for various reasons. Clashes of personality and rivalry among the leadership and so on were destructive factors. There were not enough horses, and not enough fodder for the ones they had. Of the new recruits, most were inexperienced in warfare. Many of them were barely familiar with horses and their needs, – a lot of these youngsters came from towns and cities. The list of deficiencies went on and on, I seem to recall Nicolas telling me."

"It was such a long time ago that I forget the rest of them, Nicolas did tell me I think, but this was all years ago. I remember my own part in his story because I was there and those are the images which have best stayed in my mind for so long."

"'All this was on the way out,'" Nic said, "'Almost before they had even started. The Russians were avoiding a pitched battle. There were plenty of skirmishes, minor engagements even. Finally we were able to give battle at a little place called Borodino but Napoleon held our cavalry corps in reserve as well as his 'Old Guard' and we just sat there all day on horseback watching the fighting, what we could see of it through the smoke. We may not have been able to see it all but we could certainly hear it. If you have never witnessed a battle you can't conceive of the horror of it. If you remember how the Cossack screamed continuously at the top of his voice in agony, imagine thousands doing it all at the same time. And the noise of the cannon

– deafening. And the stink of it. Guts and entrails laid bare, blood, vomit, excrement of men and horses, screaming, crying, groaning and shouting, shouts of elation, shouts of fear, shouts of anger, horses hooves and musket fire. Dismembered bodies made it all look like a giant butchers yard whenever the smoke cleared slightly. All of those things are happening at the same time. It is Hell on earth – believe you me!"' Jurgis took another sip of his concoction as Jonas waited eagerly for the story to continue.

"We learned more of the history of it over the course of the next few years from priests and travellers. They said that Napoleon had been trying to reach a deal with the Tsar but Aleksander was too clever. He had come to the conclusion long since that for Russia to progress it had to become a major player on the world stage. Settling for being a second rate country isolated from the rest would not do. He was looking westward for new lands, new territories, new spheres of influence and more trade.

He had put old General Kutuzov in charge who only had one eye and who was nearly in his dotage, but popular. He cared about his country but also about the well-being of his men. Kutuzov merely played a stalling game most of the time, preserving his army. Basically it seems they allowed Napoleon to overreach himself. As he got closer and closer to Moscow they just set fire to the buildings and withdrew, leaving the shell of the city to Napoleon.

By the time the Emperor realised he was fighting a lost cause and while he pondered on it for another two weeks autumn faded and the winter set in and he was in the first stages of a military catastrophe which finally led to his overthrow and exile. We found all this out a long time later. He did have a brief military resurgence in Belgium after three years which he lost and that was the end for him. And his downfall? – it all started in Russia but the English had a lot to do with it. I learned such a lot from that boy Nic. All sorts of politics which I was unaware of, stuff we never get to hear normally. I also began to realise how clever and resourceful the English are. They fought him out of Spain and they had undermined Napoleon and his embargo against English commerce with Europe by having an understanding with Russia to get round the landward blockade of European trading ports. The French fleet had already been destroyed by the English so they had no seaborne power with which to invade England once and for all. Nor could they set up a naval blockade of European ports. So England was a thorn in the French side. Some of this I learned from that boy. After talking to him at length I realised it was as if we were living in a mediaeval backwater, in Lietuva, a forgotten land where time had passed us by."

"Tėtis! I seem to remember years ago you did mention England to me and I never forgot it. You must have told me what Nicolas told you. You said something about it being a free country where there was no serfs like here, with large cities and industrial areas where they make iron, have big ships and a strong army and navy."

"Where is it exactly Tėtis?"

"It's not that far I believe. It's to the west across the sea. You could get to it by boat in about five days or from somewhere like Germany with its ports. From there it would be quicker. Southampton, Hull or London depending on where you wanted to go. You can get to most parts of England from Hull. They have a new system of railways, and there's always work of some sort or another to be had. They have farms the same as here too but their soil is better than ours, much less sandy. They can grow all sorts of things which we can't. Their summers are longer and the whole place is a lot warmer than here, even in winter."

"Of course, the other place is America. That's a lot further but it's far bigger than England. They speak the same language there too – English."

"I wonder if I'll ever see it for myself?" mused Jonas.

"Well whatever happens will happen but they're a very welcoming race the English by all accounts, – providing you go there in peace and work hard......."

Nicolas, over the months he was with them recovering and learning Polish, had recounted the rest of the sorry drama of his own narrow escapes. He revealed ashamedly how he had in fact already met Veronika the previous year. The family was stunned at this revelation and asked how that could possibly be. "Granny was beginning to become a bit deaf then and merely nodded," said Jurgis. "She didn't really hear very much by then."

"Nicolas told us," "'I am almost ashamed to relate it but your mother, Veronika, actually told me off when I was in charge of a forage detail. I've never mentioned it before because I don't think she could actually see me properly at the time but now I see how good and honest you all are I must be open with you. I now believe in the power of coincidences. Who would ever have imagined that the people I stole from would save my life. I must admit I did have a problem reining in those over-enthusiastic boys. But she made me think, I watched her walk off and thought how plucky she was.'"

"At that point Nicolas suddenly broke down and we all felt immensely sorry for him. '"Those poor lads, he had sobbed. Most of them are dead and I am alive. How is that possible?'"

"He uttered this plaintively in his newly acquired Polish with a lacing of French but we, the listeners, understood the gist of it quite well and listened with tears in our eyes.

Veronika put her arm around his shoulder and said,"

"'God works in his own way. Who are we to know?'"

"When he had regained his composure he told us how, on the arduous return journey, he had lost his horse. He was suffering from dysentery and had pulled up on the roadside and dismounted to answer an urgent call of nature which he was having to do with great frequency. He had left his horse standing there while he went about his business when right in the middle of it a group of Cuirassiers had gone cantering past and his horse had galloped off and joined them and that was the last Nic saw of it. At that point he got rid of his heavy breastplate and helmet and replaced them with other bits and pieces which were more practical to wear whilst walking. And there was no shortage of equipment to choose from which had been abandoned along the way. Which regiment it signified, it didn't now matter. He trekked along on foot until he fell in with Adrianus when he muscled in on his camp fire. Teaming up together they took the decision not to take the same route home as the rest of the army but to try to head home by a route further south where maybe the inhabitants of the countryside hadn't witnessed the impositions the French had visited upon them on the way out. So once they had escaped across the Berezina on foot, barely with their lives while thousands died, drowned, were killed by Cossacks or froze around them, he and his companion had veered more to the south. They left the area amid the sound of loud explosions as the French engineers blew up the bridges behind them. Nicolas and Aad realised that there were still thousands left stranded and hopeless on the other bank and that they must have been abandoned to the mercy of the Russians.

They had experienced no trepidation at calling at isolated farmhouses. The people for the most part aided them, giving them food and even shelter for the night in their barns sometimes. After all, they were fully armed with loaded weapons. Even when still trying to slog home through western Russia they found help. Even some of the Russian peasants didn't appear to like the Cossacks!

The rumours they picked up en route about some pretty fearful atrocities, exacted upon the stragglers of the retreating army, terrified them. They then decided to become even more low profile than they already were and they did more stealing, usually carrying it out in the late evening and marching on for the rest of the night, when there was an un-obscured moon, and resting up by day so they were long gone by the time any thefts were discovered. The got eggs here or a hen there and even bundles of firewood which they carried along with them. They had a couple of near misses where the barking of a dog roused the inhabitants and they noticed too that there were mounted cavalrymen who they spotted in the distance carrying lances, sometimes in Russian uniform, sometimes not, and they concluded that they were the infamous Cossacks who they had a few brief brushes with back along the route. On the whole they muddled along steadily moving closer and closer to home but keeping well to the south of the rest of the retreating French rabble. The other man was adept at navigating by the stars when the sky was clear, so they generally succeeded in heading westwards with a few detours north or south in the lonely and desolate countryside they were passing through. The days were very short only seven and a half hours and the nights interminably long at that time of year and people were loth to venture forth unless it was absolutely necessary. After nightfall there was something eerie about emerging from the house with a candle in a lantern with one's eyes unaccustomed to the darkness outside and blinking like an owl. One got this sense that whoever might have been there could see you perfectly, while you couldn't see them. So on the whole the odds were stacked in favour of the intruders whose eyes were already adjusted to the inky blackness. When there was a moon and everything was bathed in an eerie light things were slightly different."

Jurgis continued to recount the story that Nicolas had told him, coupled with his own tale until at last the point was reached in the narrative when all their destinies had become intertwined. It really started to enter their collective consciousness at the point at which the French lad's companion had experienced some kind of epiphany and had decided to take a certain course of action. He had simply left the shelter of the bivouac, sat down in the snow and, as Nicolas suspected, deliberately gone to sleep in the freezing air in order to give Nicolas a fighting chance of survival.

Jurgis slumped a bit with the effort of talking, then with a determined supreme effort gathered his thoughts together again.

"Nicolas always said that he thought that this young man from Holland, Adrianus Kwakkelstein, had done it to improve the odds for his friend. Aad had been well aware that his own feet in poor condition, wrapped in rags, were holding them both back. He had mentioned it to Nicolas several times suggesting that they split up and he would take his chances. Nicolas had always declined the offer. In fact he wouldn't hear anything about it. It had turned out that Aad had succeeded in one respect. Nicolas, and even his pursuer, was now here in our house safe and sound."

Jurgis continued, "We were all hit by the magnitude of that information. None of us in the house at that moment, when we heard that, could think in terms of giving up one's own life for another person. Your Grandma Magdalena, during one of her lucid moments, was very cut up about it. I can still see her now, eyes brimming with tears as she sat there in her tied-back headscarf. She brought one of the loose ends round to dab her eyes. I will never forget that image. She was so concerned for the poor lad's family back home. Nic went on to say that the two of them had talked during the course of their journey together and he had found out a bit about his companion. This young Dutch fellow had no family and he had been brought up in a strict manner by the charitable monks of a religious order. They had named him at random Adrianus Kwakkelstein. He was clever enough but rough and ready, and a complicated person, Nic told them. When he came of age he couldn't get away from the monastic order quickly enough. Soldiering and even stealing were things he seemed to enjoy. Nic left it there but I think that maybe it was because they were counter to the self-denial and austerity of his upbringing. It was all he had known apart from the tough education they had given him at the monastery. They had been unable to quell his natural roguishness but do you know what Jonas? Underneath it he must have had a heart of gold."

Jurgis added, "I believe Nic tried to write off Aad as someone they shouldn't get too upset about. He probably did this to spare the feelings of our compassionate Lithuanian family. But it merely had the effect of making the women feel even more sorry for him. It would have been the most immediate and personal part of the whole tragedy for Nicolas which this family had experienced too in part.

"So he was a decent thoughtful person trying to play it all down to spare their feelings with a few half truths?" queried Jonas.

"Well maybe that's what he was trying to do in a way but what he told us wasn't quite accurate. In his own mind perhaps he felt that this deception was justifiable, or maybe he even felt guilty because he saw in the other man more nobility than he himself possessed. Perhaps he realised that some of the purer aspects of what Aad had learned from the brothers, to do with self-denial and sacrifice were witnessed by his ultimate act. Nicolas however had merely re-awakened all that emotion we have all felt at church when we have celebrated Holy Communion. Every single Sunday we have done that and at every holiday and feast day. All of us immediately made that connection which was probably why we were all so emotionally overcome. Whatever Nic's thoughts were in the way he told us, he had underestimated our family's even-handed compassion. In this instance whatever he had said it wouldn't have worked because the women, indeed all of us were plainly and simply overcome by the pathos and futility of all of it. Veronika particularly isn't taken in by ego or glory. She is a wise woman who saw through all the nonsense we talked and who came up with the conclusion which worked for her, and the only correct one really – what a waste it all was. Your granny and my sister Marija – your aunt, and even I – agreed with her."

"How old did Nicolas say his friend was?" asked Jonas.

"He didn't actually say. I don't know for certain, but from what I saw maybe seventeen or so," replied his father.

"But if he knowingly made that decision it is surely admirable regardless of his age. To give up one's life for somebody else is the greatest and most noble sacrifice anyone could make."

"Yes – as Our Lord did for us," whispered Jurgis, crossing himself weakly as he sank back down on his pillow exhausted.

Chapter 6

Understanding

To Marija, Nicolas was exotic, funny and extremely handsome. He was facially different to other youths in the area. She had never really met a foreigner such as he before but fate had thrown them together and she was a little overwhelmed and she was flattered that he always seemed pleased to see her.

All through the winter months she concentrated on teaching him Polish and there being nothing like the proximity of teacher and pupil to break down inhibitions and to get to know each other they became easily familiar. The children in the house watched them, giggling.

As winter started to show signs of turning into spring. they wrapped up and started going on walks down to the lake and to the woods, returning ruddy faced and warm. Sometimes the Russian's dog Yuri came with them. He seemed to revel in his untimely, if temporary, release from military service and became quite a pet of theirs, a catalyst for the bond that was forming between them. Jurgis returned to the scene of the incident in the forest with a horse, a pickaxe and shovel as soon as he could, with the intention of trying to dig out a shallow grave for the dead Dutchman, but reaching the spot he found that it was too difficult in the frozen ground. He then just heaved the corpse onto its side and piled as much snow and ice over it as he could. He would come back when the weather was warmer and do the job properly. Gathering together all the scattered gear he could find, and the traps, he brought everything back to the farm.

The Russian had mellowed it seemed. Nicolas had continued to be kind towards Kyril and extended towards him the same respect he would have showed his own father. As life continued they shared the same board at mealtimes and sat around indoors in the warm during the evenings. The war raging elsewhere was now forgotten in most respects by both of them, except that in Kyril's mind was the thought of rejoining his unit while in Nicolas' was the determination to have done with it all and sit it out here until the conflict was over.

Kyril's personality was pretty much set in stone by his upbringing. Drilled from an early age into the creed that the most important things in life were firstly, his horse, secondly, his weapons, thirdly, his son and then his wife, – strictly in that order. The first of these were living just below him enjoying the luxury of regular food. The second, he had noticed where they had been put and was very well aware of where to lay his hands on them when the time came. The third was more of a problem. He did miss his twelve year old and somehow he had come to substitute Nicolas for the son he was separated from. He just couldn't help it, tough though he was. Nicolas' kindness and lack of animosity towards him had brought out his better side and he responded positively to their animated lively and stimulating conversations. He got to know about the enemy as a human being with hopes, fears, family and opinions, such as limited language would allow. He responded to the respect which Nicolas showed towards him and quite enjoyed this new dimension of surrogate father and son. He welcomed the opportunity to demonstrate his knowledge and impart some of his life's experience and wisdom to this eager listener. It made him feel valued and important. As for the fourth in the list, she would still be there no doubt when he got back and he just hoped she was looking after the house and his son properly while he was away. It was clear these people, these peasants who had taken him in, were a kind and generous family. They had already proved that by saving both his arm and possibly the lives of both he and Nicolas and had looked after them both thereafter, and he had no reason to suppose they wouldn't continue to do so.

By the onset of spring Kyril was well on the way to recovery from his injury. There was only so much he could do to help around the place and he yearned to see his own son and feel the embrace of his wife. He would stand under the ladder reaching up, grasping the highest rung he could then tentatively let his knees bend. At first it was difficult but as the muscles in his right arm began to be stretched and exercised he was gradually able to lift his feet from the ground. So it went on as his arm began to regain its strength.

One morning towards the end of April when spring was in full swing and the sun was shining, the ground thawing and the rivers rushing, Nicolas, as usual, took some black bread, some salted ham and a cup of yesterday's milk out to the barn and found the Cossack gone. Also missing were his two horses and all his weapons and gear. The only thing left to indicate he had ever been there was Aad's smashed watch with its chain wrapped around a ladder rung hanging down and his own small vodka jar and its inferior contents which he had abandoned in favour of Jurgis' full one.

They were all amazed and, if they were honest, relieved when Nicolas breathlessly brought the news to the rest of them. None of them had heard a thing during the night. Then their fears turned to worry as they realised that he might bring the authorities back to round up Nicolas – and even them for aiding and abetting. If that were to happen there was no guarantee as to what might happen to him.

They considered why Kyril might have gone off without saying goodbye. They concluded that it was simply because, considering his upbringing and background, he couldn't bear the thought of the loss of face. He had already been dependent on this family for nearly three months. Granny Magdalena thought he might be mildly ashamed. She thought that he may have been embarrassed by his own previous single-mindedness in tracking down fugitives. He had become easy with them all and appeared to like them. Nevertheless he was still an officer in the Russian army and the war was still going on as far as they knew. Technically Nicolas was still an enemy combatant. But they couldn't be sure exactly what was in Kyril's mind. He was a complex character whom they had a problem second guessing. It could have been that, although he hadn't taken further action himself, there was still the possibility that he might report it.

They planned a strategy that morning around the table in the event of that happening. If anyone was to approach who looked official Nic would make for the woods keeping the house and farm buildings between himself and the gate and road. They would make a cache of equipment hidden just inside the forest edge in case the authorities turned up. Two days after that had been decided, Yuri the dog appeared trotting briskly and wagging his tail. They waited for the imminent arrival of the Cossack with others. Nothing happened. The dog seemed perfectly happy to be there with them. He knew where he was well off and well-fed and he enjoyed playing with the young people there. After a week when nothing else untoward or unusual occurred they all relaxed and decided that it was the end of the episode as far as Kyril was concerned. Nicolas carried on being accepted as a member of the family as usual.

On the Saturday evening a week after Kyril had gone they all sat round and toasted his health with a shot of his own vodka, which was the only thing he had left behind, apart from the watch and the dog.

Everyone continued to go to Mass on Sundays except of course Nicolas, and thus snippets of news filtered through about the scale of the disaster which had befallen the French. It made Nicolas very depressed and he became quiet and withdrawn. Marija felt so sorry for him and longed to put her arm round him and comfort him. She could imagine what he must have been going through, and tried everything she could to distract him from his worries. He thought again of the individual friends and comrades he had made. He thought about them one by one, recalling aspects of their personalities, their likes and dislikes and their varying sense of humour or even lack of it.

He put them in categories in his own mind, those who he was sure had survived and those he thought maybe hadn't. On every occasion he finished up by thanking God that he himself had been fortunately spared – thus far. He longed for home and to see his mother and father He hoped they were well and not too worried about him. He wished that he could just be back there instantly, magically somehow. Then he came round with the thought that his life wasn't so bad after all. He was even amongst people who seemed to care for him. How fortunate he had been – or perhaps he had made his own luck!

Although surviving, he knew that it wasn't yet over. His formula for getting out of these melancholic moods was to go outside and find some manual work to do such as chopping logs, cleaning out the cowshed, or grooming the horse. Anything, as long as it wasn't too repetitive. Repetition often led the mind to turn in upon itself and dwell on negative things, so if he found himself engaged upon them he had to be particularly disciplined in his thoughts. He continued to consolidate his command of Polish by discussing all kinds of topics with them all, about nature, life in general and even religion and the Saints. Marija explained to him about the Patron Saint of Lithuania, St Kazimieras. Nicolas began to understand the complexity of the relationship between Lithuania and its neighbour. There, he was Kazimierz, a Polish prince who lived hundreds of years ago, the heir to

thrones, and yet he had been remarkably kind and generous to the poor. He died at the age of twenty five. Here, he would always be known as Kazimieras.

Nicolas commented, "Ah! That's Casimir in France. A symbol of Poland. Somehow the good always seem to die young." He then added with a self-deprecating laugh, "If that's the case, I'll probably make ninety five."

Marija immediately replied with a misty-eyed faraway look, "No! You are good and kind, but I hope and pray you will still live a very long life."

Nicolas regarded her then from a slightly different viewpoint. He sensed that the feelings he had towards her were being reciprocated.

"So Nicolas, who is your favourite Saint?" she asked him.

He thought for a moment and then replied, "I like Saint Peter."

"Why do you like Saint Peter in particular?"

"I think, because he was so imperfect. Such an ordinary man."

"Isn't that a bit of a contradiction?" asked Marija.

Nicolas struggled to understand this concept in the newly acquired tongue which he had been trying so hard to come to grips with. But after wrestling with words backwards and forwards, finally they both thought they had understood each other.

"No! Peter was basically a fisherman with the same flaws as anyone else. He was impetuous, slightly aggressive, he misunderstood things and he denied Christ at a key moment.

The whole Christian world was built upon him, and by him, because he was such a common person. He became God's representative on Earth and now he holds the keys to the Kingdom of Heaven. He was, and is, a kind of divine human being."

It was abundantly clear to them all that Nicolas possessed a strong, well informed and thoughtful faith on a worldly level.

Marija realised that she was feeling something that she had never experienced before, an emotion that whilst exciting beyond words, also made her feel vulnerable. She thought about Nicolas constantly, her every waking thought revolved around him but she also felt anxious to the point of nausea. If he were not around, her heart raced as if in a panic and for a young woman like her who had always been strong and independent this was a frightening concept. To become so dependent on one person was a risk, but in reality there was no choice to be made, this was love in the real sense, a meeting of two individuals who whether together or apart were one.

Time seemed to race by and every moment spent with Nicolas felt like heaven on earth. She delighted in his touch, his smell, his laugh, just the faintest brush of his skin on hers was ecstasy. The sound of his voice stayed with her even when she was alone. She could almost hear his thoughts because they had become so entwined in each others lives. Marija and Nicolas took every available opportunity to spend time together, sometimes it was from necessity, the chores around the farm were relentless but took on a new purpose when shared. When their workload allowed, and if the weather was fair, they would take time to talk together trying to decipher the finer points of each other's language. She laughed as he struggled with the complexities of pronunciation in Polish. Much of the time though words were not needed. They would walk for miles in the woods and meadows enjoying their growing love for each other, whilst still avoiding other people. It was on one of these precious afternoons that Marija finally realised the full depth of their love. Nicolas and she had stopped under the shade of a magnificent oak tree high up on a hill, it's wide canopy providing a glorious dappled shade. As they sat together look-ing out over the expanded vista of the countryside from their van-tage point, Marija opened the small package she had carefully carried with her containing some bread and cheese. She tore off a small piece of bread and passed it to Nicolas, he bent his head and gently took the morsel from her hand, his lips gently brushing her finger tips, it was the most sensual thing she had ever experienced. Her heart leapt as Nicolas took her hand and began kissing every finger, then her wrist, the inside of her elbow, not stopping until he reached her neck. Marija could hardly breath, Nicolas pulled her towards him until their bodies touched and then he kissed her with such gentle passion, nothing could ever have prepared her for this moment, it was unimaginably beautiful, more perfect than she could ever have imagined. She knew this was the most sublime experience she could ever enjoy with another human being. Carefully he began to remove her clothing, his strong hands caressing every inch of her willing body. She was completely overwhelmed and succumbed without hesitation or fear. Marija knew there was something uniquely special about this man, it wasn't just his sharp and inquisitive mind which had grasped the basics of the Polish language within months but also his calm, gentle nature, his easy way with horses and people and his air of con-fidence and competence not familiar to her amongst the Polish youths she had encountered. She felt safe in his arms and more of a woman that she had ever felt before. He was the reason she had been put on this earth, all her 18 years had been leading her to this point in time... to this man and when she felt him inside her she was certain that this moment would change her life forever. Over the following weeks and months these moments were repeated naturally and spontaneously as the bonds between them strengthened and Marija's anxious feelings began to subside to be replaced by a contentment that she had only ever dreamed of. Strangely though the nausea continued and in fact worsened, until one morning, two months after she first made love to Nicolas she was physically sick.......

Chapter 7

Revelation

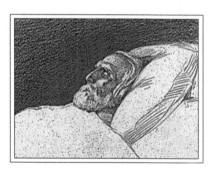

A day or two after relating the story to Jonas, Jurgis suffered a stroke and went rapidly downhill after that. It was almost as if he had given up and nature was now taking its inevitable course, and yet there still seemed to be something. Jonas noticed his father following him with his eyes in the later days with a slight frown or worried look about him. Several times towards the very end Jurgis had seemed to want to speak and his lips had moved and he was mumbling. His son had put his ear very close to try and hear what was being said but it was unintelligible. Jonas had just two weeks to ponder on the tale before his father suddenly died during the night.

Veronika found the old man one morning motionless and cold and that was the end of it. People were informed and arrangements were made for the wake and the funeral.

When it was all over and Jurgis had been interred with respect and dignity, life returned to normality.

Although Jonas was not the eldest child, but the youngest, he was still here after all the others had left to go their separate ways, so he felt himself to be the man of the house now.

"You know Mamyte," he said one evening after they had finished their meal and were sitting by the fire,

"I miss Tėvelis even though he was always too busy to really talk to me. Come to think of it, the only time he did so at any length was when he was ill and couldn't do anything else anyway."

"I wonder what else he wanted to say."

"What do you mean?" his mother responded abruptly.

Jonas detected the excessively sharp response and noted her subsequent over-softening of the voice as she belatedly sought to take the edge off her reaction with a few vague comments about Jurgis having been ill and probably not knowing what he was saying in his last incoherent rambles.

"Did you actually hear him say anything then?" she asked. Jonas sensed there was something going on in his mother's mind and his curiosity was aroused. It was now becoming clear that she knew something which she wasn't letting on about. But he knew he would have to take this slowly and carefully in order that his mother wouldn't clam up entirely.

A few days later he said to her, "I wonder if it was some more about that story he told me. We never found out what happened to the Cossack nor why the dog came back. Maybe this Tymoshenko fellow got into trouble when he got back to his unit. Perhaps he didn't make it home at all. Maybe dad killed him after all."

"Of course he wouldn't have!"

"Can you remember nothing more then about the story?"

"No, I don't know, I never really thought about it, I wasn't even there for most of it."

"Right! so you don't remember then! What about Tetulė Marija? She was here then wasn't she? I can't ask her now, God rest her, but would her husband know anything about it? Maybe she told him something before she died."

At this, Veronika's eyes filled with tears at the thought of her sister-in-law who had died from smallpox five years earlier. She and her husband had been unable to have children themselves so Jonas had never had any cousins from that quarter. For that reason Marija had lavished her affections on her nephew Jonas all the more over the years. Her visits were frequent and loving. In fact even before she had left home she had been a warm and caring person to them all particularly to Jonas, who was for a time the baby of the family.

"I don't think it would do any good to go raking over old coals," his mother said. How do you mean?" Jonas enquired."

"Let's just say that it might be better left alone."

The more he persisted, in an oblique way the more was coming out. He knew by now that his instincts had been right. I'll go over there and see Uncle Vincas, he may know something."

"When will you go?" his mother asked him.

"I think I'll leave it until after Mass next Sunday" he replied. "He's bound to be there."

He noticed his mother start visibly.

Nothing much else was said on the matter. The days passed one by one as Sunday drew closer. Veronika's head was in a complete turmoil. Jonas could tell his mother wasn't herself and just decided to let things take their course. Sure enough his patience drew results and she broached the subject again after their evening meal on the Saturday. She disappeared for a moment and came back with two glasses of vodka one of which she gave to her son taking a sip from the other before she had even sat down. Jonas took a swig of his and muttered abstractedly, "Better not make a habit of this or we'll end up like Tẽtis."

He waited, gazing vacantly into thin air until she spoke.

"Erm, look! It's only right I suppose. You have sensed something that has been hushed up for years. I swore I would never reveal it to anyone but now most of the parties are probably dead for all I know. Well some of them definitely are."

"It's all right Mamyte, carry on."

Jonas could sense his mother's mental turmoil.

"Your Papa and me........." She hesitated.

"Yes Mamyte, go on!"

"We are...... not your parents, we are your aunt and uncle, !"

Jonas laughed at first then realised that his mother was almost completely overcome by what she was saying. This was no joke, no leg pull. This must be true. Was this really happening? Had he heard correctly? His mind went numb as he floundered for thoughts, but none came. He was suspended in time and his brain wouldn't work. He automatically took another gulp of Vodka and slumped back in his chair. Veronika jumped up, tears streaming down her face and crouched beside him on the floor hugging him and apologising as he sat welded fast to his seat.

"Marija, our dear Marija, Papa's sister, was your mother..... not your aunt!" she uttered, her voice catching.

All the grief, all the burden of secrecy, the lies and the deception, all were relieved at once, the overriding load of all the years lifted.

She realised though, that she had just transferred a burden of a different sort onto her nephew. She clung to Jonas sobbing with the relief which came from unburdening her soul. It was almost like a last confession before she too would fade and join Marija and Jurgis. The lie she had been living, the facts which she had been harbouring for a generation were now lifted. She waited contritely for the backlash which was bound to come.

Jonas managed to pull himself together somewhat and as his mother drew back, managed to get up and reach for the vodka jar again. It was definitely helping. The alcohol brought out his better nature as it always did and he felt an overwhelming love for the woman who he now knew to be his uncle's wife, and no longer his mother. He felt deeply sorry for her in her present state.

"But what does it matter?" he reasoned in his mind, "We still mean exactly the same to each other as we did an hour ago. Even if all the relationships must be re-thought."

"So I take it that my father was either the Russian or the Frenchman. It was the Frenchman wasn't it? Nicolas! It had to be because of the similar ages, the Russian was quite a bit older."

"Yes you are right." his mother replied. "They were so much in love but they were difficult times, worse than now. If the Russians had got wind of it all they would have caught him and probably killed him. The only solution we could come up with was to bring the baby up as ours when it was born. Marija would still see him all the time and look after it..... him..... you!"

"We had to hide it from everyone, even the priest. Can you imagine how people would have condemned our whole family had they known?"

"Yes, I can imagine," Jonas said quietly, "But where does that leave me?" He could barely get his head round the complexity of it.

"It leaves you exactly where you are now, with fond feelings for me and Papa and for Marija, nothing changes.

And Vincas knows nothing. He must never know .....promise me he will never know. We are now the only two people in this land who know about it. It was only your accursed questioning which forced it all out of me. I suppose I owed it to you. Everyone is entitled to know the truth about themselves. It is after all a fundamental human need to know where our roots lie."

"It's just that yours lie a little further afield than you ever imagined but you are nonetheless still a Kadišius. "

She said this with a smile and he responded by seeing the funny side of it and chuckling out loud. He felt a bit like someone who has been the butt of a joke but has the good nature and good grace to smile at himself and go along with it.

In the days that followed these frank admissions he naturally wanted to know everything about his real father and where he came from, but his mother was unable to remember the name of the town in France. This information and whatever other snippets there were had been swallowed up in the mists of time and forgotten.

The details of the subterfuge involved in convincing everyone that the baby was Veronika's was complex but both she and Marija had to go far away to very distant relatives, an old couple who could be trusted to take their secret to the grave with them.

The story was to be, that Veronika was having a few problems with her pregnancy and so had been advised to go for a rest and take it easy during her confinement in case of complications. Marija had ostensibly gone to help her sister-in-law. So when Veronika came back with the baby no one thought anything about it as the baptism was carried out in Smalenai. Their loose clothing covered up a multitude of discrepancies. The rest of the family meantime had looked after themselves for the duration of their absence. Močiutė Magdalena had come round finally to the news and had stepped into the breach for a few weeks as the lynchpin of the family. She enjoyed the resurgence of standing it gave her and a new authority among her other grandchildren.

Jonas now realised why he had been so close to Marija, why she had lavished so much love on him. He knew now why she had sung that song to him over and over in a foreign language. He suddenly realised why she often cried when no one else was around. It all made sense now. On her wedding day to Vincas he had detected an underlying sadness. How heartbreaking it must have been for her! It was their family sadness. He felt a pang of nostalgia and yearning for a moment.

There was no escaping his own guilty feeling at the way he had extracted all this from someone who was clearly so uncomfortable with it. He would always see Veronika as his mother. Everything else was just an interesting but technical tragedy.

He began to understand that sometimes certain secrets are best left untold. They could cause upset and damage. People should be allowed to die with dignity withholding their private thoughts and feelings to the end. He resolved to do the same thing himself when he finally reached the end of his unimaginably interminable future life. He could see no immediate benefit in sharing any of this. It would have to be a skeleton locked away in a cupboard.

He did wonder however about his father. Was he good with horses? What did he look like? Was he still alive now? In the following days and weeks, now that it was all out in the open he quizzed his grandmother endlessly and she was only too happy to unburden herself of every last thing she knew. She went all through the whole episode from the moment when Jurgis had first brought all this excitement down upon them. She told Jonas how his father had been yearning to get back to France. Marija had told her sister-in-law about her pregnancy, but she hadn't told the baby's father so when he left he was none the wiser. If he did come back, Marija wanted to be sure it was for her and not through some sense of responsibility towards the, as yet, unborn baby. But alas, he never did return. There were a few letters which found their way to them out of sequence. Clearly they had been translated into Polish by someone but she was hurt that he had not bothered to re-copy them out but just sent the translation straight on, written in the translator's hand. So in her fraught state of mind she replied in a way which expressed the way she was feeling. But who knew whether the subtle nuances of their letters were being lost in translation and why some didn't quite add up, as if some letters had gone missing. So, Veronika thought that either there had been a big misunderstanding or that Nicolas had been distracted by other things once he got home.

Who knows what really happened as a result of the language difference, the distance between them and the turmoil still existing in their countries. And there was the shame which would have fallen upon Nicolas' own head if this had become public knowledge in his parents' household.

The result was that poor Marija was destined to spend the rest of her life separated from the man she really loved and whom she thought had loved her.

She would now have to live a lie and marry a man she may not have really cared for in the same way she had Nicolas, just for the sake of appearances. She, for ever after, must have secretly hoped that Nicolas would one day return.

Deep down she knew she would have to go through this penance for the rest of her life without ever being able to hear the word "Mamyte" from their child Jonas. She would only ever be able to address him for the rest of her life as 'Mano sūnėnas' – her nephew.

Jonas turned all this over in his mind endlessly. The conclusion he always arrived at every time was absolute pity for Marija having to spend the rest of her life unable to communicate her true feelings or to talk to anyone about it who may have understood. He tended to blame the unfair social constraints in their intimate communities which meant that her secret had to be kept at all costs. He began to think that the stigma attached to a birth out of wedlock, whilst having the effect of binding the community together morally thus ensuring that the structure of society, the sacraments of marriage, baptism and conformity weren't broken, had an appalling effect on the stigmatised girls concerned when those conventions were occasionally breached.

The old priest at the time of all those happenings had died and there was now a new one. If ever Marija had made a confession to the priest at the time, then the secret must have died with him. In any case the confidences of the confessional were sacrosanct.

"Ah well!" thought Jonas, "I may well be the first bastard in this family but I probably won't be the last."

Chapter 8

Marriage – 1853

Juozas Kadišius had known his wife Rozalia Damansks since they were both children. How they came to know each other, and later to fall into marriage wasn't unusual. She was Polish, from Seinei but her family often went to Mass at Smalenai because an elder sister had married a local man and there was therefor an opportunity to meet once a week which mother and daughter rarely missed. After church, families got together in the road in a large crowd of jostling people, all eager to exchange news. The Church was an institution which bound the people together more than anything else. From a seemingly deserted countryside, hundreds of souls would materialise on Sundays there. Where they all came from exactly was hard to imagine. There were so many in attendance that more than one service took place. Afterwards the road outside would be crowded with a seething mass of people. Individuals darted through the throng as they spied someone they wished to speak to on some matter of business or to exchange news, opinions or gossip. There was a refreshments stall set up by someone from a local house, where they could buy tea and snacks, or they sometimes took their own sausage and bread. On those days many families looked forward to the family meetings. Married grown up children, grandchildren, parents, cousins, aunts and uncles, nephews and nieces relished a social occasion. Juozas' father Jonas and his mother Ieva Kaplinskas were the same as all the other people. They loved a good gossip, or as they would have said, 'an exchange of news.' Whilst the adults talked about topics boring to the young, the children would play together and so cemented their childish friendship.

By the Monday morning one could be forgiven for wondering if anyone lived in the area at all. They were all gone, absorbed by the countryside, and back at their daily tasks, pondering, ruminating on what they had heard and seen the day before.

As the years passed and they became older the two young people met also at baptisms, first Holy Communion, funerals, marriages and religious feasts, and those very important ones held at Lent, Easter and Christmas when the faithful made every effort to attend the bigger church in Seinei. The opportunities centred around their local church were made almost continuous by the large families which the Church encouraged. At least weekly there was always someone, who had reached some kind of milestone in their life, to be celebrated by the community. The two children began to enjoy dances and festivals together, when they were old enough to be allowed to go to them.

The friendship and later attraction was mutual, and almost taken for granted. As they grew up they sought each other out, either at the church, at Masses or on market days in Smalenai, Punskas, Kalvaria or Seinei, places that were the outer limits of their world. Whenever there was some form of activity at any of these towns, they both went.

Neither had ever been very far afield until suddenly one day when he was about seventeen, Juozas was struck by a random bombshell in the form of notification of conscription into the Russian army. The entire family was shattered by this call but there was no resisiting it. He had to go. The family was resigned to it and gave him a going away party. Condolences were offered by guest after guest as if Juozas had been diagnosed with a terminal illness and in truth it was nearly as bad. His parents were heartbroken. His life in this part of the world would effectively be finished. "Why me ?" he thought. "Why should it be me to be one of the three per cent of the eligible boys called?" To be jolted out of his world just wasn't fair. At leat he wasn't being kidnapped for the army as Jewish boys were from the age of twelve in earlier times. They really did get a rough deal even now.

He reluctantly made his way to Kaunas via the nearest army post where he went through a harsh and unpleasant induction process. He had to learn afresh where his allegiances lay and to look out for himself. All conversation, reading and writing would be in Russian from now on. After weeks of training and due process he was frogmarched to an office where he was told he was being sent to the northern province of Finland. His feeling of total powerlessness over his own situation bore down on him. There was nowhere to turn. But before he could be sent to that harsh unforgiving far-flung outpost, providence intervened. After feeling drained and ill with chest pains, aching joints and shortness of breath for days he went down with a bout of Rheumatic Fever, and was then diagnosed with a heart murmur. He said he felt alright, but nevertheless they cancelled his posting and sent him to the military hospital. recommending that he should be placed on, what they considered to be, light duties. It became clear that this was to be a spell in the Kaunas garrison carpentry shop.

Back home Rozalia, at a loose end, having forlornly waited for him for a time was beset by other distractions, But letters from him kept Juozas somewhere not far from her thoughts, until finally after a further medical they told him he was to be released early from his enforced bondage. He still insisted, with youthful bravura that he was not ill. He later cursed his stupidity when they took him at his word and submitted him to a further examination. This time however, more aware and wiser now, he didn't play down his symptoms and his release was confirmed. The examining doctor told him, and wrote in his report, that Juozas had suffered some damage to his heart, would not be able to stand the strain of army service and would consequently be physically unreliable as a soldier. Juozas thought it ironic that the doctor's parting words to him were, "Remember to take it easy when you return home and don't work too hard, or you might bring on another attack which could prove fatal. Maybe not so much now you are young but in later life." "What does he think a peasant's life is like?" wondered Juozas. "They live in another world."

When he returned home, he and the love of his life met again, nearly a year after his 'abduction' as he put it. She seemed to have turned into a beautiful young woman and he had grown a little more worldly wise. After discovering that there had been a new suitor for her hand on the scene while he had been away, he professed his feelings for her anew. It had been a close-run thing after he had left. It was assumed that he would be gone for many years and Rozalia had to be married off. Her parents were ever practical, time would not stand still and life must go on. The freshly re-kindled relationship now turned into a potentially permanent partnership. From here on there would be no more snatched meetings in the company of others and no stolen kisses or clandestine assignments away from prying eyes of other youths. They could be together openly, now that he, back in his role on the land, had something positive to offer in addition to his newly acquired carpentry skills learned in the army. His experience of the force had broadened his outlook and made him mature and there was no other man who Rozalia would rather have been with. The future of their relationship was secure. And so the perennial pattern of life repeated itself yet again. Rozalia's family had already seen some of the other children take this path. Juozas saw in her parents just two older people. But they knew what to expect from life. They had lived their own rite of passage a generation earlier. They instinctively knew the protocol. But they would influence their daughter's life as much as they could for her benefit and theirs. The underlying objective, with girls particularly in this society, being to make them secure. Their encouragement of the couple was almost instinctive. Marriage would solve many practical problems. He was Lithuanian while they were Polish, and that gave them minor misgivings but looking on the positive side he could have been a Russian and that would have been a lot worse. The different nationalities were so heaped upon each other in this ever-changing border region that nothing was insurmountable. In the end it would only ever come down to guidance and advice which Rozalia might listen to, in fact probably would. But as it happened they had known Juozas and his parents a long time, which made things comfortably smooth. When he called round, he was treated like a potential son-in-law, even a son.

After a time the tacitly understood subject of marriage was broached openly. How it came about no one could quite recall afterwards, but after a vodka fuelled Juozas had poured out his heart to Rozalia's father, the man was so pleased that he brought out his special brew and gave the boy another drink. Juozas discussed his plans volubly with the parents. He was worried about his mother being left on her own and at the same time the question of inheritance of the farm tenancy came up. The couple concurred with the general feeling among family that it would be best for the pair to live with his mother after the wedding. They had taken the

boy to their hearts, especially the mother. They couldn't wait to welcome him into their family. The Wedding Mass was held at the church of St Isidore the Plough-man in Smalenai. It was packed to the rafters with well wishers and those who just needed another excuse to pray. Everyone loved a wedding and this one took place on a bright Sunday some weeks after winter had ended. The church was decked with early spring flowers. The entrance was wreathed in them. Sprigs of Ruta, not yet in flower, were everywhere giving a familiar air of pungency reminding them of their nationality. After the protracted ceremony, all the people there, without exception, took Holy Communion waiting patiently in line shuffling forward to receive the body of Christ while the priest sipped the wine representing his blood. The altar boys ministered to the priest, helping him and his assistant at every turn amid the smell of incense as the censer was swung from side to side. The entire ceremony was highly charged, emotionally and religiously and the occasional stifled sob could be heard during lulls in the ceremony. Rozalia was immersed in a romantic ecstasy of love for her new husband and religious fervour, obedience and confirmation of her faith. It seemed that everything she was meant to become in life was coming together here in this church. When the Mass was over and the final blessings had been administered to the husband and wife and the congregation, the entire party moved off in peace towards the road outside where villagers threw flowers as the couple made their way to the pony and trap which was taking them to the wedding feast. After the happy couple, came the wedding guests. They followed on carts or astride their horses, which, now freed from the harrow or plough for the occasion, enjoyed a change of role. Some were bony and scrawny others slightly better fed – as were the horses. There was one old man rattling along on a rudimentary bone-shaker bicycle with its pedals fixed to the front wheel. He was proud of it and only brought it out on

special occasions. Where he had got it or how he could have afforded it nobody knew for certain. It was guessed that his numerous grown up family must have clubbed together to get it for him to enjoy in his twilight years. It may have been a dubious gift, possibly not a good choice, judging by how wobbly he was on it, and his antics became a source of both worry and mirth. But most of the followers were walking, straggling down the well rutted sandy earth road along the steep sided river on their left, past the bridge which oddly had been built at a particularly fast flowing and deep part of its course. There were fords upstream and downstream but a previous Polish lord years ago had objected to the detour whenever he wished to go hunting in his lands across the river and had constructed this bridge at great expense to himself. It did him no good as he died a few months later and his son had his mind on other things and didn't go in for field sports, hunting or farming. He did accept the revenue from the rents though, but he left all those onerous tenancy details to his bailiff and the labouring to his serfs many of whom had specific tasks. One was a coachman always at beck and call, another was to provide several brace of woodcock or other fowl for the Lord's table every month. Each of the peasants owed a particular debt or obligation to their lord. Juozas' was to provide carpentry skills as and when required. There was no appeal against their designated roles. They had no say in it. In return they were allowed a hovel to live in and what they could make of it and all the produce they could sustain on a meagre plot of land in their own spare time. It was a type of barely civilised slavery.

Some of the Poles from the Estate mixed socially with Lithuanians, and there weren't many of those who would willingly miss the excitement and free alcohol of a wedding. These were important events in the social calendar. So there was in a limited way a mixture of different types and grades of people there on the happy day, many if not all of them from the lower orders.

Once the wedding party had arrived back at the house and assembled again and moved into the dwelling, they were regaled with a vision of colour. The whole place had been bedecked, as the church had been, with garlands of early fresh flowers and rue. Various gifts for the future life of the couple were piled up around the door. Most had been hand made. There was embroidered linen, wooden utensils carved by hand, baskets skilfully woven from osier.

The wedding feast itself when it began was a joyous affair full of dancing and drinking, speech-making and singing and charming customs and rituals which were nothing to do with the church but simply traditional. Those who could play musical instruments had brought them along and a little band was formed. Many had brought loaves, and other food to swell the feast. Places and meals were set for the recently deceased who were deemed to be present. The day wore on with revelry and songs and more speeches and dancing and Juozas at one point missing Rozalia found her outside round at the back.

"Will it never end?" her eyes said to him.

Later, when the last tipsy guests had taken their leave, and when those who had outstayed their welcome, drunken, maudlin sots amongst them, who had only come for the liquor, had been got rid of, they spent their first night in this house in the new marital bed Juozas had been making for weeks, while Juozas' mother went off with the straggling revellers to stay with neighbours for a few days. Sleeping together was an experience strange to both of them and but for Rozalia's previous resistance and her propriety, years in the making in that close-knit world of religion and parental control, they would have done so long before then. As it was they really learned about each oth-

er as they went along. It was something that would take months to get right with a little understanding.

They had the place to themselves and for the first three days of discovery they enjoyed a magical and blissful if somewhat hesitant start to their married life together. This was their idyllic beginning.

As new aspects of life and each other were revealed during the short honeymoon, they worked away seeing to the animals. In the same way that they had wished the festivities of their wedding day to come to a close, so they wished the opposite of this their new life.

Then on the fourth day Juozas' mother Ieva returned. Now that they were married at last, once they had settled down to their new life, the grimmer realities of their situation very slowly became apparent. The novelty began to wear thinner.

Rozalia had been content at first but after a while she found herself irritated at having to spend her new married life with her husband's mother as well. The day to day drudgery also got her down. There were no brothers nor sisters to share the load with here, only her new husband and a feeble old woman. There were a few minor clashes about how to cook this or how to wash that. Her mother-in-law was clearly set in her ways and still thought of it as her house. Mother slept in one corner of the main room with a thick curtain to give her, and them, some privacy but Juozas began to feel that this could only be a temporary measure. In the meantime he asked Rozalia if making the corner into a small room for his mother would make her happier and she grudgingly agreed but he knew from her reaction that this would not be a permanent solution. He had been formulating an idea for a bigger house. He would draw up a plan one day but he knew he would have to pace himself in order to avoid the heart flutters he was now learning to live

with. In the meantime he had enough mon- ey from a small loan to stock up with seed grain, a couple of pigs, a small flock of goslings and another horse to go

with Onooti. The beast was no longer a foal. She had grown into a large mare, much bigger than usual and very strong. He reckoned that as there were only three of them and Mother ate sparingly, he could produce enough food to sell and they would still have sufficient to eat themselves. Additionally he had kept his father's old gun though it was obsolete, and he had traps and snares and was hoping he would be able to augment their food in that way. At harvest time various neighbours and their children would come over to help, working from dawn to dusk and Juozas and his family would return the favour in the same way. Mother turned out to be not so bad after all. She tactfully allowed them their privacy and Rozalia began to note that she always seemed to be around to help out and relieve a few at least of the everyday burdens of life around the farm. So things levelled off into a sort of understanding between them all as the two women grew to appreciate each other's qualities. The seasons came and went and suddenly it was winter again. By this time Rozalia had borne her first child. She knew well enough what to expect, though when it actually happened to her she was terrified. This was where her mother-in-law Ieva stepped up to the plate again and the baby boy was delivered without a hitch. No doctors, no midwives, just the three of them, soon to be four. The weather was too bad for travelling and neither Juozas nor his mother dared leave Rozalia to call anyone anyway. All went well as the two young people, and Mother all over again, quickly learned a baby routine.

It was only now that their relationship really began in earnest. Starting optimistically it was more of a partnership of country people who struggled to survive exactly as their parents had done and their parents before them. The infant Vincentas was breast fed and thrived.

Chapter 9

Peasants

The main building they lived in was little more than a shack among a cluster of outbuildings. When his father, Jonas, died suddenly Juozas was the youngest and only son to be still living there. The others had all moved on. Two of his three brothers were already married and not being prepared to replicate the back breaking lives of their parents they went about exercising their new found freedom from serfdom. The very slight relaxation in the social constrictions which had plagued the peasants for centuries came early for them there in south-west Lithuania a long time ago, and had pre-empted the official decree which was to be issued by the Tsar in 1861. The noble family who had owned it all hereabouts were fortunately enlightened, or at least realistic. They foresaw the coming change of law which had been in the pipeline for years. As somebody at the time said with the knowledge of hindsight regarding the several insurrections there had been already, in other parts of the country, "It would be better to grant them something from above than to have it taken from below." There was nothing their ex-master could do about it, neither would he have wanted to, he was resigned to inevitable change.

Two of the Kadišius brothers went to Kaunas with their wives where they got lodgings and work making leather shoes in a small factory. The other brother, unmarried, the eldest, who should have inherited the farm, made his way to Klaipeda where he was earning a living as a deck hand labouring on a fishing vessel. Juozas' sister was already married. She lived with her new husband at the house of his parents just to the north of Punskas.

None of them had wanted the responsibility of such an old fashioned holding and what amounted to a hovel in which they had been raised. There was work to be done on the land and also the additional commitment to look after their old mother. Technically, while she was still alive she now owned the lease agreement on it all, even though the ramshackle building was worth nothing. The rental on the land was still being paid. There was no question of the other children being compensated for their share of the Kadišius household, there just wasn't enough value in it to share around amongst them.

It was Juozas' mother who had taken him to a Jewish moneylender in Smalenai, whom she and his father, Jonas, had been friendly with in former times. He agreed to support them under a repayment scheme without any interest repayments spread over a number of years. It was a generous arrangement generally only offered to other Jews and rendered the farm a much more viable proposition to take on and run. So he had been able to accept responsibility for all the buildings and equipment. The fifteen morgas of land, roughly the equivalent of nearly seventeen hectares, which went with it were rented. With the loan he would also be able to rent or even buy land from the adjacent farm. It was derelict and overgrown. The son who had inherited the debts and the rent attached to it had been trying to find someone to take it on for over a year. His funds were running low and his rent was badly in arrears. Juozas knew that during any negotiations, although each knew what the other would want, all the usual bargaining counters would come into play. This was only the first stage though, to discover the lie of the land and basically to pay Remigijus Bilinskas to leave.

Juozas went over to see him. As he walked up the path to the ramshackle building a mangy looking dog came up wagging its tail hoping for food. He bent down to give it a pat but it backed off and growled at him with a shifty look in its eye when the hoped-for food wasn't forthcoming. Juozas assumed the dog would be included with the farm buildings in the sell-off. He saw its master Remigijus and thought of the strange similarities there are sometimes between a dog and its owner as he noticed that Remigijus wasn't doing much other than idly whittling away at a wooden stick.

"Kaip aina se Juozas – How are you? What brings you here?" Actually he had already guessed as he had seen Juozas walking across the lower field, examining things, a few days earlier.

"I'm fine thanks, I just thought I'd pop over to see how you are."

"Thank you, I'm not too bad."

"Well, so what's new then?"

"I'm thinking of moving on."

"I heard you might be leaving."

"I've got a deal in the pipeline, – but I thought I saw you down the hill the other day. Perhaps you might also be interested, "

Juozas noticed the use of the word 'also.'

"Yes, I did have a quick look round, I could be persuaded, – at the right price! What are you looking for to go?" As he was speaking he looked around disdainfully and took in the leaky roof of the main hovel leaning at a crazy angle with its missing and cracked shingles. His gaze travelled round to the other sheds and lean-tos surrounded by a sea of mud and muck, reminders of the animals which had once been here. The household rubbish was mainly still in one heap but some had been strewn about by the chickens and scavenging wild animals. He looked back at the house and noted the empty and rotten window frames. He hadn't actually visited here for years as there had been some sort of inter-family dispute which had passed through the generations. But this was business. It wasn't as he had remembered it when he had ventured over here as a boy. He really hadn't expected the place to be so run down. Remigijus commenced the contest by plucking a figure out of the air. Juozas exaggeratedly sucked in an incredulous intake of breath then whistled it out again at length. Then he chuckled making the the other man feel foolish

"Where did you conjur that from?" Juozas opened up with. "The place itself is worth nothing and the fields are overgrown. The work I'd have to do to put it right! .... where would I start? The weeds will take years to get rid of."

"It's been lying fallow rejuvenating itself that's all," responded the seller. "I owe it to my poor late father that I really ought to ask more for these buildings and equipment."

"Mm, God rest his soul, but the work involved to get it productive again, phew! On reflection, I don't know if it's really a good idea," he said with a disdainful expression and screwed up face. "I think your father may even have agreed with me had he been here."

"I doubt it," retorted Remigijus. But nevertheless the conversation made him look again at what he was offering and he lowered his sights. He was bargaining for someone to pay off his rental debts and step into his shoes and take over management of it all so that he could get away and start a life somewhere else.

And so it continued. An offer was made, and rejected, and then a counter offer. Slowly they were coming closer to an understanding little by little. Each was careful to leave the other a face saver. Every offer was justified in some form of words. They both knew more or less that it was only the land which was important but Juozas was in the slightly better position. He knew he could afford to wait until

Remigijus came down in price. Juozas was a sharp bargainer. He was used to doing deals with a mixture of incisive business talk, incredulity at the other's offer coupled with wit together with a huge helping of ridicule thrown in. In that way he was usually able to break down the resolve of whoever he was bargaining with.

The meaning of the earlier usage of the word 'also' became clear.

The seller sprang the age old ploy. "Antanas Matulaitis was asking me last week about this place, he's already been over once and he's coming over to look again tomorrow."

In fact Antanas, had only come over to borrow some tools but there were none worth speaking of and he had ended up having to ask another neighbour. He had then told everyone the following Sunday before Mass. Juozas knew Matulaitis and his wife Ruta Matulaitienė were getting on a bit. Their family had mostly grown up and left. The one son remaining at home was more interested in playing the accordion than working the land. He travelled all over the place to dances and folk festivals, and very good he was too. So Juozas knew what Remigijus was saying was not strictly true. A man of middle age with no responsibilities would hardly take on a big project like that. He might maintain his own plot at subsistence level but he wouldn't take on this kind of extra project.

Probably they had only spoken about it generally on market day or in passing. Farmers always wanted to know what was going on. They wanted information. To know things was important in that rural community. They all seemed to subscribe to the peasant philosophy that knowledge is power. They wanted to find out much, but gave nothing away themselves.

Juozas thought, "Matulaitis won't be wanting it!"

As far as he knew no one else was even remotely interested so he began to realise that he was in a good position, maybe nearly home and dry. Juozas shrugged his shoulders as if admitting defeat.

"If that's it then so be it. It must be the will of God that it's not for me. You had better let Antanas take it over. I just wouldn't be able to afford another kopek."

Juozas knew that they were down to brass tacks but he had more up his sleeve for the important face saver.

Then, the vendor, who was now seriously worried that this arrangement might not be going through, came up with a ploy of his own. His voice developed a whine.

"Look Juozas, you and I have always got on well haven't we despite our dads? I would rather the place went to you, someone who would appreciate it. Matulaitis has part of the forest between his own land and mine. I doubt it would be practical for him no matter how much he might think he wants it. What would you say if I said I would meet you half way."

"All right Remigijus," Juozas responded heartily, "You're a good friend but you've screwed me to the wall. I don't know if I will be able to get any extra but if I can of course I'll meet you half way. But it's all going to be up to him," he said, nodding contemptuously in the direction of their landlord's house which was out of sight. This would be an agreement between the two of them, money would change hands and subject to their landlord's approval he would just carry on where Bilinskas left off. Rent would still have to be paid and so on. They were negotiating for the buildings, property and any equipment and the goodwill – not the land

Remigijus was delighted, he had been wondering how to get rid of this contract and come away with something to show for it for over a year. He desperately needed money to go abroad and start afresh. If only he could just get back what had already been spent on the land and pay off his outstanding rent and debts. He had had enough of this peasant life hanging around living off chickens, eggs and a few vegetables. What small savings he had from money earned labouring for other farmers in the Summer were nearly depleted. He wanted to leave. He wanted something more. For him the future didn't lie here in this cycle of toil. Juozas on the other hand could barely contain his glee. Feigning reluctance he held out his hand and they shook on it.

Remigijus invited Juozas in for a drink. On entering, Juozas could see immediately that Remigijus' heart wasn't in this place at all. No one around here was affluent to say the least. They were a little above subsistence levels, some more and some less but this place was positively squalid. Remigijus had always been lazy. Juozas didn't stay long. His parting shot as he left was, "Don't forget, – I may not be able to raise any extra and, it's got to be approved by the Landlord." – just in case Remigijus had second thoughts.

As he walked away he knew enough about human nature to realise that the other man would now be making plans in his mind based on the transfer. Juozas had said he would see if he could get further funds. If he couldn't, and maybe he wouldn't try too hard, then he would have to return a couple of days later and sadly tell Remigijus that the deal had fallen through because he had been unable to get any more money. Juozas though did have a little extra he could throw in. It wasn't a lot but it was still a bit of a gamble whether it would be accepted or not.

He went back a few days later with the disappointing news that he couldn't raise the entire extra sum and tempered it with the offer that Remigijus could stay at the house as long as he liked until he had sorted himself out and decided where he was going.

It all fell into place, When Remigijus accepted it Juozas felt mildly guilty but he justified his duplicity to himself with the thought that, business was business. He had achieved the arrangement he had set out for and he hoped this would open up a new future for him and his family. For one thing he could now think seriously about his long term prospects. He began to plan how he could make these extra fields more productive. As he felt inwardly self-satisfied he thought about how far he had come and the good advice his father had given him years ago when he was still a boy.

In those days Juozas had hand reared a chicken and they called at a neighbour's to sell it. This family had recently lost two chickens to a fox and they needed another laying hen.

As they drew up to the the potential customer his father had said to the boy before he got down from the cart, "Look, you must try to get the best price you can but at the same time we don't want to be too greedy and we don't want to swindle him. We mustn't do that sort of thing, others may do, but in this family we don't."

"Ask him for the price you would like plus a bit more. He will make a counter offer which will be lower and you will then ask for the price you really want."

As he walked up the little path with the hen under his arm and knocked on the door Juozas tried to get his plan clear in his mind. The neighbour came to the door and his father saw him disappear inside. When he later came out without the chicken clutching some money his father said to him expectantly, "How did you get on Juozas?"

The son told his father the story.

"When I got inside there were three of them there, Mr Kaslauskas and his wife and her sister."

"After he looked at the chicken the others had a look too examining it and tutting and saying it had this wrong and that wrong and it wasn't very fat. They opened its beak and parted its feathers and looked under its wing. Before very long I felt guilty that I was trying to cheat them by selling it at all. They told me all the things that were wrong with it as if I didn't know anything about chickens."

"So what happened then?" Juozas' father had asked.

"They all went into a huddle in the corner as the chicken ran around the floor scared and I heard them say they weren't going to buy it as it wasn't worth it. Then Mr Kaslauskas came over and very reluctantly offered me the lower price and said "Take it or leave it.""

"Yes?" said his father, "So what did you say to that?"

"I took it! replied Juozas."

His father said gently, "Juozas, this has been a good lesson for you. There was nothing wrong with your chicken, It was a very good chicken which you fed with the best corn you could find and looked after so well. That was a great bargain for Mr Kaslauskas, still, never mind we are not talking about that much difference in the price."

Secretly though Juozas' father had wondered how anyone could be so mean to a child. He had a slightly resigned look of disappointment on his face during the drive home. Even he, Jonas, old and wise and hardened to life as he was, never failed to be momentarily disillusioned by behaviour of this kind among peasants. Yet oddly at other times they could be generous to a fault.

When they returned home and told the story, his father noticed his wife's face wearing a sort of sad melancholic appearance poorly disguised by a reluctant smile. She more than anyone knew how much care her son had put into raising those chickens

As the years of his childhood faded away from his continuing train of thought Juozas considered smugly those lessons well learned and how he had come such a long way since then!

Two or three days later Juozas went up to see the estate manager of their Polish Landlord. He stood cap in hand as he explained to Tomas Gilinski about the agreement he had come to with Remigijus.

"Well!, come back in a few days . I will put it to the Count and we'll see what he has to say. By the way, you do have a certificate of patriotism don't you?"

Juozas heart sank. He knew that with his record there was no possibility of ever getting one of those from the Russians. There was no point in even asking. He was hoping no-one would ask about the certificate because he knew he had messed up his chances of ever being granted one years ago. It was a document vital in business to prove one's commitment to the Russian state. Without it no new deals could be undertaken by Lithuanians.

"I'll see about it," he said to Gilinski. Speaking about it to Rozalia, who urged him to apply for it, he told her he wouldn't. He had no enthusiasm to lower himself when he knew the answer would probably be no. Rozalia just didn't seem to understand why he should let his pride get in the way of their plans. He tried to explain it to her but she just didn't get it. "It might not make a difference. I've always been prompt with the rent and I've done good work up there."

The following week Juozas presented himself to the steward again, who said to him, " I see there's no certificate forthcoming here." he paused and thought a bit. "Weren't you once involved years ago in some serious trouble with the authorities over some mysterious dis-appearances it was thought you were behind? Juozas was dismayed.

"Yes I was accused and questioned but never actually charged."

"You were very lucky to have got away with it from what I heard."

"No! They could see I was innocent and had nothing to do with it." Gilinski nodded slowly and went on. "Yes, if you say so."

"I put your case to the master but he has other plans for the disposal of that land I am afraid."

"But ...." began Juozas.

"No 'buts,' that is final" snapped Gilinski. "That's the end of it. Good day to you." At that moment Juozas felt a surge of frustrated rage and very nearly rushed at Gilinski but he managed to contain himself with a supreme effort of will. The ache in his chest began. Through the red mist swimming before his eyes, and the frustrated sobs he could feel coming on he saw the man turn and walk away with a smirk. Juozas came to terms with his situation very quickly and by an effort of will he curbed his temper and calmed down.

Juozas departed for home feeling very downhearted, the pain sub-sided, but his self esteem at an all time low. His prodigious efforts, his willingness to work hard had all come to nought. He wasn't allowed to have any ambition or any control over his own future and that of his family by those who ruled his life. He always knew he was a slave, tied to the land. He knew that he faced a lifetime of backbreaking work in order to barely survive and feed his family the basics. With those responsibilities, a slight expansion of his existing lot was about the best he could have hoped for. Moving his family elsewhere wasn't a viable proposition as his future income was impossible to calculate and he would be unable to borrow on that basis. He couldn't even be sure that the proposal had gone up as far as Count Jozef Kwasniewski.

The Promised Land

He returned home with his body in a turmoil and the beginnings of a bad headache as his migraine began to kick in. His wife found him lying on a pile of straw in the stable after he had put the horse away. He had not had the courage to go and tell her what had happened. She drew the news from him and consoled him sympathetically but he never told her of the tightness he had felt in his chest. The frustration inside him became almost overwhelming again.

"One day there will be a way forward. It can't always be like this. We'll come through it," was the forlorn crumb of comfort from the woman who always supported her husband through thick and thin. "I've been thinking. I suppose I do understand why you wouldn't beg for a certificate if you knew it would be refused. Never mind, we will have to make do."

She went on to say, "Kwasniewski? We might as well all be chickens on his estate the way we are treated,"

She concluded, "In fact chickens are treated better!"

Juozas went to town that same evening and soon discovered that the news about the derelict land was already well-known. How information travelled quite so fast around those parts was a mystery. He felt idiotic and stupid that he had been made a fool of. He knew that many people would take a sort of perverse pleasure from his failure to better himself. Many didn't like to see others getting on. It made them feel vulnerable. They already knew him to be better off than the rest of them and their insincere advice was prompted by jealousy.

"You ought to have paid Gilinski something," said one person with a knowing look and there was a chorus of agreement and much nodding all round amidst the clinking glasses.

"You should have seen him first before you dealt with Bilinskas," said another. "You would have saved yourself all that effort."

He sat there at the inn nursing his drink as he was minutely examined by the searching looks of his compatriots. He regarded them quietly in turn. Petras the one-eyed henpecked husband who came here to escape his nagging wife. Justinas the bar-room lawyer who could barely read. Another man at the end of the table, Simas, he only knew slightly. The man's face was twitching barely managing to contain a smile. What added to the chagrin was being told by someone else in front of the assembly that the land in question was going to be let to a Russian from the east. Juozas' transparent face betrayed his emotions in front of them all as he wrestled with this sudden information delivered so publicly. They could almost read his thoughts as they occurred to him one after the other as the various muscles of his face formed themselves into expressions ranging from surprise to dismay to anger, regret and then resignation. What needled him too was that these clodhoppers could observe his innermost thoughts written on his face. And they saw that too. It gave them satisfaction.

Then his gaze shifted over to the back of the bar where Rimas sat, now riddled with arthritis, suffering a painful back and a stoop, barely able to struggle along. Still living with his mother who had told him that all he needed was lots of exercise and walking to cure his back. He was more than happy to heed her advice every evening and hobble to the tavern. He was Juozas' one true long-standing friend and to his credit he had said nothing, refusing to join in the chorus of platitudes. The two of them had helped each other over the years and they were always welcome at each others houses. Rimas had been like an uncle to Juozas' children.

Juozas rose and made his way over to where his friend sat, glancing again at the rest of the hopeless group as he passed by them. His hand was numb and he rubbed it vigorously to restore the circulation.

He marvelled at all those wise peasants, sages to a man – after the event, all living on the poverty line, exploited and bullied and accepting their lot.

Chapter 10

The Ride to Town – 1854

The pain in Juozas' hand was a seasonal stark reminder of the changing season. He absently rubbed it, as he had done about this time every year since it had happened.

His thoughts drifted back to a winter a long time ago....... when his troubles had begun.....

After a long spell of snow and freezing temperatures the day in question had dawned bright and clear. By the early afternoon there wasn't much Juozas could do around the farm and he had decided to try to get into town.

The idea of selling one of the sacks of dried peas from the summer's harvest was the only excuse he needed. Being cooped up in the house over the past few days, baby Vincentas crying incessantly, and his wife Rozalia being too preoccupied with the child to take much notice of him, he was just bored.

It wasn't market day but Juozas just needed some adult male company and an excuse for a break away from the farm. Rozalia and his mother understood him implicitly. After all, he was a hard worker on the land as they all worked hard at their various talents. They understood well enough that he felt the responsibility of their lives and of their well being and she certainly never begrudged him a small break in town. He didn't indulge himself often.

He went to the shelter specially constructed for the sleigh and the cart. It was a ramshackle affair but it did the job in keeping most of the weather off the two vehicles. At this time of year the cart was pretty well useless. It got bogged down in ice as all the weight was concentrated on the four points where the wheels met the ground, and the vehicle tended to sink in.

His wooden sleigh however was different. It was lighter than the cart but much bigger, custom made, mainly of stout ash with two wide runners of birch shod with iron which, spreading the load, slid easily over the hard packed snow. Attached to the traces and shafts for the horse was a sub framework with two shorter skis on either side. The whole substructure pivoted giving some measure of controlled steering to the sleigh. Even with that, the sleigh had a tendency to side-slip in turns as centifugal force caused it to swing round in an arc. So he had to take care to master the steering as a sort of controlled slide. The whole thing was attached to the horse's harness by the two shafts, one on either side. A huge hoop of ash fixed to the shafts looped over the horse's head and kept them clear of the animal. At the other end the shafts were fixed to the sleigh, by means of flexible leather joints. To help with both the steering and the braking, two great levers were fixed towards the rear with strong springs and a series of linkages attached to pedals in the foot-well. These could be deployed to dig into snow covered ground either singly or together to aid steering or braking. He was proud of this arrangement. He had thought of the system himself and had made the wooden parts in ash and working in conjunction with the blacksmith had fitted it all together. He was pleased that it worked so well and not a little proud that people admired his skill. The sleigh was a work of art in itself. The sight of it often prompted offers to buy it which, although flattering, he always politely refused.

In a small wooden cabinet under the seat he kept an old flintlock pistol and some powder. Whenever he set out in winter he primed and loaded the firearm. Wolves could be a problem and sometimes attacked the horses when their natural sources of food were scarce. The gun was inaccurate beyond about twenty feet but it was a useful tool which made a loud noise and would scare off most things. At this time of year, at the first sign of snow, he had his horse shod with iron crampons, like ordinary shoes but with spikes forged at the smithy into each one. Most horses were shod in the same way in order to cope with the extreme conditions of Eastern European winters.

Wrapped up in a long sheepskin coat and heavy fur hat, clad in mittens and high fur lined boots of bearskin he urged the horse, covered with a dry blanket, on into a steady trot. Onooti, was a good horse, almost a member of the family. They had bought her as a foal from an elderly horse-breeder across the Polish border. They were reasonably sure it was in Poland, the border, always seemed to be changing. The Lithuanians called the town Seinei. In Polish it was Sejny.

The two countries had once been one, a federation, the Kingdom of Poland and the Grand Duchy of Lithuania, united as the Grand Duchy of Warsaw. Then later on the country had come under the domination of Russia. Quite why this happened wasn't apparent to the peasants but they did care about it. Juozas knew that only a few years earlier his family had all been serfs, working strips of land for their lord. Now they were free but were still bound to their overlord by tenancy and were made to pay such heavy taxes and rents that many of them barely had enough left over to feed themselves. If they couldn't find money they had to pay in kind. It was a rough life in times of hardship, pestilence crop failures and famines. The prices in the market dropped if there was a glut in a particularly good year. People were looking to leave the land. Their entire existence on it was underpinned by hard work at least for all of them, or backbreaking toil for many. Both young and old had to work or starve. They made-do and mended to the point of being ragged for much of the time. They made their own clothes whenever they could and even their own bast shoes until even that was prohibited by the landlords in order to save their trees being stripped of the bark the peasants needed to make them. Getting a horse was a big thing. It opened the way for being able to have a source of muscle power and to independent travel further afield.

Rozalia's family living near Seinei had told them about the foal which was for sale. They usually visited his wife's family, the Damansks at Easter and sometimes at Christmas. Their children looked forward to it, counting down the days. The journey took hours and in the early years they sometimes stayed overnight providing they could get Juozas' nephew, Gintas from Smalenai to come over and see to the animals while they were gone. Then they would go to Mass at the cathedral and listen carefully to the sermon occasionally given by a visiting bishop from Warsaw attended by lesser priests. This experience would give them lots more to talk about regarding how to minister to their religious needs. As if there wasn't already enough to discuss about farming matters, the weather and local gossip or just simply getting on with the business of living. They spoke sometimes in Lithuanian, sometimes in Polish. Always there were Russian soldiers, policemen, and officials somewhere around. They were careful not to speak Lithuanian within earshot of them, if only to keep a low profile. The Russians would take it as an act of provocation if they heard that language being spoken, particularly as most of them weren't conversant with it. All business was conducted in either Polish or Russian and all prominent officials were mainly drawn from those two nationalities. The Tsar of all the Russias and his ministers were hard taskmasters and were intent upon stamping out the Lithuanian identity and squashed it wherever they saw a hint of it. It would be another five years before there would be any kind of uprising and that would be ruthlessly crushed. It would be followed by public hangings and even more clampdowns. Lithuanians would have to express their defiance in more subtle ways. So unfortunately for the ambitions of the Russians the Lithuanians had their own ideas and although it was forbidden to teach Lithuanian in schools, the language was kept alive by the use of prayer books and the liturgy.

Mothers told their children fairy tales in Lithuanian and it was the common language spoken in the home. Books could be smuggled in from printers in Prussia, and from the secret underground press. Clandestine language lessons were held, even though teachers and parents took a great risk they just had to do it.

Weighed down though the Lithuanian peasantry was, the Jews suffered even more. Always despised by the Russians and even by many Lithuanians and Poles, they were by now enduring real persecution from all quarters. Whatever privations Lithuanians had to put up with, even more were piled upon the Jews. True, the Jews held themselves apart from the bulk of the Lithuanian populace in the countryside, retaining positions and jobs in trade and commerce, but they were forbidden to farm. Their religion and customs and their own sense of destiny held them aloof. They kept to their own unique traditions and were also forced to remain separate in their own shtetl enclaves. Their movement and their options in life were restricted by law, except when it was necessary to come together with the peasants for the purposes of trade and business. They too overtly clung to their own language, which featured heavily in their religious rituals.

The problems of the lower orders in general, brought about by their subservient position in the hierarchy, were always somewhere in the minds of both Jew and Catholic. When they were spared briefly by some distraction, either by visits to church, synagogue or religious festivals, weddings, markets, or in alcohol; afterwards, when the effects wore off, the same old problems simply returned to haunt them all over again in a perpetual cycle.

Juozas heard a horse whinny somewhere behind and Onooti's head twitched as she replied, a flurry of steam arising from her mouth and dispersing in the cold air. He turned around and noticed two horsemen appearing on either side of the road. They caught him up and rode alongside for perhaps three minutes, one on either side, just staring at him. They said nothing. Juozas looked uneasily from one to the other wondering what was going to happen next. They were both big men even taking into account the greatcoats they wore and their fur hats. Each was carrying a gun slung across his back and a sabre and holstered pistol. They were Russian military policemen with an imposing bullying air. Juozas knew that the majority of them were arrogant and corrupt, often drawn from the ranks of the Cossacks. They were always looking to fleece ordinary people for as much as they could under the pretence of granting them a favour or privilege. They were just extortionists and this trend ran from top to bottom throughout the society that they were forcibly thrusting upon the Lithuanian people.

"Stop!" cried one of them suddenly waving his mittened hand up and down in an ever decreasing motion. Juozas obeyed and brought the horse and sleigh to a halt. "Where are you off to?"

"Smalenai," responded Juozas in Russian thinking what a stupid question it was, – the road led nowhere else. "Is that all right with you?" As soon as the words had passed his lips he regretted his impetuosity. Sometimes he just found it went against his nature to be completely subservient. "Get down," came the response. "What's in the back?" He knew they were looking for books

"No! no books, – this time," he mumbled under his breath. "What's that you peasant idiot?"

"I said 'No sir.'"

"Are you being funny?" said one of them as he slowly got down from his horse.

"No not at all, I'm just going into town for a few things."

"When I ask you a question I expect a proper answer." One of them drew back his arm as if to strike Juozas in the face but held back. It became a gesture of contempt.

Juozas just stared down at his boots without saying anything further. He felt like a low criminal instead of the respected person and hard working head of a household which was how he saw himself.

The policeman gave him a long cold stare and then with an expression of annoyance, rummaged around in the back of the sleigh whilst Juozas could do no more than stand there obediently. The officer found the sack. Taking off a mitten he undid the string at the top and plunged his arm down inside as he rummaged about. He withdrew his hand having found nothing hidden in the peas. He had retained a handful of them and threw them as hard as he could at his companion. After some coarse guffaws the first one nodded to his partner as he remounted and with backward, sneering, baleful glances they both continued along the road to town leaving Juozas to re-tie the sack and gather himself together.

The incident left him depressed. Even when they went about their normal business honest people were treated with thinly disguised disdain if they were lucky, with outright hostility if they were not.

Juozas urged the horse back into motion and continued upon his way. The Russians knew deep down that they would never break the spirit of this population and it was a thought they hated. But they would never stop trying. Although they were in charge they couldn't understand or conquer the essential character of the country and they knew it. They were even more aggravated with the situation than the people were. They were relentless though and they added to it all with the stifling bureaucratic incompetence of their administration. Difficulties were heaped one upon the other as regulations and orders issued from the Russian capital in a never ending malevolent contradictory stream.

As Juozas approached the town he saw ahead of him the unmistak
able limping figure of his friend Rimantas Bulaitis the official under-
employed schoolmaster, who was going along from the direction of
the church towards the centre. Juozas slowed the horse down with a
gentle pull on the reins and a soft cluck-clucking sound which only
he and the horse understood. The horse slowed and halted but the
sleigh continued in a slightly sideways skid as it tried to catch up the
horse when the leather straps attaching the two together slackened,
until it too came to a halt giving the horse's harness a slight jolt at the
shoulder. Juozas hadn't bothered to use the brakes as they were travelling quite slowly.

"Where are you going Rimas? Do you want a ride?"

Climbing up onto the seat beside him Bulaitis looked
around, then behind into the back of the sleigh and spotted the peas.
These people didn't miss much. He pressed the side of the sack with
his knuckles. He knew what they were.

"Are you selling them Juozas?" he asked.

"I didn't realise they were still in the back," Kadišius lied slightly,

"I meant to unload them this morning, I was just bringing them
from the barn to the house, but I got distracted, There was a bit of
a panic when Rozalia spotted the fox on the edge of the wood. Did
you see the two military policemen up ahead? They stopped me and
gave me a hard time."

"Yes I saw them, one of them spat in my direction as he rode past.
It just missed me and his mate sneered."

"Bloody Hell, what bastards they are. They're all the same."

"I'm not sure about that. There are probably one or two that aren't.
I haven't met them round here yet though."

"What are you doing in town Juozas?"

"I've come in for some more gunpowder for my old gun, I've tried
to trap that damned fox but it's too wily. Hunger's made it bold.
We're worried about the chickens. Might have to lie in wait for it. – I
wasn't going to sell the peas, but if you really want them you can have

them as a favour."

Bulaitis, keen now to get them, offered Kadišius four roubles. "Come on! the sack they're in is nearly worth that. You'll have to do better than that!" Juozas said with a slight good natured smile.

"Four roubles and you can have the sack back", rejoined Bulaitis.

"Call it six and a half and I'll throw in another empty sack free," Kadish responded to his friend good-naturedly.

"I only have five and a half," said Bulaitis laughing keeping his fingers crossed under his mitten.

Kadish thought for a moment and then said, "Alright then, but you can buy me a drink."

"Done!" said his friend, "Can you deliver them home for me?"

"Yes certainly, it's a deal," Kadisius replied.

They took off their gloves and shook hands but quickly put them back on. It was freezing.

In reality Juozas was only anticipating about five roubles. Bargaining was always expected but he was pleased with the result. This was the way things were done. He had no qualms about squeezing as much as he could from the deal. He had a young wife and a small child to support now as well as his mother. They must come first.

Chapter 11

Beaten

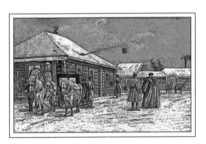

He continued with Bulaitis alongside him as far as the general store. They pulled up in front of a large wooden detached building of a single storey built of roughly hewn logs sawn into planks with a chestnut shingled roof, although you couldn't see much of it. Most of the building was coated in snow and the glass filled windows were additionally glazed with a layer of frost on the outside. A three horse carriage and a few other horses were tethered at the front, several of them munching with their faces inside nosebags. The acrid smell of horse urine and dung surrounded their hooves and areas of the snow beneath them had melted and then refrozen. The only thing Juozas wanted to do was to get inside, away from the biting icy wind. All

The Promised Land

Bulaitis had intended to buy when he set out was a bottle of whale oil for the lamps. For him it was a stroke of luck that Juozas happened along as he made his way through the snow wincing with his painful back. He lived with his aged mother who depended on her son, subsidised by the state, living in a tied cottage attached to the Russian sponsored school which few children attended except the children of Russians. Bulaitis and his mother produced no food of their own except for five or six chickens which they kept in the yard at the back. Everyone seemed to have chickens and eggs. But their food stocks had been running low lately.

Juozas stood with Rimas while he bought his oil from Mordechai Hofmann the storekeeper, a small thin man dressed in a white collarless shirt wearing a black greasy waistcoat with a row of small black buttons which were undone. Below that he wore a pair of black striped trousers with a shiny seat, and an apron, which had once been white, tied at the back. On the back of his head was perched a round, black velvet yarmulke which immediately betrayed his race to any who cared about such things. Inevitably there was a bar at the rear of the shop. After the oil was measured out and the powder was weighed and purchased one thing led to another.

There were several men in the back room, perhaps fifteen or so and a few women. While women were ostensibly quite welcome in this gathering there nevertheless existed, unspoken in the fraternity, a kind of mild humorous contempt for those husbands who were not allowed to come here alone. A roaring log fire was kept burning fiercely. It paid Mordechai to keep the place warm and cheerful, he could sell a lot of goods and liquor by providing this service. Someone was playing a fiddle and a merry Lithuanian song was being sung which everyone knew, about a hare sitting on a rock contemplating the meaning of life. After hanging up their coats and hats they started to get into the spirit of things. Fortified with several glasses of distilled honey mead, followed by a shot of vodka which Bulaitis true to the deal had bought him, Juozas joined in another refrain which had started up.

Anecdotes were related and jokes cracked. The laughter was uproarious. Juozas absolutely loved this convivial atmosphere. You couldn't find it anywhere else except in the company of other men. There was mild posturing in front of the few women, talking laughing putting the world right in their own uninformed way. The mickey-taking was happening at the expense of the Poles and Russians, none of whom were present. These ethnic Lithuanians always squared up the injustices of the day with grumbling and, in places like this, with funny and sometimes ribald criticism of their overlords. All their jokes seemed to be about a Pole a Jew and a Russian. The Russian were often the butt of the joke. Making fun of the them was, to them, a substitute for bravery, filling in the gap left by the absence of outright resistance. Lithuanians convinced themselves that somehow this levelled the score.

The warmth, the alcohol and the roaring crackling fire, amidst the boisterous company seemed to go to his head as he continued singing a Lithuanian song mocking Russians long after the rest of the singers had suddenly stopped. His lone voice continued for a while until he realised with a jolt and a sinking feeling in the pit of his stomach that he was the only person singing. Looking over his shoulder he became aware too late that a pair of Russian soldiers had walked in unannounced. His voice trailed off into a hoarse whisper and then ceased completely. It was the same two from earlier on the road. Picking him out immediately they made a beeline for him and strode across the floor in their black leather boots leaving gobbets of snow melting on the floor. Before he could properly turn around to defend himself one of them unslung his rifle in a fluid movement and jabbed him viciously with the wooden stock. The blow missed his spine but nevertheless he sank to the ground as his legs became weak and he doubled up and fell to the floor. He raised himself up with the aid of a three legged stool and as he did so he was overcome with a blinding rage and swung it at his assailant. The Russian wasn't expecting it and it caught him on the side of the head breaking off two of its legs and dislodging one of his teeth in a spray of spittle and blood. His rifle went flying across the floor. The man recovered in a fury and the two Russians both weighed in to him. No one came to his aid. The smaller of the two Russians, the one with the painful head and damaged jaw then swung his fist up aiming for Juozas' ribcage but he wasn't quite quick enough and Juozas' knee reached the end of its journey to the Russian crotch with considerable force. The tunic the man was wearing and his overcoat saved him from complete incapacity but nonetheless it put him down. Still mad with rage Juozas lurched towards the supine figure on the floor when he suddenly found himself looking down the barrel of a revolver held by the other soldier. The Russian's eye glinted malevolently behind the levelled pistol. Juozas saw the chamber full of snub nosed lead bullets start to turn.

"Don't do it!" came a shout from one of the bystanders in Russian as the soldier hesitated on the verge of firing.

"I'll see you done for murder if you do." It was Rimas. The Russians knew the schoolmaster and respected him more than they did the rest of them. In their eyes he was the nearest thing to an educated peasant and he spoke and taught Russian.

Instead of being shot Juozas just had time to see the gun being drawn up and the barrel crashing towards him before it made contact with his temple. A black veil came up over his eyes from the direction of the floor and the next thing he was aware of was being supported by several people. His chest was tight. The taller Russian soldier was looking down closely, staring at Kadišius, his hand on the hilt of his sabre, the gun back in its holster. The other one was obviously satisfied that between them they had got the better of him although at some cost to himself. The Russian's tooth was somewhere in the sawdust and Juozas dimly realised that the matter might not be over.

There were too many witnesses in that bar room though and even Russians had to go through the motions of respecting the law. No, they knew they could wait until later. This animal would have to leave to go back to its hovel at some time sooner or later.

"If I ever come across you again singing or talking in your bastard lingo you dog, I'll have you. Do you understand you filth?"

"Taip – er ...... I mean Da," mumbled Juozas under his breath.

Evidently this slip of the tongue aggravated them more and they closed in with an expletive accompanying every kick as he sat knees drawn up on the floorboards. The muscles of his arms and legs absorbed the kicks but the ridge over his eye where he had been pistol whipped was swollen and vision from that eye was blurred. Demoralised he rolled over putting up with it, curled up in a ball until they became tired and lost interest. They then moved over to the bar.

Subdued and resentful, the clientèle of the once convivial bar room lapsed into silence punctuated by a little stilted conversation in Polish or Russian. The Russians had made their point. Resistance was futile.

The two grey clad figures knocked back several vodkas, hardly paying attention to anyone else while they did so, and doing up their greatcoats and putting their fur hats back on they banged their empty glasses down on the scrubbed board counter, looked threateningly round the room, their gaze resting aggressively on random people one after another like some sort of warning. They walked away casting baleful stares at Juozas propped against the wall, one of them rubbing his head, and left the door wide open, chaperoned by the bearded, fawning store owner Mordechai. The company in the bar could hear the men outside talking then noisily mounting up, cursing and uttering profanities and shouting harshly at their horses as they rode away. They appeared to be going in the direction of their barracks.

Once the pair had left, the occupants of the bar began to find their courage and their tongues again. Gudaitis said that he had nearly intervened but it was all over before he could do anything, while Pranas Pawilaitis expressed the hope that one day they could be rid of these foreign overlords, but he said it so very quietly in Russian that almost nobody heard him.

Juozas took a while to come round fully from the assault. Mordechai's wife came with a basin of water with some ice and a cloth and kindly bathed his face and head and another woman helped her. They seated him on a cushioned chair which the bar owner had brought over. Even Mordechai realised that this could be bad for business once people found out what had happened.

Nobody had noticed the sum of money he had paid the two men on the way out, their unofficial personal retainers. For him as a shop-keeper and bar owner, and a Jew, it was still a small price for being allowed to remain in business. He must remember, he thought, to tell his customers that they must speak only in Polish or Russian when-ever they came into his shop and bar. In his own mind he took the easier option and blamed Juozas for the disruption to his trade. He co-operated all he could with the Russians – He didn't blame them at all.

Juozas for his part, initially felt injustice and shame. He, an en-terprising and respected member of the community to be belittled, degraded by these sub-human symbols of a repressive foreign regime which was determined to crush the very spirit from the people. Intel-lectuals, some of them, but with base motives, using these apes to cary out their wishes. In front of everyone too. Tomorrow the whole town would have got to hear about it. He was a proud man and the thought of it was almost unbearable.

This feeling in Juozas was followed by resentment and then hatred. He tried to suppress those negative feelings. It was his own fault. By being selfish, leaving Rozalia, Ieva and baby Vincentas for the best part of five or six hours maybe he had brought this upon himself. Guilt was always the emotion he came up with sooner rather than later. It had been ingrained into him. In this instance once again he tried to see the other party's point of view. They were only doing their job, as ordered by their superiors. No! that wasn't right. They were just thugs brutalised by their unassailable position of authority whose sadism had merely been brought to the fore by the circumstances.

Aching all over, Juozas realised it was getting late. The watery remnant of the sun, just visible low on the horizon as he had entered the building, had now set. Despite the intense cold there was a moon so bright that he didn't need to light his travelling lantern, but clouds were gathering he noticed. Experience told him that the weather would hold off until later tonight or perhaps even until tomorrow. But he felt they were in for another bout of very bad weather. He still had the sack of peas and Rimas and his oil to deliver. Looking outside through his good eye with partial sight returning to the other one, he could see that the freeze outside was intense. His friend Bulaitis helped him into his outer clothes, and through the shop to the side alley where he had left his horse and sleigh, out of the wind. The aching in the small of his back and his throbbing head was diminishing somewhat. Even his chest was returning to normal. He was a tough man. He brushed the coating of frozen rime from around the horses ears, eyes and nostrils. At least the cover had kept most of the freezing air off the main body of the horse. He scraped off the fine layer of ice from the bench seat with a scrap of wood and both men climbed up and sat down. Rimas offered to drive. Juozas appreciated the offer but he knew Onooti better than anyone and he took up the reins and clucked the horse into action. In any case Bulaitis had drunk even more than he had himself and he wasn't prepared to risk an accident. The horse, her eyes and ears already building up frost again, and with the sky relatively clear of cloud cover, was feeling the cold and was reluctant to move, but by careful coaxing eventually Juozas managed to get her slowly into motion as his back settled into a dull ache. His chest also still ached a bit but he hadn't been hit there.

Retracing his earlier route, he paused outside the schoolhouse while Rimas unloaded the sack and carried it inside on his back. He painfully decided not to get down himself and briefly paid his respects from his position high up on the sleigh to Rimas' mother Dalia Bulaitiené, who had appeared in the glowing threshold of the house.

"Come in for a minute Juozas", she urged. She couldn't see the state he was in as she was blocking most of the light from the doorway and he had pulled up a little bit further on so that Rimas could lift the peas straight down into the house. She just recognised the bulk of him looking over his shoulder perched up high on the sleigh, but it was getting even colder so he politely declined.

He continued on past the Jewish shtetl on the edge of town with its ramshackle buildings and its ornate wooden synagogue. He vaguely remembered as a small child being taken there on a visit. From the depths of his memory emerged something, quite tenuous. A slightly blurred image of him and his father being made very welcome and of a very old, old, lady with a prominent nose and dark eyes who hugged him warmly and fed him with a bowl of chicken soup and noodles while his father talked haltingly in a language young Juozas had only ever heard at the market. He had drunk many bowls of soup in his life since that day but never anything to match hers, whoever she was. He had been told as a child that they were related in some way in the distant past but hadn't listened carefully enough. He wished from time to time that he could remember more of the details but those who could have told him were all gone now.

As he drove by, he reflected on the injustice of this world and in particular on the misfortune of the Jews there who during these later years had been harried and hounded, taxed and vilified and even kicked and beaten for no other reason than that they were what they were. He himself as a Lithuanian boy, not even Jewish, had been conscripted into the Russian army and sent to the garrison in the capital. For all that he had endured there, the harshness of the training in drill and firearms, the unfamiliar way of life, he had been one of the lucky ones to be released and sent home after a year following his rheumatic illness. They still hadn't released him immediately though but they commuted it to a period of work in the garrison carpentry shop. So it hadn't all been entirely wasted. The Russian master carpenter there, Sergeant Yevgeny Balakirev was an affable man and he liked Juozas who was eager to learn and of a practical turn of mind, quick on the uptake. Although they both knew it was forbidden, Juozas explained the structure of the Lithuanian language with its Latin alphabet. He told him it had more accented letters than any other language, as well as that it was an ancient language. He trusted Yevgeny so he confided to him that all Lithuanians in the countryside spoke it as much as they could when they were out of earshot of Russians, and they read books printed in the Latin alphabet.

He hadn't had that much contact with the Jews around Kaunas during his early service but for those forcibly conscripted, like himself. He could see they were also treated as a strange breed and those he did manage to meet seemed to harbour the same resentment of the oppressor as the Lithuanians and Poles did, and with a similar helplessness. It was a sort of irrepressible universal reaction. He explained all this to his Russian military journeyman who was sympathetic and listened closely. But the man wrote off the Jews as some sort of sub-species. He too had been brainwashed, although he insisted he had nothing against them. But Juozas did learn from him something of the politics of this Russian Tsarist power bloc.

Everyone knew that many of the Lithuanian Jewish boys were kept in the army for at least twenty five years. When they were unlucky enough to be the one in five thousand who was conscripted for this length of time and were taken away it was almost as if there was a death in the family. The memory of them within their communities faded and they became Russified and estranged from others of their kind. The Jews for some reason seemed to warrant ever more extreme forms of treatment, Juozas noted, and the Russians seemed to be able to think them up in abundance. It was a deliberate policy to alienate Jewish boys from their roots and heritage. It was all beaten out of them during the quarter century they were under arms.

Thinking now about it, here on the road home, in these modern times Juozas knew full well that this discrimination was wrong but what could he do? What could anybody do? Just like the men in the bar, if he acted as an individual it would not only jeopardise him, maybe even his life, but his family also. So he tried to shut it out of his mind, to tell himself that it wasn't happening. Even the periodic frenzied mass killings, as thugs ran amok among the Jews in other parts of the country, he was powerless to influence. They never got to hear about these things until well past the event.

Ignoring it had been difficult enough at first, even before he had taken on his own responsibilities. Now in his own mind any form of sympathetic action was completely out of the question. Lately during the past years he had convinced himself somehow that the Jews were indeed a race apart and that somehow they must have brought this on themselves. From there it would have been only a small easy step to convince himself that they were lesser people than everyone else, but he hadn't taken that final leap. He did wonder though why they were so passive. They so evidently just craved a quiet life.

At least he didn't subscribe to the outright hostility felt by many people towards Jews as they unwittingly allowed themselves to become a part of the mass of public opinion. It was a brutal instinct which easily reared its ugly head when people were pointed in the direction of scapegoats for their own misfortunes. The intention to divert attention away from the true causes of their miseries and transfer their resentments elsewhere always seemed effective on the majority.

Juozas however never considered himself to be a part of the masses and he didn't identify with them. If his sympathies lay anywhere it was with the Jews. "They need friends," Juozas thought. "Although they don't go out of their way to seek them outside of their own community. Ah well, It doesn't matter, it takes all sorts to make a world."

Chapter 12

Reflection

As he continued on his way and out into the countryside, the skis hissing and scraping on the crackling icy surface of the road, both he and the horse breaking wind in time to the rhythm of its hind legs, the moonlight was beginning to dim almost imperceptibly and he was doubled forward to protect his face as best he could from the icy blast of the wind. The cold was taking his attention away from his pain and it was helping the swelling. His eye was a lot better and had stopped watering. He sat bumping and swaying there as Onooti continued along the road she knew so well – His mind wandered on from topic to topic each subject linked to the next – He thought about the peas and the money he had got for them. He might now be able to send Rozalia into town to buy the material to make a dress for the forthcoming wedding of her younger sister Ruta, due to take place in Seinei in the spring. The peas were valuable, easy to grow, and when shelled and dried were stored all year in an airy place in sacks. Soaked in water overnight they would make soup or a pease pudding which was nutritious and filling and provided some of the energy needed to survive the winter – His thoughts then recalled the strange story concerning peas passed down by word of mouth, as his mind made the connection with that oft-repeated story – French soldiers had ridden into their village many years ago, around the time his father had been born, on their way to attack Russia. Juozas, when he was a boy had been regaled by his grandfather with how, when he and his grandmother had been in their mid twenties, the villagers, forewarned of the imminent appearance of the French army, had hidden their grain and other provisions prior to the arrival of these foraging parties who had combed through all the dwellings commandeering all they could find. The hidden peas were discovered and thrown into the river. No one could ever figure out, after the mists of time had enshrouded the incident, what their motives could have been. Was it that they took all they could carry and ditched the rest just to spite the peasants? Was it just youthful exuberance? They were described in this family folklore as being only 'bits of boys'. In addition to that, they had stripped the people of everything that could be carried which might be useful to an army on the march including carts, ponies and even the thatch from the roofs as fodder for their animals. It was a desperate foraging policy because there was very little in this sparsely populated landscape. The peasants were only at subsistence level themselves. They were just serfs in thrall to their Polish Lord who deigned to let them work his fields for him in the only

remaining feudal system in Europe. These peasants were almost a race apart from everyone else on the rest of the continent.

Juozas had been told that at first the Lithuanians had broadly welcomed the French seeing them as a force who would deliver them from their bondage but after the incident with the peas the villagers were more circumspect as they continued to receive snippets of news from the east as the season wore on. The French emperor, Napoleon Bonaparte, after several minor battles and inconclusive engagements with the Russians, and more major battles at Smolensk and Borodino, fought them to a standstill, gambling on the Tsar being keen to come to terms. However, none of the actions had been conclusive. The invasion had not produced the desired result. Instead, the Russians had abandoned Moscow before the advancing French, taking everything which might have been of value to the enemy, including food, but not before setting their city aflame as its citizens retreated before the approaching army leaving a desolate wasteland as they went. The closer winter approached Bonaparte's army, the more its terrible plight became apparent as hounded by skirmishing Cossacks, the French turned towards home and began their long terrible retreat westwards.

– Juozas remembered his grandfather stressing that Bonaparte had delayed too long. If he had made that one important decision earlier, world events might have worked out very differently –

– Starving and freezing, shuffling and inching along, the remnants of the retreating army left a grim trail of frost-covered abandoned vehicles, booty they could no longer carry – and the dead! Dead animals, dead and dying soldiers and camp followers lay both amongst them' up ahead and in their wake, lying, sitting or standing frozen solid, icily petrified. Survivors were striving to keep warm and stave off starvation. Some of the injured still left alive were carried in makeshift litters or were simply abandoned along the way. All the time the remnants of that once numerous force were defending themselves from mounted Cossacks, who picked them off or captured them, subjecting their prisoners to the most inhumane treatment after first stripping and robbing them. Many of them were ritually executed in the most sadistic brutal ways, with the help of Russian villagers. A heroic defensive action was fought all the way back by the rearguard of the French army which still had some cohesion.

This mayhem continued slowly and very painfully, all the way from Moscow across the Beresina river then on and back across the harsh landscape and into Lithuania. In the Spring twelve thousand French corpses, men women and children who had died at the crossing around the hastily constructed temporary bridges would be found in the thaw. The engineering had been brilliant – the crossing chaotic.

That winter of 1812 to the north of Smalenai, as the stragglers from that terrible campaign were returning still embroiled in the ordeal, in disarray, feet and heads muffled against the harsh biting, howling wind sweeping in from Siberia, inadequately clothed, freezing and starving, the villagers heard that a family to the north-east had taken pity on a pair of them who had all but given up in a nearby wood. They had welcomed them into their own home and fed, clothed and nursed them back to health. Juozas remembered he had been told that one of them had learned the Lithuanian language and become a part of the family. He changed his name from Dubois to Dubaitis. He settled in and married, and his descendants still lived hereabouts. That family carried over from one genera- tion to the next those fireside tales of the ruthless brutality of the bands of Cossacks at whose hands their ancestor had nearly met his end in that indescribably horrific catastrophic nightmare.

Family tradition down the years in the Kadišius household too re-called that a French refugee had lived with them also, rescued by them from certain death. He remained with them for half a year but kept his own name. The lad worked around the farm keeping a very low profile. Cossacks were everywhere searching for the French. Every Frenchman, even if in a pitiful state, was fair game to them, for hav-ing dared to sully the Russian Motherland. They were without mercy Finally with the defeat of Napoleon, and the amnesty which fol-lowed, their Frenchman made his way home with a small amount of money scraped together by the Kadišius family, to see him on his way.

– Juozas remembered that when he was a child the details of the soldier's arrival and departure were cloaked in vagueness. Like most family history then, it was all hearsay and word of mouth. He had always wished to know more. His parents did remember from what they had themselves been told that when he left to make his way home, after the war had ended, he had divested himself of all trac-es of his military involvement. There was a vague idea that he had in fact managed to get home. It wasn't known how they knew – – Juozas could only speculate, riding along on his sleigh separated from the story by so many years and armed solely with scanty rumour. The story that had come down was limited. Had he been aware of the true facts he might have been thrilled and fascinated –

– The bare bones of the story handed down such as they were, were accurate but sketchy. The lad's uniform, now become rags, his weapons and ammunition and papers, were all discarded, and he was transformed into a mute Polish itinerant freeborn peasant looking for employment. He worked his way west across the Duchy of Warsaw and through Prussia and from there back to Northern France and his family's home in the Picardy countryside. – Juozas was imaginative enough to realise that there must have been great emotion there upon his return – The truth was that it had turned a French family's life around completely from a lingering aching tragedy to sudden ecstatic joy on their farm as his mother suddenly realised with a leap of her heart that her son had been spared and given back to her.

At first, when he did not reappear, she suffered unrelenting feelings of utter despair – Juozas, in his reverie, speculated on the scenario that must have existed there. His imagination could only toy with the probabilities of what had happened – For the boy's family it was a fact that day-to-day activities became meaningless and chores were carried out mechanically with little enthusiasm. She as a mother, of course, had the commitment to her other children but every task brought back memories of the eldest who was missing. Her helplessness was reflected upon the whole family and despite an outward appearance of getting on with life, confused innermost thoughts lurked in the black depths of her fear and those were all a jumble of yearning, of hope and despair. Even though her child was out of reach and out of contact she had constantly striven to communicate with him, not only by all practical means possible but also in her thoughts and prayers. The Curé helped in all this by sending her dictated letters to the army department in Paris. She spoke to returning soldiers, and asked the priest to scan news sheets and indeed she quizzed any visitor from afar. She had Masses said for his safe return. She embarked on intense periods of concentration. She made unconditional appeals to Our Lady and all the Saints. hoping that the promises she made to them would help to spare him. Time dragged by slowly. In some ways she also dreaded to ask if there was any news but was compelled to do so. There was no reply from Paris, and there was no other news.

She had seen one woman's son leave as a boy and come back as someone whose youth, seemed to have been denied him. The sight of that crippled man hobbling around the village, almost unrecognisable, disfigured, testified to the trauma of the terrible events which had gone on and what little chance she would ever have of seeing her own boy again. That poor man had been the only one of the six who who had left, ever to return to their district. Hope was dwindling. On market days and Sundays those other mothers all met up and exchanged their scraps of information about the war and their boys. Days seemed like months, and months like years and she heard nothing, yet she would happily have changed places with that surviving boy's mother. With the passing time the near physical pain would not abate. Not even at night was there any respite. She slept fitfully, always worrying about her son, especially in the small hours when everyone's fears become manifest. She relived every day of his childhood, his birth, his first steps, his first words. In her mind's eye she could see him all the time.

Her deliverance from the ordeal started with a rumour from the beyond the next village about a returning soldier. It was a hope which made her heart leap, heralding the dawn of the indescribably joyful day of his miraculous return. There was the waiting, not much work done, the catch in her husband's voice, the excitement of her other children the youngest of whom had never even met him. The tentative relief was more unbearable than the initial parting. Finally, the joy of seeing his approach in the distance on foot carrying a bundle. The first embraces were tearfully emotional. His father, with choked voice merely said with a quivering smile, "Where on earth have you been?"

Their beautiful boy was home, and in one piece. Later on, the contentment of being in the same room was coupled with the milder regret at the lost years, of not having been able to see and touch him. His mother would reflect that his early manhood years had been denied her. She had not witnessed the transition from youth to adulthood. There was also the need to know where he had been and what had happened. He told the whole story to his family.

The gratitude his mother felt to those people, those strangers in a foreign land who had saved him for her welled up inside and made her sob with an intense emotion.

Much later after the initial joy of reunion, there followed the realisation leading to a deeper anxiety that he might, one day, leave again. But in that thought she was no different from any other mother. She deeply pitied those other women of the village whose sons had not returned. She hardly dared to look them in the eye.

Her boy had indeed arrived safely home against the odds despite all of Napoleon Bonaparte's best efforts to ensure the opposite.

One single letter from this simple French woman, written out for her by the priest, eventually found its way to the Kadišius farm expressing all that she felt. Kadišiute took the letter over to Antanas Dubaitis who was now reasonably fluent in Lithuanian and Polish. He translated it for them from the French. It was an outpouring of overwhelming gratefulness from a French mother for what they had done. Although the receipt of this letter made them happy they were pragmatic in their thoughts.

"We only did the same as any other decent people would have," they shrugged. The other aspect of the situation, and its lasting effects they couldn't speak about, so they just kept it to themselves.

Juozas had heard tell of other villages where similar things had happened. Some of the lads, these 'bits of boys' who had no choice but to throw themselves upon the generosity and mercy of the Lithuanian people had been Dutch conscripts, some had been from Spain. There had been Germans, Italians and Poles. They weren't all French. There had been sixteen or more different nationalities in their army.

They were too weak and demoralised to throw themselves upon the kindness of anyone, rather it was the Lithuanians of the countryside who took pity and went out of their way to give them aid.

The flower of the youth of Europe had been depleted by the ambition or some would say, 'vision', of a few men. But there was no denying that amidst the brutality some humanity had emerged as people made sacrifices and took risks to redress the balance between evil and good, in some small measure.

The fate of insignificant poverty stricken Lithuania, it seemed, was to be always on the path to or from somewhere more important and to be the chosen territory upon which more powerful countries fought. The Lithuanian countryside, the land of marshes, forests, lakes and sand, and its inhabitants, just had no choice other than to absorb everything and everyone that fate threw at them and yet still their human resilience came through, as it always does –

– Juozas had never been very conscious of international politics until he had met Yevgeny in Kaunas but now he was more thoughtful. He had heard of England which had been such a thorn in the side of the ambitions of Napoleon all those years ago. He now knew about that country whose influence had spread across the whole world. It was a land of industry, work and wealth, for everyone, it seemed. He was aware that there was just beginning a slight movement towards emigration to that country and also beyond, – to America, especially by the Jews. He had heard that all people were equal there. It was a country where, if, given that the money for the passage was forthcoming, and the will existed to survive the formalities imposed by the Russian authorities, you could go and start all over again in an atmosphere where one would be able to breathe the clear air in freedom and enjoy equal protection under the law. Juozas had considered this option, but concluded that it was unknown territory and that he had already chosen his path, which was to work hard and make the very best of his life here. His mother depended on him. If he left it would kill her. Perhaps in the future he might reconsider it – These great men of the past and present who made ordinary people's lives such a misery. He set to pondering if their ideals, dreams or aspirations indeed those of all men, lofty or humble, were worth the loss of a single life, even if the majority were to benefit in some way. Maybe it was, maybe not. He supposed it depended on the goal. But surely those destined to be sacrificed or to have their lives ruined or changed would have a strong view on the matter? There was the grand ambition on a mighty scale which some men have and, then there was his own modest aspiration. He realised though that all ambition has a price of one kind or another which demands payment – The sleigh continued on its way guided by his sure-footed horse who had trod this route many times and who knew the way back to her warm barn, feed and rest – Juozas moved on in his thoughts to wonder if severe misdeeds such as cruelty or murder could truly be redeemed by telling the priest all about them in the confessional. Since his confirmation at first Holy Communion he had never confessed any serious issue to a priest. He always stuck to minor digressions. The more serious may have earned him a penance of say, two 'Our Fathers' and four 'Hail Marys' or a recital of the Rosary while he battled with his conscience.

He wondered what the penalty might be for starting a war or murdering someone in cold blood. There seemed to be a disparity somewhere. Did some people actually do those sorts of things knowing that a few minutes on one's knees would expunge their sins providing that they could convince themselves they were truly penitent?

And he also wondered why the emphasis was forever on sin and punishment. He reflected upon why there wasn't an ornate box at the side of the church where one could go to receive praise for good deeds done. Surely there should be a balance? How could a single sin in a person's life outweigh the many good things they had done?

To him it seemed that men, including the clergy, were more inclined to condemn than to praise. He almost felt guilty for having such thoughts and wondered whether he ought to confess them next time. He certainly wouldn't be owning up to the more serious thoughts he had had concerning revenge over the Russians who had clubbed and kicked him that evening. More hurtful to him than the physical injuries he had incurred was the humiliation he had endured. His butterfly mind fluttered on, this way and that.

As he was thinking on the charity of the Lithuanian people and pondering upon how this squared with their attitude to the Jews and the Jews' own indifference to the customs, folklore and culture of the Lithuanian peasants, he became aware of two muffled figures just ahead on horseback riding towards him. His heart sank as he began to make out their uniforms and their sabres and rifles in the moonlight. God help him! It couldn't be his two persecutors yet again – surely?

Chapter 13

Accident

The road he was upon followed the right hand bank of the river Sešupe. He had just passed the crossroads. The left turn would have taken him over the stone bridge which led to the manor house. The frozen river was wide but the stone buttresses normally had the effect of increasing the speed of the water under the ice as it rushed through, and it was also very deep.

The two riders had seen him and were spurring their horses into a gallop. The one at the front had drawn his sabre, for what reason Juozas could only guess and it frightened him. As they approached each other at an ever increasing closing speed, sleigh and riders, Juozas panicked and attempted to make a three hundred and sixty degree turn in the middle of the road. As he yanked Onooti's head with every bit of strength he could muster, both hands were pulling hard to the left. The horse gave in to the sudden stab of the bit pulling savagely at the tender part of her mouth. Her eyes rolled and she whinnied in terror as she swung left in an attempt to alleviate the pain. Whilst the horse managed to turn in a relatively small area the sledge skidded and described a huge anti clockwise slide, the horse at its epicentre and the back of the sleigh whistling around on the ice at alarming speed. Just as the two riders were reining in their horses to Juozas' left, the wooden sleigh hit them both with sickening force. The horse nearest the sleigh cannoned into the other knocking both it and its rider down the river bank, and then keeled over trapping its rider underneath at the top of the slope. The other horse and rider had been in the act of rearing up when the impact had occurred. Off balance the horse on its hind legs with the horseman desperately trying to bring it back under control as he stood upright in the stirrups, slithered down the bank, narrowly missing the trunk of a willow growing out over the river, and onto the ice which covered the surface of the water. They sprawled together for a few moments slipping and sliding as they sought to regain their feet. Finally the rider, clad in his service greatcoat but minus his fur hat managed to bring the panic stricken horse under some sort of control and slowly, gingerly began to lead it back across the snow encrusted ice to the bank. The animal was absolutely terrified and began to kick and buck. Its iron shod hooves pounded the ice again and again. Juozas who had initially been thrown out of the sleigh found himself miraculously unharmed, his fall cushioned by a deep snowdrift. He struggled out spurred on by a rush of adrenaline and managed to grab Onooti by the bit strap so that he would have a measure of control over her. He was aided partly by the weight of the sleigh which was on its side having tipped over. It was acting like an anchor now it no longer rested on its runners, restricting the horse's freedom. The first rider was still trapped under his horse which was lying very still, part way down the bank. Only his head and shoulders showed. His eyes were moving. The scene was one of total devastation in the slowly breaking dawn light. It was starting to snow again as heavy black clouds began to build up overhead.

As Juozas saw the extent of the accident, the realisation dawned that he would be blamed entirely for it. There was an ominous creaking. It sounded a little like a great tree which was being cut down at the point where the saw had crossed the line of the tree's ability to support itself. This most horrible sound was the ice beginning to crack. Unable to support the weight of both the Russian soldier and his horse, gravity had prevailed and the ice gave way in a spectacular, noisy, splashing, cracking, chaotic scenario as both horse and rider disappeared into a black hole of fast flowing deep water. Against all the odds the Russian re-emerged from the maelstrom managing to scrabble himself into a position over the turning slabs of ice where he could grasp a branch of the willow but only his head and his arm showed above water. His glove was gone and he was feeling the incredibly intense pain of his wet cold hand trying to hold on against the relentless pressure of the fast rushing water which wanted to pull him beneath the surface. The water gripped his greatcoat and weighed him down while the powerful current forced itself against its sodden bulk. Juozas took in the situation immediately and automatically scrambled down the bank, slipping a bit but his natural caution was tempered by the need for speed. Past the other horse and rider who were beyond help. he slithered to a flat rim a few inches wide at he river's edge. He had no thought of his own perilous position above the small chasm surrounding the profound black depths. Taking off his mitten he leaned forward, the other hand still in its own mitten wedged in a fork in the tree. With his bare hand he grasped the Russian's collar and attempted to pull him up and out. Try as he might, as strong as he usually was, he couldn't manage it. The beating he had received from the very man he was attempting to save had drained him.

The weight of the greatcoat was too much for the frozen Russian and his own grasp on the branch weakened as his icy hand lost all its strength and feeling. Suddenly he just gave up and in doing so consigned himself unwillingly to a quick death, following his horse under the ice. Juozas came to his senses, regained his footing and made the sign of the cross. At that instant he thought of the statue of Our Lady which stood to the side of the altar in the church in Smalenai. His heart was pounding and he was smitten with a sense of failure.

Juozas' mind was racing. How could he extricate himself from this mess. His future life or death swam before his eyes. The Russian authorities were looking for anything and they would latch on to any individual they could terrorise in their relentless attempts to suppress the Lithuanians. There were already rumblings throughout the province. He knew with absolute certainty that they would make an example of him. They would not be concerned with the rights and wrongs of the accident. If he reported it, and became involved, someone would be bound to tell them about the incident in the bar room. There would always be people looking for an opportunity to ingratiate themselves with the authorities.

With a surge of panic-stricken energy he struggled to the top of the bank again. Walking onto the road and surveying the scene he realised that the only thing to do was to clear up, get rid of all the evidence and let the weather do the rest. The effort would be a small price to pay for not being sent to Siberia at the very least or hanged, or shot at worst. His stomach churned as he thought about those at home dependent on him. He reasoned that when the thaw finally came in the spring the ground under the ice would have remained intact. There would be no sign of what had happened.

The Russian under the horse wasn't moving at all now. His eyes were closed, a trickle of blood oozed from the corner of his mouth. As his head was lower than his feet it seemed to run up his bruised cheek from his distorted lips. Juozas wondered if he was dead. If he wasn't already, surely he soon would be, crushed as he was by the weight of his horse which appeared to be lifeless.

Juozas' own hand was beginning to seize up. He looked around for his mitten but assumed he must have dropped it into the river during his blind panic to rescue the Russian. He approached the body of the horse and pushed against it with all his might bracing his feet in holes in the ice which he quickly hacked out with his iron shod heels. It moved ever so slightly taking the Russian with it as it slid fractionally down the bank, and then it stopped. He realised that if he altered his position onto the slope itself and pushed again with all his might if the horse gathered momentum he would be in a perilous position and would probably overbalance and follow it into the river.

In the upturned sleigh, still coiled in place on the inside wrapped around four pegs, was a long length of rope. There was also a spade fixed near it with two buckled leather straps. His sleigh was equipped by a kind of inherited peasant resourcefulness against most eventualities. Uncoiling the rope he thought it could just be long enough to be tied to the dead animal, looped around the tree and be hitched to Onooti who might be coaxed into providing the power to get the dead horse's carcase moving down the slope. He could hardly feel his hand as he started to put his scheme into operation. He had to make sure that once the horse was sliding, and hopefully on its way to disappearing into the river, that its weight wouldn't pull Onooti in too. She would have to be unharnessed at just the right moment.

Scrambling once again down the bank, he passed the rope through one of the two iron rings which were on either side of the dead horse's bit. The rest of the harness was firmly strapped around its head so there was little likelihood of it coming off under pressure. He looked again at the Russian trapped underneath. The eyes were fixed open. The eyeballs were covered in frost. Juozas was fairly sure he was dead.

Pulling the hempen rope through until the ends were level he slithered in a sitting position down to the tree looping the double rope around it with his left hand and retrieving it with his right despite the numbness he felt. He then inched back up the bank to the road carrying the two ends. He tied one of the ends under and around Onooti's collar knotting it tightly. The other end he left loose. Removing his horse from its harness where she was trapped between the two shafts which were now gripping her in a tangle, he backed her up as far as he could to the top of the slope. It wouldn't take much to get the Russian and his horse to follow their companions into the depths. On the top of his horse's collar were two projections between which the reins were meant to sit. He knew just how strong they were. The two pieces were actually made as one piece of cast brass. The two horns projected at right angles from a longer base bar which was curved in the same shape as the horses collar with two rivet holes on each side. The collar itself was a massive construction of several layers of thick leather, padded and stitched. It was extremely heavy as it needed to be in order to spread the horses effort over the strongest part of its body. The collar was moulded perfectly to the contours of the horse where the base of the neck met the shoulders and chest. Oval in shape it couldn't twist. Although old it was strong, a fine example of the saddler's art, and was faced with soft leather where it came into contact with the horse's body.

The brass bar was an integral part of the whole thing and was stitched, glued and riveted into the collar. It was almost immovable and Juozas was aware of this. He hauled himself up onto Onooti's back by a superhuman effort and sat astride the horse wrapping the loose end twice around the two horns. He urged Onooti forward across the road at right angles. At first she couldn't get a grip than finally the ever-willing beast achieved some purchase. He had to break a lifetime's rule and kick her in both flanks with his heels. This unusual treatment had an immediate effect as she started forward with eyes rolling, her head tossing and snorting. Painfully slowly she pulled forward against the dead weight while he held tight with both hands clenched to the rope wrapped around the horns. He reluctantly had to kick her and urge her on by threats and shouts.

Suddenly she lurched forward and fell on her front knees as something gave. At the same instant Juozas let go of the coiled loose rope end as he sought to prevent himself flying over the horse's head and it unravelled itself in a flash and shot away past him in the direction of the river. He heard the trundling crackling noise of something heavy moving on ice. Turning his head he was just in time to witness the almighty splash as the Russian's horse reached the end of its slide falling through almost the same hole as its stablemate. The rider had been carried in too evidently as there was no sign of him.

Juozas thought afterwards that he had been lucky in that as the rope shot through the ring on the muzzle of the sinking horse it had not tangled. He put that down partly to the intercession of the blessed Virgin Mary and also that the carcass sank slowly but that above all he had had the foresight to loop it through only one of the rings of its bridle and not both. The light slowly increased as the day broke and Juozas spotted the glint of a cavalry sabre on the road and threw it into the hole consigning it to the depths and it was all done.

Finding the free end of the half sodden rope he tied it to the overturned sleigh. The other end was still tied to his horse. With an effort of will as much as strength he managed to lift the side of the sleigh to a point where he could turn round and get his shoulder under it. He heaved with all his remaining energy, and with a heavy crash the whole contraption was upright again. Onooti started, but Juozas had a tight hold on the wet part of the rope where it was tied to the vehicle and the other end of which was still tied to her collar. He managed to pull and turn her towards him using his right hand and the crook of his left elbow, and after that she was alright, coming towards him quite docilely.

The job of hitching up the sleigh to the horse with one hand wasn't easy but he managed it. He then undid the rope from around the collar, bundled up the wet rope and threw it in the sleigh. He could no longer feel his other hand at all. It was still snowing relentlessly. He put his left hand into his pocket, but he still couldn't feel it.

"With a bit of luck" he thought, "If it snows all day no one will be abroad and the river will ice over again".

They found their own way home as the moonlight had been eclipsed by the approaching clouds which had heralded the snow. As daybreak had broadened, so the road was still discernable together with the layout of the landscape and certain trees and landmarks along the way. Juozas was feeling really bad now. The beating, the superhuman effort he had made, the stress, forced him into a sort of semi conscious state but Onooti, that good reliable member of the family, knew the way instinctively. Sensing that at the end of it there would be food warmth and rest for her she steadily dragged herself, Juozas and the heavy sleigh the six miles to their turnoff. She took her usual route swinging round wide. As she did so there was Rozalia swathed in a long cloak with hood, wearing a headscarf for good measure who ran alongside in her knee high boots, reaching up to grab Onooti's bridle. Looking at Juozas through the flurrying snowflakes she immediately thought he must be drunk. Annoyed, she jumped up onto the seat beside him taking the reins from his paralysed hands. She glanced at his face and was horrified by what she saw, urging Onooti onward along the track to the yard in front of the house. She called to her mother-in-law who came rushing out assessing the situation instantly and taking control. "Help him inside," she told her daughter-in- law,

"But don't put him too near the fire. Get some snow and start massaging his hands with it. While you're doing that I'll put Onooti away and bed her down."

She was marvellous. The way she had taken the lead had made an impression on Rozalia. She regarded her mother-in-law in a new light.

When Juozas hadn't reappeared the evening before, they had gone to bed thinking he would let himself in later. His mother had woken up very early and realised that something was wrong. She made Rozalia dress up warmly and go up to the turnoff to meet Juozas while she remained to look after Vincentas. Now Rozalia could see she knew exactly what to do. She herself was a mere novice. Juozas' mother had seen this kind of thing before and had learned how to cope years ago. As she was unharnessing the sleigh, hunched up against the wind and driving snow, she heard Juozas cry out in pain inside the house shortly followed by the sound of a rudely awakened baby crying. The sound was gut-wrenching to her but she knew that it was a good sign. Circulation was beginning to return to her son's hands.

Whatever could have happened last night? Only time would tell. Juozas was in no fit state to talk now. What he needed was complete rest. As she was putting everything away and leading Onooti to her straw-filled shed her shrewd eye noticed that the peas were gone, Onooti had a somewhat wild look in her eye, she had grazes on her front knees and that there was a military fur hat with a brass double-eagle crested badge on the front of it lying tangled up in a length of rope in the bottom of the sleigh.

She began to get a bad feeling about this as she prised the tangled frozen mass of icy rope from the bottom of the cart with the shovel and dragged it across the yard and into the barn.

The blizzard continued for three days without a break.

Chapter 14

Arrest

Less than two weeks later, when the worst of the weather had abated, they came for him. The first inkling the household had that something out of the ordinary was happening was the barking of the dog outside. This was followed by the sight of three armed men in uniform on horseback. One of them dismounted and addressed Juozas who was standing at the door with Rozalia and his mother Ieva peering anxiously at them over his shoulder.

"Juozas Kadišius?" one of them uttered. It was half question and half statement and the tone was very clearly aggressive.

"Yes that's me," Juozas responded enquiringly.

"We have orders to take you in to Smalenai."

"Why?" he said as the fear inside him took hold. "I think you know why." came back the cocky reply delivered in a rasping bark with ill-concealed hatred.

"Let me get dressed then," he said reaching for his studded boots and heavy coat. The soldiers, annoyed at this delay, grudgingly stood there with their hands on their holstered pistols. They clearly expected him to walk as they motioned him into moving towards the gate and the windswept, frozen road to Smalenai. As the horses and men walked toward the road Juozas noted with alarm that the third policeman, a huge beast of a man, remained behind and had dismounted and entered the house.

As Juozas trudged along on the icy road, while the other two men rode, he plucked up the courage to ask the higher ranked man what it was all about as he anxiously looked back over his shoulder, but he knew only too well. He was glad he had told the women nothing that night other than that he had been in a fight in town and had come off worst. As far as he was aware they had accepted his story. The less they knew, the better. It was now purely up to him alone how this would all progress. He knew he could lose everything, perhaps even his life, if he made a single mistake.

"You must have heard that two of our number went missing after an encounter with you at the inn. We know, – and we have the evidence – that you've killed them. The only question now remaining before you are tried and executed is how and why? and what you and your accomplices did with the bodies. And believe me you will tell us their names too."

Juozas was gripped with fear and retorted, "What accomplices? No, there were none. I haven't done anything. Yes there was a fight in town but I didn't start it. I came off worst. I still don't really know what I did to upset them that night, but they left the inn before me. I don't know where they went after that. I presume they went back to the barracks. Who told you about it anyway?"

They didn't reply immediately and Juozas felt his heart thumping wildly. A cold sweat engulfed his body and he felt sick.

"You are a bloody liar! Own up to me now and you might get off a bit lighter, otherwise we'll have to do it the hard way and beat it out of you when you get to the station. Then you will suffer pointlessly and we will win. Tell me now and it'll be less unpleasant. We'll go back and get Vlad. God knows what he's up to with your wife!"

Juozas made no reply but just shook his head again, while his stomach continued to turn over, as one of the men riding slightly behind him took his foot out of his stirrup and kicked Juozas so hard in the shoulder that he fell down in the snow. As he picked himself up he could see he was being closely covered by two guns. He dragged himself along, his left shoulder now on fire. As he faltered on his way, and when it was considered by his persecutors that he wasn't walking quickly enough, he was given another helping boot on whichever part of his body they could reach.

Thus they made it as far as the outskirts of town and by now various people had noticed what was happening and one of them went to tell Bulaitis what he had seen. Rimantas got himself ready, telling his mother he was going to follow along to see what had happened. He fell in with an acquaintance on the way who grumbled resentfully about the way he had seen Juozas being treated adding that, "Even a cow being driven to slaughter gets more kindness and consideration than a Lithuanian."

Rimantas followed the thin straggle of individuals, who were curious to see what was going on, as far as the police barracks, which most people usually avoided. It was a large wooden-logged series of buildings, similar to the other structures in town but larger and identified by the iron bars over the windows and its strong oak doors and shutters. Attached to it was another, much larger, building housing the barracks themselves and close by were the stables and a cell block, all joined together at angles.

The whole town knew that these premises were the hub of enquiries about the missing soldiers and that no-one had seen or heard of them at all since they had left the inn. They had all talked about the fight that night, but most people who knew him thought it unlikely that Juozas had had anything to do with the disappearance of the pair of soldiers.

Secretly some were a little pleased that Juozas was suspected because it took the persecuting spotlight away from them for a time, but equally, if he had done it, others admired him for striking a blow on their behalf against the hated filth, the occupiers of their land.

Back at the farm, Vladimir the soldier who had remained behind, was carrying out a search. He was thorough. He went through the building methodically, not replacing anything he moved, until finally something attracted his interest under the bed. In a wooden box was the ancient pistol.

"What's this doing here'" he roughly demanded of the two women who were terrified at the rough intrusion into their lives. He cocked it and cruelly pointed it at Rozalia. She, knowing it wasn't loaded, was still terrified by the soldier's menacing, aggressive, contemptuous demeanour. Frightened, she boldly said, "It belonged to my husband's grandfather, Jurgis Kadišius. Juozas has done nothing."

Then she blurted out, "Yes, he did come home the worse for wear after a fight in town a few weeks ago but he didn't start it. Beyond that I can't tell you anything because I don't know anything more than that. Nothing else would have happened. He is a good man. Believe me I know him better than anyone."

"Why does he keep this gun?" the soldier repeated turning it over and over in his hands. Where is the powder for it and the lead balls? What does he use it for?" He aimed it once again but this time at the crying baby awake in its cradle. Vincentas was clearly getting on the soldier's nerves. Rozalia hastened to assure him they kept it in case of troublesome wolves.

"He uses it to scare them away if they get too close."

"Too close to what?"

"Too close to the house, or too close to the cart or his sleigh when he is out."

"Where is this sleigh?" rasped the soldier. Vladimir got to his feet and lurched towards the door.

"I'll show you," replied Rozalia muffling herself up in a shawl whilst rushing to catch him up, then scurrying past him in the direction of the lean-to cart shed. The soldier looked around the sleigh, kicking it a few times and asked her if this was what Juozas had taken into town on the night in question. Rozalia replied in the affirmative and the soldier clambered up onto the seat and turned around and examined the carrying space behind. "Where does he carry this gun normally?" he said flourishing the pistol.

"In that wooden locker I think," she replied. He tried it. It was a bit stiff with the cold but he prised it open and pulled out a small greaseproof bag which he unrolled to reveal half a dozen musket balls and a packet of gunpowder. Retrieving these he stepped down from the sleigh and strode back towards the house and she followed him walking and running to keep up with this long-legged man. Re-entering the house he sat down at the table and started messing about with the gun and the contents of the bag which he had found. Every now and then he glanced over with annoyance at the bawling baby, which sensing the commotion and change to its routine, was now being comforted by its grandmother being rocked gently from side to side. But each time she thought she had calmed him the soldier made another utterance in a guttural voice which set the baby off again.

As he fiddled with the gun loading it with powder and then forcing a lead ball down its muzzle he kept on over and over, asking the two women to tell him again the events of that night. He repeatedly asked if they were sure about it as he went through the intricate procedure of getting the pistol ready for firing.

The two women were petrified as he slowly raised the pistol taking aim at the baby. Suddenly he barked out, "One last chance."

Veronika was immediately tempted to say something, anything, to save the baby and to get this monster off their backs. She remembered the Russian fur hat she had found in the back of the sleigh which she had later burned in the oven. Just as she was about to speak, simply to make this horrible psychological torture stop, the man's arm moved sideways and his aim alighted on the dog which was standing growling a few feet away from him. He pulled the trigger and the mechanical sequence was set into motion. The hammer with the flint struck the striker plate, there was a flash of sparks and the main gunpowder charge ignited.

The dog took the bullet in the chest, arched up backwards and fell dead on its side on the beaten earth kitchen floor its life-blood oozing away in a stream past its open, rapidly glazing eye. It's four legs vibrated for a few seconds then the animal became motionless.

The whole room was filled with choking smoke as the soldier, by now bored with his sadistic game, got up, moved the dog slightly, lifting it with the tip of his boot and left with the parting words, "I will be back." He was mortified that he had not managed to extract any evidence. It could have been a feather in his cap. How he detested this Lithuanian trash – peasants – and Jews!

The two women now completely traumatised by this sudden turn of events together with the crying baby huddled together on the floor near the dog and sobbed.

They never even heard their tormentor mount up and ride away with the evidence. The sound was masked by the noise of their wailing voices, all three of them.

Juozas and his captors arrived at the barracks followed, at a distance, by a handful of curious peasants desperate to know what was going on. His two captors dismounted leaving their horses to be taken away by another uniformed man and they roughly led him inside past a desk as one of them muttered to the man sitting there, "Kadišius." The clerk nodded and noted something down in a ledger. They took his coat and then Juozas was frogmarched down a corridor and thrown roughly into a cell through an open door which was then slammed shut and locked behind him. He took in his surroundings, a rickety woven canvas webbing bed with a filthy blanket and a bucket in the corner. The wooden walls had been covered in plaster and painted dark green in the past, many years ago judging by the degree of peeling that had taken place since. Faint light filtered down from a skylight in the roof. In this dank gloomy place Juozas' mind was working away but he had already concluded that there was no escape from here. Even if he could have stood the bed on end on top of the upturned bucket he still wouldn't have been able to reach the skylight. The stench inside this darkly oppressive, foetid cell was indescribable.

It was mainly a human smell of old urine, excrement, vomit and mould which hit him with a shock as he was unceremoniously thrown inside. At least the bucket was empty he noted as he felt the need to use it. It was disgusting and he wanted to be released as soon as was humanly possible. He calculated that this was just the beginning of the process of dehumanisation in order to break down any resolve left in him, for the purposes of total submission, and obedience to those who held the keys.

He was unable to bring himself to lie on the bed so he sat down on the edge of it with his back not touching the filthy plaster and with his feet on the floor.

He told himself again and again before the ordeal he knew was coming, "Remember. you did nothing, nothing. There was a fight, yes, you can admit that because there were witnesses, but nothing else, nothing else. Don't tell them under any circumstances about the accident or they'll twist it and make you a murderer."

Two or three hours passed very slowly and at last Juozas heard footsteps coming along the passage outside. The door clanked open and two men came in. Juozas stayed seated and one of them motioned him to get up, which he did. They manhandled him out of the cell and half walked, half dragged him through another passageway and into a room where there were two men sitting behind a desk. In front of them was a solitary wooden chair where he was forced to sit.

He faced the two officials. They stared at him saying nothing and Juozas was able to observe them. The smarter of the two had a totally smooth bullet-like shaved head and wore gold rimmed spectacles and sported a thick but neatly trimmed ginger moustache. He had piercing grey eyes Juozas noticed in the brief moments when he glanced up before continuing his writing. He seemed to be about forty. He was dressed in a clean well-pressed tunic. Under the desk Juozas could see he wore riding breeches with a stripe down the outside of each leg and shiny black knee-length boots. He seemed to be the more authoritative of the two men behind the desk. He was a Russian. The other one could have been a civilian, not wearing any form of uniform although he was quite smartly attired. His face was more ruddy than that of his companion so Juozas guessed he was either, out and about more than the officer or that he liked a drink. He wondered who the second man was. Would he be doing the beating and the donkey-work while the officer asked the questions?

"We know you murdered our officers with your pistol," began the officer in Russian. "We've found one of the bodies with a hole from a lead ball in him." He paused for effect waiting for the other man to translate. Juozas though, understanding quite a bit of Russian realised immediately that this was a lie, instead of answering remained silent, forming an image in his mind of his mother, wife and baby while trying to remove himself from the nightmare reality which these men were trying to create. He was succeeding in this strategy when the officer rose from the desk walked around it and up to him and hit him with full force around the head toppling him, upending the chair as it went flying. He returned to his seat behind the desk without looking back. The civilian got up and came round to help lift Juozas back onto the chair with the aid of the guard who was standing behind. "I'm sorry he did that," he whispered in Lithuanian into Juozas' ear, "He is not the gentlest of men. It shouldn't be – I hope it won't be – necessary again. Just tell them what they want to know."

The officer continued, "Why were you in town that night?"

"I went in to sell some peas and buy some gunpowder for my gun." Juozas muttered haltingly. The other man translated

"What, this one?" asked the Russian producing Juozas' pistol from his desk drawer. Juozas' mind started to work rapidly as he wondered how they had got hold of it. He then recalled the soldier who had stayed behind. He had no way of knowing what had taken place after he had been taken away. Rozalia must have given him the gun he supposed, or he had found it during a search. What sort of interrogation had she been put through?

"This gun has been fired recently."

"No, It can't have been. I haven't used it for ages. I had no gunpowder. That's why I went into town."

"Yes it has been fired. Smell it!"

With that he motioned to his underling who took the gun over to Juozas and held it under his nose. Juozas detected that it had indeed been fired fairly recently. Was this a frame-up or had they shot someone with it. His imagination ran riot as his mind raced with all the awful possibilities. He being an intelligent man though still knew that this surreal situation was being manufactured to make him talk. There was no body. They really didn't know what had happened. The ghost of a smile appeared on his face at the thought. The officer nodded to the guard who came round and punched him in the mouth and then slapped him hard on the side of his face.

"You think this is funny? You won't be amused shortly."

"Is that really necessary sir?" said the other man disingenuously to his officer in Lithuanian accented Polish.

"Why not let me talk to him?"

The officer appeared to be thinking then curtly nodded, got up and left the room. The Lithuanian motioned the remaining guard out into the corridor and adopting a more friendly air said to Juozas, "Would you like a drink?"

Juozas, although relieved to be enjoying a relatively pain free interlude, was still aware of the strategy being employed here but decided he might as well take advantage of it. "Do you have any vodka please, and would a pipe be out of the question?"

His interviewer called out and the guard returned. His new friend spoke to him and off he went returning a few minutes later with a bottle, two glasses and a pipe, together with tobacco and matches. "I don't smoke myself" said the man, "My name is Paulius Berankis by the way in case you were wondering. I help out here with a bit of translation and so on. I like to think I make things better for us Lithuanians in what are often very difficult situations."

"Yes we need people like you." Juozas said between puffs as Paulius lit his pipe for him. If it hadn't been for his dire predicament Juozas would have enjoyed that pipe and the vodka even in his pain.

"The way I see it," Berankis said, "Is that you haven't done anything wrong – but to show that clearly you have to be open and honest with them. They hate non-compliance," he said thus setting himself apart from his employers and with Juozas by referring to 'them'.

Juozas was distracted by the ache in his shoulder and his painful mouth so replied with a degree of irritation, "I've told you both all I know." Once again, although he couldn't help identifying with Paulius as the bringer of relief, the image of his family and his life was stronger than his desire to unburden his soul on this man.

"I have to go for a break," Berankis finally said reluctantly. Whereupon he left the room and the guard came straight back in. Juozas stood up to stretch his legs and the guard delivered a hefty punch into his solar-plexus which put him down on the flags. As he lay there he vomited all over the stone clad floor and the smell of the recently imbibed vodka became apparent again.

"You filthy bastard," shouted the guard grabbing him by the scruff of his collar as he dragged and kicked him towards the door. Another guard appeared, to aid the other one, and between them they hauled their prisoner back to his cell and threw him inside. He stumbled across the cell trying to keep his balance and cannoned into the slop bucket which turned over depositing its contents all over the corner of the cell. Juozas was now pleased to throw himself lengthways onto the filthy bed. Anything was better than the beating he had received.

He was nauseous and dehydrated, mentally exhausted from his battle of wills with himself as much as with his interrogators.

His cell grew gloomier and gloomier as night drew in until finally it was pitch dark but for the faint glow of flickering light coming through the chinks in the cell door from lamps which illuminated the passageway outside.

Juozas slumbered slightly, shivering in the freezing chill of his squalid predicament. He was forced by the cold, which was creeping through his bones to feel around for the solitary blanket and wrap himself in it trying to breathe through his mouth all the time and not through the one nostril which was still unblocked. Some time later, he didn't know how long it had been, he was rudely disturbed by the clanging scrabbling of keys and his cell door opened and in came Paulius again carrying an oil lamp. "Is there anything you want?" he asked, the lamp casting its light upwards across Berankis' face making him look demonic. If Juozas had questions in his mind about this man's sincerity before, then they were soon resolved by the face seen in this different light. "I could do with a drink – water please." Juozas managed to say, his mouth and tongue dry.

Berankis left and returned presently accompanied by a woman carrying a plate with a piece of bread and cheese on it and a mug of water. Juozas recognised her as Mother Consaitiene who worked for the police as a cleaner. Although God knew it seemed her duties didn't extend as far as the cells. He knew of her, that she had a reputation as a habitual gossip, so he was confident that news of his plight would soon leak out to the community at large.

Seeing Juozas' eyes light upon the refreshment Paulius said with an insincere smile, "It was the least I could do."

Juozas refrained from a reply and Berankis added,

"Have you had any further thoughts?"

Juozas grabbed at the water and downed half of it in a single draught. He then attacked the food, devouring it hungrily between further gulps of water as Berankis stood patiently waiting. Juozas began to feel better.

"Well Juozas? Shall we put an end to all this nonsense now?"

"I know you can stop this Paulius but I can't make up things that didn't happen. I've told you everything about that night. If you've got witnesses who say I did it then bring them forward, but if not, just leave me alone. Or, if you like, let them come and beat me up again, but my story won't change from the truth."

Berankis paused looking closely at Juozas pensively. He abruptly turned on his heel and left.

Outside and further down the passageway the Russian officer was waiting. He saw Berankis shake his head and said to him,

"That's it! I'm thinking we should start persuading him properly now we've tried it your way without success!"

Berankis said to him, "Do you know what? He may not have actually done anything, or if he has he's very clever. I think further persuasion here would be counter-productive. This is too local. They all know him. I'm afraid there could be a reaction. We should keep our hands as clean as we can. There's a lot of peasantry out there !"

His superior replied, "I'm not so sure of his innocence beyond all doubt. I agree he's one clever bastard. If he *is* lying then it irks me that he has got the better of me."

Then the Russian said with a thoughtful look at Berankis. "You have a point. If I start an insurrection here in Smalenai we'll both be for the high-jump. I'll hold him overnight and see how he feels in the morning. If nothing changes we'll send him higher, to headquarters. Let them deal with him. And make sure he doesn't get his coat back tonight. Now I'm going off duty."

Berankis quickly suppressed a slight smirk and nodded feeling self-satisfied in his wise counsel and began to think about going to the tavern and having a few drinks himself.

After a long cold damp night filled with doubts and fears for himself and his family, Juozas' cell grew very gradually lighter. Approximately two hours passed as the light level reached the maximum it was ever going to that day. Juozas was grateful for the morning even though he was never going to be able to read a book by its light. Still wracked with anxiety about his family, whose fate he didn't know, he heard with apprehension veering between alarm and resignation two sets of footsteps coming down the passage.

The door opened and it was Berankis again together with a brawny Russian guard. It was he who grabbed Juozas by the arm and jerked him up into a standing position and towards the cell door. The arm which the guard grabbed was the same one which was still feeling the pain of yesterday's shoulder injury and it started throbbing again. He presented a sorry sight with one arm nearly useless and his hand still pulsating from the effects of the frostbite. The night's chill had spread through his body overnight lowering his resolve further.

He was taken before another Russian Officer to an office which was warmed by a log fire which had been burning for some time filling the room with pungent smoke and heat. The non-commissioned officer before whom he now stood, sat at the desk inevitably writing and reading and re-reading a report. The report clearly referred to Juozas and his case as the man every now and then glanced up at the prisoner. This went on for at least ten minutes until at last the man said. "Your answers under questioning leave a lot to be desired and so you are now going to be taken to Suvalki for further interrogation unless of course you reconsidered and have something else to tell me."

Juozas shook his head disconsolately. He had been to Suvalki only once before, to the centre of provincial administration. It was a large town and he hadn't really felt comfortable and couldn't wait to get home. But then he was only a boy taken by his father who had some matter of business to deal with there.

Juozas was led outside and given his coat back at the same time. He put it on whilst on the move, grateful for its bulk. At last, and after the warmth of the fire, he was regaining some circulation which had been threatening to cease altogether. He was frogmarched across the snow packed courtyard at the front of the buildings towards a covered sleigh drawn by two horses. He observed with a start Rozalia and Rimantas sitting up on top of his own sleigh to one side of the square with dear old Onooti at the ready. They must have been there all night waiting for him he realised. Or maybe they had found somewhere to stay, perhaps with Rimas. The important thing was that they were here. His heart lifted slightly. His wife half stood up and Juozas observed her anxious, hopeful, questioning face looking at him her eyes looking from from one side of his face to the other.

"I'm fine," he shouted, "Suvalki," he managed to add as loud as he could while he was being bundled into the prison sledge. One of them placed handcuffs on his wrists which were slipped over a central iron bar. He was roughly manhandled and pushed in to the shouted command, "No talking."

Inside were a pair of long wooden benches on which were seated two other men in the secure confines of the space. They too were shackled to the bar by handcuffs at the far end on the opposite side to him. There was a small window at the front and another at the back, both glazed. Juozas was pleased to note this, as it would keep out the wind. The convict wagon started along its way and the three men remained in silence for an hour at least as the heat from their bodies gradually raised the temperature inside by a few degrees even though their breath still formed eddies of steam as they exhaled. One of the men opposite appeared to be dozing but every now and again Juozas caught the eye of the other man who was clearly a Jew. The man kept avoiding his gaze. He looked a bit shifty, almost guilty of something and Juozas wondered how long he would last. Finally Juozas said to the man in a low voice, "I'm Juozas Kadišius." the other man made no attempt to introduce himself so Juozas continued, "What have you done that they are taking you to Suvalki?"

The Jew replied, "Absolutely nothing." There was a prolonged silence which lasted for about another fifteen minutes.

"But what are they accusing you of?"

"I don't know. Me! a person who only wants a quiet life!"

"Did they beat you?" Juozas asked.

"You could say they were rough," the man replied.

Juozas asked him when he had been arrested and the man told him it had been late last night.

"What about him?" Juozas whispered, gesturing with a nod of the head towards the other man, who so far had said nothing and shown no outward interest in their muted conversation.

"Oh him. 'Theft', I think I heard someone say."

Suddenly a voice emanated from the depths of the third man's scruffy beard which whispered, "No!" He had not been sleeping.

"What do you mean, 'No?'" said his companion lowering his voice to the same level.

"These idiots want me to testify against you – Kadišius. I would imagine they are trying to pin something big on you. You know there is a lot going on out there in the countryside don't you? They are talking quietly in some of the inns about a revolt. There are quite a few young bloods who want change. Trouble is they are not well organised, nor even armed. The Russkies are blackmailing me with accusations of theft which I am innocent of. But luckily for you there has obviously been a mix-up and they have put us all together in this sledge. I doubt that was supposed to happen but, because of the changeover of officers overnight there must have been a lack of communication. Typical. The Russian left hand doesn't know what the Russian right hand is doing. That's the only saving grace with these bastards sometimes – their sheer incompetence."

"How are you going to handle this then?" said Juozas betraying the trepidation he felt in his quivering voice.

"I'm not," said his companion.

"I would no more shop an innocent man than I would skin my own grandmother. And.... they won't keep their word anyway. There might be another way"

"So what do you think then?" asked Juozas worriedly.

"I am just going to act like an idiot. If I give answers like a half-wit they might just let me go because I believe I could have proved I borrowed the horse they accuse me of stealing if the owner hadn't died meanwhile. I have borrowed it from him several times before and always returned it better fed than when I found it. I have witnesses who can vouch for that. But I wasn't to know he had sold it to someone else just before his death and neither did his wife who gave me the permission. Some men don't tell their wives anything. Unfortunately all the details died with him. The authorities have grasped it all full well, but you are the key person here. They have two missing soldiers to account for and what with this talk of dissent amongst Lithuanians – and some Poles too, they are desperate to pin something big on someone as an example – and it's just your misfortune it's you."

"So," Juozas thought, "I'm a pawn in an important wider game."

He didn't know however that following along at a distance were quite a few people from Smalenai, all Lithuanians, with not much else to do at this time of year, for whom this was a major event in their repetitive lives. Who would be the first to carry all the gossip back to Smalenai and be the centre of attention? Amongst the number of the followers were his friend Rimantas Bulaitis and his own Rozalia.

After hours of bumpy slithering travel the sledge stopped, the door was unlocked and the prisoners unmanacled. Russian guards appeared and re-handcuffed the prisoners taking them in separate directions into the stone building which stood on one side of the main square. One took charge of a packet of sealed orders given to him by the driver of the sleigh. Juozas remembered the square vaguely from his youth but had no time to glance around to get his bearings before he was hustled quickly inside.

The cell he was accompanied to was cleaner and less rank than his previous incarceration of the night before. He remained there for two hours at least before being escorted through tiled corridors to a room with large tall doors. Waiting inside, standing behind an ornate desk was a heavily built man whose age Juozas put in his early fifties. He motioned Juozas to sit on the other side of the desk. The man said,

"Allow me to introduce myself. I am the Margrabia, Aleksander Ignacy Jan-Kanty Wielopolski of Kraków. And you are, I believe, Juozas Kadišius from Smalenai."

As soon as he opened his mouth his language confirmed him as Polish. This was a better prospect than if he had been Russian like the previous interrogators who had done him no favours. Juozas thought that as the interview had started in a civilised way he should respond accordingly in a civilised way.

"Yes Your Excellency," he said respectfully in his most fluent and well-spoken Polish.

"Call me 'Sir' from now on." the Margrave said.

"Now, I have a report from our station in Smalenai that you are suspected of terrorism and of doing away with two Russian officers. If this is true you've got yourself into serious trouble. It doesn't look good for you. I want the full story– and no lies."

The Margrave looked piercingly deep into Juozas' eyes. Juozas summoned up all his self-control, and looking suitably humble he replied, "Your Honour, I am only a farmer. I have no interest in terrorism and I haven't killed anyone sir. I am not capable of it, I wouldn't be able."

"But they tell me you were singing in Lithuanian to provoke a fight and encouraging others to join in. And what was to follow? Were you hoping for backing from the others?

"No sir."

"You might think we are all villains."

"No sir not at all," Juozas grovelled.

"I do understand and sympathise a bit with your point of view. I suppose no-one could blame you for wanting your freedom? You would want to be able to make your own decisions and farm the land for yourselves and not for someone else. You would, no doubt like to bring up your families as Lithuanians?"

Juozas looked startled. He was inclined to nod, to agree, to discuss it with this man who was someone who appeared to understand the problems and might be sympathetic. But instead Juozas ventured to say, "Sir, I simply went into town for something to do. The baby was crying, getting on my nerves. There was no work I could do outside, with the weather being so bad. I was having a good time at the inn until it all happened. Yes! I was singing in Lithuanian but I didn't see your men come in until the last minute. I would never have done that if I had seen them. I'm sorry for that. As for their disappearance I am completely ignorant of where those men might be."

The official looked at him. He was aware the man had been beaten up already and he believed him. But nonetheless he spoke again. He thought he might be able to use the prisoner.

"You may not believe this, but I myself have been struggling against injustice all my life. I do believe in the diplomatic path to change though. I am touring these provinces to assess things and see how we should progress. The Polish nationalist movement is doomed. It is going to be derailed and the Lithuanian one along with it. We will make sure we forestall any insurrection. There are many Lithuanians who share my point of view. You are intelligent, you could be one of them – one of us. There would be certain benefits."

Juozas may have nearly fallen into the psychological trap which Wielopolski was laying for him, but just at that moment there was a knock on the door and an orderly came in and quietly spoke to his superior. The two then walked to a far corner of the room, out of Juozas' hearing, to an ornate window overlooking the town square, leaving Juozas to reflect on what he had seen when the door had just opened briefly. Outside in the corridor Juozas had spotted Berankis standing. He had his back to the room but Juozas would have recognised that duplicitous turncoat anywhere. How he had got there Juozas didn't quite know. He must have ridden there later judging by the travelling clothes he was still wearing; but any softening of his own defence which Juozas may have been contemplating was hardened again as he realised with foreboding the compromising position he was still in.

The orderly left after a few minutes and Wielopolski returned to his seat behind the desk.

"I personally have been responsible for a gradual transfer away from serfdom towards the renting of farms to the peasants. The Tsar is going to abolish serfdom eventually anyway."

He paused awaiting a response.

"We are indeed grateful for that sir."

"And as you may know I also enforced conscription for up to twenty years to forestall any future disruption to this beautiful country. There's nothing like a spell in the army to dampen down revolutionary ardour and for young men to get their priorities right. If there should ever be a revolt, then nobody wins."

"I agree wholeheartedly Sir. I served in the Imperial army in Kaunas. I was taught to be a carpenter. My best friend there was a Russian, who helped me a lot."

"Well then, this is a mystery. What are you doing here? You couldn't have served for very long at your age."

"I was invalided out with Rheumatic Fever after a time," explained Juozas, managing to sound suitably regretful.

"So you seem like the sort of man who could help us keep the peace and work with us to retain order. Tell me exactly what happened that night, just for the record, and we can forget all about it and work together. It could be worth your while."

The Margrave was aware that the witness sent from Smalenai had proved to be worthless. The interview with him earlier had ended in a fiasco. He intended to leave his case and that of the Jew to be dealt with later on that day by somebody else.

He began to realise after getting the measure of Juozas that they had picked the wrong man here. He seemed incorruptible. But it was one last throw of the dice to see if there was any truth in the accusation against Juozas which he had been presented with by his inferiors. He had to do it to be sure. If he thought the peasant mentality might leap at such an opportunity to ingratiate itself, but he was mistaken in the case of this particular individual.

Money would never sway Juozas. It wasn't in his personality. He was unable to succumb to bribery nor betrayal. He was too honest, and during this interrogation he hadn't lied – technically.

He just repeated the same story yet again which he had now memorised by heart keeping all the details exactly the same. The Margrave looked at the written report and his final throw was, "I'm told there are witnesses." To which Juozas replied, "I am sure they mean well but they are mistaken sir – whoever they may be."

Wielopolski noticed the slight sarcasm of that last sentence and envisaged the torture procedure which was still available to him but tended to veer away from that option. He was a reformer at heart and believed in persuasion in the true sense of the word and not coercion. At that moment both men became aware of a faint noise coming from outside. It sounded like the continuous hum of human voices heard on market days. It rose and fell. But this was not one of those days.

The Margrave strode across the carpet to the window and looked out. He returned to his desk and rang a small hand-bell. The orderly came in straight away.

"What are those people doing out there in that crowd?"

The orderly bustled out smartly and returned several minutes later out of breath. "It appears Sir that they are singing, protesting about a prisoner. they are becoming more and more rowdy."

"Which prisoner." asked Wielopolski.

"This one Sir – Kadišius Sir. They are saying he is being victimised, and that he has been set up and is innocent."

"Mmm, as a matter of fact, this interview is just about over. The prisoner is to be released anyway. What time is it?"

"Nearly three o'clock Sir," the underling informed him.

"Get him ready, give him back his coat and get rid of him as quickly as possible. I don't want to provoke an insurgency."

The prospect filled him with mild dread. Any such eventuality might jeopardise the future plans for reform which he held dear.

"Very well sir." The orderly motioned Juozas to follow him which he lost no time in doing, while the Margrave walked over to the window and looked out.

After Juozas had gone he went into an ante room, whose door was ajar, and where Berankis was waiting. "You heard most of that did you Paulius. What did you think?"

"Yes sir I did. I'm surprised he didn't take up your generous offer, he may have proved useful."

The Margrave looked at him with contempt. "Did it never occur to you Berankis that some men are honest? and that bungling by you lot in Smalenai could have caused the very train of events we are desperately striving to avoid in this province. That man is not subversive, no leader and not a collaborator. Your witness was worse than useless. I find no fault with him and much to admire. Now leave!"

Out in the square Rimantas, Rozalia and the others had been anxiously waiting. At first the sparse crowd had been viewed with curiosity by passers-by but once the gist of the story got round more and more people paused to witness the outcome. Somebody from a nearby building had set up a stall selling hot drinks and snacks to the overcoated and fur-clad crowd who were standing or stamping their feet in the cold icy square, the steam from their breath rising in eddies above them. An atmosphere of common cause developed as the crowd absorbed the plight of the prisoners and began to relate to them. Why was it always the Lithuanians who were trodden underfoot all the time? Somebody began to sing a Lithuanian refrain which was taken up as if by a choir. There was safety in numbers and the singing continued despite attempts by Russian soldiers to bring it to a stop. A person was clubbed with a rifle and the mood of the crowd began to grow more ugly. While this was happening, Rimantas found himself stretching his legs on the corner of a pavement. It was quite a novelty for him and he was feeling happy that there was solidarity. Nearby was a small group of men one or two of whom he vaguely recognised. He may have glimpsed them in the market or somewhere he couldn't quite place, he wasn't sure. Suddenly one of them started talking garrulously to a Russian in a slightly slurred voice referring to the circumstances of this case, telling him that he came from Smalenai himself. The Russian, more concerned with the mob blatantly singing in Lithuanian, fortunately wasn't really interested. The man then turned and caught sight of Rimas staring at him. He screwed up his eyes and opened them wide again peering through an alcoholic haze.

"Just a minute, don't I recognise you from Smalenai. Aren't you a friend of Kadišius?" he mumbled too loud for comfort.

"No not me. I just came along for the fun." replied Rimantas anxiously looking round to see who was listening. He noted with relief that the Russian soldier had been swept out of earshot by a slight surge of the crowd. The drunk then lost interest and edged away.

As soon as he had uttered that denial Rimantas Bulaitis felt heartily ashamed. But he also knew that if he had admitted knowing Juozas he may well have been arrested too. There would be no point in putting himself in harm's way without any purpose.

Suddenly, for no apparent reason the singing died down and then ceased altogether. An official had come out onto the steps of the civic building where Juozas was being held. Paulius Berankis read out a statement in Lithuanian to say that no fault could be found in Juozas Kadišius and he would be immediately released. Of the other prisoners, one was a madman and the other only a Jew. There was now no reason for the gathering and they should all disperse.

Shortly thereafter, Juozas emerged to the increasing cheers of the crowd who having taken the rare opportunity they had been given at last to express their resentment at their wretched lot in life at the bottom of the social pile. They bore him away like some kind of hero, amidst much back-slapping, to a nearby inn cheering wildly. He was bloodied and bowed The peasants and townsfolk seemed happy, fortified with alcohol, the other two prisoners forgotten. They had finally expressed themselves against their rulers and given themselves a modicum of self respect.

An ill-fated revolt was to follow throughout Lithuania five or six years later with ensuing brutal reprisals, but no-one knew at this point what was coming – only that here and now there were stirrings in their hearts against the authoritarian régime which was governing their rude lives. They had given themselves the confidence which is gained from the anonymity of the crowd and had won a tiny victory.

As far as Juozas was concerned any struggle against the massed ranks of Poles, Russians and renegade Lithuanians would be too big an obstacle to ever surmount without outside help. The nearest their tiny nation had ever come to that was when Napoleon and his Empire had once offered a brief glimmer of hope to the entire continent.

From the moment of his release Juozas realised that the only practical salvation open to peasants like himself was total conformity or escape. It wasn't so much that he was himself damned, but it was the thought of his children suffering with it for all of their days which filled him with despair.

He heard later that after the Margrave had returned to Kraków, one of the other prisoners had been transferred to a lunatic asylum in St Petersburg and another one, a Jew, after questioning, had been shot by a firing squad for an unknown crime. Back in their various farms and hovels most peasants discussed the latest gossip. They talked about Juozas, offering their various ill-informed opinions to each other and speculating endlessly. Some were curious about the lunatic. An absence of facts didn't get in the way of the wild rumours which went round. Only Juozas seemed to care about the Jew. One or two of the peasants laughed about it. Juozas, ignoring the gossip nevertheless felt anew the leaden weight of the life they led. The scapegoats whom the Tsarists had seemingly picked on in lieu of proof of Juozas' guilt, made him feel culpable. More importantly it reinforced the obedience of the peasant majority in this district to their overlords. The lengths to which the Russians had gone in punishing someone for something, anything! proved effective to calm the majority.

The Jew dying on a trumped up charge, the other man sent to a life of bedlam and Juozas' own close call, were events which had sprung from nowhere. How could matters of life and death introduce themselves so suddenly? The answer to Juozas' questions, why three men had died and another was condemned to spend his life with the insane could not be answered by him, without the contribution of a philosopher. All that was left was to fully blame the iniquitous imperialism of the Russians for it. It had all started, simply because he had sung in his native language. He still remained in grave danger of losing his self-respect whilst gaining the additional burden of a kind of heavy, guilty responsibility for the lives of people he barely knew. That burden would communicate itself to others closer to home.

As his children were born and grew up, he became wiser.

Juozas Kadišius, was a man whose hopelessness nevertheless still included intelligence and peasant practicality. He was well aware that his whole life's pattern was dictated by his birth. He had begun to believe he would never climb above it himself.

To his family he advised caution, adding by way of justification, that as long as they were able to think, all was not lost, they would have the high ground. Their beliefs and secret opinions would never be taken away. But to resist in an uncontrolled manner could never bring success and would only let the representatives of the Russian State know how you felt. "Fighting back," he used to say, once got him into a predicament, one he barely escaped with his life. The only possibilities for success for the downtrodden would not lie in collective action during which people might die, but in total escape – emigration. Juozas counselled the softer option to his children.

"If you are unable to change the causes of your ills then the better way would be to remove yourselves from them."

For those who remained, if their identity was to be abused at least they still had the Church to fall back on for the salvation of their peace of mind and their souls. But the State, its system and his own immediate responsibilities had persuaded Juozas. He would never himself ever be going anywhere. He would just get on with his life and raise his family as best he could.

Chapter 15

Farm Girl – 1882

Elzbiéta lay on her back in bed gazing up at the ceiling bewildered and apprehensive as she clutched at the limp white sheet which came up to her chin. Its all enveloping folds tucked up to her neck were reassuring, despite the pain in her head, and she held it up around her neck with both fists clenched. On top of that was a warm patterned quilt. She began to feel safer now as she relaxed knowing she was secure in her home. She could hear faint familiar voices as she fought to make sense of her surroundings, the flickering shadows which came and went and the murmuring which rose and fell. A jumble of dream-like thoughts and images filled her head. In brief interludes of clarity, which lapsed more often than not into obscurity as she began to fall asleep, she sensed fleeting impressions of other events in other times in far distant places.

She felt warm under the quilted eiderdown which covered her. Mamyte had painstakingly shown her how to make it when she was younger. It was a folk skill learned from her own mother which she had in turn imparted to Elzbièta.

She had done the same thing many times before with younger sisters of her own and with Elzbieta's own older sisters. They were all schooled in it, the necessary knowledge passed on.

"Look Elzyte ! I'll show you first and then you try one," her mother had said. The child watched as she lightly sketched out a design on a large piece of white linen she got from a wooden chest. She planned out and copied the designs from a dog-eared old book with a torn cover inherited from her husband's mother. Taking a fine needle from her little sewing box, and going over to the window she passed the end of a piece of green thread through the eyelet at the third attempt. Elzbièta looked over her shoulder attentively and could hardly wait until it was her turn. Mamyte had started the stitching along the outside of one of the lines. The young child had then been patiently coaxed in the intricacies of sewing and decorating with the pagan designs unique to Lithuania, picked out in fine coloured, delicate cottons in a style which seemed to be part of an unbroken link with the past. The finished artefact sewn into a number of puffed up panels and stuffed with goose down wasn't exactly perfect in its execution but both mother and daughter were extremely proud of it. It was this same eiderdown which covered her now.

A hazy face appeared and a cool hand was was placed on her forehead followed by a cold compressed cloth. Someone had come to soothe her fevered brow. Her eight year old head pulsed with one of those familiar periodic bouts of agonising thumping and she felt sick as her dear, gentle mother bound a damp rag around her forehead uttering calm soothing words of comfort as she stroked her daughter's soft brown hair. Elzbiéta felt the need to tell her mother how she felt, confident that she would know what to do. "Mano galva scauda Mama," she muttered, feeling the pain acutely.

"I know, I know my angel," her mother replied lapsing from Lithuanian into her own native Polish. "I'll be back soon, just go to sleep." As she made her way to the door she stopped briefly and quietly, on the way out to pull the homespun flaxen curtains across the small window obscuring the weak evening autumn light outside, plunging the tiny room into gloom. She told the other children quietly to keep out of the room. Elzyte's elder sister Juoza, who shared the room and indeed the bed, was none too happy but there wasn't much she could do. She was the sister who wore her heart on her sleeve, always bursting into a temper without thinking and then immediately regretting it. Her personality was in direct contrast to that of Elzbiéta, who always shunned the limelight. Juoza was the opposite, craving attention, loud and uninhibited.

Elzbiéta had always suffered like this with headaches. She was a sensitive, thoughtful soul and also a worrier. The slightest problem became magnified in her fertile, imaginative mind and other people's worries became her own. Whenever she felt the first signs of the onset of this affliction, if she happened to be near the hill of Žemyna, she would head towards it and slowly climb, getting higher and higher. Gradually she would see the landscape of this remote Russian province unfold, stretching further and further before her until she could sit under the huge oak tree which crowned the hill's summit amidst a thicket of bushes and saplings, offspring of the mother tree. That tree had been in existence since before anyone could remember. It had always been there, an unbroken link to the time of Mindaugas under whose rule, for the sake of some important political expediency, but now long forgotten, the old gods were formally denied. The ancient pagan ways, the gods of nature and of every living thing were superficially consigned to folk memory.

Even though there were many reminders of the new faith dotted in the landscape, people by custom continued to appeal to the god Perkunas in time of need.

Elzbiėta, like the rest of her family had been nurtured in the arms of Catholic doctrine and brought up with the acceptance of the newer faith as the only true path. She had no other choice and knew nothing of other faiths. It had been only four hundred years earlier that Christianity was embraced by the aristocracy, albeit slowly and reluctantly, and a long time after that by the peasantry. She had never known anything else but what she had been taught, so she accepted it unquestioningly. There was no doubt that their religion was a strong source of support to the peasants who lived across this ancient land and it helped to offset the debilitating effects of poverty, drudgery and the weight of the persecution they were all forced to bear.

Their lives continued on through the seasons for year after year, child after child, crisis after crisis and through all the petty jealousies and rivalries in the agricultural community. From famine to famine their existence lurched. They were told everything was in the hands of God and who was to say that wasn't the case? But nevertheless some people still strove for something more, even just to have a little more control over their own destinies a bit more to pass on.

Underlying everything however was the affinity with the natural world, its nature, the weather, the cycle of the seasons, the landscape and its healing powers which were somehow ingrained in the Lithuanian subconscious.

All was peaceful up there under that tree and she could look out across the endless expanses of forests and areas of wilderness. The wide vista of fields and lakes was faintly streaked with thin wisps of smoke rising from the numerous farmsteads dotted about. Foremost of the sounds in summer were birdsong and the buzz of insects filling the air amidst the forests of birch

and pine which extended in great and lesser swathes right across the landscape. Branches bent and creaked and the wind had its own sound. Strange unidentifiable noises came from the woods and long grass. On still days a person could be heard talking loudly or a dog barking or the sound of hammering from miles away. From her vantage point at the summit of her hill, she could see the many lakes sparkling like bright sheets of silver in the intense heat of the sun. Up here there was a light breeze rustling the leaves above, as the great tree gently moved and shifted its form. She would listen for the sound of cow bells faintly, woodenly, tinkling around the necks of her family's animals. Further afield others could be heard but she knew the sound of their own bells which had a particular familiar pitch. They had been carved by her father from blocks of wood in previous years during the long winter months in the warm, smoky atmosphere of their two roomed farmhouse, as the fumes from the oven eddied upward and found their own way out through the rafters. He used as a model for the bells those which had survived from the time of his own grandfather. Some had cracked and split after long exposure to the wind, rain and sun but he could remember clearly the patterns which had faded and he showed the children how to sketch them out and how to colour them with various ground up rocks mixed with egg white and oil.

Back in those days, when Elzbiėta was no more than a toddler, they had all lived closely together in the two roomed home which the family had occupied for generations. The house was falling down, leaky, draughty, long past its useful life and crowded. The smaller room had been added at some time in the past but it was little more than a very large cupboard in the corner with a ramshackle door. When she was about five years old, her father Juozas after endless discussion with her mother, over some years, decided that they would try to re-fashion a new house. Once they had discussed the feasibility of such a project mother and children went to stay with neighbours for

three months. During that time, using the old house as a core, her father and her twenty-five year old eldest brother Vincentas had camped in the outbuildings and constructed a new dwelling around the old, made of thick wooden planks and split logs. They had gained the help of various friends who came when they could. This time they made improvements on the old design. They built the new house with more rooms and a brick and clay chimney to vent the smoke properly from the new oven to the outside. The floor they made from planks elevated above the level of the previous beaten earth floor. There was now an upper storey within the roof which was accessed by a shallow ladder with wide rungs. Two projecting dormer windows made the best of the available floor area above. There was even a large porch fitted with glass windows which was built out with the eaves which were themselves given additional support by wooden columns forming a sort of covered colonnade at the front. They now had two bedrooms, a living room and a passage downstairs and two more small rooms upstairs. But even with rebuilding, the available rooms needed to be apportioned among the large family and Elzbiėta still had to share with Juoza. The two girls as children, were barely compatible. One very tidy, the other not. Elzbieta was continually clearing up the room and tidying whilst Juoza didn't consider it to be at all important. She just did what she wanted to do. They shared the bedroom because

there was only two years age difference between them, Juoza being the senior and therefor in charge. Elzbiėta was a girl who really needed her own space, such was her nature.

In later years Elzbiėta would wonder whether the improvements had been worth the stress in her father which seemed to have been brought about by the endless bureaucracy he had waded through to achieve the necessary permissions from the Russian authorities. All applica-

tions had to be made respectfully, cap in hand. Various payments were necessary and they were mostly unofficial. It was demeaning, corrupt. The process was a challenge to Juozas' self respect. What kept him resolute throughout was the need to do the best he could for them all. That powerful factor forcing him to comply with the unfair system all peasants had to struggle under. He had learned that hard lesson years ago when he was young, realising with a shock that the system could not be beaten even at great personal sacrifice.

Once pride had been swallowed yet again, the tedious and depressing application procedure had been gone through over months. Afterwards there was the endless toil necessary to make the money in order to repay the loans and to pay back in kind the favours that friends and neighbours had done him in giving their labour and advice.

In summertime during the intense heat, the ancient tree of Žemyna spread its comforting shady canopy protectively over her head. She would think about the tree and wonder if it could feel her presence. As she listened to its whispering leaves and leaned against its gnarled trunk, her body responded as her mind gradually shed its load of cares one by one and her inner turmoil grew less as her concerns and worries eased and became lighter. After a while, restored in mind and spirit, she would whisper a prayer of gratitude to Our Lady and make the sign of the cross as she retraced her steps back down the winding hill pathway ready to face her numerous noisy family again.

On this day though the leaves had already turned brown and mostly fallen and there was a sharp chill in the air. The best remedy for her troubles at this time of year was to lie in the small double bed, shared with Juoza, which her father had made from pinewood. With the resin from it still oozing, the room was permeated with a subtle fragrance. The aroma of woodsmoke from the main room still found its way under the wooden door her mother had gently pulled to. In the other corner was a single cot for her younger sister, named after her mother, Rozalia. But before she could allow herself to submit to the pain, Elzbiėta had to complete her allotted tasks around the farmyard. It fell to her to let out and feed the chickens every morning and put them away in their coop at night and to draw the evening two buckets of water from the well having to go out through the gate and along the single track earth path which led to the main road about three hundred of her strides away. This was the road that led to Smalenai about ten versts distant. She was also put in charge of buying honey from their priest who was also a beekeeper. That was her favourite job but she used to feel sad when she thought about the effort that each bee had made to take the nectar back to its hive only to have it taken by humans. But being a child, as well as thoughtful, she loved to chew on the honeycomb, and the liquid had all sorts of other properties apart from sweetening. People said it was very good for you and they used it as a disinfectant salve for various physical ailments. This was a characteristic running through the family and especially in Elzbiėta, one of respect for nature. They depended upon it to stay alive.

She had carried the two elm buckets, even though her head was thumping, suspended from a decorated curved wooden yoke of wood resting across the back of her shoulders. Her father had carved the yoke and the staves for the buckets himself from a piece of ash, which he had got the blacksmith to put together at the village forge with riveted iron hoops, and attach handles.

Shuffling back in her wooden clogs, the load evenly distributed, Elzbiėta bent her knees and unhooked the buckets one by one leaving them down outside the back door under the open wooden lean-to. She covered each one with its own wooden lid which hung on the outside wall, leaving the contents protected from investigation by the chickens, cats and dog. Slipping off her clogs outside she stepped into a pair of plaited birch bark slippers then made her way through the kitchen feeling nauseous, with her head still pounding. She tried to ignore the attention of her siblings. The youngest of them, was singing talking and playing while the older ones were helping their mother who, as she walked in, spotted her daughter's discomfort immediately and instinctively knew her problem. She quietened the other children and guided Elzbiéta to the room which three children shared and to the small double bed in the corner, took off her daughter's bast shoes, putting them under the bed next to the other shoes and sabots thrown at random there, and helped her under the covers.

Finally here she was, motionless on the bed, lying on her back covered by her sheet and quilt. This was the moment she had been anticipating through all the continuing headache, the retching and the endless tasks she was determined to perform before she gave in.

Her mother helped her, cared for her and soothed her. She settled her daughter down and then quietly, on tiptoe, left. So Elzbiéta lay there and pictured a glowing halo encircling her feet. Gradually it moved up along her body towards her face, relaxing every part of her as it passed over until it had travelled as far as her chest and shoulders. The higher it came the less she felt the parts of her body it had already passed and they became relaxed. When it reached her head and started across her face, the pain diminished and she lapsed into a slumber. She imagined in her dreams that winter was raging outside but that here tucked up in her bed she was warm and snug and secure.

Chapter 16

Family

She awoke some time later to muffled sounds, subdued laughter and clinking noises coming from the main room. Her head was clear, she was a little weak but otherwise she was fine. Her clear deep set blue eyes now sparkled as she swung her legs down onto the bare wooden planked floor and gingerly tiptoed across to the door in her bare feet. As she crept through into the main room not wishing to draw attention to herself, most of the family were sitting round the table on wooden chairs. Her nose was assailed by the smell of cooked pork and vegetables. She knew what it was. Their pig had been killed a week earlier and it was going to last them well through the autumn and into winter. For her, this yearly event was always tinged with sadness. The family could never carry out the actual slaughter themselves, but at the same time couldn't afford to be sentimental.

Usually they called in a friend who was expert at it. It was fairly quick and painless for the pig. It was done with a knife and the blood was collected in a pot as the animal expired.

The family had spent two days scraping off the bristles with boiling water, cutting it all up and rubbing salt and a mixture of herbs into the meat before hanging some of the pieces up around the main room on hooks to cure. The rest was stowed in large chunks in a barrel full of salt. No part of the animal was wasted, everything was used for something or another. Even the intestines, after they were washed, were used to make pork sausages and the blood mixed with onions and fat for black pudding. The brains of the animal were used to make brawn and the head was boiled to make soup.

The pig was a sow, about three years old. She had been covered by a boar belonging to one of the neighbours about eighteen months before. Two thirds of the ensuing litter had been given to him as payment. It was a price worth paying as the boar was of known and reliable pedigree and always produced fine, strong piglets. Their share of the litter, three females, had been weaned and lived in the old sty fifty feet from the back of the house which was necessarily slightly downhill and downwind.

It was situated in the same general area as the family's latrine. That consisted of a small outhouse sturdily built, again with wooden walls and a single pitched chestnut shingled roof sloping down towards the back. Any rainwater dripped into an elm gutter under the eaves to the rear and was channelled away to a gully further down the slope. Beyond that was a deep stretch of forest commencing about a hundred strides away on a narrow front which then became wider and wider the further it extended. The children knew the parts that were within earshot of their farm but they were never allowed to penetrate much deeper into the woods than that. Inside the hut was a deep pit over which was an ancient low box in the form of a sort of long wooden commode with two circular holes in the top side by side, one smaller than the other. Each had a hinged cover over it. To the left was a heap of sandy spoil and a shovel, and on the wall was a spare hurricane lamp and a wooden box of Vestas. The whole edifice was mounted on small solid wooden wheels, with a gap at the bottom which made it fairly easy to move to a new location when the pit under it was full, if the whole family put their backs into it.

As she emerged into the room she was spotted, and amid enquiries as to how she was feeling they all shifted up along one side to make room for her. Juoza yelled out in a concerned but very loud voice,

"How are you feeling Elzyte?" The boisterous shout was almost enough to set her back again but she was expecting it, so she steeled herself as she screwed her face against the noise and politely replied.

"A lot better thank you Juoza," She said it in a whisper as if encouraging her sister to lower her voice and then added, indiscreetly as she soon realised. "Would you mind tidying your stuff up and putting it away? You've left your shoes all over the place, all over my things. I've sorted out folded your clothes away tidily in your box for you." Juoza looked a bit miffed.

"I'll tidy up in my own good time and not when you say so!"

This was the sort of response Elzbiéta had come to expect, the usual reaction. She wondered why she had bothered to say anything at all. She didn't want another argument over her personal space.

In the middle of the table was a large metal pot. Everyone was reaching across and eating out of it with wooden spoons. Alongside that was a board with a huge loaf of hard, black wholegrain bread baked the day before. There was also a deep wooden bowl of sour cheese which Mother had made from milk curds encased in muslin left hung up to drain for two days. Elzbiéta thought she had never tasted anything as delicious in all her life as a slice of that slightly sour bread covered with cream cheese. The rest of the meal consisted of carrots, onions and turnips. They had been produced in the well drained, well manured plot, not far from the house, by the youngest son, Jonas. It was his job to sow them in their fertile vegetable patch as soon as winter had turned into spring with its usual unheralded suddenness, and to nurture them to maturity and harvest them in late summer. He knew how to store them in the cool dry vegetable shed in clamps so they could be eked out throughout the winter. The surplus, if there was any, they sold on market day, which was held on Mondays and Fridays in Smalenai. In bad years though there wasn't even enough to go round for them, let alone any left over.

Some of the children were drinking milk from wooden beakers, others water, while the eldest brother Vincentas and father Juozas were quaffing home brewed ale from white china mugs which they had bought from a Russian pedlar the year before. She noticed writing on the bases as they were lifted each time a gulp was taken. After discussion and deliberation Juozas thought it said 'England', which he supposed was where they were made. The half dictionary they kept hidden away in the rafters confirmed that 'England' did in fact mean 'Anglija.' It was lucky this time that it was the latter part of the dictionary which had gone missing at some indeterminate time in the past. It was a source of fun that never lost its worth, this half-dictionary joke; as they often took pot luck as to whether the word they were looking for would have been at the front or the back of it. They would all groan laughingly and pretend to fall on the floor if the word they were looking for turned out not to be there. Juozas kept meaning to ask for a new one smuggled from Germany but never got around to it.

He was by now middle aged, a thickset man with a prominent nose and wide solid chin. His heavily greying auburn hair was beginning to recede and thin but was compensated by the short coarse beard he had grown, even more white flecked than his hair. The usual fashion was a walrus moustache in men but Juozas always had to be different. The clear blue eyes his children had inherited were still bright despite his advancing years. His face bore all the signs of one exposed to the elements. The complexion was reddened and browned in equal measure. The skin at the corners of his eyes betrayed the evidence of continual squinting against the sun during the short summer and the sometimes bright ultra violet light reflected from the winter snow.

His forehead was creased and lined. When his eyes relaxed the white crows feet at the corners became clear. His nose and ears were becoming larger than they had been in his youth. He was still immensely strong and his barrel chest and huge arms and hands bore witness to it and Elzbièta was childishly confident that there was nothing he couldn't do on the farm or make for the house. He in his turn seemed to love his young daughter a great deal. In her own way she helped him do various things around the place and occasionally accompanied him to market. Sometimes, in the autumn when they had geese to sell they would drive them along together and have plenty of time to talk. They would discuss what was going to happen to the geese once they got to town. All the geese which other farmers had brought in would be put together in a flock together with theirs. When there were enough, their feet would be coated in tar, like little boots, and they would all be walked together to the border and across it into Germany in time for the Christmas market. Her father, kindly as he was, didn't dwell for too long on the purpose of their walk in order to spare his daughter any heartache. He would quickly change the subject and tell her various stories his father had told him about life in the past. He talked to her about nature, plants, trees and animals and abstract things concerning how one should be responsible for one's own future happiness. She came to realise that this country wasn't the complete extent of the world. She began to be aware of the practicalities of keeping animals and the reasons for it and the shortness of their lives and the harsh, limited horizons available to peasants.

She could sense the longing in him. He instilled in her very slowly and unintentionally the notion that things needn't be that way and if things were wrong there was always an alternative. Life could be made better if you wanted it badly enough. As she grew older she became more aware of their situation both in terms of the landscape and their social position and the pattern of her own education. She had attended school on and off in Smalenai until the age of seven, after which she went to Kalvaria twenty five versts away once or twice. But it was too far. Her official education came second when she was needed at harvest time or haymaking and when the roads were sometimes impassable for several months of the year. During the long winters they were occasionally snowbound and the river was frozen solid to a depth of six inches. So Elzbièta's education was gained mainly from her parents, particularly at her mother Rozalia's knee and consequently she learned to read books printed in the Lithuanian language.

Since 1863, after the uprising, it became illegal to print anything other than Russian Cyrillic text, so they had got around that by smuggling Lithuanian books printed in Germany, in the Latin alphabet, across the Prussian border bearing false imprints dated before prohibition. The language they spoke among themselves was almost exclusively that of the peasantry. In previous years their immediate Polish overlords had never needed to communicate with them directly except through their estate managers. Every now and then travelling pedlars doing the rounds across the countryside would visit each homestead in order to sell goods and to pass on news. One or two would even teach, and some of them smuggled books. But punishment by the Russian authorities was severe if ever they were caught encouraging any kind of peasant nationalism. Beatings, fines and maybe imprisonment and thereafter persistent hounding of the entire family, or even the whole village, by the Russians, were the penalties they risked. However the underground network of discreet defiance was too well disguised round there, so they managed to avoid the worst excesses of Russian sanctions or punishment.

There was a twenty year gap between her eldest brother Vincentas and herself. Separating them in descending order there were six other brothers and sisters and Rozalia who came after her. Some were still at home, one or two had already left and were making their own way. There were two or three others who had died in infancy. Elzbiėta's arrival eight years ago on June 18th 1874 had been a pleasant surprise and she was doted over accordingly.

However, on this day of Elzbiėta's latest attack, and the falling temperature which was heralding the onset of winter, Juozas was again beginning to feel the recurrence of the old problem which had come about early on in his marriage. Year after year his left hand would start to ache and turn white when it grew cold, a stark reminder of his place in society. He was forced to rub it vigorously to help the circulation. Whenever he felt it every autumn he remembered bitterly again how it had happened. He would talk vaguely to his family about it, only if they asked him, but giving them a version so mundane that they wouldn't bother to expand the discussion. Inwardly however he felt extreme resentment as the painful memories came flooding back.

His wife was aware of most of the various setbacks he, indeed both of them, had lived through over the years, if not of the more painful details of some of them. Some things he shared with her although not aspects which he was too ashamed to reveal, which he thought might make him seem less in her eyes.

He need not have worried. She understood more than he knew, with an intuition which became increasingly reliable as the years passed with an increasing rapidity. Days, weeks, seasons, seemed to be gaining momentum passing quicker and quicker for the couple until they seemed to be flying away at breakneck speed.

It seemed to be always in retrospect that they noticed it. They made comments concerning events from time to time which younger people couldn't really grasp, "Where did that time go?" or "It seems like yesterday that this or that happened!" or "Look how she's grown. The last time I saw her she was only this high. Look at her now!"

Juozas and his wife were both hastening onwards towards an unknown future. One thing they knew for certain though – it would be owned by their children. They would succeed – it was what the couple had worked so long and hard towards.

Chapter 17

Parting – 1894

Daybreak arrived just like any other April morning in Suwalke. The false dawn, then darkness, then light again, and the deafening chorus of birds which roused Elzbiéta from the deepest level of sleep. With the early morning light filtering through the window to the sound of scuffling animals outside begging to be attended to, came a further level of awakening. Most of them, the chickens, ducks and geese just wanted food. Some needed to be let out and the cow had to be milked. As Elzbiéta awakened she vaguely remembered there was something unique about this day.

Late the night before, after celebration, storytelling and merrymaking, there had been tearful farewells. Her friends and relatives had gone back to their homes and the house returned to near normality. There was still an undercurrent of uncertainty, of change. As she collected her thoughts she developed the butterflies in her stomach which had lately been coming and going. The misgivings she had felt for the past few months and weeks took hold again.

She was going on an adventure. Now at the age of twenty she recalled her father Juozas' almost dying words. "You must do what I never had the courage to do, dear Elzyte, make a better life, go to the West, go to America. There is nothing for you here." He had forced himself to say those words, and they came out with an air of deep regret. He was putting her future above his own in exactly the same way he had done for his sons. Some of them had indeed gone and sent back glowing reports of their lives abroad. She had known all her life that this had been his deepest personal ambition, left too late to achieve himself. Before he had paused to think about what was happening he was married with responsibilities and assuming that he could improve his lot and his family's standing in their native country, by faith, hard work, honesty and application, or that somehow things would change and life would become better. That hope had been dispelled. By the time he had acquired a handful of children and debts, he knew he had missed his chance. He came to the realisation gradually, then came to the emphatic conclusion that it couldn't be done under this régime at this stage of his life. He should have done it when he was young, unmarried and with no commitments.

That yearning for freedom however had never gone away. It was always welling up inside. The many injustices in their lives relentlessly made it a frequent occurrence and he had constantly spoken to his family making them aware that they didn't necessarily have to accept oppression or servitude all their lives and that there could be another path out of it while they were still young.

Privately he recalled the depressing moments throughout his life when he had been forced to swallow his pride and conform to what the tyrants demanded. To bureaucracy and awkwardness of official-dom, was added contempt. There was hostility and bullying at every level. He put up with it all for the sake of his children. After that first incident so long ago he had never again gone out on such a limb.

He had hated himself for being so subservient. He lived with it. He had witnessed more outwardly spirited, opinionated friends paying a heavy price for even the slightest hesitation in conforming. The pun-ishments meted out by the Tsar's representatives were dire, ranging from being hauled up on the basis of some trumped up misdemean-our, to being beaten up, and even to being forced off their land. And some of these so called transgressions were as mild and reasonable as just wanting to speak and read their own language or to better them-selves. The edicts and decrees which had periodically come down from the top to the bottom of the social hierarchy were so unreason-able as to become almost tedious if they weren't so serious. All the peasants, were truly up against an entirely weighty, crushing system.

Lithuanians speaking their own language in the home behind closed doors was something the Russians could never fully combat however, and most people were just content to wait and hope for better times to come. He had been thinking about these issues most of his life and his whole family were aware of his views. He voiced them often enough – at home. It had been one of his regrets and he had instilled it into the children as they grew. Every time he mentioned a topic remotely connected with it all, they sighed and smiled at each other as if to say; "Here we go again." But at the same time he knew he was con-demning himself and their mother to a final future of loneliness and heartache without their children and future grandchildren if they did listen and take his advice, but the yearning for them to be happy and prosperous outweighed all that. For him, there was no way out but death. He wondered if he was ever going to see his utopian dreams for them come to fruition.

His rheumatic illness, when it happened again, came at the end of a lifetime of toil. He was still hauling logs and making fences when he ought to have been relaxing more in front of the fire and leaving some of the burden to be shouldered by his elder sons. They did help and pull their weight, but they were young. The older girls helped too, but around a farm there was always work to be done. Everybody pitched in to do their bit towards the continuous daily routine, and jobs which had to be completed at certain times of the day, and there were always unanticipated things to do. There were too, the calls to help out collectively, on other people's land. Their lives were mostly, drudgery and routine. There were certain jobs in the house which Juozas had to undertake. Making, mending, and improving things. There were still other tasks which only women seemed to take responsibility for; cleaning, cooking, tending chickens and in Elze's case, sewing and looking after the beehives. They were all in this life together, each person contributing in full. Above all he felt his position as the head of the house and he would pull his weight.

When he noticed the ache in his arm and breathlessness while he was at the haymaking, typically he continued to exert himself, thinking he could work it off somehow and it would pass.

The end for him, when it came, was very quick. Elzbiėta saw him fall and at first, in the distance, she thought he was taking a rest. The wooden pitchfork he had been using methodically to turn the hay had now fallen uselessly to the ground. As he was suddenly consumed with the gripping, wracking pain which burst forth from within his chest the dim realisation clarified into reality and hit him. "Dear God! I really am sick this time. Don't let me die, there are too many things......"

"Elze, Elze," he whispered faintly but she had already seen him and came running over ready for a game with a slight smile on her twelve year old face. He was always playing funny tricks on her. He was usually an amusing companion.

"Tevolis, Tevolis, stop larking around.

"Get some help," he whispered weakly through his blue tinged lips.

"I am very ill." She looked at him and realisation dawned.

As she ran she began to sob and by the time she reached her mother she could barely gasp out, "Mamyte! It's Tevas, he's suddenly been taken ill – over there," she said pointing to the meadow. By the time they both ran back, Rozalia with a cup of water, they were barely in time to make him more comfortable with some hay bunched up under his head and shoulders. His wife seemed to know in an instant that this was the end for him. She was distraught and felt helpless. She had been worried by his earlier Rheumatic Fever all their married life.

If she had summoned aid she would only have been able to get him to bed at best, but here he was already lying down.

He whispered weakly, " Look after them all Rozalia, don't let little Elzyte work all her li..." His face screwed up in agony and then relaxed as his lips stopped moving. They hugged and kissed him, sobbing as they did so. Suddenly he looked old and white and frail and still and cold. Rozalia stayed with him while Elzbiéta went to summon more help, she felt helpless but she continued to murmur reassuringly to her by now lifeless father. They brought an old door and gently placed him upon it covered with a sheet and bore him back to the house. Rozalia sent Vincentas on the horse into town to summon the doctor. They returned an hour and a half later, the doctor in a two wheeled trap. He brought his bag down with him and went into the house, but inevitably, after a short while he emerged shaking his head sadly. He advised Rozalia that she should go and report the death as soon as possible and then he produced and signed a document for her to give to the authorities.

Rozalia went the next day to Smalenai with Vincentas in the cart but was confounded by the lack of sympathy expressed by the officials she spoke to. She then had to go to Father Motiejunas who was a pillar of support for her. He took it upon himself to relieve her of the worry of funeral arrangements. He would inform the Seinei Diocese within the next couple of days.

Elzbiéta could scarcely take it all in during the time leading to the funeral. There were so many people coming and going, so much talk about him and what a man he was. Anecdotes and reminiscences fuelled by the provision of drinks resurrected him in a way, keeping him alive for a bit longer.

This was particularly so with his body laid out in the next room, eyes closed, hands lying one on top of the other across his chest. These times of hospitality and support from friends and neighbours served a purpose and provided a shield against reality as his family and friends became used to his demise.

She wouldn't know the really deep pain of loss until after most of them had gone. She did know though that she had lost her best friend, the person who had always been able to spare endless time for her, the man who used to talk to her as an adult above her years, making her think, filling her head with ideas. And for him she had always been a joy and a captive sounding board.

During the subsequent days the thought came into her mind more than once, "I must go and tell the bees what has happened."

And then, bitter-sweet images and events came crowding into her mind of the day when they had discovered their first bee colony, just the two of them together, father and daughter. Her mind wandered back as if she was there again......

She had been quick to spot it in some woods about an hour's brisk walk from their house. There was an area in the depths where mushrooms proliferated. No one seemed to know about this place but her and she enjoyed going there alone, returning with a bag full of them. During one of these trips she had happened to look up as her eyes scanned the forest floor. She had seen bees before but in this instance clouds of them were coming and going through a small crack just above waist height in the bole of a dead tree, Fascinated she watched them from a safe distance marvelling at their industry. When one flew towards her buzzing loudly with a sort of high pitched whine she ran away, flying like the wind, her free arm wildly flailing while she carried the bag with the other. The bee was persistent and chased her for a long time until it eventually gave up. As she returned panting and hot towards the house she saw her father coming along with the horse and told him all about it. The enterprising father, really interested, took Elze up onto the horse in front of him and together they returned to the woods where she showed him the tree, from a safe distance.

"Mmm," he mused, "I wonder if we could get them back to the farm and have our own honey?"

So they returned home again and that evening he went over to the church and spoke to Father Motiejunas, who kept some beehives behind the church in his garden. After explaining the situation and without waiting for the priest to say anything he added "I would like to keep these bees myself and start an apiary for little Elzyte."

Any thought the priest might have had regarding possibly augmenting his own apiary were immediately discouraged once he saw Juozas' intention.

"Right, I'll give you a hand," he said kindly. "What's the diameter of the tree?"

"It's about the same girth as a stout man but it seems to be dead".

Juozas went on to explain the situation of the nest.

"Alright, if I said that the best way to get them to your place is in the tree they already live in we can go from there. What we have to do is to approach the tree and stop up the entrance while they are all inside. The best time is in the early morning before they start foraging. Most of them won't come out until the temperature rises and they warm up."

Juozas was interested and intrigued by this. He had never given the topic much thought before but had merely bought honey or wax as and when they needed it from the one or two local beekeepers. He had always kept away from any hives he saw, thinking them dangerous. Beekeepers though were always treated with the greatest respect, on a par with priests. People raised their hats to the beekeeper as he passed by. He had even known them to be asked to sit in judgement in matters of local contention or mediate in disputes.

"What we could do then is to remove the whole tree after cutting off the top." the priest went on. "They are probably in a large hollow space above the entry hole, because the bees always tend to move upwards, only moving down to get out. Has Elzyte seen this nest before?" "No she hasn't, and she would have done because she goes there quite often."

The priest then responded, "Well now! the chances are that this is a new colony which has swarmed from another hive and recently settled in this tree. This is going to be the ideal way for you to start up beekeeping, as the colony will have a queen laying eggs. She would have led half the bees in a swarm in the search for a new home. My guess is that she has already mated and egg laying is in full flow."

"We should be alright if we can get the whole lot back in one piece without the bees getting out. It's sufficiently far away from the nest to your house that they will adapt to the new position. Any closer and they wouldn't, but would simply fly back to where their tree had been in the forest and just crawl around on the spot and die there. Bring your cart to the crossroads tomorrow just after dawn. We will need an axe-man and a two-person saw."

Early the next morning Juozas harnessed up the horse and cart at dawn taking two sons and Elzbiėta and they met up with the priest at the crossroads. They then all proceeded along the track to the forest guided by Elze.

Once there the priest donned a hat with a veil made from muslin and tied it around his upper body and under his arms. Examining the entrance he then opened his bag and produced a piece of muslin, doubled over, and a hammer and nails. This he nailed over the opening explaining that the bees needed to breath and remain cool. The bystanders noticed him twitch several times as he was stung around the hands by one or two bees which had emerged to investigate the intrusion, but he just carried on regardless. Picking a point some way above the hole he and the men took it in turns to use the axe and the hatchets to finish off chopping part of the way through the trunk, which did not take long as the bole was not very thick. On the priest's advice they had picked a solid area above the hollow part of the trunk where the bees were by tapping with the hammer until it felt solid.

They started their cutting with the saw a little way above that, standing on the ladders they had brought with them. When they were most of the way through it they hitched a rope to it as high as they could and pulled the top of the tree over. With the help of a bit more chopping and sawing the dead part of the tree above the colony space gave way with a crack and crashed down leaving the stump. They could hear the angry bees inside as they applied Juozas' two-man saw to the base. Whilst the two lads sawed away the priest held the top of the stump steadying it as they made the last cuts and the whole block, with the bees inside it came free.

Elzbieta remembered sadly how it had all been brought home in the back of the cart and set upright in a small meadow some way from the house. The priest then bade them all go away and wearing his protective headgear lit a small fire in a pot he was carrying until it smouldered with a thick cool white smoke which hovered around the hive as the priest waved it back and forth. He cut the muslin patch away from the colony entrance and retired while they all watched fascinated. A few bees slowly emerged and seemed to be carrying out exploratory flights while the priest advised them all to leave well alone and keep clear. The next day when Elzbiėta eagerly looked out she saw the insects coming and going just as they had in the woods. This time she kept a respectable distance away

From that day Elze had never looked back.

Her father went over to see Father Motiejunas many times and at his suggestion made another wooden hive out of a thick hollowed out tree stump with a heavy wooden lid. Removing the lid they spaced a series of sticks coated with wax set into notches which they cut in the thickness of the trunk perimeter at regular intervals across the central third of the circular area. The sticks, they were told, would form the basis for the bees to build and draw down their honeycomb which later on Elzbieta and her father would be able to access to harvest some of the honey. The new hive was placed near the original and eventually it was filled by a swarm which Father Motiejunas had collected from a tree in his own church garden which had come from one of his own hives. He shook the heavy honey-laden bees into the top of it from a large basket, thousands of them, muttering, "Don't worry, no-one will be stung. When they swarm they always fill themselves up with honey first. They are so full that they can't bend their bodies to sting, I hope we haven't lost the queen during the transfer!"

But there was no need to worry, the queen was there and the colony started to thrive.

Elze was thrilled to see the face her father had carved on the front of the stump and the thatch on the top of the lid which looked like hair. It seemed to her like one of the ancient forest gods. Father Motiejunas got Juozas to drill down through the top of the forest hive using as large a bit as he could find, until it just went through. they placed a wooden box, which the priest had brought along, over the top with an entrance hole just aligned with the drilled hole. Then banging the base of the hive, they drove the bees inside up into the box. When they deemed that most of them were there they closed the box up and put it to one side. Then they sawed the top off the forest hive revealing the comb. Some of it was slightly damaged in the sawing but Father Motiejunas assured them that the bees would soon repair it. The hive now had its own lid with a drilled hole in it which was then sealed up. All this was done wearing protective clothing with muslin draped hats, towards late afternoon. Opening the box of bees again they left it nearby and retreated. The next morning the box was empty but for a few stragglers and most of the bees had returned to the forest hive.

Gradually bee keeping lore and it's practical uses sank in as she made trips to the church to meet the priest together with her father, when he had the time, to learn about bees. Father Motiejunas told her of the legends and even folklore surprisingly, about the gods Babilas and Austeja and how ancient people had held the bees and humans as equals. The hive colony was called 'the family' and the queen was referred to as the little mother – 'Motina' .

She learned Father Motiejunas' method of building a fairly new type of hive he had read about in a series of articles in magazines from the Lithuanian community in Chicago in America and he passed this information on to Juozas who then made the most traditionally ornate beehives over the following Winter months decorated in the old way but with removable frames which could be inspected and replaced.

Previously in years gone by, they were told, a hive would have to be completely destroyed and the bees killed with poisonous smoke in order to get the honey. Now they could imitate the priest, wearing the same garb as he, and gather some of the frames, cut out some of the blocks of the bees honey stores and press out the honey through muslin wrappings, in an old apple press, as the honey itself ran into a container from where they poured it into jars. Or they could just cut up the comb into blocks and drop it all into a pot with a large stopper. It was a messy process but they never took more from the bees than they thought the colony could replenish before Winter came. The priest guided them through all this and finally after mass one Sunday he said, "Well it seems you are now proper Beekeepers." Elzbièta walked home on air that morning feeling so proud of herself and of her father.

In return for all his help Elzbièta supplied the priest with wax for his candle making and used to feel a quiet satisfaction at Mass when she saw the candles he had made burning without spluttering.......

Those visions of happier days gradually faded from her mind and turned into thoughts more melancholy.

There was a local woman whose job it was to lay out corpses ready for burial and Juozas was placed in an ornate open coffin dressed in his best clothes, head and shoulders slightly raised, hair combed, eyes closed, garlanded all around with flowers and ruta. His pose appeared similar to the one in the field but somehow he now looked tidier, smarter, more peaceful.

The day before the funeral, they, the family and all the mourners, including old women who had come from miles away and who attended most funerals, stood sadly in a circle around the coffin outside, paying their respects to the deceased.

Elzbiėta noticed many bees buzzing around, flitting around the body and alighting, settling on the garlands' flower petals.

It seemed that somehow they knew already, but she would go and confirm it to them later on anyway.

In the months which followed, once life returned to its normal routine, Elzbieta just felt a yawning gap inside her. Questions which came into her mind remained unanswered as she realised with an empty feeling that he wasn't there any more. She wouldn't see him again for years to come. But see him she would. She knew that with an unshakeable certainty. But the future stretched away ahead into an indeterminate void which she couldn't fathom. There was so much to this world that she didn't understand yet, so many marvels, the bees had started to teach her that. But try as she might to resist, her grief became deeper. Her mother was a great comfort and sometimes they talked about Juozas and cried together. Time she spent on her own however made her increasingly depressed. Everything she saw, every change in the weather and seasons reminded her of her father. Now and then she would see something or think of something to tell him, only to suddenly remember with a pang that he didn't exist any more. Occasionally, when she was very low she would lapse into complete paroxysms of weeping and her migraine would return and the endless cycle of bed and rest and recuperation would take place. Except that sometimes when she awoke the headache was still there. She lost weight and became thin and red eyed. The tree of Žemyna however was always there, just as dependable, just as comforting when she sat with her back against its trunk. But the solace she could gain from it during the warm months faded with the onset of autumn and winter. How she longed for spring again and communion with the tree and the bees and nature. How she yearned to indulge again and be at one with the natural world which her father Juozas had left her.

After six months of intense grief lasting throughout the winter something happened to the child which precipitated her slow return to normality and gave her a new focus. It was during the following summer while she was visiting her father's grave with some ruta plants for him. She had sown the seeds early in the year in a wooden tray. With her green fingers she had nurtured them through to the point where they could be potted on into small terra-cotta flowerpots and then into bigger ones. As she knelt and worked away at the soil on his grave she knew she was doing something positive as a bar against her own grief. The mourning process was coming to an end. She turned over thoughts in her mind and imagined his kind and understanding weatherbeaten face. His often repeated words somehow seemed to enter her mind, and she could imagine him, and hear him, speaking them. She sensed the timbre of his voice with the pauses and emphasis. "Seek a place where you can do well, a place of freedom. Get away from here, Go! because it is never going to change! There is a promised land somewhere! Just recognise your opportunity when it comes and take it while you can!"

For the first time since the tragedy she felt peace. She would do as he had suggested and then they would both be happy. She knelt by the grave and taking out her rosary she prayed. She felt strongly that he was also there praying with her. She made the sign of the cross and taking a look all around at the cemetery and the church across the road and then down again at the grave, she made her way home under a clear blue sky with a lighter heart.

The eight years which had passed since that day of revelation had now brought her to this crossroads. The ending of one life and the beginning of another. The hierarchy had changed in the homestead.

Two brothers had since made their way to America but had stopped off in London. There had been a mix-up with their tickets but they didn't seem too concerned and more importantly they had work. So her eldest brother was committed to the farm and another brother was now old enough to shoulder much of the burden and between them they had taken their father's place in the running of things. She had worked away towards her ultimate goal – America. It would be a passage built on honey, lots of it, sold to some Jews in Seinei who re-sold it on in town. She was confident enough to drive a bargain with them. They were amazed that a slip of a girl should have bargaining power as good as theirs. This was her moment. There was no turning back now. She took out the letter and re-read it.

6, Winterton Street
Stepney, E
London
1894m. balandžio 3d.

Miela Elzyte

Tikiuosi, kad Tu ir visi tiki jauciatės puikiai.
Perduok linkejimus visiems, o ypač Mamai.
Kumi malonu girdėti, kad gavote mūsų
siųstus pinigus. dabar leuksame mūsų
sekti kino Londone litg minieg. Nes
leuksime jusų iš. Kotrynos prieplaukoje.
Mūsų laivas „Ango" atvyksta 22 dieng,
vakare, sekmadienį. leikokite mūsų Keyside
patrankeje. Jei vėluotume, leuk mūsų ten.
Tikiuosi, kad laivas atplauks laiku, bet
jei ne, tai ne beda, nes mes gyvstojse tokioje
vietoje, iš kurios matosi prieplauka, kuria
plaukia laivai temse. Bus sekmadienis
ir nereikės dirbti, taol turesime daug laiko.
Tau ir Juozui radome kambarį šveiu
namuose, kuriuo olati nuitis, tai atvyluite.

Dievo palaimos Jums. Iki pasimatymo.

Pranas ir Jonas

Looking at it again gave her renewed confidence. She and Juoza would not be on their own. The way had been marked out already by her brothers who had taken their father's advice and blazed a trail two years before. They were doing very well in London. There was an established community from Lietuva there, so none of them was going to be lonely nor isolated once they arrived in Londonas.

Her mother Rozalia came into the room. "Come on Mazute, Juoza is already set. Do you have your luggage ready? The luggage, such as it was, consisted of a large canvas bag and some smaller ones containing her personal items. In one of these was a small rag doll which her father had made for her when she was little.

In the larger bundle made of a heavy patterned material cloth was her goose feather filled bedspread and some clothing. There were bags and a case belonging to Juoza also. In addition her mother had prepared a large quantity of food for the journey which included two large cheeses, a loaf, a bottle of water with a stopper and some salted pork wrapped in a cloth. This food Elzbiėta and Juoza were intending to save for the voyage on board ship. Money she had in her bag and about her person would pay for food along the way to the border and through East Prussia, Germany, as far as Hamburg and beyond. Juoza was kitted out in a similar way. Elzyte's elder sister was carrying most of their money. She was very good with it and it was thought it would be safer to split it unevenly.

"We must hurry, Mr Kershook will be here soon with his cart." Isaac Kershook was a travelling Jewish trader who came and went across the border. The guards there knew him and for a small consideration they would turn a blind eye to any passengers he had who he would refer to as his 'assistants' or sometimes his 'daughters' or 'sons.' The border guards were well aware of the real situation but Russian petty officials at these outposts didn't earn much. They could boost their pay by being shrewd. The system was completely corrupt. Elzbiėta didn't concern herself too much about the details. It was the passengers who paid the bribes indirectly and Mr Kershook took a cut too. In times of purges or crackdowns Isaac had an alternative plan, which was to cross the border where it was un-policed, sometimes at night following the book smuggling route into Prussia. He still took his cut from his passengers. The other way of doing things was to request passes and permits from the Russian authorities in advance, but these were not always easily forthcoming. This could take months of bureaucracy. There could be rigorous checks because there were many young Jewish men fleeing westwards in order to avoid the Russian draft. If they were caught in that particular trap they could say goodbye to the best years of their lives often extending for a quarter of a century. So when they returned to their village after their army service time was up, if indeed they ever did, all connection with their standing in the village had gone. Their kith and kin and relatives had moved on or had died, women their own age had already been spoken for and some of them were even grandmothers now. Their customs and practices would be difficult to find again. Additionally the Russian army tried to carry out the unthinkable to Jews under arms, which was to do its best to Christianise them. This was attempted first by persuasion, a pointless exercise, and then by force, the potential converts being made to run a gauntlet of Russian blows and abuse. This was intolerable persecution that cut to the very heart of Jewishness. It was a terrible fate which Jews were seeking to avoid more and more. The authorities were well aware of this, so all applications were thoroughly scrutinised including those of Poles and Lithuanians but especially Jews, male and female alike. The documents could take six months to come through – if they were approved. Regulations changed wildly from one extreme to the other and then back again. It was akin to living with an unpredictable caged tiger. The other approach was often taken. So the Jews tended to go as families by the illegal roundabout routes. Sometimes motley collections of people went posing as families when they weren't even related. The majority of the Lithuanians who travelled, however, consisted mainly of single people hoping to earn money to send back. Many were intending to do a round emigration and return home when they had enough to pay off any debt. A labourer could earn nearly three times as much in England as in Lithuania; and in America, the wages were nearly fourfold.

Elzbiéta's brothers, the ones still at home, appeared with their mother while they waited for the cart to arrive. Tears were shed by all of them but there was also mock cheerfulness and attempts to play down the enormity of what was happening. Unusually Vincentas seemed the most upset of all of them. He wasn't going anywhere. As the eldest he would inherit the farm and he already had effectively, unofficially taking it over when Father had died. He was partly aloof from this course which many young Lithuanians were adopting, caused by this tie which held him to the farm and obliged him to look after his mother. Other brothers had gone already and now these two sisters were off on an adventure and a new life. He was both sorry and envious at the same time. Even so there was a feeling that this wasn't to be permanent and they would be returning after a time when they had made good.

"We will all meet again when I've made my fortune". said Elzbiéta to her mother.

"Or married into one," Juoza came out with. "When that happens Mamute we will send for you or we can come home rich."

"I wish Tetukas was here he would be so proud of you and excited." Her voice quivered, "Your father would love to see you setting out to achieve the very thing he always wanted to do himself."

"What a day, to see my two lovely girls embarking on a new life." She turned away, as she felt her voice catch in her throat. No one saw her face contorted in an uncontrollable grimace of sorrow. Her mouth twitched as tears welled up in a rush from her sad eyes.

At that moment the sound of horses and the rattle of iron shod wheels was heard outside and a voice shouted. They all turned away and rushed outside. All except Rozalia who went to the bucket mopping her face with a rag doused in cold water and composing herself before she too started for the door bringing one of her daughters' bags with her. She made another trip but this time Elzbièta went with her for the last three bags. She felt the same emptiness as her mother.

"Don't worry Mamyte we'll be alright. Mr Kershook had made this trip many times before. When we arrive we'll be met at the docks in London, and....," here she paused expectantly, then her voice rose excitedly, "I'll be coming back next year to see you, when I have earned enough." This made Rozalia feel slightly better. She wasn't going to be alone. She had her other sons and daughters who at least for the time being, were still with her. She had her friends and the rest of the family, nieces nephews, a married son, two grandchildren and all. Juoza wasn't involved in this conversation. She was more pragmatic, less imaginative, more outgoing.

"Come on Elze", she cried, "We'll be late."

They climbed up onto the seat at the front with Mr Kershook and their bags and baggage thrown in the back of the four wheeled wagon. Isaac urged the horses forward and the cart trundled out of the farm-yard and onto the road. All the time Elze looked backwards while Juoze looked forward excitedly. Rozalia followed the road out as far as the gate, as the cart turned right heading off towards the west.

Elzbièta looking back, continued to watch her mother waving, getting smaller and smaller and more and more blurred. Then the image was sharp again as she blinked and then blurred but smaller. Elze con-

tinued to watch her mother until she was just a tiny speck in the distance and then she was gone from sight.

They passed by the field where once it was ploughed in furrows, when, as a child, she had lost the knitting needle lent to her by her friend. Worried almost to death she had searched and searched to no avail. Going out at night and praying to Saint Anthony she had, after a time, seen the missing needle glinting in the moonlight in one of the furrows. She turned her attention to Mr Kershook. "How has all this been worked out she said?" She looked over her shoulder at the wagon with Juoza sitting on some bundles in the back. There was a frame construction over them of three or four wooden hoops joined together by rope tied and tensioned to the cart, with rolled up canvas attached to be used in bad weather. That canopy wouldn't be needed to keep off rain. The weather they could see was set fair for a few days at least.

"I work for a company, Leizer Gershenovitch and Israel Krisovsky in Vilna who have a deal with the steamship companies in Germany. They employ many people like me to help smooth the way. Being a pedlar I draw very little attention when I travel. When we get to the border I'll give you your train tickets and ship boarding passes. Do you have your passports?" We should be alright at the border. They know me, they welcome me. I've made this trip so many times before."

"How come? Will they let you through?" said Juoza.

"They'll let us through alright. They are getting to be quite well off you know, which reminds me, you have to pay your extra bit now. How much money have you got on you?" A warning bell sounded in Elzbiéta's head as she delved into the deep pocket of her dress. "Not much – enough," she said, which was not a lie because she reasoned that quantity and wealth were all relative. She brought out some of what she had wrapped in a purse, – two roubles and some kopecs. He took them and gave her back some of the smaller denominations and asked Juoze the same question. As sharp as a button she said, "Here's one," and gave him the coin.

Quickly wishing to divert the Jew's attention, Elzbiéta asked him what he was doing out and about on the Sabbath. "Oh I don't hold as much truck with all that as some people. Also the roads will be less crowded and you will find a seat easier on the train. The majority of Jews will not be travelling today, but some will be. The Russian authorities deliberately try to make sure business is conducted on the Shabbot just to be awkward. By the way, that letter from your brothers in London is very important. You may have to show it to someone along the way to prove you have got somewhere to stay when you arrive. Did you manage to get someone to translate it into English for you?"

"Yes, our priest got the Bishop in Seinei to do it for me. I have it here. At least we now have the proof in both languages."

> 6, Winterton Street,
> Stepney. E
> London
>
> 3rd April 1894
>
> Dear Elzyte,
>
> We hope you and everyone are well. Please give our love to everyone especially mama. We are glad and relieved to know you got the money we sent you. Jonas and me are so looking forward to seeing you again next month in London and we will be there at St Katharine's Dock to meet you. If we should be late wait there for us. I hope the ship will be on time. It wont matter if it isnt, we can see the dock from where we are staying. We can see the ships coming up the river. We have a room for you and Juoza to share.
>
> God Bless
>
> Pranas & Jonas.

They trundled on for what seemed like hours during most of which the two girls were lost in their own thoughts. During the first few miles they recognised the countryside they were seeing for the last time and waved at people they knew but these became fewer and farther between until the country became strange and new to them as they passed through villages, skirted lakes and passed across bridges.

"How long is it going to take?" Juoza asked impatiently.

"It's eighty three versts", he replied so that's about nine hours. You had better take it in turns to ride up here as it's more comfortable in the back, you could probably nod off."

"What are we lying on in the back?" "Ooh not much, just a few soft goods and furnishings which I might try and sell in Eydtkuhnen on the other side of the border. I must just mention that if there is a problem getting you across we may have to get you over by an alternative method." he replied tapping the side of his nose with a finger.

The girls were a little worried but slightly thrilled at the idea.

Juoza thought back to the time when she was thirteen and Elzyte was eleven when they had heard something very exciting. Some Cossacks were coming to the town and there would be a dance. It was the most wonderful thing she had heard for a long time and she talked and talked about it to her younger sister who hung on her every word.

"Shall we ask Tetukas if we can go?" "Ooh yes, shall we?" replied her sister excitedly.

"You do it then Elze, he'll listen to you!" She remembered how they had crept up on their father and hidden behind the barn and she had pushed Elzyte forward and out into the open. She had watched as they spoke together and Elzbieta came back.

"What did he say?" said Juoza.

"He said, 'Go and tell your sister behind the barn to come and ask for herself next time, but in any case the answer is No! You're both too young.'"

"What shall we do then Juoza?"

"We'll go and ask Mamyte."

Their mother was sympathetic. She just said something like, "Wait and see." They found this very encouraging. When the evening in question arrived they carefully avoided their father and did each other's hair and put on their best dresses. Father had thought they had gone to bed and was sitting near the oven smoking a pipe and supping a drink from a small glass. He had drunk several of these and had sunk into a doze and they could hear him snoring now and again. They heard a tapping on the window and looking outside they saw their mother who helped them both through the window.

"Off you go, and don't be late back."

It had been one of the most exciting evenings of their young lives and Juoza had fitted straight in, dancing with young men when asked, whilst Elzbiéta just watched timidly from the back of the throng as the Cossacks danced and sang. It was unforgettable for both of them. Towards ten-thirty they had set out to walk back. They had only got a short way when one of the neighbours came past in a cart and they got a lift back to the top of their road. Of course they had then seen, with dread, their father talking to that same neighbour after church the next day. He walked over looking at them with a mock frown. But then he just said, "I think it's going to rain." As they ran off as fast as they could go Juoza thought she heard a chuckle but dared not look back.

Juoza remembered all this with excitement and eagerly anticipated the social life she would enjoy once they got to London.

Chapter 18

Gentile & Jew

Now and again Isaac pulled in to the side of the road or just off it and stopped. They walked about and stretched their legs a bit. Every time they did so, he saw to the horses first, getting nosebags from the back of the cart and a large bucket for the horses' water which, filled from a stream or pond, the animals shared.

It was during one of these stops that Isaac said a very strange thing. "How is it that the basic root of your name is Jewish?"

"What do you mean?" hedged Elzbiėta.

I mean your name is Kadišius. Did you know that the Kaddish is a

Jewish prayer for the dead and you seemed to have been named after it with the little Lithuanian bit added on. How is that?"

"My mother advised me never to speak of it."

"Come on! I'm interested. To tell you the truth there are some Kadish's on my mother's side of the family. Could we perhaps be indirectly related?"

Elzbiėta thought to herself, "I am leaving the country. So why not? Let's give it an airing to a stranger for the one and only time!"

"Legend in the family has it," she began, "That many years ago my granny's granny," she paused, screwing up her eyes, "or somebody, was living on a farm. We think it may have been the same farm we come from, although we are not certain, we have always lived in it."

"I wondered about that," said Isaac.

"Yes, it was rented for a long time and then the family bought the buildings some years ago and added to it."

"Anyway, it appears that this girl, when she was young, formed a friendship with a Jewish boy from the Shtetl. What has come down to us is that he intervened when some Russian youths were torment-ing her on her way to the fields. They were throwing things at her and calling her names. It reached such a pitch every day that she was terrified to go out."

"Kids can be cruel." Isaac replied, "particularly Russian ones. They listen to their parents talking. They hear how they address people, you Lithuanians and us too. They have an attitude against everyone which is typical of so many, if not most Russians." He stopped to al-low her to continue the story.

"So he somehow protected her. He started coming to meet her there every day and walked with her past the boys. They kept on call-ing him 'Jewboy' repeatedly until finally he chased after one of them, caught him by the hair and nearly yanked his head off. As the kid ran off screaming he also got a kick up the backside. When he was a safe distance away he turned around and shouted that his father would be there the next day to sort them both out and give them a jolly good hiding. She went home, told her father and the next day he went with her, plus two of her elder brothers, all carrying cudgels and pitchforks. I don't know the rest of the details, it was all very hazy. There was trouble with the Russians and neither our family nor the Jewish one was very happy about the friendship and tried to stop it. It didn't work of course. The more they tried, the closer the pair became and they continued to see each other. By now our family was earmarked by the Russian police and things were very uncomfortable for our family for ages. Some time later, the two of them, the girl and the Jewish boy ran off together."

"Oi vay!" muttered Isaac incredulously inadvertently staggering backwards and tripping over the bucket. He regained his balance.

"Her father went straight after them. They had been together for three days before he caught up with them. Who knows where they had been in the meantime. They came back with him in the cart and on the way the father got to talk to the Jewish boy and came to know him a bit better, he realised how much they meant to each other."

"You keep saying 'the Jewish boy' did he have a name?"

"Yes of course, similar to yours Mr Kershook."

Isaac Kershook smiled, intrigued. "Oh! – Isaac Kadish then?"

"You nearly got it? More or less – Itzhak Kadish," Elzbieta said. "It gets even better. You can easily work out the rest of it can't you?"

"Yes I think it's reasonably clear. Itzhak must have converted to Catholicism and her family..... your family, took him in. That would have been the way of it, not the other way around. We Jews will, under duress, take a man into our families – if he converts, but not so much a woman, because we believe Jewishness is passed down through the female line, – to us that is everything."

"Eventually it all died down and the connection faded from official memory. Even now we don't talk much of it. We have always been told not to publicize it as it could make things really, really bad for us with the Russians," explained Elzbiéta. "It's now very unlikely that any of our boys would be conscripted, at any rate not on account of any Jewishness but you never know. Although Tétis was called up now I come to think on it, for a time anyway. So it's a legend that has almost died out. I think I am one of the few who has been told, and then only because my father and I were interested in all this sort of thing and talked a lot. Juoza for example, over there, couldn't care less about the family. She just wants to enjoy herself and have a good time and borrow my shoes to go out in."

Juoza, who had been listening to every word and upon hearing her name mentioned shouted, "Come on! Can we just get moving again?" As they climbed back up onto the seat Elzbiéta looked at the man and said, "So now you know our history Mr Kershook. What do you make of it all?"

He looked all round, at the goods and bundles in the back and at his two passengers, making sure nothing had been left behind before easing the pair of horses out onto the road again. He drove on a bit before giving voice to his thoughts.

"Oi yoi yoi! It must have been quite a business! You know, I can well understand his family not wanting to have a mixed marriage. Every mixed marriage is a nail in the coffin of Judaism. We must keep our line pure to survive. We are the chosen people of Yahweh." He uttered the name of God almost under his breath like a sort of sigh.

"Oh! I never thought of it like that. I feel sorry for you all though, being so ... sort of ... isolated in the landscape."

"Yes I suppose if I look at us all from afar, if that's possible, others may find us a strange race. A race and a religion all linked together as one identity. We do want to preserve that and our way of life and our faith. I think other peoples see us as a threat because they don't understand us, and they resent our enterprise. But we are not all wealthy. Look at me for example, scraping a living as a pedlar and traveller and a part time agent for a shipping company in Germany, indirectly. We are absolutely forbidden to do certain occupations. We Jews are hated and despised by the Russians – and nearly everyone else. We have been badly treated throughout history – everywhere."

"Yes, in a way you have my sympathy." responded Elzbieta. "But I'm glad you're doing this for us." Isaac went on, whining a little,

"We don't really have the physical toughness to take up jobs on the land, so we are tending to make our living by other less strenuous means, but believe me, our chosen occupations are often mentally exhausting. As Yahweh is my witness, what I'm doing is both – Oi vay! the worst of both worlds. But I am thinking that this is a subject about the past, a bit of your heritage you would like to hide."

He transferred the reins into one hand as he felt around in his coat pocket, his hand emerging from the depths with some coins.

"Here is one of your roubles back."

"You are kind," said Elzbiėta a trifle ironically, knowing he had been paid already by the agents anyway.

Juoza, who had been listening, finished the conversation suddenly and cruelly with a smirk, as she realised there was going to be no re-fund for her, and said rather abruptly,

"Yes, we Jews must all stick together."

Throughout the day Elzbiėta concentrated on trying to memorise the towns they passed through. Down their farm track to the main Seinei - Sipliške road and turned right. At the point where they reached the main road was where Elzbiėta had looked back barely making out her mother waving before she was lost from sight as they pulled out. Then onwards after a fair time and several versts through the town of Smalenai. Then they turned right on the road to Kalvarija past the woods on the right and marshes on the left. The road passed across newly sown farmland until a turnoff to the left towards Sala-paraugis then on through Lubiava round a bend until they met the Vyštitis - Kalvarija road.

This dragged on all morning as the sun rose higher and higher to their right. The shadow of them and the cart and horses gradually shifted round from the side to the front with a few variations for slight detours from the south-east to north-west route. The sun beat down upon their backs and the shadows shortened. They stopped briefly about every hour to rest the horses and to take a breather. On one of the stops Juoza asked if one of the canopies could be opened out and stretched over the frames to give some shade. Isaac concurred with this as he was feeling hot himself. Between the three of them they managed to throw a canvas over the first two frames and tie it down, which kept the worst of the sun off them but allowed any breeze to flow through at the same time. They took a left turn some way along this road and then a right turn to Bartininkai. Then they turned left in the direction of Užbaliai. Isaac knew that there was now only a right turn and then a left towards Virbalis and they would almost be within spitting distance of their destination, the railway station at Kibartai.

Chapter 19

The Fainzilbers

It was by now mid afternoon. As they commenced leaving Užbaliai, after turning right there onto the Virbalis road, they could see in the distance a wagon with a party of people trudging towards them. As they got closer Elzbiėta noticed with alarm how disconsolate they looked. The woman had obviously been crying and the two children amongst them looked dejected. The two parties drew near and stopped opposite each other. Isaac spoke to them in Yiddish and the elderly man among them responded in the same language in a low voice but in a plaintive wailing way.

"What's happened?" asked Juoze.

"They have been turned away at the border." replied Kershook in

Polish after speaking to their driver. "Their exit papers, are not in order so they won't let them out of Russia. This man is called Moshe Yurkansky but he is not a trader like me. He is just a driver. That is Mr Fainzilber and his wife Sarah and their children Shmuel and Rachel." The sisters nodded as they themselves were introduced by Isaac. But there was scarcely a response from the Jews who were clearly used to holding themselves aloof.

"Oh my good Lord." said Elzbiéta, persisting, "Is there anything we can do?"

"They're on their way back home to Kalvarija."

"What was their final destination?" Juoza enquired. "Whitechapel." Isaac assured them after a further exchange of words.

"Where on earth is that?" she replied, "Is it near London? That's the city we're going to. It's supposed to be a big place, the biggest city in the world."

"Doesn't matter," thought Isaac, seeing a way he might be able to help out and also make a bit for himself. He spoke for a lengthy period with Moshe, the man with the black beard who was clearly the one who had been hired to get the others to Kibartai. The rest of them also joined in animatedly but discreetly. The party consisted of him and a married couple and two teenage children. The boy seemed desperate with his head held disconsolately in his hands as he rocked from one side to the other moaning softly. "I wonder what the matter is with him." Elzbiéta thought staring at his strange demeanour. As if he could read her thoughts the father said, switching to Polish, "He is due for the draft. The orders came through a few days ago. We did apply for the emigration papers last year and got them only three weeks since. The rest of the family urged us to leave, right away, before the draft started to be put into effect. It was either that or we wouldn't see him again for years.

"Did you offer them money at the emigration office?" Juoza asked in the same language.

They discovered from the replies they got that the family had hint-ed at the border office that there might be some money for the officials. Once they realised how much it would be though, they either would not, or could not, pay the amount that was demanded. Their biggest problem was that the official clerk had deduced that the boy was about the right age for the draft and guessed why they were so desperate to get away. He assumed they would be concerned enough to bribe him handsomely, knowing he had the bargaining advantage.

They moaned that they had made him a lesser offer which he refused. He was certain they would be back once they had reconsidered and maybe sold something to raise the money. The wife wanted to try to raise the money, the husband did not.

The family were retracing their steps while they thought it over, together with their driver, and wondering what to do now. Thus they found themselves in this impasse.

Isaac explained to the sisters that he had a plan but that it might put their own timetable out a bit. Juoza started to get a bit animated. "Look! We have paid you good money to take us to the frontier. It is not our problem that these people have messed up their own arrangements so badly is it?"

Elzbièta cut in, "Hang on a minute Juoza, Let's show them the meaning of Christian charity and at least listen to what Mr Kershook has in mind." There was a pause and Juoza seemed to calm down.

"What's the plan then Isaac?"

"If we can get them across the Liepona river into Prussia they can then bypass the frontier control post and the Russian emigration officials. If they can approach the train from within Ostpreussen at Eydtkuhnen, which is just the other side of the border, they will find that the Prussian officials are far less demanding. They may however have to lie a little bit about where they are coming from, I'm afraid that can't be helped."

"But why would the Germans be more accommodating?"

"Because Germany has its own interests at heart. It wants to encourage trade, which includes looking after its own shipping lines.

The passenger trade is massive. They want to make it easy for emigrants, not more difficult. After all they are mostly passing through Germany. It's all to do with the economy of their country." Also the differences between the German authorities and the Russian ones are huge. No wonder there is a kind of mass movement out of Lietuva and the rest of Russia. The exodus is becoming almost biblical.

The sisters grasped the logic of Isaac's explanation. He was a shrewd man Elzbiėta was beginning to realise.

"So what do we do now?" asked Moshe.

"I know a spot where we might get you across the Liepona. It's quite narrow at some points and it forms the border between Russia and Germany. The crossing place is a bit off the beaten track. Normally a good fit man could jump across it if he took a long run up but I believe I know a place where cattle go down to drink."he continued somewhat cagily. "The bank there is worn down flat. Where the cows have tried to scramble out sometimes on the other side, that is also worn, but has been fenced by the Prussians. I am wondering if I could get your cart across for you. It's not very deep. In fact at that point it looks like a pond but its a gradual slope down and then up again. If we all help we could do it maybe, but from then on you would be on your own as I have to get back on the legal route with these two young ladies. The other alternative is to go further south. The road goes over the river but then the river veers away from the border and we should be able to just cross into Prussia with no obstacles.

By this time the hopeless consternation of the Jews had died away to be replaced by a more hopeful outlook and they even started to converse haltingly with the sisters in a mixture of Polish with a smattering of Lithuanian which they didn't speak at all well.

At this point Juoze, forever one to think on her feet, made the suggestion, "Why not do that on the way back after you have dropped off my sister and I, we're nearly there anyway? One horse and six people ought to be enough to push the cart across, you won't need us too?"

"Mmm" mused Isaac out loud. "I'd rather do it now and get it out of the way. This family has lost enough time already it seems to me."

He could see the wisdom of the old adage 'a bird in the hand is worth two in the bush'. While he had the family there he had the possibility of making more money for himself. Those people were a bit of a windfall which he wouldn't willingly let go of.

"Oh no!" expostulated Juoza. "You're not doing that! You will do it my way or not at all." She began to take on the appearance of a boiling kettle beginning to splutter. There was clearly an explosion pending. At the age of twenty one she was beginning to appreciate her own qualities as a woman and would brook no nonsense from this man whom she was paying to do their bidding. She also had a loud voice and had already raised it by an octave or two above the level of what was seemly. Isaac sensed she was about to have a full blown rush of blood to the head. Being a mere man, and terribly weak when it came to confronting women about to explode, if not to undergo a bout of pure hysteria, Isaac collapsed and conceded. The imagined sight of steam coming from her ears was enough to convince him.

"Yes! agreed, agreed, agreed!" he muttered. And with more authority, "Moshe! you and your clients pull off the highway and have a rest. Then carry on along the road towards Pajevonys. In fact it will be better this way. Go straight through Pajevonys and continue as far as the crossroads. You can go no further without turning left or right. To the right is Kaupiškiai. To the left would take you to Girėnai. Pull off the road at the junction and wait for me there. I will see you in about three hours from now. It will be dark by then but there is a moon tonight and we will be able to get across pretty much unseen under cover of darkness. Once I get you to Eydtkuhnen you can pay me what you offered the emigration official and you will be home and dry. Well! not exactly but you will be on your way."

After a quick consultation with his charges Moshe turned back to Isaac and in Yiddish, accepted the offer. The girls could tell by the happier demeanour of all concerned that they had succeeded and their route out of Russia would not be impeded, at least not at this stage.

They said farewell to the family and wished them luck and their cart resumed it's journey towards Kibartai.

"Will three hours be enough"? asked Elzbiéta.

"Oh yes," laughed Isaac. "I won't come back from Kibartai this way. After I have dropped you off I'll take the more direct route from there to meet up with them via Matlaukis. That particular road runs south, almost parallel with the Liepona and the Prussian border.

"I am amazed, how do you know all these roads?" asked Juoza.

Isaac replied, "It's my job, and I have a good sense of direction. And also I have this map printed in Germany."

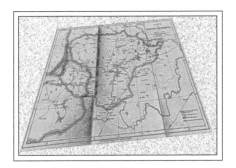

Chapter 20

Kibartai

They were quite tired by now, all of them, and it was way past noon so they pulled up at the side of the road for something to sustain them on the rest of the trip. The horses were attended to first one at a time with water from a nearby stream in the wooden bucket.

"Would you like some cheese Mr Kershook?" Juoza asked with a mischievous smirk. "You did say earlier that you weren't strict."

Isaac looked at her through his shrewd narrowed eyes. He could tell racialism a mile off, and he was suspicious, he had spent his entire existence smelling it out.

"No thank you, I do have something with me," he retorted somewhat sharply.

"Juoza, don't be stupid," Elzbiėta whispered very quietly, "You know they can't eat anything but Kosher food. He might be working on a Saturday but they do draw the line at some things."

"Sorry," Juoza mumbled.

The sun had moved around quite a bit as they continued on their way. It became late afternoon and the girls had no idea where they were, nor how far they still had to go to get to the train. They had never even seen one, only in books. This was all new ground for them. It was already an experience beyond anything they had ever known and they were doing it alone. In fact they were totally in the hands of the Jew. The discomfort of the cart was alleviated somewhat by the changes of scenery which the girls looked at with amazement spotting farming that was being done in a slightly different way to what they had known. They saw a contraption in a field with wheels and a huge metal cylinder which had a cylindrical chimney coming out of it.

"You see that machine over there with the wheels?" Isaac said, "The steam train you'll be going on is many times bigger than that".

They were all agog.

"How many carriages will it be pulling?"

"Scores" he replied, " But I warn you it will be packed. Once you climb on, get yourselves two seats together somewhere and don't leave them until you get to Berlin. Do the same on the train to Hamburg. Always make sure that one of you is there to keep an eye on your baggage and to save the other's seat for her."

"What about the paperwork and tickets onward from London to America?"

"I'll give them to you when we get there".

"Where?" asked Juoza. "Kibartai" he answered.

"Where is it exactly?" Elze asked him. "On the Prussian border. It wasn't always a town until the railway was built and then it became more important than the nearest other town. Most people going west leave from there or go through it. The Tsar keeps a train there they say, hidden away somewhere. He uses it on trips to Prussia and England to see his Royal relations. I doubt if you will see the train though – or him. Just as well really, the place would be swarming with soldiers."

"What about you"? asked Juoze, "Don't you ever fancy leaving and going across the border to see what it's like"?

"I know what it's like, I do it all the time. I trade goods on the other side and bring imports back and sell them over here, or the other way round, depending on prices and availability and exchange rate. People will pay good money to get things that are scarce on their side. That's how the border guards know me so well, they look forward to seeing me – always on the make."

"It is a good thing that they do know you then."

"Yes, it's what sometimes gets my passengers past them and across with no trouble because they tolerate me, as I do them favours."

"What favours?" "Well they like Schnapps and certain fruits, and many other things they can't get, and I can get them."

"So it's dishonesty which gets people like us across is it?"

"Something like that," responded Isaac. "They are rough with people when there's nothing in it for them but they don't earn much so can easily be persuaded to make things, 'go a lot smoother,' especially if they trust you. That's the way of the world, which you will learn before too long. Not far now," Isaac said, as if to close the matter.

By the time this conversation had died away they began to notice other carts on the road. Many were carrying goods but they saw that others also carried people. As the farming land gave way to houses more densely placed they could also see a few travel weary individuals, mostly young men, carrying bundles and trudging in the same direction as them. Some called out for a ride but Kershook ignored them.

They headed into the town of Virbalis and noted the town had obviously seen better days. As if reading their thoughts Isaac informed them that the town of Kibartai, where the station was to be found, was only half an hour away. He explained how the town had taken over from Virbalis when the railway had come to the border with Prussia, and as a result Kibartai had grown up at the border and station and become a very prosperous place with people coming and going, a customs house, ticket offices, lodging houses and a huge bustle going on. It rather reminded Elzyte of a beehive. By the time they threaded their way through the throng on the road and entered Kibartai, Elzbiéta was thoroughly bemused by the crowds and the noise. Great houses lined the streets, some were of stone and some of red brick and stucco. They could see, as they passed the side streets, that there were plenty of more ordinary looking dwellings made of timber in the traditional style with people walking up and down there too. The main street, when they came to it, was lined with large mature trees which gave some degree of shade from the hot sun. The buildings got bigger. One was an imposing wooden synagogue but there was also a small church in the Lithuanian Baroque style, and another further on with the distinctive onion domes of the Russian Orthodox.

There was a clamour of human voices. Groups of Jews were walking up and down, others standing in circles arguing and gesticulating dressed in long black coats and tall black hats. People on bicycles passed along, with every so often a motor car chugging by. Along the dusty edges of the road around the station, carts, horses unharnessed, were doubling up as makeshift stalls as people plied their wares. But there was no Jewish trade going on. She could hear what she thought was German being spoken in the babble of human syllables which assailed her ears. Amongst it too she could pick out Yiddish, Russian, Polish, as well as her own language. It was as if chaos existed here in Kibartai. People stared at them momentarily from time to time looking them up and down curiously. She had never been anywhere

so busy. Even Seinei was not in the reckoning when it came to confusion. Jews stood in circles in their typical all black attire wearing the perennial black Homburg hats, most of the men with long beards, debating it seemed, with lots of raised voices. But they did not seem angry. Others were sitting passing the time of day drinking water. The incessant sound of a myriad of voices in vari-

ous languages, Yiddish, Polish, German, Russian and Lithuanian was overwhelming. It was the Tower of Babel all over again.

"I'll take you as far as the passport control and wait outside until the train is safely on its way with you both on it." It was reassuring to hear their guide say this.

Isaac drove his cart up outside the station, a huge, grand imposing building of two floors with an impressive approach to it. People eyed them while they continued their conversations seamlessly as Isaac took down their bundles and bags and carried them as far as the entrance. Elzbiėta herself felt extreme trepidation. She was more or less on her own for the first time in her life. Yes! she had Juoza it was true, and she supposed there would be a degree of mutual support through whatever lay ahead of them from now on. Isaac gave Juoza a package containing their tickets for the train and for the boat when they reached Hamburg. Their passport papers she already had. They were solely passports out of Russia. She knew that they wouldn't be required after that. They wouldn't be needed to gain access to either Germany or England. There were trains five times a day and they had allowed enough time to catch the last one.

They found themselves at the end of a queue of about twenty people. There were two or three different officers dealing with the travellers. Some passengers were allowed to go through without a hitch but others were directed towards a door which led to another part of the building. They waited for about twenty minutes until it was their turn to have their papers and tickets scrutinised. They were dealt with by a gimlet eyed man of around fifty with a florid complexion and a permanent frown. He looked at them over the top of a pair of brass rimmed spectacles as he held out his hand without a word. Juoza and Elzbiėta looked at each other bemused until he rasped in Russian "Papers." Juoze proffered the package and the clerk riffled through the contents until he came to the passports which he studied meticulously. He handed them back. "Go through there!" he snapped, pointing to the door on his left.

"Juoza, what have we done? where does this lead to?"

Juoza said nothing but grabbed some of the baggage from the floor and headed in the direction indicated.

"Next!" shouted the clerk.

With sinking hearts they passed through the door and found themselves in a large hall with more doors at one end which seemed to lead to offices, and a line of hard wooden benches outside with people already seated in a line. They took their places on a vacant part of the bench at one end of what was obviously a seated queue.

The people sitting there consisted of a few families plus what appeared to be single people travelling.

Every so often a uniformed guard came out and called the next batch in. A whole family consisting of two adults and four children went into one office together. Into another went four young people and the doors closed. Elzbiėta and Juoze moved along the bench as their turn drew nearer. They watched as one of the doors opened and the family came out. They comprised a Jewish man in long black coat his wife wearing a check shawl and a voluminous dress. Guards were called and two uniformed militiamen came and escorted the family away as the wife sobbed, dabbing at her eyes with a handkerchief and the man wringing his hands and the four children looked glum. Elzbiėta noticed that there seemed to be an extra tiny child toddling out. She could have sworn there were only four children going in but there were definitely five coming out. They looked pathetic as they were hustled out under armed guard. They had no time to ponder on this before a loud voice shouted, "Kadišius!"

They followed the shout into the office with their bundles and baggage. They were not asked to sit down, as yet another Russian said to them brusquely, "Your passports are not in order. It will require thirty roubles to put them right. There are conditions you haven't complied with." "What conditions are they?" said Juoza, her voice shaking.

"It's too complicated to go into. Can you read Russian? You haven't got the right signatures. Yours hasn't been signed by the governor, only by his deputy."

"Yes but that's what we were told to get," said Juoze in very bad Russian. Her voice, which was shrill now, was quivering and rising.

"Since this was issued the regulations have been changed," the official countered.

"Keep calm Juoza I'll deal with this," said Elzbiéta sounding more confident than she actually felt. "So what can we do?"

"It's obviously a genuine oversight unlike the Shimberg family just now. They actually had the audacity to try to smuggle a child through under her mother's skirts. They're now for the high jump. They will be prosecuted for attempted fraud." He said in a bullying tone.

Elzbiéta felt a void in the pit of her stomach as she thought about what that would mean for the family. But her first concern was for their own plight.

"You can wait until Monday morning, find a place to stay while this is sorted out when the office opens again. The passport will have to be re-issued and it will cost you at least thirty roubles plus a legal fee. – Each!"

"Is there no alternative?"

I could perhaps pull a few strings and get it done by tomorrow morning but it will cost you the same, but then I would need a fee as I would be doing it in my own time."

"Can we have a moment to talk about it?"

"Juoza I don't think we can do it," Elzbiéta said very quietly and rapidly in Lithuanian. "We just don't have enough money. The money we have has been hard earned by Pranas and Jonas – and our bees.

What little there is we can't afford to waste."

"There could be another way." Turning back to the official she said in her halting Russian, "We will have to go outside and think about it. I believe we may even have to go home again."

The official shrugged.

"Next," and looking down at his paperwork, "The Sackevičius family," he shouted looking past them towards the door. The four youthful Lithuanians went in as the Kadišius sisters were going out, and closed the door. There were two girls and two young men. They looked nothing like each other.

Juoza and Elzbiéta exited the station building and wandered down the steps looking this way and that for Isaac who had said he would wait for them and see them safely on their way.

"There's his cart," cried Elzbiéta. "But where is he."

Seeing their consternation a Jewish woman passing the evening with her friends interrupted and asked if they were looking for the man who owned the cart. They went on to say that he had told them some time ago he was going to the synagogue for evening prayers and shouldn't be long. "Where is it?" enquired Elzbiéta. "Just down there to the right but why don't you wait here with us until he returns?"

They sat with the women and before long had told them all that had happened to them.

"One of them muttered with a knowing smile, "Oy! It's like this all the time. The poor families who get persecuted here, we see them time after time. Some have to go home, but some are sent away for further interrogation. Some get through but the Russians are on the make the whole time." As she said this she rubbed her first two fingers together as if sprinkling something. "Did they ask you for money?" Elzbiéta nodded. "Ah I thought so. What excuse did they make up this time? something to do with passport irregularity." She nodded knowingly. "Why didn't you just pay them?"

"We don't have it," replied Elzbiéta.

"Well there's no arguing with that," the woman replied.

"It's the likes of us who are harassed the most. You can almost predict the number of Jews who get turned over compared to the rest. The gentiles get off lighter even when they have broken the law but the Jews? Never!"

As if to prove her point the four youthful Lithuanians could be seen wandering down the station steps with their baggage looking bewildered and lost. Juoze could almost read her sister's mind.

"No Elzyte! Let them sort themselves out, we have our own problems to contend with." They wandered away from their new friends past the station buildings complex in the direction of the synagogue indicated by the Jews.

Just then they saw Isaac walking back along the street as the train was pulling out of the station. It trundled away with a hiss of steam very slowly at first and with a shunting and screeching and slowly increasing puffing exhalations. They were transfixed by this monster the likes of which they had never seen before. In the growing twilight they could see sparks flying up into the air from the top of the engine and all was obscured momentarily in clouds of steam and smoke. The endless stream of carriages gathered pace but still seemed to go on and on for ever, as the small white faces at the windows looked out becoming a sort of blur. Finally it was disappearing into the distance and then it was gone and relative peace descended on the street. They both knew they should have been on it. Elzbiéta had never been as lonely and disappointed as this in her whole life. She felt an emptiness inside. Isaac approached looking concerned. "What happened, why are you not on the train?"

"Passports," responded Juoza desolately.

"There is an alternative she added decisively. "You will get us across the border with the other lot. You're going there now aren't you? We'll come along and join them."

There was no arguing with Juoza and it was a sensible and logical next move. They all walked back to the cart and Isaac loaded their baggage into the back again. They climbed aboard as Isaac took the nosebags away from the horses and placed them and the empty water bucket on the hooks at the back of the cart. They trundled away south onto the Kybeikiai road which ran parallel to the border between Lithuania and East Prussia.

The two country girls , never having done anything underhanded or illegal in their lives before were full of trepidation once they had had time to reflect on it. Isaac noted their quietness and rushed to reassure them that it was a necessary and inevitable thing to do, especially as the Russians had cheated them in the first place.

"We are heading south to meet the others at Girėnai. This will take us across the Liepona where it swings eastwards back into Lithuania. There will be a bridge and we won't have to ford the river to continue south to meet them. We then just turn right and head across to the border which is not guarded for its whole length. There are occasional patrols though.

It was beginning to get dark, but as promised the moon was rising to light their way.

"There are five trains every day usually, I'm not sure about Sunday but if we can get you to Eydtkuhnen by about seven tomorrow morning you should be alright. There are a couple of days grace before the Kirsten Line ship you are booked on sails from Hamburg. I allowed plenty of time for eventualities such as these. When we get a bit further we will stop for the night and make our bid for the border tomorrow before first light.

The passed through Kybeikiai and were heading south for Matlaukys when they spotted a familiar sight coming towards them. It was the Jewish family, the Fainzilbers and their driver.

"Well met Moshe." Isaac shouted in Yiddish. "Sorry I'm late what with prayers and so on. What great foresight you had coming to meet me. But as you see I still have my charges. They had similar problems to yours, so now they are all in the same boat. Then in Polish, "Well then, let's all of us pull off the road here out of sight and make some kind of camp until the morning." They swung the horses round heading off the road, Moshe and the family going first, followed in his tracks by Isaac and the sisters across some flat sandy uncultivated ground until they came to a woodland thicket through which they drove their carts and stopped in an open space surrounded by trees and undergrowth where they were safe from prying eyes.

"This means that we will now have to get across the Liepona which is the border along this stretch," Isaac told them all. "It will be the shortest route. But I know the crossing point."

Moshe and Isaac went about unharnessing the horses while Moshe was muttering, again in Yiddish about Yahweh forgiving him for working on the Sabbath. "Don't worry," Isaac said, "You can make atonement when your good deeds are done. I am sure the great and good Yahweh will forgive you." Once again he spoke of God with extreme respect, almost like a soft exhalation of breath. The sisters understood very little of this except the words 'work' and 'Sabbath'. But they were quick to cotton on.

"We'll do the women's work. At least that will be something," Elzbiéta offered. Yitzhak Fainzilber's wife Sarah showed very little reaction apart from an almost imperceptible nod. They gathered dry wood and soon had a fire going and made hot drinks with water from Isaac's water jar heated in a steel kettle. The Jews also had their own food which they and Isaac shared. Elyte and Juoze discreetly didn't offer any of their cheese and rye bread and especially not their pork this time. Then Isaac suggested they all wrap up and settle down where they felt most comfortable and he would wake them on the following morning at dawn.

The next day as it became light he had them all roused and going about their final preparations for the illegal border crossing. They gathered themselves together then made their way west towards the river, skirting woods and using sandy roads where they could as the river gradually came into view.

"Now where was, – is, the best place to cross, I must just get my bearings." Isaac thought for a while and then decided on a right turn and they travelled along the east bank of the river making slow progress. Up ahead they could just make out some vegetation and a few alders and willows around the river.

"The Lord be praised, I got it right!" exclaimed their guide. They could see that the river's banks were too steep to negotiate and the river just too wide to safely jump across so they were relying on this crossing point. They finally entered the wood, following a cattle track and eventually it curved down towards the river.

Suddenly they heard voices and shouts in the distance and Isaac gave the signal for them to stop, holding his finger up to his lips at the same time. They all froze as the voices got louder but whoever it was, they were so intent on their conversation that they paid no heed to anything else and the voices gradually diminished and finally died away completely. The owners of the voices must have been on foot without horses as the travellers' animals harnessed to the carts did not whinny to others of their kind. Leaving it another five minutes Isaac told them all to wait while he went ahead. He was gone for a good fifteen minutes before he returned.

"All clear, move forward slowly following the path and we should be able to get the wagons across."

As they emerged from the shelter of the woods they could see the area on both sides which had been trampled and flattened over the years by cattle. Although the river looked wider here, it was shallow on both sides. It was only in the middle that the river bed dropped more than a metre below the surface. It was the ideal crossing place. The footing was firm, there hadn't been much rain and they could see the river bed was stony gravel. The first cart, which was theirs, went across without much trouble being pulled by the two horses. The girls remained dry on top. The second one was more problematical with only one horse, but the men and the Fainzilber boy taking off their shoes or boots and most of their lower garments added their weight against the wheels and that too made it to the opposite bank and up the other side. Isaac had already uprooted the fence on the opposite bank and drawn it to one side, the poles still attached to their wires. After they had all passed safely through, albeit some of them soaked, he replaced the posts and hammered them in again with a mallet he kept in his cart. They quickly dried themselves off and then taking a shovel from the same place Isaac discreetly disguised with loose mud the marks which the wheels had made at the water's edge. They then continued in a north-westerly direction toward Eydtkuhnen until they encountered the main road.

"We're in Prussia! Phew, we made it!" said Juoza.

"Not quite," said Isaac in reply. "We must now get our story right and make sure we are all agreed. Your passports will not be necessary any more, the Germans won't be interested. All you need are your rail passes and your embarkation tickets. If or when you are asked you must all pretend to be neighbours from a town in Prussia." It was a bit weak as the girls spoke no German. "Let me give you the address. I know people here, we will use their address. So make sure you get it absolutely right in your minds – all of you."

"What about you and Moshe, how are you going to get back?" a worried Elzyte asked.

"No problem. We will just drive straight over the frontier at Kibartai back into Lithuania. I am doing it all the time in pursuit of my trade selling goods across the border. Moshe can pretend to be my assistant. The guards will have no idea that we didn't go through yesterday. They are on a rotation and for all they know we passed across the border at Kibartai yesterday. They don't check passports for people like us. In any case we can always grease their palms with silver, which brings me to a good point. I will have to charge you for the extra time and trouble and the risk I have taken so let's settle up now. It will be ten roubles for the two of you."

Chapter 21

Eydtkuhnen – The Train

The weather remained fine as they continued to make their way towards where Isaac said the road to Eydtkuhnen lay. Following the edges of fields. and sometimes rudimentary paths, the wagons occasionally became stuck and had to be heaved out with the efforts of everyone working together. When they finally reached the road Isaac had told them of, another two hours had passed.

"In a few versts we pass under the main railway line and then we will be turning right for Eydtkuhnen where you will board the train. I think you are going to be lucky – no big health checks as there has been in the past when there were outbreaks of cholera and they were being careful to examine everyone before they were even allowed onto the train for Berlin."

"What shall we say when we get on the train? Will they ask us where we are from?"

"I don't think they will. Let me have another look at your papers. I hope they will just ask to see your train tickets. You have valid tickets from Kibartai-Eydtkuhnen which is pretty much the same place except that the river and the border passes between them but you are already through the border and into Prussia. You will get on the train there along with the hundreds of other people. You'll find the officials just want to get rid of you and speed you on your way. You will see that it is totally different to Russia. Just remember that you can change your money at the station into Prussian Thalers. And a few coins placed in the right hand goes a long way!"

Isaac reached into his pocket and sorted through his own paperwork and gave them back their railway tickets and the tickets for the voyage, which Juoza put away inside the lining of her coat. She looked at them first but couldn't understand the writing.

They joined a stream of other traffic on the main road into the town and found themselves in the company of all sorts of different people. There were German traders heading to the border post with cartloads of merchandise and others from Lithuania coming in the opposite direction. They could hear their own language being spoken as the carts passed each other. They could also make out other small groups and individuals on foot heading for the station. Once again they could hear many languages being spoken, including now German, which they couldn't follow at all.

Juoza and Elzbièta were bewildered and awestruck. It was something that was completely outside their life experience so far. They and the Fainzilber family and the two carts just seemed to blend in with the general traffic effortlessly. The carts pulled up outside the station and they all got down. Their baggage was lifted out for the second time and they said their goodbyes to Isaac and thanked him and he wished them good luck and once again assured them he would wait until the train had gone. They were now on their own.

The Fainzilbers separated from them and clearly wanted to go their own way. The two girls joined a long queue, carrying their baggage and shunted it along as the number of people in front diminished and they drew nearer to the head. The closer they got to the beginning of the queue the more Elzbiêta's heart was pounding, but she need not have worried. The inspector, a young man of about twenty-five years of age, gave a cursory glance at their tickets but spent more time looking them up and down. He blushed slightly and asked them in German where their final destination was. Not understanding they hesitated until someone behind chipped in and translated into Lithuanian for them. Juoza then replied, "Londonas." confidently and with an endearing and encouraging smile. She then asked the people behind when the next train was and learned that it would be arriving in about fifteen minutes and would be departing half-an-hour after that

The young man waved them through with a shy smile and looked as if he wanted to ask them something else but never seemed to get around to it. In a few moments they were through and he was having to deal with the next passengers in line.

The sisters walked through the station buildings amidst a stream of other people, men, women, youths, children, young and old alike, seemingly desperate to get away. They were all following the signs which said 'Berlin' in Gothic script and indicated by arrows pointing towards a platform teeming with people. Many of those were carrying large amounts of baggage, bundles and suitcases. Some had folk with them who appeared to be relatives seeing them off and many were the tears being shed as families took their leave of each other. Some would probably never meet again but others would no doubt follow along at a later date. Elzbiêta wondered how much money had changed hands to facilitate all these people somehow arriving on the other side of the border and embarking from within Germany.

They sat down on their bundles and a little later Juoza got up and went to change their money and buy some tea and bread while

Elzbièta surveyed the different types of people waiting here and listened in awe to the multiple languages being spoken, some of which she was able understand and others which she couldn't.

A huge proportion of the passengers appeared to be Jewish and she realised that they must be pretty desperate to undergo all this with their children and in some cases their parents and grandparents – elderly infirm people past their prime who were bravely travelling this tortuous road in their quest for something better. Their situation must indeed have been terrible. She pondered on her own reasons for making this journey. She was going mainly to keep faith with her father's wish that there was a way out of their downtrodden, and at the very least, patronised existence. She could show them by doing this that they didn't own her and at the same time open up a new horizon of opportunity and maybe also earn the means of one day returning and helping her mother have a better old age.

Juoze returned with two glasses of tea and some black bread and cheese. They just had time to finish their meal when they heard the distant sound of the train. There was an expectant hubbub from the crowd on the platform. The general level of human noise rose as people sought to be heard above the enormous noise of the train. The sisters had never been close to a train before and were almost overwhelmed by the bulk and power of this mass of steel. Trailing along behind it screeching and clanging were scores of carriages already containing a mass of humanity. The train stopped in a hiss of steam and a handful of people got off and pushed their way through the throng as they made their way to the exit. Elzbièta and Juoze were swept along helplessly with the crowd in the direction of the platform's edge until they found themselves near a carriage door and they pushed their way, or rather, were pushed from behind, through it and into the train with the rest of them. The supervising guard was ignoring the cries from within that there was no more room. He just smiled knowingly and pushed ever more people into the carriage. The two girls preceded by their bundles squeezed into a corner of the open carriage and tried to edge nearer to a window. The four benches running the length of the carriage were already occupied by twice as many human-beings as they were designed to take. The heavy atmosphere inside was thick with the smell of unwashed bodies. Elzbièta was glad they had managed to position themselves in a slight draught between two open windows. The people they were closest to were regarding them with mild approbation for invading their personal space and muttered to each other very quickly in Russian which neither girl could quite make out. There was no mistaking their objection to losing a part of what they thought of as their carriage. The selfishness of people who wanted to hang on to what they considered they now owned struck Elzbièta as being ironic. She supposed it had something to do with territorial space and fear of strangers. Once this nearby group had stopped glaring at them and rearranged themselves and their possessions and turned away, Elzbièta allowed herself to discreetly examine them. They consisted of three children, two small girls and an older boy, a young couple, obviously their parents and an older woman whom she deduced to be the mother of one of them. They were reasonably dressed in what looked like their best clothes. They were definitely townspeople and not from the country. But they were in a third class compartment. At least it wasn't fourth. The engine's whistle blew a few short loud blasts and the train juddered into motion. Very slowly, almost painfully at first the great leviathan gradually increased its speed. Elzbièta could feel the enormous weight of the carriages that the engine was attempting to set in motion as some people near the windows on the platform side, the last people to squeeze on, waved at their relatives and friends still on the platform. Elzbièta had no hope of doing the same, not that there was anyone to wave her handkerchief at but Isaac Kershook, wherever he may have been. There was no window at the spot where the girls positioned themselves but if they stood up and peered across the carriage through the heads and luggage somewhat obscuring a good view, they could just make out the station buildings disappearing and the countryside passing by as the carriage settled into a regular, monotonous rhythm.

Elzbiéta gazed again at the family and one of the little girls stared cheekily back and gave a little smile holding out a small dolly for Elzbiéta's inspection. She remarked to the child in Russian in a very simple voice how beautiful the dolly was and stroked its hair. The child looked fiercely protective and snatched it away.

"Her granny made it," said her mother, smiling indulgently at the child. Thus was struck up a conversation in which the woman confided to the two girls that they were going as far as Berlin to start with and might continue on further after a time.

"Where have you come from, and why are you leaving?" asked Juoza curiously, desperate to create a rapport.

"We have come from St Petersburg where our family has lived for years but we just can't stay there any more. We are Pashkovites – Baptists! and the State is making it increasingly difficult – almost illegal, to practise our faith. I wouldn't mind, it's not that different to the Orthodox faith, but it is our faith and why should we change it? That would be a personal denial of what we believe in."

Her husband nodded and added, "Under Tsar Alexander – the second one – things were not so bad, We were quite hopeful, but under his son things got steadily worse and worse. The Russian government seems to think that somehow we are undermining the official religion and therefor must be a threat to the Empire. They call us 'religious dissidents' and with the increase in police powers have taken many legal measures against us. As a religious group we have become more and more demoralised."

"It seems even Russians suffer under their own masters' yoke. It's not just us then, the whole Empire is rotten for all of us." Elzbiéta remarked sympathetically.

"I hope you find the freedom you are looking for."

"Thank you," said the woman. "My name is Olga, this little one is Tatiana, our other girl is Vera and our son Vladimir. This is my husband Pyotr and that is his mother Elizaveta."

"Oh that's the same name as mine. I am Elzbiėta and this is my sister Juoza" The older woman and the husband nodded in a reserved but friendly way.

With introductions all round completed, and the beginnings of friendship established, they settled down and Elzbiėta felt suddenly very tired and rapidly dropped off to sleep encouraged by the soporific sound of wheels clanking over the regular joints in the rails.

She was rudely awakened a few hours later by the cry of 'Koenigsberg', 'Koenigsburg.' being shouted up and down the platform of a station where the train had stopped. It was dark outside but the platform was illuminated periodically by the glow of gas lamps which the sisters had never seen before. Their new acquaintance Pyotr looked at his watch and declared it was four in the morning. "I would advise you and Juoze to get off and stretch your legs," he said, "We'll look after your stuff and then perhaps you would be good enough to do the same for us."

So Juoze and Elzbiėta made their way to the carriage door and stepped out and down onto the platform along with others. They found the ladies washroom inside the station buildings, joined the queue and eventually availed themselves of its facilities performing a few basic essentials including washing their faces, cleaning their teeth and redoing their hair.

Thus refreshed, they returned to the carriage while their three new friends, leaving their still sleeping children in the charge of the sisters, did the same. When the train eventually continued on its way this procedure became the pattern of their journey. There was more space in the carriage now that some of the passengers had alighted at their destination. Things became even more comfortable for them after Elbing and Simonsdorf when more passengers got off.

It was the most exciting thing the girls had done in their lives, particularly when they crossed the river Weichsel on a bridge which must have been a mile and a half long. They passed through strange places named **Dirschau, Staargart, Schneidemuehl,** names they could hardly read let alone pronounce, until they reached Kreuz late in the day when it had got dark again for the second time. Once again they got off to stretch their legs but this time were able to buy a loaf of rye bread and some sausage with their German money from a seller on the platform. They refilled their water bottles for the continuation of the journey. At dawn they crossed the Oder river at Kustrien and reached Berlin at around nine-thirty in the morning.

Once again they had to say goodbye to their new acquaintances who had an address they were to go to. Off those people went to hire a horse and carriage outside the station to take them to it.

Because the train contained so many emigrants a guard walked up and down informing them that they were to take another train which would be departing later, at an hour after noon. They were told that those who had tickets for Hamburg were to leave their luggage, labelled in the baggage room and were also informed which platform their train would be departing from. After leaving their valises and larger bundles in the baggage room, in the care of two baggage handlers they took their receipts, and seeing that the system was quite secure, decided to look around Berlin for the duration of the morning. Once again they were overawed by this metropolis. They had never seen anything like it. They felt rather like pygmies amidst this bustling sophisticated place. Smart carriages being pulled by horses with glossy gleaming coats and bigger than anything they had seen back home in Lithuania. Impeccably dressed soldiers in uniform were walking. The wonderful shop windows caught their eye. They wandered along stopping every now and then to point out some fashionable – they assumed, piece of clothing or some luxury item. They were amazed by the many and varied goods and objects on sale. They walked in the park with its manicured lawns and found a café where they sat down and ordered coffee, two plates of zweiback and some cheese. They did most of this by pointing at the menu and sign language. Luckily the waiter understood a little Polish and was able to put them at their ease. They nevertheless felt slightly self-conscious as they still had their smaller personal bundles with them which was unusual and they were attracting a few stares from the regular clientèle. Their mode of homespun looking dress was different from that of Berliners and they were clearly foreigners. They paid the bill, trusting to the honesty of the waiter to take the correct coinage from Juoza's outstretched palm.

Noticing a clock on the summit of a big department store and seeing that the time was getting on, they made their way back to the station, found their platform and there was the train. Checking with the guard that the luggage would have been loaded they climbed aboard and this time found a seat. The train set out at one in the afternoon and arrived in Hamburg around nine.

Once again instructions for emigrants were given by railway guards walking up and down and the travellers were led to a large six storey building in which, they were told, they would be staying overnight. They noticed that the luggage had also been unloaded and was being taken to the building on carts by railway porters.

Once in the building the sisters found the luggage room and reclaimed theirs, then joined the queue again as it snaked up the stairs and they were separated into three groups, women, men and families as the floors were occupied by emigrants starting with the lower floors and working their way up. It wasn't until the fifth floor that Elzbièta and Juoza found themselves at the head of the queue and peeled off into a dormitory-like room.

They immediately claimed adjacent beds by putting their bundles on them and then looked out of the window. Once again they were overcome by a new experience as their gazes wandered across the entire city from this great height.

"It looks as if our train fare and embarkation ticket covers all this said Juoze."

"I know, I didn't realise it would all be as involved as this and we're not even on the ship yet let alone in London. I have heard that the ship doesn't sail for a few days.

Somebody came round to tell them there was food available in a dining room on one of the lower floors so they went there and partook of the food which was on offer and for which they had to pay. They then went back to their dormitory and went to bed. The next morning they again visited the dining room after which many of them were conducted to a Lutheran church nearby where they took part in a service for an hour and a half. When that was finished the rest of the day was theirs to do with as they liked so they decided to go on a trip to the zoo they had heard about.

Leaving the emigrants building they walked along a wide boulevard until they saw the sign for the zoo. This sign they understood as it began with a 'Z' and had pictograms of animals on it.

They walked in the direction indicated and eventually arrived at another botanical garden, similar to the one in Berlin, which they had to pay to enter. They wandered around it as if in a wonderland. It was just like being children all over again to actually look at animals in the flesh which had only previously been seen in picture books. They were in turn fascinated by the elephants, terrified by the lions and amused by the antics of the monkeys. It was wonderful – another of life's highlights.

They fell in with another group of young Lithuanians they recognised as the Sackevičius family from the station and as they all walked along together they discovered that they were going to London too, to a place called Wapping. Somehow it made them feel more secure.

"How did you make it through the passport control?" Juoza asked. "We stayed outside in the park for the night but decided to pay them the bribes they were asking for the next day. There were different officials on duty and they asked for less. We must have been on the same train as you on the Sunday morning."

The following day another trainload of emigrants arrived. The whole building became packed and they got separated from their new friends. Every bed was taken, They rubbed shoulders with hordes of people whichever facility they availed themselves of. At every turn the sisters were charged a fee until they began to wonder how long their money would last.

On the following day they were organised by officials and the women were herded into an area of ablution-rooms and made to strip and shower while their clothes were taken away to another room and fumigated. The reason for this evidently was that there had been some suspected cases of cholera fairly recently and the authorities could not afford to take any chances. As they were passed towels by female attendants who didn't get too close, they were re-united with their clothes. Most people had separated their valuables when they undressed and had put them and any money into waterproof bags they had been supplied with. Who knew how many other valuables were stitched into linings of the now divested clothes.

So confusedly sorting their clothes whilst wrapped in sheets and in a damp state they re-dressed and were led through to see a doctor. The examination by the multi-lingual doctor was cursory and concerned things like eyesight and questions about general health. Both girls passed and were told at that point to find their luggage. There was a porter in charge to help them identify it by its labels. After scanning the piles and piles of baggage they spotted theirs and were reunited with it. They were then sent outside where they saw a succession of horse-drawn buses lined up. Some at the head of the queue were already loaded with people and were pulling away. They were directed towards the next empty one at the front. Juoza and Elzbiéta on foot were following others. People were also coming along behind them and the bus quickly filled up with them and their luggage. It set off obviously heading towards the docks. The passengers sat there on top and below taking in the sights of Hamburg along the way. They themselves were as much an object of curiosity to the people of Hamburg as they stopped and stared and children pointed and laughed. Elzbiéta felt rather silly perched up there with people looking and pointing. She was self-conscious, never one to seek the limelight, but Juoza couldn't have cared less.

Chapter 22

Hamburg – The Ship

The horses pulling their omnibus jogged along for perhaps half-an-hour in what was the direction of the docks, for after a while, groups of drab buildings, warehouses and cranes became visible as they drew nearer and nearer. They finally arrived at the quayside on a wide river. There was no ship in sight and Elzbiéta began to have concerns. They were asked to alight and then led to the edge of the quay and for the first time really they became aware of a funnel with traces of smoke coming from it and some masts, the tips just projecting up slightly above the level of the quay. The now empty bus turned around and continued with its shuttle service back to the emigrants' building.

Once again they had to show their tickets and were then doled out pins to affix them to the front of their clothing as they and the other passengers were firmly ushered down a set of wide floating steps and onto the small steamer moored at the quayside. They descended to the broad deck and from there were directed into a saloon with wooden seating. There they sat and waited for fifteen minutes until another busload of emigrants appeared above them followed closely by another. Once everyone came aboard and were packed in, not all of them could be seated . The people were of all types, peasants, Jews and a class of better dressed folk. The sailors cast off fore and aft and the boat raised steam and drifted out into the middle of the river and then under full steam down towards the sea. "Is this our ship?" asked Elzbiéta. "Surely it can't be, it's very small," Juoza answered.

Turning to a crewman Juoze asked him what was happening. Having overheard the conversation he laughed and said in halting Lithuanian, "We just taking you out to ship in deep water."

The boat continued for about three quarters of an hour as the waterway gradually opened out to reveal a sort of estuary. In the distance was the biggest man made steel structure the sisters had ever beheld, even bigger than the train. As they drew ever closer it took on astronomical proportions towering above, dwarfing them into insignificance. As their ferryboat rounded the stern of the ship they could see a wooden staircase, similar to the one at the dock but larger, coming down its side and at the bottom a wooden floating deck at about the same level as the deck of their ferry. Once again there was all the hustle and bustle of tying up to it and being conducted off the ferry, onto the floating wooden deck and up the staircase through an open steel half-door and straight onto the deck of the monster.

Standing there Elzbiéta felt a bit queasy and strange as she caught the tang of the sea borne on the wind. It ruffled her hair and she felt chilly. She noticed the baggage being lifted by crane up onto the deck in a huge rope netting bag and deposited on deck. Without being given much time to look around they were all lined up and their tickets properly examined by a steward who glanced from each one to its owner as if to ascertain its accuracy. What had been a polite greeting at first, became abrupt when steerage passengers were revealed as such, and not as being saloon class. They were roughly directed further forward up the ship. They clustered around the baggage area as people identified their own property and claimed it. The two sisters, just part of a long chain of people and not being aware of exactly where they were supposed to be going just milled around with the other steerage passengers and their luggage until a sailor was sent to lead the way towards the front of the ship and to a passageway with a staircase which led down into the bowels of the ship. This he achieved by grasping harshly the shoulder of the first woman he came to who was somewhere near the front of the throng. As she followed the crowd and then descended through a hatch Elzbiéta looked up and saw cabins above with well dressed people lounging indolently looking down at them over the rail in much the same way that Juoza and Elzbiéta had watched the animals at the zoo.

Reaching the bottom, there was another turn and a second staircase going down, it seemed, into the depths of Hades. At that level each person was handed a metal plate, a mug and a knife, fork and spoon by another steward as they passed by him. Coming down the final few steps they could see the layout of the space below them. Families and individuals, after their tickets were inspected, were being separated and sent to different parts of the accommodation, but not before having to pass another rudimentary doctor's inspection. In the case of Juoze and Elzbiéta it consisted of a cursory glance up and down and a level gaze into their eyes by a florid faced man in a waistcoat. They were pronounced fit and waved past with a slightly irritated dismissive gesticulation. They were then brought before a man seated at a desk who quizzed them on their names, ages, professions and so on. He was German and didn't appear to understand much. Elzbiéta suspected that he wasn't familiar with Lithuanian names as he seemed to write down something else when she gave her name. She could see that the spelling was wrong but such was the press of other people behind her and the irritation of the officials that she felt obliged to accept whatever they decided to do and just move along. Juoza seemed to forget all traces of civility at that moment as she gave the clerk a withering glare but he didn't seem to notice. As they made their way down the final few steps they could see that some travellers had already made themselves at home in the various alcoves fitted out with bunks one above the other. The alcoves though were still openly communal and offered very little, if any, privacy. There were still some of these alcoves with berths free in the part where the sisters were told to go, so Elzbiėta and Juoze having already scanned the room even before they had reached the bottom step had a place earmarked. Arriving at the bottom and stepping off the first rung of the staircase, which was more like a ladder, heaving their chattels before them, they headed straight towards the alcove and put their baggage on the two spare bunks. A table firmly anchored to the deck in front of their alcove with a storm rail around the top delineated the space as theirs after they placed a few small items on it. Their table space was part of a much bigger surface running the length of the cabin cursorily divided into segments by thin rails. They agreed to stay there until the ship was full, for fear of losing their berths. The quarters they found themselves in were way towards the front of the vessel where the space available became rapidly more constricted the further forward one went. The smell down there was sickening and seemed to be overpoweringly tinged with the smell of vomit mingled with food and the foul stench of the lavatories somewhere on the deck above. Wafting up through a hatch from below was the aroma of salted and cured fish. It was an overwhelming atmosphere added to by the unwashed and travel stained bodies already in residence. It was barely slightly improved by the opening of the portholes occurring at intervals along the sides. Doing that, just added the smell of the salty estuary water to the mix. It also allowed the sound of lapping water to be included in the general clamour of passengers of all types and families chattering and shouting, babies screaming, children crying and the oaths and cries of members of the ship's crew.

On their excursion down the precarious descent, manhandling baggage and bedding bundles between them, they had passed a wooden butt half full of water. It was presumed for drinking, as it had a tin cup attached to it by a chain. Next to that was another barrel which appeared to be half full with the rotting detritus from the previous voyage's passengers. The old food and other rubbish inside it did nothing to enhance the atmosphere. Disgusted, heartsick, homesick and exhausted they just lay down on their bunks with their baggage strewn around the alcove. Juoza having climbed into the upper bunk.

Exhausted, they both dozed off until rudely awakened by the vibration of the ship's engines suddenly starting into life. Other harsh mechanical noises and shouts and the slightly pitching movement which caused everything – themselves, their bunks, the cabin, – everything, to rise and fall slowly together creating for the passengers an experience, which most of them had never encountered before. Juoza disappeared and came back twenty minutes later with the news that they were to be fed stew, potatoes and tea shortly. When the stew arrived it was being carried in a huge bucket by two men and the passengers were served from it into their metal bowls with a huge ladle, by a cook – judging by his white overalls, who gave the bucket a stir each time before doling out a portion into the crudely shaped receptacles eagerly held out by the diners. The cook was closely followed by his assistant with the potatoes and slices of bread. They tucked in with an appetite and found the greasy concoction actually quite delicious, as no-one had eaten for quite some time, and hunger ignores a multitude of shortcomings in the quality of food.

"There is a place where you can wash your plates and things up near the lavatories" Juoza said. "Also there is a washroom, but it's for both men and women and the water is pumped from the sea."

Having finished her food Elzbièta decided to go and check on these other facilities and going up to the deck above she found herself at the back of a long line of people with the same intention as herself, to wash their eating utensils. The tub for this purpose was being presided over by another steward. Although filled originally with hot water, by the time it was her turn it was only lukewarm and had already dissolved the grease of plates and dishes belonging to at least twenty people with ever decreasing effectiveness. Globules of fat floated on the surface.

"Could I have some fresh hot water please?" asked Elzbieta. The steward must have taken a shine to her because he winked and heaved the tub over and the cloudy water with all its floating bits cascaded away down a drain. He replaced it on its stand and then topped it up again from another bucket of warm water, which although not exactly piping hot by that time was at least a marked improvement on previously. The people behind her said "Well done." The couple just in front of her who were still in the vicinity of the ablutions turned round noticing this and looked slightly bitter and disappointed.

Later on in the evening Juoze and Elzbiéta made their way up onto their part of the deck which was roped off from the saloon passengers area. At least they were clear of the fug of their accommodation. They leaned on the rail as the cold night wind riffled through their hair and they picked out the twinkling lights of the coast they were leaving behind them. To Elzbiéta this departure seemed so drastic and final and she resisted the urge to suppress her tears at leaving all she had ever known. Her eyes filled and two small runnels trickled down her cheeks. This was symbolically leaving the country of her birth but also truly departure from the baleful state she had been constrained to live under all her life. But even here in this sub-standard accommodation, thrown together with all these unknown people also seeking something more, she was feeling a new spirit of adventure and freedom which she had never experienced in her life before. She thought of her mother who would be sitting by the oven about now, sewing, patting the dog, harking at the sounds of the night outside, and she felt a knot of regret and loneliness in the pit of her stomach.

Her nostalgic reverie was interrupted by Juoza who suddenly said,

"Come on. it's getting cold here. Let's go back downstairs the sea's beginning to get a bit rough." And indeed it was. The front of the ship was buffeting the water as it beat its path towards England and the receding twinkling lights were moving up and down at a faster rate. They made their way downstairs and on the way encountered a member of the crew going in the opposite direction. He paused, bidding them "Good evening," in Lithuanian and Juoze, glad to be able to speak to an official who was also a countryman stopped him to ask how long the voyage would take. He replied.

"We had a delay to start with but now not more than a couple of days. The Argo is quite fast and you should be seeing the Pool of London the day after tomorrow."

"You mean we have to put up with those conditions down there for that long?" muttered Juoza.

"Listen! Just be thankful you are not going to New York. You would have to bear all that and be cooped up for anything up to two weeks. You would probably be going first up round the west coast of England and then to Ireland to pick up people there followed by the voyage across the Atlantic. And can you imagine putting up with all that Irish music and dancing en route? They are a very noisy race. Depending upon which ship you go on there might be livestock on the deck above. In bad weather the water penetrates the deck and mixes with their manure as a sort of farmyard slurry and drips down onto the passengers on the decks below. It can be a tough, unpleasant journey. The sisters looked a bit shaken.

Elzbiėta replied, "Once we've got some more money together we will be making that trip anyway. The passage to America is all included on our tickets. But if it's as bad as that, we'll pay the extra to go saloon class. It's clear that they are far better treated than we are."

Yes! Money speaks many languages," replied their new found friend. "I'm Justinas by the way. I work in the laundry. Let me have a quick look at your tickets." While Elzbiėta was looking for them Juoza took it upon herself to introduce both of them to him.

"Do you understand German?" she asked. "Can you translate?"

"Yes, let's have a look." He scrutinised the documents. "I'm afraid to say that these tickets will only take you as far as London. Unfortunately it looks as if you may have to pay for any further journey.

"I knew it!" said Juoza with fury. "We've been had." Elzbièta was calmer and said, "Perhaps there's just been a mistake. Isaac seemed honest enough. Anyway we may prefer Londonas."

The crossing was relatively calm and there were only a few cases of sea-sickness on board. Elzbièta imagined what it could have been like had the sea been rough. The next two days and nights settled into a routine which was just short enough to forestall too much monotony. Nevertheless it was still an uncomfortable voyage even amidst the other Lithuanians. There were also Jews, Poles, Russians, Germans and Scandinavians. Some of them, with whom they had managed to communicate, had terrible tales of hardship to relate. Stories of pogroms, when mobs of angry, crazed thugs attacked Jews in their own homes brutally killing many and driving the rest away from their villages. There were also reports of more subtle persecution stopping just short of murder, and false accusations of crimes committed levelled against them and wrongful imprisonment and the balance of the law weighed against them. Their freedom of worship was continually under pressure and laws passed to make their lives even more desperate. These were crimes against Jews, ignored and even encouraged by the Russian authorities, which had made it so pressing for them to leave. It was serious for ordinary peasants too trying to get away. Some had had their applications turned down, some had been swindled. The worst cases were of the families who had been forced to make the decision to split up because one of their number was deemed unfit in the course of the many medical inspections they had undergone. The decision had to be taken whether they should all stay, or maybe some of them should continue on their journey and hope the child's or the wife's or the sister's ailment cleared up and they could be sent for later. The sisters had indeed witnessed for themselves the agony of some who were rejected on grounds of bad eyesight, or health, or because they were considered undesirable characters. They had seen a traveller, who some people said was a thief, apprehended and escorted away to a secure place on board in handcuffs, to be dealt with on arrival in London and probably sent back. This flotsam and jetsam of society only seemed to continue their own personal odysseys at the whim of the fates. That they were all prepared to undergo this in order to get away spoke volumes about their desperation.

Elzbiéta and Juoza became friendly with a particularly outgoing Jewish girl, Leah, travelling with her entire family, and marvelled at some of the Jewish humour which the girl exuded. Even there, down in the dismal, dank hold, the sense of relief of some of the passengers, as typified by her, was palpable. She was young, about the same age as them and did more to acquaint the sisters with the deprivations the Jews had to put up with than they already knew. Elzbiéta would always remember Leah by the self-deprecating jokes she told her. One in particular stuck in her mind.

"Why do Jewish men always wear their hats indoors?"

Elzbiéta had thought for a while, then shrugged expectantly.

Leah replied with a smile, "Because we never know when we might have to move on at a moment's notice."

They all chuckled together but Elzbiéta was still amazed that Jews could find such humour even amongst all the troubles they had to bear. From the outside they often seemed aloof but she realised that inside they were like anyone else. She noticed that Leah's father was in fact wearing his hat – and so was her brother.

The ship steamed on. To add to Elzbiéta's already anxious mind was the realisation that there had been a delay in departure from Hamburg, something about missing the tide, and the rumour had spread early on that they would not be arriving in London until the Monday and not the day before as had previously been thought. She fretted that their brothers would be worried when the ship didn't arrive on Sunday. Juoza assured her that everything would be alright.

Chapter 23

Welcome to England

On the afternoon of their third day aboard, the passengers were abuzz with the news that England's coast had been sighted off the port bow. Some of the emigrants had climbed the stairways and crowded to the rail for a glimpse of the promised land which represented itself as a faint mysterious black smudge on the horizon. As the ship forged on, they passed another vessel going in the opposite direction. Both steamers sounded their foghorns in greeting. The other ship looked magnificent and Elzbiéta wondered if its majestic appearance concealed the same squalid conditions which they were enduring aboard the Argo. Surely though it would be nearly empty of people as it returned to the continent for more passengers, perhaps carrying other cargo – maybe cattle?

They passed close by some fishing boats under sail as the smudge became more discernible as a coastline. Fishermen shouted up at the ship as they passed by and members of the crew shouted back. Elzbiéta caught a word or two but couldn't understand any of it so she just waved. Presently they came around a headland and she could see one or two yachts skimming along close to the coast and heavier boats like barges with huge red sails making their way slowly along. For a young woman who had never even seen the sea before arriving at Hamburg docks, this was fascinating and exciting.

"Let's go down and get our belongings together," suggested Juoza. Elzbiéta went with her, knowing that soon they would be off this boat with its lack of privacy, class ridden hierarchy, bad food and squalor.

As Juoza raced ahead Elzbiéta suddenly felt a tug at her dress. Turning around she became aware of a fat Jew leering at her.

"I've been watching you my dear." he intoned. "Have you got employment when you land in London?"

"Why no, I haven't, not yet," the girl replied honestly.

"How would you like a job in a very good part of town with good wages and your food and lodging paid for?"

Juoza had passed out of sight by now and Elzbiéta and the Jew were alone on the landing. Feeling a little disquiet Elzbiéta nervously, for the sake of politeness asked him what the job entailed.

"All you would have to do is to look after various guests – gentlemen! – keep them happy and supplied with drinks and generally make sure they don't need anything. So you would be a sort of exclusive hostess. You might have to see them home in a cab if they are the worse for wear and see that they are alright. You will soon get the hang of it and just for doing that you could become very rich. We would supply you with the latest in fashionable clothing to wear and you would want for nothing. That would mean a lot to you in a strange land. And we could also send you for English lessons."

Elzbiéta thought it sounded quite an attractive proposition but demurely, politely replied, "I don't think so, thank you very much all the same. My brothers are meeting us in London and they have everything sorted out for us."

"Look! I have these rings," he said brandishing his chubby hand in front of her eyes. "These would be yours if you decide to give it a try."

"No, I am not sure. I will speak to my sister and see what she says." replied Elzbiėta.

Just at that moment Juoza appeared after retracing her steps. The Jew faded into the background.

"What was that about?" Juoza asked her.

"He was offering me a job when we arrive in London."

"Oh yes! doing what?" her sister asked ironically.

"As a hostess."

"A '*hostess*?' Juoza barked. "do you know what that means?"

"Er I thought maybe we could send the money home.."

"No! you're not even going to think about it. It's out of the question. You have a lot to learn, I can see that. If that man appears again let me know. I'll give him what for. He'll get an earful from me."

They gathered together all their belongings making good everything into bundles and bags again and progressed up to the deck. There were many others like themselves on the rails gazing expectantly at the estuary they were now entering with land on both sides. As the steamer forged its way up the channel the land on either side drew closer and closer until they realised they were in a wide river heading upstream. The land on both sides was very low-lying and they began to make out buildings at the water's edge with boats and small ships in varying stages of building and repair. The river was a hive of activity with vessels and craft of all kinds plying their way up and down the flow. Some boats under sail made their way across from side to side, both in front of and behind them. It was a busy thoroughfare and had a slightly different atmosphere to Hamburg.

The further the ship went, the more foggy became the air. But through it they could make out warehouses with cranes and ships docked alongside them. They gazed at vessels of all kinds, steamships, launches, three masted schooners, together with a myriad of barges in strings tethered to each other. Some were anchored together and some were under tow up and down the river. Amidst the hustle and bustle of this waterway was once again the whistle of steam and the shouts of the lightermen, stevedores and dock workers.

Straight ahead of them they could see a brand new massive structure of a bridge gleaming in cream coloured stone with twin towers built in a style which neither of them had ever seen before and beyond that was a huge white stone building bigger than anything else which someone told them was 'The Tower.'

Their ship, its engines cut to a bare tick-over slowly edged in towards the quayside aided by two tugs which pulled it and nudged it alongside until at last it was still. The tide wasn't fully in and the ship was too low for them to see what was going on. But they could hear the sound of a brass band somewhere up there. The lively tune it was playing boded well for the passengers. Elzbièta realised with a surge of optimism that it was there to welcome to England those newly disembarked. Elzbièta, her sister and the rest of the steerage passenger were told to wait until the first and second class passengers had disembarked. The Steerage passengers were treated in a completely different manner, once again being roughly directed off the boat and up the gangplank in groups according to gender and family. They edged up it with trepidation clutching their pathetic bundles.

She noticed after reaching the level of the quay that the higher class travellers must have made their way out of the dock area with relatively little fuss and dispersed leaving the emigrants to be processed. She could no longer hear the band. Firstly, they were told, they must go

through the immigration buildings and be checked. Again they had to suffer the indignity of close scrutiny while their names were ticked off against the ship's manifest. They were made to pass through several rooms and answer various questions relating to how much money they had, whether they had jobs to go to, who was meeting them and so on. Elzbieta produced her letter and the translation as proof that they had somewhere to go to. Then there were the eye checks again, just in case they had picked up something en-route.

Finally they were through, away from the ignominy of steerage class and free, left to their own devices in their new country.

The two girls stood at the exit to St Katharine's Dock, lost, looking around for their brothers. The remnants of the band were disappearing into the distance clutching their instrument cases. Suddenly from nowhere the Jew of the previous job offer experience appeared. This time he was accompanied by a blowsy looking Englishwoman and another man. They advanced upon the sisters. Elzbiéta saw him now with an air of distaste and caught again the whiff of pickled herrings and tobacco breath as he came up to them. Juoza too began to feel quite alarmed as she sought a way to extricate herself and her sister from this potentially threatening situation.

"We have a carriage for you if you just tell us where you are going," the Jew said to Elzbiéta. The three of them crowded round the two girls and started to bundle them towards the carriage. Juoza looked extremely angry and Elzbiéta was terrified. They were two helpless girls in an alien place being bullied by people of superior strength and there was no-one at hand to help them. They found themselves hustled towards the back of the cart amidst cajoling tones and curt sounds which they took to be curses and their own shrieks and shouts.

"Do you need any help?" a voice yelled in Lithuanian. It was Elzbiéta's friend Justinas from the ship.

"No! mind your own business," the Jew shouted back grabbing Juoza's bundle as he and his two associates continued to hustle the girls up against the back of the horse drawn conveyance.

Looking behind him Justinas shouted, "Gintas, we have a problem here." There was the sound of running and Gintas appeared. He was the biggest man Elzbiéta had ever seen. Realising that things was probably not going to go their way the blowsy woman jumped up into the driving position on the carriage closely followed by the other two hot on her heels who threw themselves through its open rear doors. The horse was whipped savagely into motion by the woman. The carriage clattered off over the cobblestones and into the early evening, its occupants thwarted, as the girls stood there out of breath with their hearts pounding.

"They really ought to do something about this, it's happening all the time here. The young girls who become inveigled by the lure of bright lights and easy money," exclaimed Gintas.

"Thank you Justinas, and you too Gintas, our brothers are supposed to be here to meet us. I don't know what's happened to them."

"Very well, what address do you have to go to?"

"Number six, Winterton Street, Stepney".

"Alright, we'll see you there," Gintas reassured them. They waited around for a bit to see if Pranas and Jonas might turn up, while just in case, Justinas went off to ask an English person exactly where Winterton Street was, leaving Gintas on guard. He went back to the offices and one of the staff showed him on a street map. As they left the dock area, all four of them together, they walked along behind the dock buildings which faced the waterfront, between those and another level of warehouses further back. Every now and then the buildings were connected by narrow bridges and there were cranes everywhere.

"What is this ugly, ugly place I have come to?" thought Elzbiéta. "Whoever would have thought a place could be so depressing, hideous and filthy?" she said.

"It's not bad her sister replied. "I'm certain it won't all be like this."

They reached a maze of narrow mean looking streets with dwellings all crammed in one upon another in rows. There wasn't a single wooden building as far as they could see. Everything was brick and stone. Every chimney, and there were many, had a plume of smoke coming from it. But this wasn't the smell of wood smoke which they were used to but the acrid smell of something else. It was the same as what was being burned on the ship, but unlike at sea, where the smoke was soon dissipated into the air, this stuff seemed to linger and hug the ground. Everything they could see was covered in grime and soot. They could see no trees nor grass anywhere. The nearest things to the natural world they had recently left were the grey and dejected looking nags pulling the carts and wagons through the cobbled streets and a few stray cats and dogs sniffing around.

They passed along a terraced street and past an open upstairs window. The occupants having heard the travellers speaking in Lithuanian below decided to welcome them with a greeting of their own. The party was assailed by a torrent of abuse, which put succinctly urged them to return to the country from whence they had come.

Elzbièta had absolutely no idea of what was actually being said but there was no mistaking the tone and if there had been any doubt at all it was soon dispelled by an avalanche of dirty liquid thrown from a pail upstairs followed by a packet of flour which burst on Juoze's shoulder in a cloud of white. Justinas hammered and kicked at the door. Unsurprisingly there was no response.

Once they had hurried upon their way, and the two men had ceased yelling defiance, they brushed themselves down and reflected on their predicament. Justinas turned it into a joke and said with a wry smile, "Welcome to England." It was by this time evening and they observed with fascination a lamplighter at work. The faint glow the lamps engendered seemed to highlight the murky atmosphere of the dirty damp fine particles which hung in the air. A little further on in the failing light they just made out two men walking towards them.

"It's Pranas and Jonas," Elzbiéta exclaimed in recognition as the figures got nearer. The two men broke into a run towards them and they all embraced rapidly under the yellow light of a street lamp, and quickly, the words tumbling one over another, brought each other up to date regarding major developments both here and at home. As they walked along and became calmer, they got down to more pragmatic topics. They spoke about how they would survive until the girls got jobs. They agreed to pool whatever financial resources they had and try to eke them out as long as possible. Between them all they had the two rooms which comprised the bottom half of the house. The good thing was that both the lads had jobs making slippers which brought in enough money for survival.

"If we all pull together we can make it work," Pranas assured them with the air of confidence of a man expert in these matters.

They arrived in Winterton Street at the door of number six and were let in by another man, a Pole, introduced by Pranas as Kazis from one of the rooms upstairs.

"This is your room," Jonas said preceding them through a door on the right. You are sharing it. They surveyed the dingy room critically.

"Where's the oven?" asked Elzbiéta scanning the room.

"No, it's not quite the same here, there isn't one." he replied. "There's a coal fire in that black iron stove over there. It does the same job really as our oven at home, cooking and heating, but it's not as good. As you can see it's too small. We cook on that as best we can but there is a gas ring for boiling water. You have to buy coal for the range and put money in a meter for the gas. You'll find the whole place strange at first. It will take getting used to! It's not like Lietuva."

"You are telling me," Juoza retorted peering round the sparsely furnished room. The shabbily curtained window looked out onto the dingy street. The only bed nearly filled the room. "Well maybe it's not that different," Juoza murmured. "It is a little bit like old times. I still have to share a bed with my sister!"

Chapter 24

Planet Street

After arriving on the shores of England, Elzbiėta spent the next few days trying to make sense of her new environment. What she saw of her new country didn't immediately endear itself to her as she timidly walked around the filthy, crowded streets in order to get her bearings. She felt self-conscious. Occasionally she went with Juoza, but found that the two of them going out together attracted attention when they were heard speaking their own language. Passers-by looked them up and down. The rest of the time they spent cleaning and

tidying their room, and that of their
brothers, and buying food, as they
figured out how things worked and
how they could best get to grips with
washing and ironing and generally
just existing. They were left to their
own devices most of the time while

Pranas and Jonas were out making shoes at another house for the best
part of the day. Elzbiéta ventured into a few of the larger shops just to
have a look. They were mostly Jewish owned but at least they had a
common language, Polish, and depending on exactly where they had
come from, sometimes Lithuanian. Commercial Road, which ran
across the end of their street, included the church of St Mary and St
Michael which they soon found without much trouble. The priests
there were mainly Irish with an Italian also, none of whose accents
they could understand. But Elzbiéta soon learned to follow the Mass
when a Lithuanian woman she was sitting next to, who had been in
London for some time, helped her with it. Much of it was in Latin.

Very soon however practicalities set in. Their money began to run
low. Their brothers were suggesting that they either get jobs or think
about getting married. Elzbiéta had never thought of herself as part
of a cattle market before but it *was* true there were many single men
from Lithuania round and about. Looking for and finding one whom
she might like seemed quite adventurous. The emphasis back home
had always been on marriage as soon as possible for eligible girls and
so it seemed logical to her that it should be the same here. The alternative was not a particularly good prospect. The only employment for the unskilled speaking no English seemed to be either as
a worker in the rag trade, run by Jews, or as a domestic servant in a
well-off household, once again these would be mainly Jewish. The
problem with the latter option was that she would probably have to
live-in, perhaps in another district and could be put out of touch
with the rest of her community. This had already happened to oth-

ers and their lives had been made miserable. There was of course the other alternative she and Juoza had so narrowly avoided at the docks, but that didn't bear thinking about. So she was paired up with various suitors by well-wishing friends and acquaintances. She either rejected the prospective matches or things didn't work out. Then she was introduced to Juozas Kurtinaitis.

In her eyes he outshone all the rest. One year older than herself, cultured, musical and hardworking, no one would have guessed that he also came from the land, from a farming family near Vilkaviškis. Even if he didn't exactly sweep her off her feet he certainly impressed her in his quiet way and she felt comfortable with him. He was kind, attentive, romantic and full of plans and ambition. Above all he was witty and funny but in a gentle dry manner which she loved. So everything merged together. When they went out for excursions by bus on Sundays after Mass, she was oblivious of their surroundings and of other people, as they recounted stories, anecdotes and news about their homeland while the horses clip-clopped along. They didn't notice when people stared at them as they spoke softly to each other in this seemingly unintelligible language. There were trips out to places which were nicer than Stepney that gave her a fresh outlook and sense of wonder at the different sights. In the evenings he played her songs on his accordion which reminded her of home. The buildings, parks and trees in other parts of London made her realise that the slums of Stepney were only a small part of the picture this interesting man was painting while he successfully wooed her.

As she got to know him over a few weeks the certainty grew ever greater that this was the man for her. He looked forward to being with her. She felt the same, and her savings were running out.

They were married at the church of the Holy Martyrs in Prescott Street on 26th December 1895. It was Boxing Day and a public holiday and the factory in Hackney where Juozas usually picked up his work was closed. So he carried straight on afterwards on the following day without missing a stride. He couldn't afford to turn down work anyway, even around his wedding day, in case it was subcontracted to another outworker. So their married life commenced as it was meant to continue, with the will to work hard and to try and achieve something in their lives which their parents back home had somehow never quite managed to do.

Juozas took on the rental lease for 59, Planet Street. At first they shared the house with a Polish family to whom they sub-let the lower floor. When their tenants, the Ambrosiaks, moved on, they occupied the whole house. The slipper business was going well and all was set fair on the path to their next goal which lay across the Atlantic in America. Two brothers of Juozas, had come to stay with them briefly en route for that transatlantic destination. Kazys. the elder of the two had gone on ahead leaving his wife whom he sent for later, once he was established. The other brother's arrangements took a bit longer. But while he was still staying with them Elzbiéta noticed something quite odd.

"Why do the others refer to you as Simon sometimes and to your brother as Juozas, is it some kind of joke?"
"I suppose you could say that in a way," he explained.

"When '*He*' was born," he said, jerking his finger towards the adjacent room, "my mother wasn't well enough to attend the baptism so my father stayed behind to look after her. The details of the name were entrusted to my father's friend Gintas Raulinaitis. He liked a drink, to say the least, but the occasion was too much for him and he surpassed himself, even before the main event. By the time the priest asked what the child was to be called, Gintas was sozzled, couldn't remember, and said the first name that came into his head – 'Juozas'. When my mother later found out that she now had two sons officially called Juozas all Hell broke loose. So from then on they all used to call me 'Simonas' and sometimes even 'Vincas'. I hated those names and as soon as I got away I changed it back!"

"At least, all three are Saints," said Elzbiėta with a slight smile.

A lot had happened during their first year together. The brothers, and Kazys' wife, had been and gone, The little Kurtinaitis family had settled down to a routine pretty well after the arrival of baby Joe. It had taken a while to adapt to a child but they managed with the advice and help of their neighbours, who were mostly newcomers themselves. Juozas became a leading light in the Lithuanian community always involved in initiatives, societies and clubs and was respected.

The two of them used to talk about their plans until well into the night when the house was still. They dreamed of their next move, getting away from this ghetto and branching out elsewhere.

Even though there was a certain security among their own kind here in London in this small area of Stepney, they both realised deep down that their future lay somewhere out there. Shortage of money was an inevitable drawback. After paying the rent, buying food and clothes and other essentials, paying for the gas lighting and the coal, there wasn't much left, but they were steadily saving a bit week by week. Maybe they would indeed be able to continue on to America. Juozas' brothers were set up there now and also cousins from both their families, the Cernauskas family and the Schwartzes. They all sent back letters glowing with gossip and optimism. Having made the initial leap to England in 1894 it was now 1897 and time to go on to that land of opportunity. It was an alluring prospect.

But here they had housing, an occupation, and a young baby. It was a big decision to make and one which they deferred from week to week. It was never *quite* the right time. Learning English was an obstacle too. They couldn't afford lessons, even had they known anyone willing to teach them. They were also too busy, so they picked up what snippets of language they could as they went along but they were often at a disadvantage with other East-enders many of them Irish. In the course of running his little cottage industry, Juozas would go to the factory in Hackney to collect the materials – the silk and the soft kid leather. He had his own lasts, bradawls, needles, thread, scissors, sharp knives, hammers, gluepots and brushes. He brought the raw materials back to the house and, together with other Lithuanians from within this small enclave, cut and glued and sewed it all into an array of white or pink coloured top quality slippers. The men sat on stools holding the work in construction hard down upon one knee by passing a leather looped strap over it and with the other end held down by the foot, kept it taut. The lasts were used initially to set up the work but most of the process was carried out using the knee as a workbench. Thus these sub -workers would sit down on a stool or box anywhere they could find and produce as many pairs as they were able to at the required sizes banging the glued parts to shape with a hammer. At the end of the day Juozas gathered up all the completed slippers, tied together with thread at the heels, checked the quality and slung them over a long pole in pairs for transportation back to the client. The money earned was then allocated proportionally to the rest of the men.

It was the sort of co-operative venture which might have presented great potential had things worked out differently.

One Friday evening Juozas came home from Hackney Road with the money for the week's work. A couple of pairs of slippers had been rejected but that was pretty good going in the circumstances. He quickly stopped off at home where Elzbiéta and Agnes Baukis were

chatting with their babies. Greeting them and gently pinching Joe's chubby cheek he said, "I'm just popping over to sort out the wages," and then walked the few paces across the cobbled road to the 'Star'.

Striding across the bare floorboards to the mahogany bar he asked the landlord for a drink. It was a good way of breaking down the half-sovereign he

had been given as part of the payment for the completed slippers, so that he could settle up with the other workers. It wasn't often he saw a gold half-sovereign and it made him feel important.

"Half Porter please sir" he said, proud of his ability to communicate. The landlord took the coin, put it in the till and then pulled the beer. He glanced down at the money in the drawer, then looked at it again for a long time. He suddenly snatched it up from the drawer and held it closer to his eye. His expression changed from seeming mild irritation at being given such a large coin for a small drink to one of anger, as his face flushed.

" 'Ere what's this?" said the landlord. "Passing me a dud 'n are ya?"

Looking now at the coin which the landlord held in his hand Juozas could see that it didn't look right. The gold colour was slightly different from the gold he had sometimes glimpsed from time to time. He hadn't noticed it before. The publican however never missed anything to do with money and his takings.

"I no see."

"Well we'll soon see," muttered the man, "Oi Ned! Nip aht and see if yer can find a copper!"

The boy Ned did as he was bid as Juozas attempted to walk out of the pub. He was not thinking straight, the landlord still had the coin.

"Not sa fast me lad, 'ere George, 'Arry, stop 'im leavin' 'til the old bill gets 'ere will ya?"

Juozas couldn't get his thoughts straight. He had never been in any trouble before and he knew he was of good character. It was all a misunderstanding. As it became clearer he realised it must have been his supplier, and his employer effectively, who had passed the coin on to him. He would never be able to prove it but could only rely on the man's honesty. Perhaps he in his turn would remember who had given it to him and clear Juozas of any blame. Ned returned some time later out of breath. " 'E's on 'is way. I told 'im we 'ad 'im 'eld fast, so 'e's gorn fer the Black Maria."

The commotion drew a small crowd as people who had been walking past lingered. Elzbiéta was knocked up by Mrs Gold and went to the scene where she found Juozas looking dejected and embarrassed in a corner of the bar with two stevedores between him and the door.

"Whatever has happened Juozas?" she cried plaintively.

"Elzyte it's a mistake, I haven't done anything, they think I'm a forger or something. Go and get Father Kerwin from the church." The people in the pub looked hostile as they saw these two communicating in a lingo they didn't understand. They felt excluded and consequently adopted an aggressive atitude.

"Oi! speak English Johnny! None of yer fancy tricks in 'ere, ta very much." Elzbiéta made her way out and through the throng outside in as dignified a manner as she could amongst some muttering which included comments such as "They comes over 'ere, nicks our jobs," and a few louder catcalls, "Go back 'ome you forrin gits!" Elzbiéta understood very few of the words but she got the gist of it. There were also a few quiet words of encouragement in Polish and Russian, and some which were defiant and a few decibels louder. Once she was clear of the crowd she made haste the length of Planet Street towards the main thoroughfare. As she ran down towards Commercial Road and started along it she saw a Black Maria pulled by two sweating horses trotting along in the traffic on their way coming from Whitechapel in the opposite direction. She saw a boy run out into the road and stop it. He spoke animatedly to the driver who then pulled the horses around and started to make a turn towards Winterton Street. In a real fluster she hurried, running and then walking when her breath became too

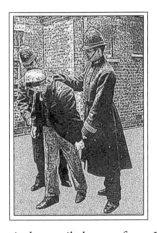

short. Eventually she stumbled as far as the church, ran up the steps and burst through the doors, past the vestibule and into the nave. Making her obeisance quickly before the altar she ran around looking for a priest, but there was none. The only person she saw was a woman arranging flowers in front of a statue of St Michael slaying the dragon. Elzbiéta grasped the woman's arm, hot, flustered, sobbing, but the flower arranger instinctively recoiled away from Elzbieta, and was in no frame of mind to try and understand a word of what the distraught woman was trying to tell her. Back in the pub two burly policemen had arrived. They briefly listened to the publican then went over and laid hold of Juozas and started to manhandle him to the door. In the melée he struggled and squirmed and his hat fell off and as he turned to try to retrieve it someone took off their own greasy cap and slapped it on his head as they bundled him out. His ignominy was complete as the onlooker's laughs and jeers and general hubbub were cut short by the closing pub doors. Meanwhile, panic stricken, leaving the church, at her wits end, the Lithuanian, woman in a foreign land and with no communication, stumbled, sobbing, back the way she had come along the road to Planet Street just in time to see the police wagon come round the corner pulling out into the teeming traffic of Commercial Road and head in the direction of Whitechapel. She craned her neck but couldn't see inside it through the bars which covered the tiny window at the back. She limped down the last bit of the street. She was almost oblivious of her own discomfort but assumed she must have strained a muscle in that sudden burst of activity. Her hair was awry and tears covered her cheeks with dirty smudges. By this time the crowd had dispersed, excitement over, and a degree of normality had returned to the scene. She lurched against her street door and it fell open as she half tumbled into the passage. There was her good and reliable friend Agnes hurrying down the passage carrying both her own child Antanas and baby Joe, each little three-month-old securely nestled in opposite crooked arms. Both were fast asleep as Elzbiéta overbalanced onto the floor. Amazingly the children continued to slumber untroubled.

"I heard what happened and have sent Mr Sikorsky's boy for the priest from the Polish church Elzyte. Have you been to St Mary and St Michael? I've been worried about you. Come in here and sit down and I'll make you some tea." She deftly laid both babies down side by side on the bed. At that moment there was a soft knock on the door. Agnes opened it and after some muffled words at the door the sound of firm striding footsteps came down the parquet floored passage. Agnes came in and sounded hopeful as she announced with some relief, "It's Father Odrobina." The priest entered the room and sat down on a wooden chair. He was a dignified looking man about sixty years old who had been in England for over twenty five years and spoke excellent English. Before that he had attended the university of Warsaw studying languages, law and theology. He was no pushover. Elzbiéta brought him a small glass of Starka and then they rapidly blurted out the story.

"All right Mrs Kurtinaitiené," he said, "They will have taken him to Whitechapel, I'll go round there now. There's clearly been a mistake of some kind. Please don't worry any more, I will do what I can to clear this up. Just try not to worry, everything will be alright."

"Thank you Father," both women replied in unison. Before he made his way to Whitechapel he strode the ten paces to the 'Star.' There was no doubt in his mind that Juozas had been the victim of some kind of fraud. On his frequent secondments to the other church in Commercial Road he had seen Juozas often standing as godfather to various new infants. He knew also that the Russian community looked up to him. He was obviously of exemplary character. He couldn't figure out though by whom the scam may have been perpetrated. It might have been the employer, but equally may well have been the publican who could have palmed the good coin behind the bar, exchanging it for a dud one. He was aware that this trick had been pulled before with foreigners in other circumstances.

The publican came round the bar uneasily and sat down together with the priest at a table in the corner.

"Tell me what happened with this coin?" the priest asked. "You're an Irish family are you not, I seem to remember seeing you at the church a few months ago for a funeral?"

"Er that's right but I...."

"Before you go on, I am often up at St Mary and St Michael's but I have only seen you the once, has your faith lapsed?"

"No Farver me faif ain't lapsed. I'm still a right good Caff-olic. I knows I should be going but I always seems to be bus......."

"Busy? Too busy for the word of God and what is right?"

His voice then softened slightly. "And what do we call you my son?"

"Patrick, farver, Patrick 'annon."

"Were you born here?" the priest went on, taking the initiative.

"I take it you were, as your accent is that of a true Londoner."

"Yes farver, me grandad came over after the famine in the 40s. Me grandfarver worked in the docks labouring and me granny cleaned. Me dad was their fourf kid."

The priest then asked the man exactly where in Ireland they had come from. The publican told him that they had come from County Sligo, from a small village not far from Ballymote, in the west of Ireland, a place called Culfadda.

"I think I have heard of it," the priest said.

The priest went on, "And I doubt things were straighforward for them when they arrived. I can well understand the difficulties they must have had to bear. You know that Ireland is very much like

Lithuania where Mr Kurtinaitis comes from. It is small and has about the same number of inhabitants. They are also both oppressed and many of them from both countries have come here to make a better life. Is it possible that we who have been here for longer could forget that we were once like them, alone and afraid? But these Russian people don't even speak the language to boot. Come on man! Put yourself in their position. They need all the help they can get. They certainly don't need this. But just as both nations are also equal in their strong faith in the Holy Catholic Church I am going to ask you to carry out an act of charity towards Mr Kurtinaitis. You will be a better man for it. I want to ask you......," and at this point the priest looked deeply into the other man's eyes. "I am going to ask you to reconsider whether or not you may have been mistaken. Did you perhaps, wrongly, believe that the coin in your till was the same one which Mr Kurtinaitis gave you? God will forgive you if you have made a genuine mistake as I believe you did?"

Patrick Hannon looked away shiftily and from side to side not wishing to meet the other man's gaze.

"I'm sure that he give me ......"

"You are sure? It sounds to me that you are not sure."

"I would say that would be the view of all the Russians, and the Poles who frequent your establishment. Why would you imagine that they would continue to come in here if they thought that they too might become the victims of a – 'mistake'?" The priest emphasised the last word in a scornful tone. This sorry tale will have to be related after Mass to the congregation."

"We have a duty to all our flock, including those who have come here recently, to warn them of the dangers of living here in this city where – 'mistakes' are often made."

"I would imagine some won't be coming into your pub any more if this comes out. Of course, if you come with me to the police station and say you were mistaken and you don't know who it was, then maybe I could persuade the canon not to mention it at any of the

Sunday masses." I will also be expecting to see you at Confession and Mass regularly from hereon in."

The publican was relieved that the priest hadn't actually asked him if he had been lying nor suggested it. He didn't want to go down that road of accusation and denial.

"Farver forgive me, I may 'ave been wrong abaht it."

"I am pleased we have got to a good place. Now please get your coat and come with me right now."

Once they arrived at the police station and Father Odrobina had spoken to the duty sergeant, the publican then officially withdrew his accusation explaining that he hadn't noticed the coin until he was closing the till. There were two others there apart from the dud. He hadn't been on duty all day anyway and it could have been anybody who had given it up. He quickly made himself scarce to the words, as he went out of the door, "...wasting police time..." Juozas was released from his cell, was given back his belt, bootlaces, scarf and second-hand cap and the rest of his money. One of his main concerns even at that stressful moment was how he was going to make good the half sovereign to pay the wages tomorrow morning. Elsewhere, the thought had crossed Patrick's mind that maybe he should have just left it at that and not called the police. Maybe he had over-egged the pudding. He wouldn't be doing that again. Now he was saddled with going to church if he didn't want a visit from the priest. He knew Father Odrobina would be watching out for him like a hawk. Towards eleven o'clock that evening Juozas returned with the priest, dishevelled, but free, albeit with his pride injured and he was a half-sovereign lighter. They spoke briefly on the doorstep where Father Odrobina told them that this test had been meant to happen and was a trial of their faith which they had successfully come through. He then produced a half-sovereign explaining that the publican had admitted he wasn't sure if it was Juozas who had given him the counterfeit. He had then been obliged to return a good half sovereign at the priest's insistence into his keeping. Father Odrobina departed feeling really contented, He was a good, kind, shrewd man and a pillar of the community, a rock they could all lean on. Agnes had already gone home and Juozas went straight to bed, while Elzbiėta stayed up to feed the baby. The words of the priest kept going round and round in her mind. Had God some purpose? Was all this happening because he intended it, just a small part in the great plan? What part could they, honest, simple, humble people, possibly play in all this. She was not one to question the priest though. She just accepted it. She knew they could never know what was intended. Elzbiėta looked down at little Juozas now sleeping again contentedly and wondered what life had in store for him. He would be the best, the fittest, the finest, the most wonderful son ever. He would prosper and do well here. Everything she did, she did it for him. He had a bright future.

During the early hours of the morning Elzbiėta began to think her time of the month had come again. She felt acute stomach pains and it slowly dawned on her that she must be suffering a miscarriage. She already knew the signs, she had seen it happen back home to various women. Sometimes it seemed to be caused by overwork, or it was just an act of God which no one could explain. But like all God's work it was supposed to be for the best in the end, they were told. She was ill for several days, in and out of bed but just carried on stoically as best she could. Agnes came in and tended to her gallantly and was there with her when the contractions began, leading to a sad conclusion. They couldn't afford a doctor and indeed she knew there was nothing much to be done anyway, but as always Agnes was there to lean on. Elzbiėta treated her own ills and worries with thoughts of the tree of Žemyna so far away and now almost a distant memory from another time and another age. It brought her through that period of deep depression and the aching sense of loss that went with it. When she was up and about again she continued to ponder on the priest's words She concluded that it was all meant to be and that there must surely be some greater plan, some grand design which they must accept. Everything was for a purpose.

Chapter 25

A Trip to the Country – 1913

It was a warm day in early September when Elzbièta decided to go to Brentwood to visit her youngest child. The autumn term at Julie's school hadn't yet started and Joey was between jobs. Julie and Joey needed no second bidding to agree to a day out.

Since Juozas had passed away in March the previous year she had been to St Charles' once before by carrier's cart along the main London to Chelmsford Road. She had caught a tram to the outskirts of Romford a place she had never been to before. As she got off there at the conductor's prompting, he told her where to go to pick up the cart to Brentwood and the cart driver had then taken her right to the door of her destination.

Previously the furthest she had been along this route was to St Patrick's Catholic Cemetery in Leytonstone. She had been there far too often; to bury her own babies, her friends and the children of friends, but most recently her husband. In terms of magnitude of grief this last loss was very nearly impossible to bear. The two of them had been a partnership for seventeen years, through thick and thin, shouldering the crises and tragedies together but knowing joyful and pleasant times too. There was now no money, other than by the kindness of friends, and charity. There was no companionship, no discipline for Joey no chance now of a new life somewhere else. Now Juozas was gone, she was no longer one half of a couple and she had sunk into an abyss of deep depression and loneliness. She felt like a haystack that had begun to fall apart at the seams, at the whim of the wind or some malign force; She was merely a child of fate.

She got work from Levene's a Jewish tailors in Commercial Road sewing the linings into gentlemens' trousers. But not before Mr Levene had asked to see some samples of her work. She had carried down the quilt she had made as a child which had followed her everywhere. She had been explaining to him that she was only a girl when she had done it. Nevertheless he still seemed impressed and gave her the work. So there was now a small amount of money coming in, but she had to work really hard for it until the early hours of the morning, the room lit only by a candle, and seated on the tiny wooden stool which her husband had made for Julie.

It was seen by many around her though that she was struggling to cope with her own mental condition. During the course of her troubles Father Matulaitis suggested that perhaps the burden on her could be eased slightly if she allowed the Church to help in some small way. He went on to say that there was a charitable Catholic institution in the heart of beautiful countryside not far away which would be prepared to take one of her children, her little boy, and look after him until such time as she felt she could cope with him again. This would help with the finances and benefit the child. That was the way in which the case was set out. In this suggestion the priest was supported by some of the sisters attached to the convent of St Mary and St Michael who visited Elzbièta on several occasions talking things over with her in words of comfort and understanding.

"It would be like a holiday for him in the country where the air is fresh, no smogs, no dirty streets and he will receive a good education and be all the better for it."

She thought and thought about this prospect. On the one hand she couldn't bear to part with him, but on the other, and this was frequently reinforced by the priest, she was being selfish in denying him an opportunity.

"Who in their right mind wouldn't take up this offer?" the priest finished up with, after yet another discussion with her, prompted by him after Mass one Sunday.

Her friend Agnes was against it. Her view was that he, the unmarried priest, couldn't possibly understand the finer points of a mother's love and her instinctive feelings about her own child?

"He is just a man and not a very worldly one at that, none of them are, as far as we are aware. He's single, How can he know?"

Elzbièta veered towards feeling in some way disobedient to the will of an authority but she still pondered, "I've been here before. Authority, people dictating to me, bending me to their own will."

"Now surely I am being uncharitable, this is hardly the same as then, Father Matulaitis is giving me his genuine heartfelt advice. Am I being churlish and headstrong in not listening to him?"

One evening he called round yet again, unexpectedly. As she answered the knock and saw him standing there she noted that it was still raining outside, an event which always made her feel low anyway, especially if it was cold and dismal too; and it was that night. She had spent the afternoon thinking, which led inevitably to nostalgia, melancholy, anxiety and sadness. She was bordering on depression.

In being so turned in upon her own woes she had burned the vegetable soup she was making for all of them and would have no money to buy more food until the day after tomorrow. Her great respect for God's spokesman in the East end and her feelings of guilt, as well as him happening to find her that evening at such a particularly low ebb finally led her to agree to it, reluctantly, out of pure despair. He had worn her down. She just wanted to get rid of him, having no more stomach for resistance. The priest went away inwardly pleased. He tended to feel automatically that his will had prevailed over hers in the sensible advice he had offered her. This was the way things should be. He would give advice and his flock should and would accept it. The parish of St Georges-in-the East would pay for it.

Admittedly he had become a little frustrated along the way that she should so overtly disagree with him. He had begun to fear that if his advice was ignored it might have a bad effect on how the rest of the congregation viewed him. These were subtle thoughts and perceptions in the depths of his subconscious which he was scarcely aware of himself. Although he would not admit it, even had he been aware of it, he was revelling in his success. Or as he would have perceived it, he was satisfied. This had been more to do with his pride in his calling and the triumph of common sense over the emotions of a humble parishioner. He knew he had done what was right.

So Pranas, or Frank, as he was sometimes known in English, had been taken into care by the Catholic nuns at St Charles' Home in Brentwood in Essex. Two of them called round late one morning soon afterwards and Elzbiéta entrusted him into their care amidst suppressed tears. She did make a supreme effort to compose herself as they were leaving, just for Frank's sake. She couldn't bear the thought of him going off unhappy. They just told him he was going out for the day. He seemed contented with that little white lie.

It was only meant to be a temporary measure. He was very young, between three and a half and four years old. The thought of him going, weighed together with the collective plight of her family sent pangs through Elzbiéta's heart.

But today she was happier. She was going to see little Frankie and going with her eldest son and daughter. Evie couldn't go because she was working at Scheiners the manufacturing seamsters in Whitechapel. She would soon be bringing something in. The company seemed happy with her progress and would now consider paying her a bit.

This time, Elzbiėta thought they would try the train. Someone had told her that there was a station at Brentwood. She hadn't been aware of this before, so on this September morning the three of them walked to Liverpool Street Station. She bought their tickets with the coins she had scraped together.

She wondered why the carriages had become so packed after they had secured their seats when they arrived early for the train and got on at Liverpool Street. The station was filthy with grime and soot. Smoke from the trains hovered high up in the station's iron and glass canopy. More and more people of all shapes and types had appeared. Each time someone got on, Elzbiėta and Joe had to move their legs sideways to let them through. They weren't moving from this end of the compartment though, because they wanted to see as much as possible on their journey even though the windows were cloudy. There was already a gentleman seated at the other end by the window anyway. The next nine of their travelling companions had managed to get seats whilst another three stood holding on to the parcel shelf because Elzbiėta had thoughtfully squeezed up with Julie to take up only one seat so that another adult could also sit down. Both windows in the carriage were half open, each heavy sliding window glass held by the punched thick leather strap with one of its holes fixed over a brass stud inside the carriage.

They conversed a bit amongst themselves keeping it quiet in their usual modest way. As soon as this strange tongue was heard though, albeit that it was almost whispered, it was followed by the usual stares and a few audible comments, but they heard them mutter softly "foreigners" and, "humph, we're standing while they sit." Elzbiėta was still trying to come to grips with England and the English after eighteen years, but Joe understood well enough. This was nothing compared to the name calling and mockery he had endured at school. In order to fit in he had made a conscious effort to become as much of a Cockney as anyone else, so bystanders were often surprised when the person who had been speaking in a foreign language responded with a few defensive comments or even expletives in some cases, responses they could readily understand. On this occasion though, being with Julie and Mother, he held his tongue.

The train clanked on at a slow pace twisting and turning out of the station and through the litter strewn area where the signal boxes were and from where men changed the points directing trains onto the appropriate tracks. High above on either side were dirty buildings, warehouses factories and offices. Forty years ago and even further back when they had first been built, their bricks had been yellow but now they had taken on the filthy patina of the age of open fires, steam and soot and were a dirty grey black colour. The acrid black smoke curled up relentlessly from forests of chimneys to right and left.

A faint buzz became obvious above their heads. somehow amidst this grimy background a bee had entered the carriage through the opposite window. Shrieks of consternation filled the air as people frantically waved their hands up and down in their clumsy attempts to keep it away from them. It flew towards the opposite exit and alighted for a moment on Julies forehead. "Just keep still Julie" said her mother, "It won't hurt you." A few seconds later the bee flew towards the open window whilst a man in a cap leaned over and aimed a blow at it with his rolled up newspaper. He missed but the bee disappeared from the carriage through the open window and to freedom. Elzbièta knew that even had the man not missed, it would have made no difference to anything. The solitary bee was just a tiny part of a bigger entity.

Eventually the unkempt and condensed city around the station disappeared and was replaced by a sort of drabness as they watched the backs of the shabby tenements speeding past, each with its own mean backyard. Every so often Elzbièta spotted one where the residents had tried to make things nicer by the addition of flowerpots filled with bright blooms. Strange how people all over were really the same. She compared them with her own back yard in Planet Street. The red and the pink geraniums bought in Watney Street market a few years ago which she had kept going by propagation each year. Her pot of Rue with the tiny yellow flowers reminded her of home. Yes, she still thought of Smalenai as home even after all this time. She hadn't been able to spot any Ruta on the way out of London.

Finally these prospects gave way to suburbs of a different nature. They could see fairly new terraces similar to their own in Stepney but somehow more open with gardens and small trees which had started to become established.

"This is what I always hoped for here," she mused. "To live somewhere like this." But the thought of leaving her friends and fellow countrymen in Stepney filled her with trepidation and even fear. She longed for an escape but yearned for security more.

When they reached Romford the train stopped in the station high on the bridge above the town and Elzbiëta could just see some of the streets below through the smoke and steam of the train. It must have been market-day in Romford, it looked busy. It was the closest she had ever been to an overall view of an English country town. The buildings seemed old, but not in the same way as the ones around the East End. These houses mixed with a few of more recent times conveyed to her a scene of real interest and a whiff of antiquity, as if taken from a picture in a history book. It was all centred around a cobbled open area she could just see in the distance. There were pens full of cattle. People thronged around them or stood in groups talking amidst the lines of stalls which she could see were selling all kinds of goods and produce. It must have been market day. She had viewed it from the bridge above through the steam and smoke of the train as it slowed and prepared to stop in the station. She saw a small network of back streets and alleys which seemed to lead to the centre like a sort of spider's web with the market place and the church as its focal point.

Awkwardly leaning tiled houses and shops lined the cobbled square with its wooden enclosures and fences set out.

She could see for herself that this market was not so very different from the one she remembered in Kalvaria or Punsk or the one in Seinei. These places were the same the world over. But where were the Jews? There seemed to be none there.

The difference she felt here however looking at a familiar scene was freedom. Underprivileged she may have been in her impoverished condition but no worse than she would have been back home, apart that is, from now being a widow. But despite all of that, here she felt a sense of what real freedom was. From her vantage point high up on the bridge she felt, as she used to at Žemyna, looking out across the countryside; for a moment, almost omnipotent.

Large numbers of people got off here when they drew to a halt amongst much squealing, hissing of steam, clouds of smoke and metallic banging. The final halting jolt was followed by the slamming of heavy carriage doors and then by the passage of many people crowding by on the platform. She and her children were sitting at the platform side of the compartment so they were able to watch the people as they walked past. A little face appeared at the window as a small child stood on tiptoe and looked into their carriage. All that was visible was her little nose and upper face and her eyes moving from side to side as she surveyed the small family huddled by the windows. A taller figure suddenly appeared as the little girl was whisked away in a hurry as suddenly as she had appeared. The child put her in mind of Evie when she was little and she felt a slight twinge of sadness at the thought of her slaving away in that factory sweat shop.

Elzbiëta and her children, Joe and Julie, now had more room. After a long delay whilst various goods were unloaded and some baskets and boxes loaded into the guard's wagon, and most of the people had left the platform, they heard the long blast of a whistle and the train slowly began to move again. The massive iron wheels turned, slipping slightly on the steel rails as the train painfully started to pick up speed. As it left the station they could see over the town again but this time from a different angle and Elzbiéta noticed the old ship-lapped inn on one of the corners leading into the market. She saw it and it called to mind the bad memories she had of the 'Star' on the corner of Morris Street. She had seen enough drunks coming out of there over the years and sometimes went to sleep to the sound of community singing and people being sick outside towards closing time. But many Lithuanians and Poles seemed to enjoy a drink and she supposed that at least they could forget their worries and troubles for a time in there, until the next morning. Her own family had kept well clear of the place since the incident with the half-sovereign which had been the bringer of so much trauma. Now here she was, a widow in a foreign land. It seemed a lifetime ago that Juozas' brothers, and indeed her own, had departed England for the United States and one of the Kadišius brothers to Brazil, but she had no wherewithal to follow them. Too much commitment here, graves, schools, friends, Frank in a home. Julie and Joey, not to mention Eva. She couldn't leave, but only try her best to raise her children in the correct manner despite all the drawbacks. One good thing however was the sub-letting of the house to her sister Juoza Daugirda and family.   This made things a lot easier for the time being as Peter, Juoza's husband intended to go and pave the way for his family in America and would send for his wife and their children when the time was right. Elzbiéta knew that by the time that happened she would be more settled, she would have the whole house back and something would have turned up.

The train continued on its way and the countryside seemed to her to become ever more exhilarating. There were farms, cows, sheep, woods and isolated groups of houses joined by small unmade roads beset on either side with tall hedges of elm, oak, hawthorn and ash.

Sometimes the country they passed through was wilder and more wooded. Julie noticed her mother looking longingly out of the window intent on seeing everything.

"Wouldn't it be lovely if we could come and live here one day Mama?" Julie mused. Unlike Julie, Joe never noticed the salty tears which had clouded his mother's eyes as she continued to gaze, with blurred vision at the passing countryside. Julie didn't miss much.

The telegraph poles alongside the track were fascinating Julie. She let her eyes rest on the wires and fixed her stare upon them as the train hurried along. The wires fell and rose, fell and rose as their length was periodically interrupted by a wooden pole.

There had only been a handful of people on the platform that day when they got off at Brentwood and Elzbiėta had asked Julie to find out where the home was. The child went to the stationmaster's office and asked in a perfectly refined English accent. The man looked up from his desk at this child whom he guessed to be about nine. The stationmaster was impressed with this posh little girl and respectfully took them all outside and up the stairs. Pointing up King's Road and with an Essex burr he said,

"Go up the hill yonder past Queen's road on the right as far as the crossroads and you'll see the High Street on your right. Carry straight on through the country towards South Weald and you will come to St Charles on your right, off the road up on a hill. It's about a mile and a half."

"Thank you very much," replied Julie."

"There is another way you can go if you are early and want a nice walk where you turn left at the crossroads which would take you to Honeypot lane then you could sweep round to the right to get there, but I think you would be better off to go the way I said."

Julie translated this for her mother and the stationmaster looked quizzical. Joe kept quiet as he knew that if he had spoken, Julie, young as she was, would have been annoyed at him spoiling the effect with his Cockney enunciation.

"I hope you don't mind me asking you this, but, you're not Belgian are you?"

"No we're Lithuanian explained Julie.

"Where's that?" the man asked.

"In the Baltic," the erudite Julie responded, with that slightly condescending facial expression she often adopted.

The man still looked blank as Julie thanked him and they began to walk away leaving the man scratching his head.

"Mamute, he thinks were Belgian she laughed."

They were all tittering and smiling as they walked off in the direction of the crossroads. They had been called many things in the past but never Belgian. Their semi-exclusive nationality gave them something to feel slightly unique about, together with a feeling of solidarity and a touch of superiority.

They walked up the unmade road, the three of them, Julie holding her mother's arm, until they reached the crossroads where on the left was a beautiful old shop with curved glass windows. There were a few carts and a trap and an open topped car coming up the hill from their left into the town and on through to the High Street, so they waited for these to pass then carried on past a line of newly built yellow brick terraced cottages with red brick detail, on the left. They continued down a winding lane with a few houses here and there, some obviously very old, and then magically, suddenly they were in the countryside. Elzbiėta was surprised that this quite busy town should be so close to such a contrast. There were no suburbs to speak of. One minute it was town, the next minute it was undulating farmland.

The dusty road they continued down was overhung with trees and bushes. Sometimes through the hedge they glimpsed rolling fields covered with stubble. She marvelled at the productivity of this land as she regarded it with an almost professional eye. She compared it to the unfolding Lithuanian scene in the 90s when she had absorbed the last views of her native land slowly passing by from the cart and more rapidly from the train taking her to Berlin and then Hamburg.

The feeling of sad nostalgia came over her again as she saw a rabbit and became aware of the cacophony of birdsong. But once again she resolved to try to look only forward to their future. As her mind wandered, she mused that this was surely a country where they could indeed all have some kind of a decent life to look forward to. They did need money though and she realised that to get it, her children would need education. She could see that future for them mapped out in their versatility and in their skills with language. What she could do to augment that was to bring them up with love and with the right set of values. Teaching them the pursuit of money for its own sake would not be her priority as a mother. She had already seen distant relatives in her youth, who had that unacceptable trait, and who were shunned and despised, sometimes envied by their less well off neighbours because of it.

"How much further is it Mama? I'm getting tired," Julie asked as the hint of a whine crept into her voice. She added, "You've been here before so you should know." in an accusatory tone.

"I can't be sure," replied her mother, "Just a bit further."

"Do you think they'll have anything to eat when we get there?" said Joe, "I'm starving."

As if by a miracle a few seconds later and a few yards further along the road, a pear fell from a tree just in front of them. They all stood looking down at the pear. Joe went to pick it up.

"Just a moment," said Julie, "Who does it belong to?"

They looked over the fence, but could see nothing, then up again at the tree above. There were many more there, ripe, waiting to fall.

"I think it's a wild pear tree" said Joe opportunistically.

"So it wouldn't be stealing if we ate it," said Julie.

"No it wouldn't. I'll climb up and shake down a few more then," replied the boy. Before they could stop him he had pulled himself up into the tree climbing to the upper branches where the fruit was ripest and started to shake one of them. Half a dozen more pears fell and Elzbiéta and her daughter picked them up.

"That's enough," shouted Julie. Joe pretended to get ready to jump from the high branch he was standing on, to the gasps of his mother and sister, but he was only joking and came down the same way as he had got up. They then sat down by the roadside shaded from the hot sun on the grassy bank amidst the wild flowers for a while as Joe produced his penknife and they proceeded to wipe the pears on a handkerchief before cutting them up and eating them. If ever there was a little bit of heaven on earth in England then Elzbiéta experienced it here in this rural idyll. Afterwards, they picked themselves up refreshed and continued on their way. Further on through a wooden gate set in a break in the hedge they could see a large, long imposing brick building on the crest of a mound.

"That must be it," shouted Julie excitedly, then she repeated the same thing in Lithuanian.

"Yes that's it," replied Elzbiéta. "We're on the other side of it. When I came before, the cart came to it from over that way."

They could see a small road going up to the home which seemed to start towards the building much further along the road they were walking. Elzbiéta decided they would take the short cut through the field nearest to them in which some cows were grazing. They passed through a gate and closed it behind them but her mother could see that Julie was timidly afraid of the cattle. To her they looked so big. So she went back with Julie the long way around while Joe headed straight across the field. Joe had never seen cows this close before in their natural environment, but being game for anything he wasn't afraid of them. These cattle had previously been content to graze, searching about with heads held low sweeping from side to side for the next succulent tussock. They had been moving slowly forward across the field intent upon their vital occupation but most of them had now paused with heads raised, regarding him curiously. Some looked over their shoulders at him. Joe was fascinated by them, by their bulk and angular frames. He had sometimes seen them being driven to Smithfield along Commercial Road but this scene was more relaxed. The sight of theses beasts and his thoughts about their one-way journey made him feel desperately sorry for them. Compassion was an innate part of Joe's soul. He was a complicated, but kind and thoughtful sixteen year old. It struck him how unfair it was to inflict this treatment upon them. His spiritual beliefs went back to before he could remember. Even so, he couldn't always make sense of some of the things that he had been told were true. He paused and then stood motionless for a while and some of the cows, no longer curious or afraid of him, resumed their foraging. Joe went into a sort of reverie of imagination. Was it right that cows and even human beings should be influenced without question by people and events outside their control? Joe stood there reflecting on the unfairness of life and his mind wandered on to ethereal things. A pang went through his heart as the memory of his father came to him without warning. Losing him and then being suddenly thrust into the real world of responsibility left many unanswered questions. It wasn't fair. Life wasn't fair. Neither was the world. Joe stood in that field and dwelled upon his first job at the solicitor's practice which had ended in tears after three months when he was wrongly accused of stealing stamps. Ever since his humiliating departure from that office, he had wondered what it really was which had led to his dismissal on a trumped-up charge. But then, he supposed, they *had* taken him on. But there again, his interviewer was not the same person as his day to day colleagues. They could have seen him as different or as a tearaway with a mind of his own. This may have unsettled their routine. And it was true he did have values unique to him. Maybe he just didn't fit in. He had always known that life was full of perversity. And so it was for these cattle, he thought. There was no need for any trumped up charges in their case. People could just do as they liked with them because they appeared to accept their lives unquestioningly. As long as they could eat and drink and gaze with their beautiful dark brown eyes they seemed to be content.

Chapter 26

St Charles, Brentwood

They all met up again outside the steps leading to the front doors. Elzbiėta and Julie looked at Joe with the mud on his shoes where he had stepped into a ditch, and at the bottoms of his trousers covered in dust with pieces of grass caught in the turn-ups. "How did he manage to always look so scruffy?" wondered Julie as she cast her eyes up to heaven. All the while his mother just looked kindly, stooping and brushing him down a bit.

"Where have you been?" Julie asked him, her eyes looking at her mother whilst her head was inclined towards Joe. He retorted,

"I have been thinking that you're getting on my nerves!"

They were met by a young red haired priest who came down the wooden staircase and introduced himself as Father Drea in a soft

Southern Irish accent. He was clearly expecting them, as Elzbiéta had written a week previously to say she was coming, to which he, as the new secretary there, had responded by return of post. He now conducted them up the stairs and into a large hall where they sat down while he hurried away. As they waited, in the distance they could hear a boys choir singing to the accompaniment of a piano. Father Drea returned presently with little Frank looking a bit apprehensive, who was so excited as soon as he saw his mother, that he came running at breakneck speed clattering in the new hob-nailed boots he had been given. About half way across the hall the boots lost their purchase on the shiny floor and he finished up sliding towards them on the seat of his shorts. They picked him up as he started crying. The emotional shock of seeing his loved ones and of falling over was too much for him. His sobbing went on rather longer than Elzbiéta would have expected. She wasn't happy about it.

"Is it alright to take him out for a walk with us?"

Elzbiéta had framed these words as a question but she meant it more as a statement. Joey translated it to the priest before Julie could get in, as, "We would like to go for a walk." Julie, even though she was only nine years old gave Joe a sharp look. But from that moment on it was to Joe that the priest looked when he wanted to communicate with Elzbiéta.

The priest was clearly undecided about this change of procedure. He knew what the régime here was like and he was sympathetic, but by the time he thought about it, the moment had gone and the little family had reached the stairs and were heading down.

"I ought to say this is irregular," he said as he caught them up. "Usually you have to stay in the visiting room, but he must be back in time for Benediction."

Father Drea was a kindly young man of about twenty five years of age who had been here for approaching three months. Some of the procedures here he wasn't altogether happy about, thinking them too severe. He also thought that one or two of the sisters were very dictatorial and noticed that other sisters and members of staff seemed to defer to them. It appeared to him that there was something going on. But he couldn't quite put his finger on it. He detected a sort of sub-culture here, a climate of authority similar to that he had observed amongst the staff and inmates of a gaol, when he had briefly been a prison chaplain, where there existed a sort of hierarchy amongst them independent of those at the very top of the staff structure.

"Good Heavens," he thought, "They even have supervised visiting times, just like prison with a warder always present! God forbid that one of these kids should attempt to escape."

This underlying unease led him to agree to give Mrs Kurtinaitis some leeway. Why shouldn't she enjoy time with her children?

As he watched them going out of the main door, Father Galvin appeared suddenly at his side and asked him what was going on. Galvin seemed to be one of those whose word was law.

Father Drea told him that they were just going for a little walk as it was such a beautiful day.

"Discipline and obedience! that is the credo we live by here I must remind you Father. Get them back."

"It can't do any harm surely?" He replied, making no move to obey.

Galvin looked a bit hot under the collar. He certainly didn't like being told anything or crossed, particularly by somebody he considered to be a subordinate

"No! We decide what's best for these boys as we see fit."

Then he added as an afterthought,

"For their benefit, of course. This is not a holiday home but a Catholic children's home involving ... er... guidance and education. for boys. Who knows what the child will be telling them?"

"What do you mean Father?"

Galvin rather ignored the question and launched into a short sermon to the younger man.

"You have surely seen in your *short* time here haven't you? that the sisters must run this place in their own way for the good of the residents and for the good of the Church and the Faith. We as two of the priests assigned to St Charles' must support them. If we have people coming and going willy-nilly and discussions going on, all order will be lost. This home which has such a good reputation would become chaotic. These boys need discipline, and order. Why would he not be happy here? I doubt he's been chastised yet. He seems a good boy."

"Chastised? what do you mean, 'Yet?' Do you mean told off. Or are you referring to another punishment?"

As he was speaking Father Drea recalled hearing one of the boys talking in the corridor about the cartwheel which someone had been tied to and beaten by a local farmer brought in specifically for the purpose. He hadn't taken it in at the time, and not given it any credence as he already had his hands full with other pressing matters of administration and he had put it to the back of his mind. But now he remembered it with alarming clarity.

"Oh, never mind just now," replied Father Galvin hastily, "Give them ten minutes then get them back."

Drea realised by the other priest's demeanour that there was something more about this régime which, against his will, he knew he should force himself to find out. But now, with misgivings about the running of the whole establishment confirmed in his mind, he knew that sooner or later he would have to bite the bullet and confront it. He knew he was on a difficult wicket. He was one small cog with the massed ranks of mighty Church authority machine ranged against him. He might have to place himself in a position where he was immune from the persecution he knew would follow if he pursued this course. Going down this path, his continued position, and indeed his future Church career, would be untenable. But he had to be true to himself, it had to be done.

Their discussion had taken place at the foot of the stairs and, as it was now at an end they went their separate ways.

Drea went upstairs and sat in the bay in the front window

looking out for the family's return whilst Galvin went through to the classrooms at the rear. Father Drea was certain however that he had incurred the other priest's displeasure. It was a portent of things to come. He knew that only too well. He continued to read his book, but the words did not sink in as he periodically glanced out of the window wondering why they were so strict here.

Downstairs, Joe emerged from the corridor leading from the washroom he had been in urgent need of. He had paused for a considerable time before coming out into the lobby. Typical Joey, he had eavesdropped on every word.

He followed his family down the steps where they were waiting at the foot. "Mama, I just heard them talking and I get the feeling that it is very strict here. But Frankie hasn't done anything wrong – has he? How could he? So why is he here?"

"Of course he hasn't he's only four years old."

Joey went on, "They were talking about punishment here. Father Drea seems to be quite a nice man but the other one is a lot harder."

Her previous doubts now came flooding back into her mind with a sense of alarm. Normally she was reasonable, compliant, submissive even – sometimes, but this was the one issue over which her maternal instincts took priority. There was really no contest and a resolute determination took shape in her mind.

Softening her voice somewhat insofar as she could, she stooped down so that her eyes were on a level with Frankie's and asked him gently if he liked it there. The poor child at first didn't reply then reluctantly, in a tremulous Lithuanian, he responded in the negative.

"Why don't you like it here?" "Is it cold, are you hungry, is your bed warm and comfortable?"

"Yes Mama, but sometimes the sisters smack children with a ruler, but I'm only hungry sometimes"

She had questioned him on her previous visit but the answers this time were slightly different to those he had given then when he had only been there for a week. But this time she wasn't at all happy with his answers and became certain that she should have been more thorough. But then she had been incapable of being more searching, she hadn't been herself, as life was overwhelming her at that time.

It had obviously been a traumatic departure, for a child so small, to be away from his mother but now there was a misery about him which her previous visit had failed to reveal. What was that faraway look in his tear-filled eyes? Was it despair she detected in him, was it rejection? Elżbieta didn't quite know, She had assumed on her first visit that he would settle in. Her own desperate condition and nervous problems at that time had prevented her from making a proper judgement, but this visit had made her sure. Now she thought about it. The badgering from the priest at home. Her own instincts then. She began to wonder why these visits had to be under supervision

Being wintertime during her last trip here, she had not remotely considered taking him for a walk outside so she now realised that her conversations with him had been monitored and she recalled feeling stilted and over-respectful by another presence in the room even though it was one of the sisters who was supposedly not showing much interest and mother and son were conversing in Lithuanian. Frankie must have been the same. She couldn't be herself with her child with that nun there, and Pranas had kept glancing nervously and a little fearfully at the attendant black robed figure, the Sister of Mercy of St Vincent De Paul.

It all came back to her as her stomach churned and she blamed herself for agreeing to this in the first place. But now they were outside,

"No Mama, I don't like it." he wailed in a childish voice.

"I want to go home."

As some ideas occasionally come from nowhere and mushroom, becoming stronger and stronger, so this was such a resolution which rapidly formed in her mind. She would take him home here and now! No going through channels. No asking and no waiting. He was coming back to Stepney with them right now!

She shepherded them all back up the steps and they stepped once again into the lobby at the foot of the stairs. "What about our walk, Mama?" enquired Joe, "We didn't go very far!"

Father Drea had only just settled down to his book again having barely found his place in it, when he happened to glance out of the window and his thoughts were interrupted by the sight of the four of them returning up the steps. Putting his book down, he clattered down the stairs again to meet them.

"That was a short walk."

She smiled at him and turned to Joe, saying in Lithuanian,

"Listen! Joey we are taking him home, what do you think?"

"Yes, I think we should."

She repeated it, this time in broken English.

Father Drea nodded understandingly.

It was as simple as that. The decision was made, no one and nothing would now dissuade her.

Father Galvin, hearing the steps on the staircase and the voices again, now reappeared with two nuns behind him.

Looking past the officials the small family could see six boys walking past carrying huge loads of washing. They looked very regimented, and none too happy, bowed as they were under their burdens.

Father Galvin and Father Drea and the sisters listened to all this discussion, most of it in a foreign language, not understanding much but sensing the consternation. Elzbièta was trying her best to be diplomatic but somehow it was being lost in the translation.

"Joey, tell him, we miss little Frank and he misses us and we would like to take him home again – and ask the Father to bring down his things – no, actually he didn't have anything but for those few tattered clothes he came here wearing,"

Joe did as he was bid, except that he just said to the priests, "We would like, ... we are going to, take him home!"

Joe enjoyed defying authority provided he thought he was in a good position or that he had support. He had already sensed that father Drea was on their side.

"Are you sure about this? What are your reasons, why do you have doubts? "What did your child say to you?" said Galvin.

The other priest just looked concerned and thoughtful. Father Drea could see exactly where this mother was coming from and he realised that she had more courage than he did. Joe translated Galvin's questions to his mother.

Elzbièta responded, "He said nothing. He is too young to decide for himself but something is not right, he is much too young. I should never have let him go! Whatever was I thinking of?"

An older nun who had been hovering in the background looking in a cupboard appeared in the circle and introduced herself as Mother Emmanuel. She had heard Joe's statement and it had made her angry and extremely concerned that their authority was being undermined.

"You just can't do this Mrs Kurtinaitis. You will have to go home and speak to your priest." She said addressing herself straight over Joe's head to Elzbièta.

"I am sure he will give you all the reassurances you need." Her remarks were wasted on Elzbièta.

Elzbièta, not understanding turning to Joe asked Joe what she had just said – "Kąs ji sako?"

Joey, irritated, mistranslated what the sister had said as, "She's not very happy but there is not much she can do about it."

Julie looked aghast but Joe gave her a sharp look.

Elzbièta couldn't explain what was on her mind in English so she said to Joe in Lithuanian;

"Tell them this Joey, thank them for agreeing to release him, but he is my son, I sent him here voluntarily and now I have changed my mind. He's not happy here, I can sense it, and he is coming home. He will be better with us. Thank them for looking after him but I don't want to get into a protracted conversation about this."

Having heard the private exchange of the two priests earlier Joe had got the picture of the régime which was in place here but wanted to spare his mother any further upset. His one aim, like his mother, but armed with a greater understanding of the situation, was to get Frankie away from here. Joey translated it to the assemblage of officials as,

"We are going, we are all going together including Frankie and there really isn't anything more to be said on the matter."

Joe could sometimes look quite mean and on this occasion he had started to lose his temper and his face was flushed. This had solved many problems in the past as people who were trying to get their own way with him were left in no doubt that they had pushed him to the brink, so they were slightly taken aback. He was also a strong wiry character exuding an air of Head-of-the-Family and chief translator. They sensed all this so didn't argue much, particularly as they knew they were on slippery ground anyway, legally. They walked towards the outside doors. Mother Emmanuel, ungracious in defeat said with less than perfect charity,

"What about the clothes he's wearing. All he had were worn out, we gave him those, they are expensive and they could do a child?"

"We could send them on once we get home," said Joe

Joey translated into Lithuanian for his mother,

"They said he didn't have anything when he came here. But Mama it doesn't matter. I think we can keep the clothes he was given. I think they would wish us a safe journey home!"

Elzbiéta realised by the expressions around them that she has missed something here. Nevertheless it was the sort of thing she wanted to hear, so gathering Frankie up in her arms she led the way and the family trooped off down the steps and back the way they had come along the lengthy path towards the road. On the train home Julie asked Joe why he had told lies at St Charles. Joe screwed up his face in irritation and replied, "Keep quiet Julie, you're getting on my nerves."

A few months later Joey happened to be reading a copy of the 'Universe' when he noticed a small article on page twelve, just a couple of lines under a small headline at the bottom of a column;

ST CHARLES SCHOOL, BRENTWOOD.
Father Drea will be leaving his
post as secretary of the above
school. A new secretary has
been appointed

Joey later discovered from Mary Newbury opposite, who did evening work at the church, that while she had been cleaning the corridor outside the vestry she had overheard Father Odrobina talking to Father Matulaitis about Father Drea. He had said that the Bishop had wanted to transfer Father Drea to another parish but that Drea not only refused to go but had made a point of principle out of it, threatening to make such a fuss that a compromise had been reached. The Bishop had been forced to agree to an enquiry into the systems in place at the school in Brentwood and had undertaken to look at ways to improve it. One of the clerics had been replaced and sent to another parish. St Charles was getting a new Mother Superior. Father Drea had evidently resigned the priesthood and had now gone who knows where?

As life resumed once again for Elzbiéta and her children, she noticed that Father Matulaitis was always a little awkward with her, if not slightly distant. He rather held Elzbiéta responsible for all this. Not being able to understand how a woman could be so devout and yet not submit to the will of the clergy he couldn't quite come to terms with it. So he put it all down to God's greater plan which he assumed included his own intervention, which must have been for a purpose. That Father Drea's role might also have been a part of this, and for the better, never really entered his mind. He was unable to calculate into the equation a mother's overpowering maternal instinct having never experienced anything like it himself. He loved his flock, his family, mother and father but it wasn't the same. He rather regarded her action as wilful disobedience of the Catholic Church's authority – and not part of God's plan at all.

Chapter 27

Enlistment – 1915

Joe Kurtin had been in the first wave of enthusiastic young men to volunteer for the army in 1914. It was all rather a lark and it was said it would be over by Christmas. When he got to the head of the queue he was turned down. He wasn't old enough to have fun or to see the world just yet, nor even to die.

He came away from the recruiting office disappointed in which state he reflected on his own circumstances.

Since his father had passed away three years earlier, quite a bit had happened, most of it bad. For an intelligent boy he might have been considered as wayward, involved in escapades and gambling. He did sometimes tread a fine line between authority and his own personal set of morals and he picked and chose which rules he would obey and why. That wasn't quite as bad as it sounded, – he was just a bit rebellious – mainly because of his age and the lack of a father.

When he was still only ten he had passed the scholarship to gain a place at Saint Ignatius College a Catholic grammar school for boys in North London, run by Jesuits. There he had once again walked the tightrope between obedience to the Jesuits who ran it strictly, and defiance in going his own way. This frequently led to corporal punishment administered for even the slightest infringement of the school rules by the violent application of a steel and leather ferrula.

The death of his father, followed by the difficult circumstances which had befallen the family, forced him to leave that school which he had been attending since 1907. Having then got a job at the Solicitors' practice in Mile End Road, what had seemed to be the start of a promising career had been abruptly terminated after the alleged pilfering had been discovered. After that he worked as a labourer and delivery boy here and there. The money he earned helped out slightly with the housekeeping at home, but the family still struggled to keep its head above water.

Elzbiëta, nominally now the head of the household, was still burning herself out sewing Mr Levene's customers' suits.

To her, even though it seemed like half a lifetime ago, the schooling in needlework she had received from her mother when she was a child back home, came into its own now. The tailor, was grateful for her fine work but not grateful enough to demonstrate his appreciation in practical terms, and he still only paid her a pittance.

Young Frank now back from St Charles, was another mouth to feed, Julie was still at Johnson Street school and Evie was progressing at Scheiners as a machinist. She hadn't earned anything while she was learning, but now Mrs Levy the forelady, had decided she could make a profitable contribution and she was being paid a very small wage.

Joe did step up to the plate insofar as he was capable but for him tragedy, disappointment and responsibility in life had started early. The first two he could handle relatively well but the latter was difficult to cope with for one so young. The consolation for him was his faith and his ability with languages. Already speaking Polish and

Lithuanian at home as a small child, he had picked up English as he went along, while he played and integrated with other children.

Whilst he had been at St Ignatius he had taken French and German at which he was always top of the class. This was no mean achievement in such a respected establishment. He was helped in the German language by the family of his friend Jonny Miesner whose parents ran a small German Delicatessen in a side street on the other side of Commercial Road. It was welcome entertainment for Jonny's parents helping this English boy. They originated from Hamburg and had been in London for twenty five years and had become British citizens. Their four children had been born here in their adoptive country.

Joe's quickly absorbed skills in those languages had led to him being singled out at school to help younger pupils. Already speaking three languages made the introduction of two more easier for him. He absorbed them rapidly. In German, with the help of the Miesners he could hold a serious conversation. All this ended when he had to leave school in order to try to earn some money.

Both his sisters' opinions carried great weight with his mother and his future was decided there and then by them, even though all his siblings were younger than he. There were now two girls, a woman with little English, a baby and the advice of priests to contend with. So Joe's future and that of his descendants were mapped out for them all there and then in March 1912 with the death of his father. All future education for him would be gained only by life's experiences.

It was in March 1915 nearly eight months after the outbreak of war that his friend Jonny's family had been driven away.

The Kurtinaitis family were sitting upstairs in their main room at 59, Planet Street one evening when they heard the street door being opened and slammed and someone clattered up the bare wooden stairs. Evie burst in upon them out of breath.

"I've just come past the Miesners'. There's a mob outside, a rabble of women and men throwing stones and bricks. They've smashed the windows and kicked in the door. They seem to be looting the shop. I only just managed to squeeze through."

"Oh those poor people," cried Elzbiėta, her face fixed in a concerned frown. "Are they alright?"

They were all speaking at once, and there were gasps of dismay. To an English ear it would have all been an unintelligible babble of Lithuanian, but the lamenting tone of concern was obvious. Evie went on, "There was no sign of them! but people were hurrying away carrying groceries. I saw people stealing black bread and sausage and coffee, cheese and butter. There was a burst sack of flour trodden all over the street by many feet!"

"Why are they being picked on? They're not really German," said Julia. "they're just like us!"

"I'll go round there and see," Joe worriedly muttered.

"Be careful Joe, don't get involved, remember they can't tell one foreigner from another over there. Just remember Mama isn't an English citizen. Don't provoke anything"

Joe walked as fast as he could down to Commercial Road. He made his hurried way in the direction of Aldgate, passing hoardings and walls plastered with posters urging young men to join the fight against the Hun, until he came to Jonny's street on the other side. Walking down to the Miesners' shop he could see the police were there but it seemed that things were dying down. The shop was open to the elements and the pavement was strewn with glass, paper, broken crockery and other debris. Even the upstairs windows were smashed. There were scruffily clad individuals running in and out, looting. Some chairs had been turfed out into the street and were lying smashed at the side of the road. Joe spoke to a policeman, a middle-aged uniformed individual with a

walrus moustache, whom he recognised from church. Joe approached him and asked him where the family was who lived there.

"Why, are you friends of theirs?"

"Yes I am, I know the son, he's my mate, we used to be at school together at Johnson Street."

Joe knew this man, a sergeant, who when he was out of uniform was a member of the choir at St Mary and St Michael's. Clearly the recognition wasn't immediately mutual. The man took off his helmet to reveal a bald head glistening with sweat. He wiped it away with a handkerchief which he then replaced in his pocket. He put his helmet back on before he deigned to answer the young man's question.

"I'd forget about him if I was you sonny".

Joe was thoroughly narked by the policeman's offhand manner and the way in which he had addressed him.

Joe then assumed an accusatory tone replying. "Why?" in a long drawn out single word question with an insolent inference which wasn't lost on the copper. The policeman looked at Joe and his face went through various visible emotions as he worked himself up.

"You cheeky little so-and-so. Don't use that tone with me. Watch yerself – whippersnapper. Any more insolence from you sonny and I'll run yer in fer obstructing a Policeman in the hexecution of 'is duty."

Joe wanted to hear the full story and he realised that confrontation wasn't the best way of going about it. "I'm sorry about that," Joe said through gritted teeth. "I'm just worried about them that's all."

"Well, all right then. They've gorn away," the officer reluctantly continued, "They got pelted with their own rolls and jeered at as they left. We did what we could but the mood of the crowd was ugly! We did try but there were too many. I got thrown to the ground and my helmet was knocked off. I'm waiting now for re-inforcements. It's too late now, they've dispersed mostly." He went on to add in a plaintive tone, "We couldn't do nuffing. They was really worked up about the Lusitania. Once we stopped 'em pushing the Miesners around, – well we 'ad to really, – and they let them be, we got 'em through the crahd. Then they stopped shouting about the bloody Lusitania and just concentrated on nicking all they could. Me partner did take one cove away back to the station leavin' me on me own."

Joe left the company of the policeman with the remark, "Maybe I'll see you on Sunday morning." The sergeant scratched the nape of his neck as he began to place where he had seen Joe before.

Crossing the road Joe approached the opposite pavement to where a woman was looking out of an open ground floor window. She was dressed typically in the working class way with her blouse sleeves rolled up, wearing a grubby pinafore. Most of her hair was concealed by a turban knotted at the front and on top. She was obviously quite young judging by the strands of fair hair Joe could see protruding from the edges of the turban but somehow her face looked older, lined, more careworn. Joe noticed her doorstep brilliantly, gleaming white in places but its pristine quality was now marred by some scuffed black smudges where the crowd had overrun it. There was white powder all over the road too and some of it had been blown and stamped up and down the street. The whole scene was a mess. In a way Joe was glad he hadn't been here earlier. There would clearly have been some decisions to be made which would probably have got him fully involved.

"What happened to the Miesners? Did they get any protection?" he asked the woman.

"The police *was* 'ere as the crahd was gaverin' before the shop was smashed up, but they just stood at the back an' did nuffing. They've gorn, the Miesners. Took to their 'eels wiv a few bundles. Lucky to get past the crahd, but the coppers 'elped 'em get frough, there was only free of 'em. That's the last we'll be seein' of them bloody Germans. I fink they must've went to the country somewhere. I 'ave 'eard 'er

---

talking before abaht 'avin some family aahtside London!"

"Did you buy bread in there ?" asked Joe.

"Yeah, I used to, but not no more. Specially after them 'Uns marched into Belgium, the so-and-sos. I stopped goin' in there. I 'ave to go rahnd the corner for it nah to the Yiddisher place."

Joe gave up in despair and went to walk home taking with him the sorry tale of how the police had given the unfortunate Miesners very little protection. He passed the sergeant again who said, "I've just placed yer. You're foreign yerself ain't yer? I've seen yer wiv yer muvver. Yer from Planet Street ain't yer?"

"Yes, I'm from there, but no, my mum's Lithuanian not German, for Heaven's sake don't get them mixed up. The Lithuanians round here are on Britain's side. That's going to be dangerous lumping all foreigners together. People round here can't always tell the difference. Someone once thought I was Belgian!"

"So you'll be thinking about joining up very soon will yer?" the sergeant came back with, his eyes narrowing.

"Yep, I'm joining up next week. But when are you lot going to start doing something about protecting the innocent better? The Miesners are all British, every one of them. They have been for years."

"Maybe they should change their names then," retorted the sergeant. "So what's your name son?"

"Joseph Michael Kurtinaitis," replied Joe.

"Mm, could be German. 'Ave you fought abaht changing it so's it sounds more English?"

"Good point, but maybe the Royal Family ought to change theirs also. Saxe-Coburg-Gotha's a place in Germany. Doesn't sound very English does it? but I don't see anyone attacking them in the streets."

"I'll fank you to 'ave a little more respect for 'Is Majesty, if yer don't mind Mr bloomin' Kuskinitos."

There was nothing Joe could do and he wasn't wasting any more time on this ignoramus. He returned along Commercial Road. When he got back he reported what had been said while his mother made them all a cup of tea. As an additional thought occurred to him he advised them all to keep their conversations to a minimum when they were out together and to try and speak in English. He was beginning to realise that if you couldn't rely on the guardians of the law to demonstrate a bit of intelligence then the mob could hardly be expected to. They would all be better to keep a low profile.

"Why don't we just shorten our name to Kurtin?" Eva suggested.

Two weeks after this, and with the events of the wrecked delicatessen still fresh in his memory, several months after his first unsuccessful attempt to join up, Joe found himself at just barely eighteen years old walking with his friend Anthony Baukis down to Commercial Road. They went across and through the back streets to Mile End Road where they traversed the cobbles and tram lines to the opposite pavement and queued up at the bus stop. The line of hopeful travellers also waiting there facing in the direction from which the bus was coming. That way they could give themselves hope, and read from a distance the number of the vehicle approaching and its destination from the board above.

They could have caught either a bus or a tram. The first to come along was a number 63 tram heading east. It was a huge rounded thing with 8 wheels set in two separate bogie clusters securely nestled in the tramlines. The windows however were of flat sheeted glass with the driver's compartment separated from the rest of it.

The tram became full up before Joe and Tony reached half way along the queue. If there was one civilised thing the British public adhered to it was the principle of queueing.

The next vehicle to appear was an open topped bus with its spiral staircase curling round the outside

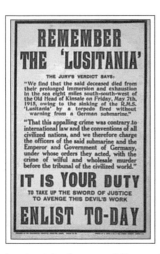

to the upper deck. It was a number 25 plying between Aldgate and Romford.

Joe had once passed through Romford the market town outside London. He had seen it from a distance briefly on his train trip to Brentwood, to visit young Frank. Today they would not be going that far on the bus. Aldgate and the East-end he knew like the back of his hand. Stratford was only a penny bus ride away. As they waited for passengers to get off, the driver was level with them and Joe and Anthony chatted away to him telling him in slightly raised voices over the clatter of the motor, and looking all round as they shuffled along, that they were going to Stratford to join up to do their bit.

"Well done lads" he shouted with a wink, "You'll have all the girls fighting over you once you're in uniform. I was in South Africa during the last one, they were great days and I got to see the world a bit. You had better make the most of it! It'll all be over by next Christmas." Joe idly noted that they had said that last year. But for a fleeting moment they and the bus driver were comrades.

Just then a number 61 tram pulled up behind and the people in the queue in front of them surged forward abandoning the bus in favour of it, as it seemed there were more seats available there than on this bus. These were split second decisions people had to make. In these circumstances the hierarchy of the queue was abandoned and if you could overtake someone else in the sprint which followed, that was all well and good, because for the runners, the old queue no longer existed and the new one had not yet been formed.

Joe and Anthony stayed on in the existing, and by now depleted, line and entered the bus and had to stand inside as all the seats downstairs and upstairs were taken, but as soon as they heard two people clatter down the stairs and alight at the next stop they moved back down towards the rear of the bus and up the staircase. There were two seats available in the aisle and Joe sat down on the slatted wooden seat on the left hand side. Anthony was two seats in front on the right. At the next stop Joe's unknown travelling companion got up to get off and Anthony was able to join Joe on the same seat so that they could now look out for girls walking on the pavement. Because the bus was so full, and as they were so well brought up, they wouldn't be shouting down to any they saw on the way. Their youthful optimism and a joking demeanour would have to be held in abeyance this time. Maybe the bus would be emptier on the way back.

Both boys had been brought up on stories of the Boer War and tales of derring-do from the heyday of the British Empire. They had been drilled in it throughout childhood. They had learned to read with sentences such as: "A' is for Africa coloured in red. 'E' is for Empire on which the sun never sets,' etcetera. They knew that Britain was superior to any other land. They were British. This was their country of which they were intensely proud.

They never realised it at the time but they were sleepwalking into a new future with a certain lack of imagination and limited forward thinking. For the two of them it wouldn't be much of a future.

Their parents were more realistic. They had left their homeland to escape the constant oppression, the relentless day-to-day drudgery of farm life and the heavy restrictions on their personal freedoms which went with it. Now they were being included in something they would never have chosen to be involved with, had they had a choice.

Germany they were ambivalent about. They always preferred that country to Russia. It was more progressive, they had obtained all their surreptitiously printed books and periodicals from there, from East Prussia as it was, in the old days. They had travelled through it and departed for a new life from its ports on its shipping lines. It had been their gateway to the future, to a better life, or so they had believed. Now they were just the older generation hampered in London by their limited linguistic ability in English, relying on their own children to translate for them, scraping a living doing opportunistic work for other people who were making good.

In the case of Joe's mother without her husband, the translation and the letter writing which the children took on had progressed into actual decision making. So Joe, Eva and Julie, possessing the full ability to communicate with everyone from school teachers to council officials, held the power in the household, or to be more precise Elzbiéta wasn't able to exercise it. In addition Julie was seen to be so competent that she was asked by all and sundry to write letters for them. English people also sought her services. She was literate even by their standards. Typical of this family, they never asked for recompense for the favours they did people. They did these things willingly, even naively, for nothing and were happy to do so.

As it became clear that Joe wasn't interested himself in taking much of the share of responsibility, Eva and Julie took it all on. Their mother just took the soft option for an easier life. In 1914 by now aged 40 she had been a widow for two years. She had tried hard to master English. She spoke what she had learned in a charming soft pidgin way. But for most of the time she spoke her native languages. Around the house she spoke to her children in Lithuanian or Polish and more often than not they responded in Lithuanian, but more and more, in their own native language – English.

These children of Lithuanian parentage even though they were born in London were unable to speak English when they first went to school. It had presented the nuns established here two generations ago, with a huge problem but one which they managed to overcome given their total dedication to their profession. To them these were difficulties posed by the Almighty which were simply put there for them as a test or a challenge which they rose to admirably.

At the turn of the century the whole Catholic infrastructure around Whitechapel was highly efficient, supported by a convent full of nuns, mostly Irish, drawn from a previous influx of immigrants from beyond the sea. It was based around a local church, part of a larger diocese. This was of massive support for these people from this Baltic Sea state who were Catholics themselves. In a similar way the Jews had their own network of worship, support and various charities.

It was to help ease them into British society within a couple of generations. There were few recriminations amongst this community consisting of so many different elements. With minor exceptions, each recognised the right of the others to live, trade, communicate and worship in their own way according to their own customs. English, Polish, Lithuanian, Jewish, Irish and Italians in that small enclave lived together accepting each other for what they were.

On the whole it was a veritable crucible of tolerance. The people themselves just took it as read. Something which marred this to a slight extent was the obduracy of the Diocese of Westminster which clashed with the resolve of the Lithuanians to have their own church.

In their ignorance of geography and national pride the English diocesan hierarchy had believed it was enough for the Lithuanian community to attend the Polish church. They were very wrong. After months of lobbying to no avail, things came to a head when the Lithuanian congregation put its foot down and went to church armed with sticks in order to assert their right to have Mass said in Lithuanian. So at last they were taken seriously and land was found and eventually a church for them was built in 1912 at the Oval, off Hackney Road. It was just in time for Juozas' funeral Mass.

Elzbiéta's husband when he died was the first person to have his funeral service held at the church of St Casimir. It was quite fitting as he had played a major part in raising the money for its construction

 against a background of his own deteriorating health. Lithuanian men had a tendency to die young in this city. Whether this was caused by the shock of coming from an unsullied environment into the concentrated smoke and fog of the London metropolis could only be speculated upon. But Juozas was no exception and he too succumbed to the almost inevitable acute Bronchitis which led to Aphasia, and death followed. Short of moving to the pure air of the countryside, where there was no work, there wasn't much else they could have done.

Who could have known it? but the young Lithuanian priest Father Mantvila, who conducted the funeral mass, was himself to perish crossing the Atlantic on the Titanic a week or two later, kneeling on the after-deck of the ill-fated leviathan together with Father Byles leading the doomed souls of all denominations in prayer.

When this terrible news was announced at church on Sunday the people were shocked. There was a murmur, and a flurry of movement rippled through the nave as people made the sign of the cross.

The other event which changed and ruined everything was the outbreak of war, as people became more suspicious and looked for the enemy within, their fears stirred by newspapers and propaganda.

Even Lithuanians were looking over their shoulders. Their own particular age of innocence was well and truly over.

Once Joe and Anthony got off the bus at Stratford they had asked the way to the local recruiting office and were directed towards a large municipal building bedecked with flags and bunting, with posters on stands on the pavements and arrows pointing along the road. Turning a corner they came upon a press of young men blocking the way stretching back towards them. At that moment there was a small surge and the men at the back straggled forwards about ten yards and then stopped again. They realised they were in a group who had evidently arrived there with the intention of joining up, like themselves. Men were wending their way in their direction having clearly succeeded in being inducted into this élite fighting force. You could just tell by the smug expressions on their faces and their excited chatter that they  felt they were doing their bit. All except one. This particular man was walking disconsolately in the gutter towards them muttering "Dash it! Dash it!, Blast!"

"What's up mate?" said Anthony as the man drew near.

"I'm too old they told me. I wouldn't mind but I lined up here for two hours. They are quite choosy. They rejected a few schoolboys telling them to come back next year. At least they will qualify then maybe, but I never will!"

"So what do you do for a living.?" Joe asked the distraught man.

"I run a pie 'n mash shop in Green Street."

"Well I wouldn't worry then, that's an essential service. That's probably why they would prefer you to stay at home. People will still need to eat round here." chipped in Anthony. Joe smiled to himself as the man gave Anthony a sidelong glance as if deciding whether he ought to take umbrage or not but must have concluded that Anthony was serious. It made him feel slightly better about it as he walked on mumbling, "Yeah that's right! I can still do me bit."

Joe and Anthony got separated in the scrum as they finally entered the building and were channelled in opposite directions by men in uniform carrying clipboards. They little realised how this arbitrary selection would send them on differing paths which would change both theirs and the lives of others for ever.

Chapter 28

The Crater – 1917

The high pitched shrieking scream filled the night sky. Startlingly sudden, it rose in pitch culminating in an ear splitting explosion of noise high in the sky from the source of which burst forth, like an expanding galaxy, a spherical ever-increasing mass of white hot magnesium particles in a climax of heat, light and sound. Slowly it fell bathing all below in an eerie white glow. It was followed intermittently by others. Some moments later a salvo of shells arched overhead, tracing their irresistible path through a night sky, betrayed only by faint whooshes. The earth seemed to tremble as they fell behind the lines and exploded with dull thumps. Tony knew that men may have been dying behind him even as he cursed the progress of his own life which had brought him to this point, and which he feared was about to end here.

As he half crawled, half squirmed across no-man's land pushed on by the instinct of self-preservation, driven by the fear of being blown up, drowned in the mud or being shot, skewered on a bayonet, gassed or bitten to death by the vermin which clung to his body, the answering fire was already under way from the other side as high velocity projectiles whined through the sulphur saturated air en route to their explosive destiny.

So unless Tony kept his head down he could have been caught by the blast from a shot from either side. Small arms he was used to on these raids but it was unusual for big guns to be fired at night. It was rumoured through the British lines that something big was brewing and the gunners were a bit jumpy. They would find out in due course exactly what had been dreamed up by the top brass who were supposed to be leading them wisely. In the meantime he thought he had taken just about all he could. His nerves were frayed beyond understanding, shot to pieces. He couldn't bear the noise any more nor the carnage the stench and the squalor of it all. The perpetual itching from the lice which covered his body biting away for all they were worth under his armpits and round his crotch and ankles must have been worse than wearing a hair shirt of penance. Out here in this desolate wasteland he felt he was at the lowest ebb a human being could descend to.

He had these confused despairing thoughts every time he found himself out here like this. If he ever managed to get back to his own lines he would collapse into the sleep of exhaustion with the hope that his body and mind might be able to repair and prepare itself for the assault on them again tomorrow.

The rattle of small arms fire which had started up from the German side coming from somewhere ahead, was joined, in this cacophany of sense-deadening sound and luminescence, by further eruptions of starshells bursting with ever more revealing candour. The activity died away and the whole battlefield reverted to intermittent starlight.

The three days of rain which they had suffered had eased off this morning. The clouds were scudding across the night sky sometimes obscuring the moon and stars for long periods at a time. The Germans must have seen movement among the small reconnaissance parties who had been sent out under cover of darkness to cut the barbed wire in preparation for the attack to come. His two companions in arms on this expedition, Private John Wedge and Lance-Corporal Keith Jones were somewhere out here, he didn't know where exactly. Miraculously unscathed he inched his way across what might have once been an orchard judging by a few small evenly spaced stumps of blasted wood left standing, slithering on his belly down into the stagnant water of a shell hole. It was bigger than usual, formed from three or four separate blasts that had rendered it into one big irregular pond shaped rather like the Ace of Clubs. He sat in the darkness on a piece of debris jutting out from the side amidst a most repugnant smell which attacked his nostrils and permeated right through to the back of his throat in the usual familiar way. He knew what it was. He would never get used to it, the smell of putrefaction, sulphur and death. Something, or maybe many things, were beneath the surface, had been there for weeks probably.

He clutched his Lee Enfield .303 ensuring he kept it above the level of the water. The bayonet was fixed. Inevitably any encounter with an enemy patrol out there amongst the craters was settled with the bayonet, a wooden club or even a shovel rather than the bullet. Such an offensive course was ugly, brutal and quiet. He may have accidentally already killed a man in this way. His scouting party, reconnoitering the wire, had stumbled upon an enemy patrol doing something similar. In the ensuing melée in almost total darkness, lashing out in all directions he had struck the man almost unwittingly in the adrenaline fuelled frenzy of self preservation before the action broke off and died away as each party fled from the other. He had been turned into a potential killer by necessity and against his nature. Up until this point he had only shot at the enemy from a distance.

They may as well have been fairground targets in Victoria Park. He had though, certainly witnessed the full horror of what modern science could do to the human body. He could never get used to it. It induced nausea, sometimes leading to vomiting, when he saw some of these gruesome sights up close. Legs with no body, a single head coated in mud, torsoes cut in two by machine gun bullets with intestines spilling out white, smeared with crimson or scarlet. He had heard the plaintive cries and screams of dying agony of the wounded men and schoolboys out there, both types calling for their mothers regardless of age. These horrors, communicated to him by each of his senses, and in combination all at once, often brought him to breaking point. He frequently saw it as he felt it, as he heard it, as he smelt it and tasted it, all at the same time.

He had never been required to go over the top as his army-taught skill was in communications. He believed that he had survived thus far because he must have been in some way blessed.

Sometimes, upon receiving letters from home he noted with a wry smile the news that Masses had been said for him and the other Catholics whose lot was to find themselves out here prematurely in this hellish inferno.

Father Matulaitis had written to him, and to other soldiers, from the Lithuanian church. He told them that everyone was thinking of them and their brave comrades and were praying for them. Ironically Tony knew it wasn't bravery which motivated him but cowardice. The fear of what would happen to him if he refused to obey an order. The fear of the shame of letting down his mates.

In his communications capacity he had learned to read Morse code and semaphore and operate a field telephone. He intended to get a job in this newly emerging industry, when he got back home after the war was over. Lately however, because of losses in the regiment, he had been ordered to go out with the wire parties. In effect he was working a night shift. The absolute stress and physical exertion of these nightly forays into no-man's-land from nine in the evening until three in the morning was rapidly driving him to insanity. His body clock was all over the place and it was difficult to sleep comfortably in any manner other than in the arms of sheer oblivion bordering on unconsciousness during the day. The guns and smoke and noise made it difficult but he had a dugout shared with his pals. Holed up inside with ears plugged with lint, a lot of the sound was kept at bay while he slept. He and those of his companions who managed to make it back every morning were all grievously afflicted by sleep deprivation and disorientation. Gaunt and hollow eyed they were mere shadows of the people they had once been, most were on the brink. The others were indeed quietly insane. Their own mothers would have had to look twice in order to recognise them. Still they were sent out night after night. Some of those who could take no more, the active and vocal ones who had been driven completely over the edge had been taken away and a few who had fled and been caught had been tried and shot for cowardice. At this moment Tony felt totally, miserably, desperately alone, suspended in a kind of desperate shit-infested nightmare from which there seemed to be no awakening.

He started, as he seemed to hear movement in the crater. His mind began to imagine all sorts of things. He thought he could hear a sort of shuffling and squeaking and a splash and what he thought might have been a human sound. He couldn't see though as the other side of the hole was a long way away and the moon above and behind it in that quarter bathed it in shadow. The tension increased with his heart rate. He grasped his rifle tighter and lowered the muzzle pointing it in front of him. It all went quiet again and the moon seemed to move in and out from behind the clouds. He became calmer and Tony's eyes re-adjusted to the darkness as the astral features of the night sky became starkly visible again. He looked up and studied the stars in the gaps in the cloud cover. They were brighter than he had ever seen them before and beautiful. He studied the surface of the moon. For all that was going on here on earth the combat was happening in the depths of the countryside but if it could have been seen from above one would never have realised it. All natural life and beauty had been obliterated by the hand of man to be replaced by churned mud as if in a nightmarish other-worldy landscape pockmarked with thousands of craters, which bizarrely formed a sort of perverse mirror image of the lunar landscape above.

As he sat there soaked through, the cold penetrated right through to the marrow of his bones. He shivered and his teeth chattered uncontrollably. His testicles had shrunk away somewhere inside his body. He could no longer feel his feet. The intense cold had forced the need to urinate but his hands were icy cold as he fumbled to undo the buttons and he let it go without moving from where he was.

Forlorn, desperate and demoralised in this stinking hell-hole miraculously his mind sought to clutch at happier memories as he waited for the bombardment to subside. He laid down his gun and put his face in his hands.

In his mind's eye he gradually envisaged that sunny day he had caught the bus in Mile End with his mate Joe on their way to enlist. From the top of the bus they could see posters plastered on billboards on the side of other trams, buses and buildings. Flags were flying from every available fixing, single Union Jacks on flagpoles and strings of red white and blue bunting strung between lamp posts.

Young men were walking around in uniform. Even old men were wearing their medal ribbons from previous wars when we had shown the foreigner who was boss.

They were both caught up in the patriotism, the mood of a great part of the nation, with the exception of most mothers. He recalled the line from a song, "We don't want to fight but by Jingo if we do..." These boys were heroes already in their own minds.

When they got to Stratford Town Hall he recalled their surprise to see that they were just two among hundreds and hundreds queueing up to enlist. He and Joe soon lost track of each other. Every volunteer was quizzed by a sergeant about his age and general health and filled up the recruitment form which amongst all the personal information required asked for the recruit's preferred options as to choice of regiment. There was also a box on the form as an option for the Navy and then, if ticked, any particular reason why the applicant should be considered for that service was to be added. But the closest Anthony had ever come to a boat was to watch them being unloaded in the Pool of London. He had bad memories of the rowing boat on the lake in the park where he had splashed some girls in another boat with an oar and toppled over backward fully clothed into the four foot deep water and nearly drowned. He still felt silly every time he thought about it. He couldn't even swim. So he left that option on the form blank. Then it was a medical. A full examination by a doctor in a cubicle and then shuffling round semi-naked clutching a clean bill of health. They seemed to spend an inordinately long time examining teeth. He wasn't to know that the authorities were just making sure that each recruit would be able to cope with and digest future rations of the army's staple fare on campaign, bully beef and hard tack. He thought though that they evidently wanted you fully fit in what he took to be this élite army. They needed only the very best, the cream, to swiftly put the Hun to flight.

Finally each man who had passed all the tests was given a strip of paper with a long number on it with the rejoinder, "Remember that number as if it's your name. It's your service number.".....

After returning home there was a long waiting period when nothing seemed to happen. It wasn't an altogether pleasant time as the sight of a young man in civilian clothes sometimes drew disapproving stares from passers by. At one stage he saw a young woman approaching him with a white feather but he quickly dodged away from her and made himself scarce. Tony felt guilty when he had nothing to feel guilty about.

Finally they had received orders to go for basic training on Wanstead Flats and had set out with a bit of trepidation mixed with pride. Being thrust together with all these other youths in a huge camp was quite fun. It was very much like a huge boy's club at first as they all milled around exchanging jokes and wisecracks until they were sorted out into sections by middle-aged and elderly NCOs who had been speedily co-opted into these roles for the expertise they had gained on battlefields and in army camps far away. Additionally all the competent regular soldiers were already abroad on active service and couldn't be spared for that kind of job. They were all in this together. Many different types were there, with differing personalities. A real cross section of the youth of London. During the course of their training a few would be earmarked as being potential officer material, others as NCOs but most were destined to become private soldiers. Then it became worse than school, – much worse, as the army machine started to crack the whip. It was a shock to them all.

Having achieved the exalted position of adult after what seemed like an eternity of being told what to do by parents, teachers, priests and policemen and even people such as public baths attendants, and the majority of adults they encountered, they had graduated to being addressed as 'Mister' as they left childhood behind. Only recently had they begun to revel in the new respect accorded them by their age when all of a sudden they were thrust back into the subservient position of not being respected again. It was difficult, and some coped with it better than others. Now they were referred to officially by their service number and surname and their rank – 'recruit'. That form of address was later to be elevated to either sapper, private, driver, bombardier and so on.

Issued with itchy uniforms, they were told how to wear them and keep them immaculate by a battery of NCOs who all seemed ready with sarcasm, or at the least, mickey-taking bombastic bullying. Various recruits were singled out by them for ridicule. Among them was his pal Joe who was asked by Sergeant Claxton yelling at the top of his voice whether he had shaved with a knife and fork that morning. When Joe innocently started to answer, in his ignorance not realising it was only a rhetorical question, he was silenced with a, "Shut up you 'orrible little man, I'm doing the bleedin' talking," which was delivered at maximum decibels into his ear. This drew a few stifled nervous sniggers from amongst the ranks. They all knew beyond any doubt who was in charge.

"Keep quiet, eyes front!" he bellowed, and they all stiffened with fear again.

"Strange how old Claxo tries to be funny then falls on you like a ton of bricks when you answer." Said Joe later that evening in the mess tent. I don't know if he wants to be loved or hated.

"Oh I don't mind him" Anthony said.

"I reckon his bark's worse than his bite."

Sergeant Claxton and soldiers like him were all a part of the deliberate disorientation process. The army certainly didn't want recruits who had minds of their own. All individuality had to be stamped out. But it wasn't personal. It was necessary they should obey every order without question. The RSM had said to the captain in charge upon being asked how they were shaping up,

"This is a good batch sir, they'll make very fine soldiers yet sir,"

"Just as well," responded the officer,

"There are thousands more needed across the channel in the next few weeks. It wouldn't surprise me if they brought in conscription."

Sleeping on camp beds in tents erected row upon row, Tony and his companions started to become accustomed to military life, and military food, which wasn't at all bad, before being attached to various regiments, seemingly at random. He himself had been assigned to the Essex Rifles and his mate Joe to the Royal Field Artillery. Perversely none of the lads he knew had been sent to the regiments of their choice which they had indicated when they joined up. He had come to realise by now that this was probably deliberate. Just another way to let them know that they had absolutely no say in anything. They were just there to obey orders. The shine was beginning to wear off as he began to harbour doubts as to what he had let himself in for. But still, he had the travelling to do. He had never been abroad before and was looking forward to it.

"Such a shame" he thought, he loved animals and would have liked to work with horses as it seemed Joe was going to do. But their ultimate allotted regimental destinations had been decided on that first morning at the recruiting office

After six weeks they were given a week's home leave as the camp's infrastructure prepared for the next batch. Tony and Joe travelled back to Stepney together carrying their kitbags, getting the tram from Wanstead and got off at the London Hospital, Whitechapel. They both walked through to Commercial Road and then along and across and down Planet Street at four o'clock in the afternoon. It was warm and sunny and all the street doors were open and children were thronging, playing outside after school, at hopscotch, whip and top, skipping and marbles – all the innocent pastimes of childhood which Tony and Joe had only recently left behind them. Outside some of the front doors of the small terraced houses, wooden chairs were placed as old girls sat outside gossiping. The arrival of the two caused excitement. Children stopped what they were doing running alongside them. Housewives spoke to them. Everyone was smiling. Joe's little sister Julie saw them from afar and forgetting her natural reserve for a moment, came running down the street her long brown hair streaming out behind her and Joe grabbed her as she reached him and used her momentum to hoist her up into his arms. She could smell the newness of his uniform. He felt like a returning hero.

Tony made his brief farewell to Joe outside No 59 and continued round past the Star and through Watney Passage and into the next street where he lived seven doors along on the opposite side.

He was just the right age for all this. Very nearly eighteen years old, full of the brash confidence of youth.

He was a man technically but still enough of a child to be moulded by square bashing sergeants major into one tiny cog of the mighty military machine which was being assembled. He had seen how the girls round here reacted to lads in uniform and he wanted some of the same. It had to do with peer pressure, it had always been like that.

There was an air of superiority among those who had already enlisted. There was also an unspoken standoffish demeanour, a sort of palpable air of disapproval in girls towards those lads who still hadn't taken the King's Shilling.

The following morning he spent indoors helping his mother tidy up and looking at the Daily Mail translating some of the news from the front into Lithuanian for her. The more he read out the more agitated she appeared, uttering small worried gasps or groans so he switched to reading domestic items which weren't to do with the war but there were not many of those. His father was round at the Cernauskas house in Morris Street helping to make small leather shoes. There were a few of them doing that. The remaining days of his leave continued much in the same vein. There was an uneasy air of expectancy in the house. They were all on edge. Tony was keen to get underway on his new adventure but his mother and father were dreading it with a sort of feeling of inevitability, even helplessness.

Tony's orders which came in the post a few days later ordered him to present himself at Victoria Station where he would be catching the 11.14 for Dover. When he arrived there he would be given further instructions at temporary battalion headquarters outside the town ready to be inducted into his unit and prepare for embarkation. To where exactly, they didn't elaborate. When he disembarked and found his unit, together with hundreds of other new soldiers, they were formed up outside the station and marched into the Kent hinterland to the camp which would be their home for the next three weeks

On the day of his departure from his home, he had been armed with a packet of sandwiches made by his mum and an apple and an orange wrapped in brown paper plus essential necessities such as washing equipment a hair brush and comb and some spare clothes, handkerchiefs, a sewing bee and so on. He also carried along with him, the resigned muted pride of his parents and the cheers and best wishes of the whole street. He walked around the corner to Joe's at number fifty nine and took his leave. Joe was out somewhere, probably playing snooker or gambling but Joe's mother shed a tear, as she hugged and kissed him and gave him sixpence though she could ill afford it.

In the evening after he had gone, the house round the corner seemed empty even as Tony's mum and dad sat round the range in their back room with Elzbiėta and Julie, reminiscing, all in the Lithuanian language. The older ones remembered the celebratory drinks in the 'The Star' when he was born. How Mama had to help her husband home as he staggered along in an alcoholic haze singing merrily. Admittedly he didn't have to go far before he could collapse onto his own bed, out for the count, but not before accidentally wakening the new baby which was being looked after by Juoza Daugirda, heavily pregnant herself. She then made her excuses and left, consigning the responsibility of Tony back to his mother who started to see about feeding him. She was using cow's milk bought from the grocers – Gold's the little Jewish shop on the corner. The horse and cart delivered the milk there every day and it was dispensed into Gold's barrel with a huge ladle which dangled off the back of the cart just behind one of the iron shod wheels, a few inches from the dusty roadway, as it trundled through the streets. Why so many babies died around the East End in their first year of life was a mystery but they thanked God that Tony hadn't been one of them.

As they sat there nearly eighteen years later they laughed as they sought to find humour in the middle of concern. They remembered the congratulations of family and neighbours. Each of them, both father and mother re-lived in their own minds the slightly different memories of the happiness and sense of fulfilment they had experienced then, when they were young, when they produced him for the first time for the neighbours to see and admire.

"It all seems like yesterday said Agnes."

"Do you realise we are talking about the last century?" said Elzbièta in Lithuanian. "This is a new era." She spoke very softly and unhurriedly in her native language and Agnes thanked God she had her for a friend. She was always so calm and wise, even philosophical. She was the ideal person to know. Her advice was always good and she had a calming influence on all who knew her. She had certainly mastered the meaning of life and it showed.

"Oh yes! it was eighteen ninety seven they were born wasn't it?" "Those were the days, – when is Joe off?"

"He hasn't heard yet, – soon I would imagine"

"How I wish Juozas was here now," thought Elzbièta as she looked at her friend. "We were all just kids then ourselves. – not much older than Anthony is now"

She sipped her tea. How comforting this simple drink was in almost any situation. She could see the worry in her friend Agnes' face, behind her smile, and she noticed the slight catch in her voice. There was nothing that either of them could actually do to change this situation which had inexorably arisen. They were all in the hands of some power greater than them.

They both felt the same sympathy for each other. From that, they drew a reassuring collective strength.

Agnes' mind strayed again into nostalgia. Eighteen years had passed. Eighteen years of keeping Anthony safe, making sure he was warm and not hungry, teaching him to walk, to talk and to read. They taught him values, instilled the faith, showed him how to treat others with feeling and kindness. He got a special treat when he had been particularly good or helpful, perhaps an ice-cream or a lollipop. These good simple people taught him, mainly by example, how to behave, and all the other values which he now accepted without question.

From the very moment Ruta, his five year old sister, had been allowed to hold him for the first time she had become almost a second mother. He was her very own real live dolly. Except he gurgled and smiled when she tickled him, and cried when she teased him When she went to school the other kids asked her all about him. The teacher, with her Irish accent, made a big thing in the classroom, about Ruta's new baby brother Anthony.

The children had to draw a picture of him and write a little story. They loved him, they spoiled him and they were proud of him. Later on when he was an altar boy at St Mary and St Michael alongside Joe, he could be a little bit naughty, the constant spoiling had seen to that, as well as Joe egging him on, but he was funny lad with a dry sense of humour and he had a kind and sunny temperament.

Planet Street was a real buzzing neighbourhood of friendliness and support. Amidst the deprivation, the struggles, the overcrowding and the poverty it was a real community which pulled together.

The blackness of the night was beginning to diminish. Somewhere, afar Anthony heard birds beginning a chorus. Even here life went on.

The 7.92 millimetre bullet struck him in the forehead without warning. There was no inkling, no hint, no sound. His nervous system never had time to register anything before it shut down as he jerked back and then slumped forward subject to Newton's third law of motion. Blood, tissue and gore from his shattered head burst forth and spilled down his back soaking into the already wet khaki cloth.

A mud-bespattered infantryman in field grey with a roll of wire sitting diagonally opposite fifty feet away in the shadows on the other side of the shell hole with his levelled smoking Mauser rifle, never gave any further thought to the individual whose existence he had just terminated so arbitrarily, beyond muttering, "Got the bastard" and then in the direction of the enemy, "Take that Tommy." He felt the relief of knowing that he had saved his own skin and the thrill of doing his duty to the Fatherland and to the Kaiser.

He left his roll of wire where it was and made his way circuitously round the rim of the crater to the corpse he had created. It was slumped half in and half out of the water. He went through the pockets which were still above water. The German realised there was nothing of value amongst them. He threw the collection of assorted papers into the middle of the crater with an expression of disgust. The photo of Anthony's mother, amongst the assorted detritus floated for a while on the shining surface before it became water-sodden, overcame the surface tension and sank from sight.

The shelling had stopped now, it was not yet dawn and safe to think about returning to his own lines before it got light. He negotiated the rim of the shell hole. Twisting as he pulled himself slowly upward towards the slimy rim of the crater easing the roll of wire before him pushing it over the top, he peered left and then right into the darkness. As he did so the moonlight illuminated his brutish smallpox ravaged face, which resembled a miniature battlefield all of its own as that old familiar nervous tic started up again near his left eye. And then he slithered away as flat as he could go on his belly, taking a zigzag course back to his own lines. He headed towards the three tree stumps which were level with his own unit. He paused some way away and called out the night's password a few times until he heard an answering counter password quietly uttered. He left it for a few moments and then crawled forward and dropped over the parapet into the comparative safety of his own lines.

"Rosenkrantz, you're back you rotten bastard! A disappointed sounding voice uttered. "We were hoping you might have been detained out there for good! Ha Ha!" A few bystanders also laughed ironically, humourlessly amidst grunts of agreement. His own face remained impassive. He usually tried not to laugh – not that he found the greetings funny. His difficult birth had destroyed a nerve in his face which pulled it into a twisted grimace whenever he found something amusing and inadvertently attempted a smile. They all hated him and he knew it. He was an unpopular man who was cold, with no soul, nor any generosity of spirit. The bad feelings were mutual. He despised them all too. In his view they were a stupid bunch of fools with no ambition.

The Promised Land

His transfer application had been approved by his Commanding Officer only the week before. The CO was well aware of the negative influence one man could have on the orderly running of his unit. He was only too eager to be helping him on his way. Rosenkrantz was always at loggerheads with his comrades and obsequious to those in authority. At least now he would be free of the man's sickening sycophancy. Maybe the soldier would be better off as a runner.

The faceless, anonymous, characterless, and now lifeless, enemy form which the German had glimpsed in a brief flash of moonlight, the nonentity in a bedraggled, wet, blood-soaked, khaki uniform and tin helmet had been contemptuously toppled sideways into the oozing water by his executioner, leaving only a few ripples on the surface of that unspeakable depth.

Antanas Baukis, aged nineteen, second generation Lithuanian from Winterton Street, Stepney in London; was left all alone in the stinking muddy soup which filled a shell crater in no-man's-land. He would present no threat to anyone ..... ever again.

Back home in the family abode just off Commercial Road, Agnes Baukis, unable to sleep, could just hear the lamplighter coming down the street extinguishing the gas lamps. As she bustled about her chores she glanced out of the window and up at the sky, full of optimism. The sparrows were chirping. A new dawn was breaking.

Chapter 29

Transfer

"Kurtin!...Get yer 'orses and report back ter me, AT THE DOU-BLE," bellowed the stentorian voice.

Driver Joseph Michael Kurtin was already at a low ebb, drained and depressed. He had received a letter from home yesterday morning which contained a bombshell. His best friend Antanas was reported missing in action. Joe hoped against hope that Anthony would turn up soon. He had read and re-read the letter from Julie, and the added snippets from his mother in which he detected the anguish hidden between the lines of their local gossip and good wishes. He took it out, unfolding it, re-reading it again and replacing it in the cheap envelope it had arrived in. He muttered a few prayers as he felt his way along the rosary in his pocket.

He thought he was supposed to be resting but evidently now others had decided that this was not so. He could have kicked himself for hanging around the battalion instead of going for rest and recreation further back. But then again, they would only have come looking for him if this was for something important.

There was no point in arguing with Sergeant Metcalfe. That fellow always wanted his own way. Still, Joe realised already that the man was in his element in this situation, a born autocrat. Outwardly he was missing both friendliness and warmth. What he was really like he never revealed to the men. No one opposed him. This wasn't the time nor the place to challenge him, in fact he could never be challenged. The man indirectly had the power of life and death over him in this situation. Maybe after the war was over Joe would be able to choose to decline association with these types, depending on circumstances. Joe's nerves were fraught and ragged and sometimes he didn't really care what happened. Depending on his frame of mind at the time, his own life or death didn't always concern him. Every aspect of service here seemed designed to demoralise and break the spirit.

His mind raced over all the possibilities involved with this summons. Was there more bad news from home? Had he committed some infringement of military discipline? Was it the Crown and Anchor game they had found out about? He weighed it all up but couldn't think of anything other than his love of that blooming Crown and Anchor. Maybe it was his own guilt. The authorities in the army frowned on it, particularly when it left soldiers cleaned out, separated from all they owned. It could have a negative effect on discipline and attitude. Joe did understand this viewpoint but it wasn't exactly banned and Joe was addicted to the whole principle of gambling. To him the faint hope of winning big was a distraction from war. It gave him a sort of thrill of anticipation only now and again fulfilled by a rush of adrenaline through his veins. In civvy life with the best of intentions he had started out to make good money by working for it.

But try as he might to get a decent job he just couldn't. He had no particular qualities which an employer could use and labouring skills were competitive in his world. The Docks were all sewn up. He wasn't a particularly big bloke, five foot six and a half with narrow shoulders. But although incredibly strong for his size even in this field he was at the bottom of the food chain. Other opportunities for un-enterprising boys like him just didn't exist. So here he was in the market not for a vocation but for work of any kind.

He had never been brought up to strive for money for its own sake and an additional handicap was his honesty, which was only dented by his gambling habit and the game. But strangely, that was coupled with his lack of responsibility. Around Whitechapel, Stepney and the East End people hustled and bustled to scrape a living, himself included, but without an eye for the main chance he really was up against it. There had been no father to emulate, no business to inherit, aside from the little cottage industry slipper-making enterprise. But there he was, already being exploited by other, bigger fish. Further up the line was where the real profits were made. The coming of war was the temporary distraction which was to give him some sort of regular wage, board and lodging and adventure away from Stepney in some green field far distant, or so he believed. He had jumped at it, seizing this opportunity, to rush off and join up taking his Crown and Anchor skills with him.

The British infantry supported by the Royal Field Artillery had just completed a massive assault on the Germans which was preceded by a concentrated bombardment of the enemy lines, during the course of which Joe had played his small part along with tens of thousands of other ants. Now situated well behind the new lines achieved by the Allies, the guns, the 18 pounders and the howitzers, had been brought forward dragged along the best possible route by tractors and sometimes massive teams of horses and men with ropes, and drawn up to their new positions where they could be entrenched in batteries as quickly as possible. But this still wasn't fast enough to prevent the enemy from re-deploying to new positions of their own and they too brought their guns to bear again.

The Germans had been allowed to retire to a new line by default. As usual, the British had been overwhelmed by their own success and had been painfully slow in following up the almost unexpected gains and with the enemy artillery pulled back to a safe distance, their new targets and trajectory re-calculated, the whole thing was starting all over again, but two miles further to the east. The Allies had not been given much time to sort out the communication infrastructure or the transport of the ammunition up to the guns in their new positions. The British ammunition dumps were now even further behind the guns and consequently the munitions would have to be brought up from a greater distance until the whole dump could be moved bit by bit up towards the artillery. The railhead would have to be re-positioned and advanced to a new terminus with subsequent supplies and ammunition unloaded there further forward.

The ground to be traversed by the ammunition-carrying wagons with their iron shod wooden wheels was not always suitable over the newly won terrain, so men and individual horses was the fallback method of ammunition transport, each horse carrying two or four huge shells slung on each side of the beast. Such a heavily laden animal could only be led, not ridden, so men and horses had to pick their way over the hard packed jagged earth and get across old trenches with the aid of the Engineers who had hastily rigged up makeshift bridges across which they would tentatively pick their way. This amounted to two trench systems to traverse, their own old ones and those of the Germans after that. But between was the great hardened morass of craters, some dried out a bit, with parts of bodies,

equipment, wire and horses and skeletons partially obscured but with jagged pieces sticking out of the drying mud, sometimes with bits of old rags attached, occasionally khaki but other times grey or blue. Shards of steel, beginning to rust, occasionally visible as rifles, but otherwise just shapeless pieces of metal doing their best to dissolve back into their basic chemical elements. Grass shoots and greenery were already beginning to sprout over the old terrain. Nature was taking over again. Wild flowers forced their way through the hardened mire as nature sought to reclaim its earth.

What lay behind them was a network of old Allied trenches and German ones which had been overrun by the British and French and a hardened sun baked muddy morass which had once been no-man's land. A newer no-man's land was forming up about two miles ahead. Joe had been involved in this chaos for many months now. Shells which had landed in soft mud last Autumn and Winter and which had just sunk in with their contact fuses only partially tripped, were now encased in baked mud, which itself transmitted any vibration to the fuses causing random explosions. Shells had become mines.

The tension was always there, heart in mouth sometimes, a tight feeling in the chest. The alternating of fear with relief had long since started to render men mentally unstable. Lack of sleep, exhaustion, bad and irregular food made most men mentally taut. Some broke down under this pressure becoming crying wrecks and acting irrationally. Only these men at the front really understood what it was like and sought to protect their comrades from retribution by the higher ranked officers based well behind the lines who were partly divorced from the day to day grim reality of it all. Even officers nearer the action were in a cleft stick, most doing their best to maintain discipline whilst remaining understanding yet, at the same time, being made only too aware of army regulations.

To this latest all-out assault, the enemy had been rather yielding at first but eventually mounted an effective counter attack which halted the British in their tracks. Joe owed his life, such as it was, in some degree, to his role in this confusion, fetching ammunition from base camp up to the guns. Originally he had been up there with the batteries but in early 1916 he was transferred to the ammunition column. This meant a  different kind of danger but at least he no longer had to suffer the pain of being on top of the ever-thundering guns.

'The noise! the noise! the earth reverberating with unendurable sound! All the time – day and night,' as he had written home. His eardrums and his whole head seemed about to burst. And Jerry wasn't just sitting on his hands while this was going on. Jerry was forever aiming to pinpoint the British guns. One minute, men might be feeling relatively secure running backwards and forwards servicing the guns like busy bees and in the next moment they could be blown to smithereens without warning. It was like God's huge foot stamping them out of existence.

Until that posting to the ammunition column came through, Joe's personal Hell was relentless all the time he was up near the front lines. Being sent to the ammunition column saved him. Now some of the time at least he was back at base loading shells, looking after horses and ferrying ammunition, and sometimes people, supplies and food, up to the front. But it was to be his ability to speak French and German passably which may well have saved his life.

During periods of respite which often descended into monotony, headquarters had made it possible for those who were interested to learn French. There was always an element of the French population, middle aged, ex school teachers or professional people who were too old to fight with the allies but were only too pleased to be of service, to feel important and to be respected again. Joe enrolled in one of these groups as a diversionary way of alleviating the tedium of rest periods at the rear. This had been fine when the war had been fairly static. There was some continuity in the lessons.

Joe found that his tutor whilst not speaking much English himself at first, was keen to learn about England and the English and he picked on Joe, who being one of his brighter students was only too happy to explore ways of explaining various things. They, the students, started by being taught 'La Madelon' a French marching song. All were encouraged to sing it together with the teacher's wife and some children joining in. That broke the ice and removed any inhibitions the Tommies may have had. Then they went through the vocabulary and grammar. Joe already had a large mental store of vocabulary but he benefitted from unravelling the grammar, and above all the colloquialisms which could only be really picked up with a keen ear by being there in the country speaking the language, which he did whenever he could.

Monsieur Martin his tutor was a man about fifty years of age. He was born not long after the Franco-Prussian war in the early 1870s and had been brought up on war stories and the tales and opinions of his parents. He remembered by hearsay the age of the French Revolution at the turn of the eighteenth century and the years of greatness, followed by the return to the status quo. And there was the later revolution of the 1830s and what followed. But he understood that this present war was necessary to prevent Germany's supremacy.

He had noticed Joe right away. He was expert at spotting a student with aptitude and interest.

Thus a sort of intermittent friendship sprang up between the two of them which developed into Joe teaching Monsieur Dubois, 'Maurice' by this time, English, as much as the other way round.

"Je veux apprendre le Francais Maurice. Vous devez le parler avec moi!" muttered Joe one day when he thought the language being used was too one-sided, – Strangely Joe found it more comfortable not to use the familiar tutois form of address. He believed in respect for the older person although Monsieur Martin insisted he called him by his Christian name – "Yes alright," replied Maurice, "But I think it will be necessary for us all to learn English in the new age which is coming. The Germans will lose this war now that....." He paused here and Joe could almost see the thought processes written on his face.... "Les Américains are...... here."

"Yes" replied Joe" concurring with Maurice's wishes.

"I think the Germans might lose their empire, such as it is. La France will also gain. She'll get back Alsace Lorraine and the British will go from strength to strength. I think English is going to be the language of the future, spoken all over the world."

"Talking of English, would you like to learn 'Crown and Anchor' – a little English game? Maurice gave him a sharp glance and Joe dropped the idea, wondering why he had even mentioned it.

This pupil–teacher; elève–maitre relationship went on for months on and off whilst the war remained static. During Joe's periods of rest behind the lines he used to seek Maurice out and they exchanged their news in both languages. All this was taking place against the disorder of the countryside surrounding the trenches, the shortages of basic necessities, food, clothing, fuel, even of water, the turmoil and chaos.

Now everything had moved forward and new billets had to be found, new friendships forged among the French. A few of the French people who had once been behind the German lines and who helped to provide the support network to the national enemy in all sorts of ways had fled at the onset of the assault or had hidden as the battle raged past them but were now slowly re-emerging and living in the ruins. They had nowhere else to go. The natural sympathies many had developed towards their erstwhile German occupiers now had to be transferred to the British who filled the gaps left by the retreating Germans. A very strange situation indeed. French people, allied to the English, who had grown to like many of the German lads they had met even though they were the enemy. Now they were compelled to try to like the English, their allies.

Those amongst them who had been deemed to be too friendly with the Germans in some cases were ostracised now that the Germans were gone, and they were victimised and some earmarked for even more drastic action. War had played havoc with friendships, loyalties, the Law and even reason itself.

So on the day when Joe heard that rude, raucous call to action before he was ready to start again, he felt the old familiar sinking sensation. Mentally he had already geared himself up slowly to his known timetable of periods in action followed by periods of rest. He paced himself in order to gain the maximum benefit from his self imposed therapy. He wasn't due back on for another two days but in reality he knew every man was needed. Four or eight shells per horse per journey would mean an awful lot of trips backwards and forwards as a muleteer, because that was what the drivers had become, purely animal handlers, draymen, labourers. In Joe's case the two horses he was assigned were good ones. Great tall black creatures, one was named 'Cherry Blossom' and the other 'Boot Polish'. They were the pair which were always harnessed closest to the limber as they were the strongest. The latter now had a jagged hole through one of his ears. Joe always said the bullet was intended for him but he was saved by his own instinct of self preservation. By always walking between the two of them at all times their vast bulk shielded him from unspeakable horrors. They were both about as good as he was himself under gunfire. All three of them were shattered by it. The unexpectedness of it sometimes. The bursting of a shell or grenade too close for com-

fort, the staccato rattle of machine gun fire, the starshells at night, the whizz-bangs and the continuous noise caused one or both of the horses to rear up, ears laid back, snorting with flared nostrils. At those moments Joe was in as much danger from the flailing hoofs and huge bulky bodies moving on either side as from blast or shrapnel. He could quite easily have been squashed between them but that was just a chance he was forced to take.

There were certain parts of the terrain during the previous long period of stalemate through which it was necessary for Joe to take his horses where he regularly came under sustained German shellfire. There had been a particularly firm pieces of ground damaged in some places but shored up, patched and even screened by the Royal Engineers, which provided the firmest footing for man and beast from the ammunition dumps up to the guns. The Germans knew all about them and regularly shelled them for two minutes, and because of restrictions due to shell shortages, with a four minute break. So methodical were they that the British could have almost set their watches by them, those who could afford them, and not many of the lower ranks owned one. That was the window through which Joe and his companions had to make their way at breakneck speed. A mad dash to beat the shells, day-in, day-out. Relentlessly, repetitively dicing with death. Nerves were on edge with such heart-palpitating regularity that the feeling became almost permanent.

Unless the road had been recently hit and damaged it was usually possible to charge a wagon and horses flat out with one driver sitting on the lead horse and another on the wagon itself holding the reins.

Joe's introduction to horses had been, in a way, brutal.

These terrifyingly large, immensely strong animals with minds of their own it seemed, were daunting to city lads who had never actually dealt with them physically. The millions which had been commandeered from all over Britain had to be managed by someone. The entire war hinged on horse transport. Joe and his mates were taught how to harness them, how to groom them and how to hitch them up to a wagon. Then they had to learn how to sit on them and even ride them. It was a huge task for a boy who had only ever been to school, worked briefly in an office and, who had been lately, an errand boy and finally a labourer. Now he was a groom too and learned how to muck them out and what to feed them. He and the other drivers had to know about shoeing and horse's ailments. They learned how to tether them to a picket line in the field and how to pick a sheltered spot for them, how to make them comfortable and to put their needs first, above their own.

Once more the continual shouting and criticism bullying and mickey-taking played havoc with his sensibilities. During training he fell off his horse once as the sergeant came over and quickly screamed, "Oo said yer could dismaant?" The worst part was that his mates who had been lucky enough to retain their seats smirked. They did so due to an odd mixture of sycophancy towards authority and relief that this moustachioed would-be villain was not directing his sarcastic wit towards any of them – at that moment, but at the erstwhile Charlie Chaplin. Joe of course just felt stupid as he lay there on the grass with the wind knocked out of him. A year later he would have given any-thing to be lying again on that turf in England at Preston Barracks, gasping in the sea air, being ridiculed.

Instead, he was continually coming upon the aftermath of un-speakable atrocities that had happened in a slightly earlier timeframe. He was walking on corpses, friend and foe. He could sometimes tell which was which by the accoutrements and type of weaponry scat-tered around or the uniforms or the dead horses nearby. German horses had distended bellies due to the greenstuff they were fed. Brit-ish horses were the opposite. The British fed theirs with dry oats and hay which made the difference. Other times he was unable to tell, bits of bone, a badly damaged boot with a foot still in it. A faceless head. Sometimes it wasn't possible to know what he was treading on or in. There were clues to be interpreted when his foot stepped on something yielding, its softness accommodating the shape of his boot, signalling to him, reaching his brain via his nerves, through his sole. It was a fragile arrangement. Repulsion, resignation the compulsion to look down. The stink of putrefying meat and shit was another clue and clouds of egg-laying flies. One stumbled through one whiff and straight into another almost impenetrable, a wall of gases designed by the Almighty to warn unwary humanity of the dangers of associating with the source too closely.

No callow boy should ever have been made to confront such a man-made nightmare. These were the scenes and experiences one might only encounter in the worst extremes of imagination or after death at an advanced age, and only then to be punished with it if you had led a particularly sin-filled life.

It was Dante's Inferno, the world's most hellish stage. It was never-ending, grinding on and on. It was impossible to remove oneself from it. It was now this boy Joe's entire way of life.

He and all the other youths were damned by being there and would have been damned had they run away. There was no escape. A litany of low points followed by more lows interspersed with brief rest periods when the guns could still be heard. Those hard metal, remorseless, relentless, unforgiving guns.

If ever any gains of territory were made, curiosity often led some of the lads to explore the German dugouts for souvenirs or injured soldiers from both sides. One young man, a Methodist who had already been put through the mill in England as a conscientious objector and had been placed in the Royal Army Medical Corps after a hugely demoralising and traumatic fight to defend his beliefs, went down into a recently vacated German dugout. Hearing a plaintiff mewing noise he saw on a table at the end, a kitten with its paw nailed to the wood. "Those bleeding German bastards," yelled the distraught boy. He took his pen-knife and prised away the bent nail holding the cat's paw. His two medical colleagues crowded round seeing if there was anything they could do, as the grenade booby trap fixed under the bench exploded in his face killing him instantly. The two others behind him were luckier. They had been shielded by the first boy. One lost his right eye, his nose, an ear and a hand but the third escaped with just burst eardrums and severe chest pains and breathing problems caused by the pressure of the blast. Again this probably saved their lives ultimately as they were first taken to a field station and then invalided out to Boulogne on the coast and from there back home to a hospital in Britain.

These tales went round like wildfire, which suited the military hierarchy. Distrust or even hatred of the enemy couldn't have been more welcome at Headquarters. Unplanned incidents had occurred at various parts of the line on two consecutive early Christmases, the makeshift truces, exchange of presents and the singing together of carols. The goodwill towards men, had been bad for discipline. It was most unwelcome to the High Command.

"One just couldn't have the troops taking matters into their own hands. It was highly irregular, bad for discipline and for morale."

Any fraternisation would, at the least be heavily discouraged, and at worst severely punished. Consorting with the enemy could be interpreted as treason. A couple of examples made would soon put paid to that. Anything which would concentrate the minds of the troops, into despising, even hating the enemy. The sure and certain knowledge of reprisals by army authorities if orders were even slightly misinterpreted was to be made absolutely clear.

It would be spelled out in official orders and justified by army chaplains at church parades.

Chapter 30

Cherry Blossom, Boot Polish

"Dont worry Kurtin, you aint goin' forward, yer goin' back."
For a moment Joe was uncomprehendingly blank.

Metcalfe read the puzzlement on his face.

"It's 'cause yer speaks French don't ya?"

"What a stroke of luck this is," thought Joe. "Maybe some cushy little number further back, safer, better for my nerves. But how did they know I speak French?"

"Take yer 'orse and ride 'im dahn ter Columnbear. Go from there to the big 'arse. That's the new HQ.

Take the uvver 'orse an' all. Keep 'em as a pair. An' you'll need all

321

yer kit wiv ya. Them nags is evenly matched ain't they?"

"Yer gonna be a messinger ain't ya?"

"How do I know you stupid git? Am I ?" mused Joe – silently.

"Sergeant?" He responded aloud, inquisitively, crisply.

"Ain't yer 'eard they lost a bunch of 'em to a direct 'itt, day before yisterday, all their best Froggy speakers?"

"What an idiot," thought Joe. "Calling those beauties nags. The big arse? He must mean Colombières and the Chateau," Joe concluded. Joe was outwardly servile and inwardly scornful. He wasn't aware of it, but it came across openly sometimes.

Then he got to pondering on the sergeant's mispronunciation. In the case of his own Cockney accent, Joe was putting it on to fit in, but he knew Metcalfe's was because he was badly educated.

"Metcalfe is a bit of a silly arse himself," he thought.

"Yes sar'nt, right away sar'nt" he smartly said.

As Joe disappeared with alacrity, Metcalfe watched him go. Calling his corporal over he said, "That forrin sounding bastard Kurtin, what jer make of 'im, I sees contempt in 'is eyes?"

"I fink 'e's a piss-taker Sarge," replied Corporal Shepherd, sensing the reply Metcalfe was looking for. " 'e seems to 'ate orfority, trouble is 'e don't akcherly do nuffing wrong but I reckon yer could get 'im fer dumb insolence. 'e overdoes the 'Yes corp, No corp' bit. 'e seems to be mocking arf the time, the cocky bugger!"

As far as the spoken language was concerned both of them were masters of the glottal stop.

Joe for his part knew that although these two had some jurisdiction over his destiny, it would only last at most, as long as he was forced to serve in this army. He hoped that he would never set eyes on either of them again. But he knew well enough that he would meet their equivalents wherever he was destined to go in his future life.

As he rode away on Cherry Blossom he couldn't break the habit of seeking protection from flying metal projectiles. He made sure he led Boot Polish on a tight rein almost alongside. At least that way his lower body would be protected on one side at least. As he jogged along rising and falling in the saddle he became aware again of the intense itching. The more he thought about it the worse it seemed to become. Where *did* the lice come from? On the occasions when he got to water and managed to shower the lice and the dried skin off his body there was still the problem of clearing vermin from one's clothes before putting them back on. The lice seemed to hide in folds and seams, the crafty little devils. Rows of stitching was their sanctuary.

The ablutions were set up at supply railheads and camps, barracks or temporary billets behind the lines. They were often makeshift and basic. He tried to think about something else and the irritation diminished slightly. It was mind over matter. His mum had taught him how to do it with the personal technique she had learned back home in Lithuania. "Just think of something else, slow down your heart rate, calm down and all will be well." The itching faded into the background.

That afternoon Joe had arrived at the Chateau in Colombières. Identifying himself at the gatehouse he was taken straight before the duty officer, Captain Scannell who sat there slowly reading the despatch which Joe had handed to him. Joe stood to attention.

"At ease Kurtin, at ease! Monsieuer Martin tells us you were the best French speaker amongst your group. We need you to be a messenger between us and our French colleagues elsewhere. Although most of the British Officers here speak French, the telephone lines are often down and messages need to go by hand with someone who knows the language. Do you think you are up to it?"

He said this last sentence in French to which Joe immediately responded in the affirmative in the same language adding, "I can also speak Lithuanian and Polish and some German and Yiddish too sir," The Captain started as he was caught a little unawares by this development but figuring out what had just been said, looked at Joe with renewed interest and responded,

"That may not be necessary at this stage. You are now relieved of your driving duties as such and you will be transferred here to head-quarters forthwith. I see you have brought some horses too and they appear to be well-cared-for beasts. They have been looked after pretty well haven't they? How is that? Have you been with them all along?"

"Yes sir, thank you sir, it must be something I've inherited. I've always loved horses but in the East End of London I've never really had a chance to work with them."

"The East End eh? I take it by your name and the languages you speak that you are not entirely English."

"Oh yes sir I am, I was born in Whitechapel but my parents came from Russia"

"Fascinating," said the Captain in a posh voice.

"The paperwork will go back to your old unit tomorrow. In the meantime see to your horses, put them in that outbuilding over there with the others. You will find hay and straw there and some bran and oats. There is a well over there," he added. pointing outside.

Take a bath, wash your clothes and smarten up. This is HQ you know. We have many important staff officers here and of course high ranking French officers too.

Joe saluted, took his leave and made his way over to the little group of outbuildings some way away from the main house.

Two privates and a corporal were sitting outside in the afternoon sun. They greeted Joe in a friendly manner. After enquiring who he was and why he was there they confirmed that there had been a mishap two days previously when two of their French speaking messengers had accidentally 'copped it' in what was almost a freak incident. They explained to Joe that rarely did they ever come into contact with the front line and Joe wouldn't even have to go up to the guns. Their job was to take the messages between the outposts of the High Command, mainly between the French, the British and the Americans.

Evidently those poor men whom Joe was replacing were making their way over an old piece of churned up ground when a dud shell mostly buried had suddenly gone up taking them with it. Fate had decreed which group of soldiers would live and which would die, and when they would meet their maker and which parents and loved ones would therefor be chosen to receive dreadful news.

There wasn't much left to find, let alone bury but it had been forced upon the unit to do the best they could with some alacrity as the weather had been warm of late.

Dave Winter, one of the surviving messengers, introduced himself to Joe in a friendly manner and said, "We can't have you bringing your nits and lice in here, we only just manage to keep our own at bay. Wear these togs while you wash and dry your others," as he delved amongst some dried clothing from a washing line.

They fired up the copper and told him to bring his own water in a bucket from the well. After a few trips to and fro, and while that was heating up, they gave him a cup of tea and some bread and jam and a couple of slices of corned beef from a tin.

Luxury, luxury. Joe relaxed in the tub of steaming hot water. Standing up and rubbing himself down with the chunk of carbolic soap he found in a dish beside the tub, he mused upon how civilised this was, more so even than Planet Street, where he had often wished himself back over the previous two years. He realised that there must be more to life than he had thought as he enjoyed for a moment one of the things which he now realised his betters took for granted. "How the other half must live," he thought.

There were now six of them in the billet. But there were eight beds arranged in two rows of four, with a pair of them still unoccupied. To Joe these new quarters were completely satisfactory. He was normally used to even less privacy than he was enjoying here. The spot occupied by his bed and his locker was the equivalent area of an entire room in Planet Street.

Once the euphoria of the bath and food and clean clothes had worn off he found himself reverting to that anxious, fretful, depressed state of mind. As he lay there warm and cosy he could hear the continuous droning roar of the guns far off. There must be another offensive in the offing he thought. "What if they send me back? What if now I am no longer in the RFA they send me to the front, to the infantry?" As this thought struck him he felt queasy. Then he thought about Anthony and his friend's poor mother. Then his mind flitted unaccountably to his lack of a trade or occupation if he didn't include the slipper making. How would he help his mum when this was all over?

It was about 2.30 am, that time when all one's worst fears and nightmares come to the fore in startling, blinding clarity. He lay awake staring at the blackness. His mind was taking over, jumbling with his emotions. The thoughts of what he had already seen tumbled over other thoughts of worry for the families of those poor souls whose lifelessness he had seen with his own eyes, not just individuals, not tens, nor scores, but hundreds upon hundreds. Why were they dead? Where had they ended up in eternity, in God's great scheme?

"Stop this now," he thought as he turned over. "Don't open your eyes, don't admit that you are nowhere near asleep. Count sheep, imagine a fence. Here comes a flock butting up against a gate. Here's the first one, he jumps over it. Here comes another one. That jumps it too. Where have those two gone now? This is not working. I must sleep, I am wasting sleeping time. Turn over. I need to sleep. Too much has gone on, I have too many thoughts. Lie on your back, keep warm, slow down your breathing. Breathe slowly, slowly, slow, slower. The bright hoop of light is near your feet, it encircles them. It is moving up your body. As it does so your feet are relaxing, now your shins and calves now your knees and thighs. Then your hips, stomach and chest. Slowly, slowly your body is relaxing your breathing is slowing, your heart rate is very slow now. It's working. It's passing outside your head. Now it is like a halo." Oblivion.

It's daylight! Dave is there.

"Are you all right mate? Time to get up."

Joe swung his legs out of bed. The sun was shining. He was still clad in the underclothes he had been given the day before. His uniform had dried on the chair at the foot of the bed. He got dressed and got his shaving gear out of his kitbag. There were clothes in his bag still, which he would have to go through and de-louse. At the end of this block was a small scullery type washroom and, wonder of wonders, a tap. It only ran cold water but to Joe this was an opportunity. He shaved in the cold water using his cutthroat razor, working up a lather with the carbolic soap and he was happy to do it.

When that was done he checked his rifle. The old standard issue Lee Enfield .303. Mainly wood surrounding a steel barrel, brass trimmed stock, an adjustable rear sight, a sling, one end attached to the stock and the other to the upper part of the gun. He checked again the 8 clips of five bullets he carried in a pouch. Each clip and its bullets was arranged in such a way that the edge of it could be engaged in the top of the breech and the bullets pushed out of the clip with the thumb, down and into the magazine. The magazine held ten cartridges and one could include an eleventh shell 'up the spout' as they used to say. He checked all this was operating correctly by opening and closing the bolt and ejecting shells with repeated actions but without pulling the trigger. Using a small can of oil he applied drops where he thought it necessary. Then he fed a long wire down the barrel inserting a small piece of oily rag through the slot on the end once it appeared in the breach. He then proceeded to pull it back up the barrel twisting it slightly as it was withdrawn. He checked the magazine already fixed underneath the weapon. The spring was working well. He loaded ten of the ejected bullets back into two clips then reloaded them into the rifle. The odd bullet he placed in the breach. The safety catch had been on all the time and the gun pointed away from any person. He checked the movement of the rear sight and slid the mechanism up and down. It was working. He hinged the whole assembly flat against the barrel again. He had already previously zeroed in the foresight to his own eye at the rifle range set up near the last rest area. It had needed a tiny amount of tapping with a toffee hammer from right to left to make the gun align properly with Joe's eye, the rearsight, the foresight and the intended target.

Joe had no intention of dying because of some oversight on his own part. Even though he had never used the gun in anger it was really the only protection he had against a hostile world.

Breakfast was cooked on top of the same coals that the copper of water had been placed on. Instead of the copper was an iron frying pan set lower down on the coals. In it they fried some bread and some eggs. There seemed to be a plentiful supply of those, with some lard from a jar. This was even better than making money on the Crown and Anchor game. He would have to show these lads how to play. No, no! how could he? They were decent types he wouldn't be able to bring himself to take their money from them. He recalled those games behind the Front where the pot sometimes stood at £50. You could almost buy a house for that. And to think, he helped to run the whole thing! His portion of the winnings didn't remain in his pocket for long. The other organisers always seemed to take the lion's share.

He went to check the horses. He could have sworn they were pleased to see him. He watered them, found some hay and put it in a manger where they could reach it. Then two buckets of oats left at their feet. They had not had quite such good conditions for the past two years and neither had he. There were other horses there mostly fine specimens well fed and glossy-coated, officer's horses.

Joe wondered who looked after these other horses and he soon discovered from Fred Humbles, a corporal messenger, that, most of the Frenchmen who had been servants in the chateau or worked on the estate had been drafted into the army. Many had been killed at Verdun or had died on the Somme and the rest dispersed to who knows where or back to German prison camps. The menial and manual tasks and the grooming were therefor done by the female servants and girls who stayed with the house. They ran the farm. Two of them, Hortense and Mathilde, were permanently assigned to protect and look after the chickens of which there were many and to milk the half-a-dozen or so cows who had calves. Pigs, geese, goats and chickens still had to be looked after and fed but they were more expendable than the cattle and so were sometimes slaughtered by an old man, a butcher specially brought up from the town to do the job and were then cooked and eaten up at the house by the officers and staff billeted there. Having always been well behind the front line the house had managed to escape any major military action. It had retained all of its paintings, chandeliers, thick pile carpets, polished floors and sumptuous bedrooms. It had sustained no damage, and consequently it had remained the ideal place from which to conduct a war in a civilised manner in relative comfort, with all of the modern conveniences to which staff officers were usually accustomed.

Chapter 31

The Men in Field Grey – 1918

Joe did his apprenticeship at messengering for two or three weeks mainly going backwards and forwards between elements of the High Command. He was much safer from the nemesis which had been hanging over millions of men for over three years and for many with fatal results. He even had time to write home and hoped that letters from Planet Street might eventually find their way to him via the ammunition column. Then one day there was a change in the pattern of things. German shelling followed a different formula. There seemed to be more German reconnaissance aircraft around which led to dogfights in the sky above them as aircraft warily circled each other striving for that one position which would give them mastery and send their adversary plunging earthward. Evidently there had been more balloon observation also visible from the Allied lines. Something was pending so all available reserves and supplies were brought up in preparation for an expected onslaught. Suddenly it happened one morning. All was in continuous confusion up ahead for a couple of days and Joe was pleased not to be involved in it. But he wasn't immune to his baptism of fire as a messenger. It would come very shortly.

They were four miles behind the lines at Colombières and everyone at Joe's level, used to taking things for granted, was a trifle complacent. The battle lines had only fluctuated eastward and westward very slightly since the beginning of the War, so there was little preparedness when up ahead the Germans had launched this last ditch offensive catching the Allies very suddenly, and then the Germans started to dig in, constructing fresh trenches on their newly won ground. Unusually for the British and French but probably because they had been gaining in confidence with the arrival of the Americans on various fronts, which gave them more resources and more latitude to consolidate their forces, they managed to finalise their plans and launch their own brilliant offensive. The Allies committed everything they could to this counter-attack. The Germans, by this stage of the war, stretched in both manpower and supplies, were taken by surprise and overwhelmed. Briefed by intelligence the Allies had assumed that this was a last ditch German effort and that if we acted swiftly enough they would not be able to consolidate. Or if they were expecting a counter attack they wouldn't be able to deal with it. The enemy had bet on this last throw of the dice. It had soon become clear that this was part of an overall offensive along the entire front. Now having made the effort, to be faced with another battle before they had recovered sent German morale to rock bottom and they withdrew, sometimes in good order and sometimes in confusion. In some areas it became a free-for-all, an every-man-for-himself situation until the Allied counter offensive petered out for lack of firm and adequate continuing supply logistics. The Allies had been so successful that they had outrun their own back-up. When both sides paused and took stock, the Allies had not only recaptured the ground they held before but had also overrun enemy lines and the hinterland behind it to the depth of at least a few miles. Areas of countryside behind the German lines which were controlled by the Germans which had been behind the war zone were now part of it, but so swift had been the action that much of the civilian infrastructure was only mildly damaged and some near intact, although of course the civilian population had fled further eastward away from the fighting.

Towards the end of the main action Joe was summoned by one of the sergeants who arrived outside the billet, and was shown an aerial map about two weeks old. It was explained to him roughly where he would be able to find the intended French recipient of the message to be delivered. He was shown by the sergeant roughly how far the Allies had managed to get. There hadn't been the time to do any photographic processing from further aerial reconnaissance as yet in order to update the maps. But the sergeant also gave Joe verbal instructions. Joe looked at the written message. It had been drawn up by a French speaking officer. Translated it said, "The messenger bearer of this despatch is fully authorised to deliver his message verbally." Sergeant Phillip Boddy, a cut above the rest of them and blessed with some insight and understanding continued, "You are to go on a horse up to the front. We are not quite sure at this moment where the French have deployed to exactly, but when you find the new lines, make your way as far as you can up the chain of their command and let them know verbally that we have no more support to offer as yet. There will be no more support. Got that? We've used all our available reserves. They are to hold their positions at all costs." Joe suddenly experienced a sinking feeling in the pit of his stomach. He needed the paper in order to deliver his verbal message but what if he was captured? This was a devastating message it appeared to Joe. To put it mildly, this tenuous new position was the result of a do-or-die counter offensive. We had overreached ourselves! The image of his own possible impending fate must have been visible on his face.

He had never been told to take messages up to the very front before. Until now it had been backwards and forward behind the lines either in a motorcycle sidecar, on a bicycle or sometimes a horse. Never this though. Sergeant Boddy must have read Joe's mind. "Kurtin, don't be concerned, the Germans probably won't attack again. You seem a bit worried. Have you ever been close to the actual sharp end, bayonets, whites of their eyes, kill or be killed and all that?"

"No," replied Joe and Sergeant Boddy affected not to notice the non-acknowledgement of his rank.

"Only shelled from a distance but it was more than enough, too much really. Hah! I thought it was a bit safer here," Joe said with a grim chuckle then realised that he was moaning and groaning. It was the same for most of them there.

"Go to the stores and draw a Webley if it will make you feel better. I am bound to say though that if you are captured, the message in your head must not fall into enemy hands. If it looks like they're going to get you, destroy the paper. They will think it was the actual message. Have you got a lighter?"

"No, I've got matches and cigarettes."

"Fine then. Off you go and good luck. Report straight to me when you get back."

Joe made his way to the stores and duly signed for and took charge of an officer's pistol with case, belt and lanyard and strapped it about his person. The stores NCO showed Joe how to load the pistol before he went off to saddle up Cherry Blossom. He preferred that animal to Boot Polish as it seemed to him that the second horse in the team was suffering from battle fatigue. His huge eyes rolled quite a lot lately showing the whites and every now and then it reared up looking alarmed, whinnying in panic at some imagined situation or noise. Not surprising really, it had been shot a couple of times, not fatally – obviously, but enough to terrify the poor creature at the slightest sound. But here, well behind the lines the horse was reasonably happy, as was Joe. Men and horses were very similar. Joe and his horses had formed a real affection for each other.

The guns were now only a distant rumble as they had been moved forward even further and were pounding the enemy far less frequently due to a chronic shortage of ammunition. Joe mounted up and made his way at a trot along the well-made roads that led up towards the front. The horse was going along briskly picking its way surefootedly and seemed happy enough. He was glad he hadn't risked the other one now. As he began to draw nearer to the previous theatre of battle he could see just what the situation was. The usual supply lines one would have expected to be re-stocking the combatants up ahead was almost non-existent. Clearly they would build eventually but until then Joe realised the situation was quite serious and dreaded being the person to deliver the bad news.

He and the horse picked their way as far as the previous Allied trenches and he was glad to see that they had been bridged in places by wooden causeways and he carefully edged Cherry Blossom across and into the churned up maelstrom of dried mud on the other side. Looking down as he crossed he noticed uniformed bodies both German and French which hadn't yet been taken away. He passed working parties of soldiers detailed to clean up the mess, clearing wire and carrying away corpses. The whiff coming up assailing his nostrils was fearful. He was used to it though and didn't give it much thought other than to wonder about what religious denomination the dead might have been. He could see that the British and French when driven from their trenches had reformed and, with reinforcements, counter-attacked so quickly and effectively that the Germans had not had time to re-adapt the trenches to warfare from the other direction. The spy holes and firing steps were all pointing the wrong way. For the Germans it was a short lived achievement. Driven back and across their own previous lines they fell away in disorder towards the town before they managed to regroup into some sort of order in the face of the weakening allied attack which finally ceased as they dug into new positions. Many men from both sides died in those two days but a feeling of doom and desperation was quickly spreading up and down the German lines. What the outlook was in Berlin Joe was unaware of but the appeasers were beginning to make their views heard. For the moment however more bellicose voices prevailed. The German war effort continued.

There were a few burial parties wandering about and some tractors which had been used to pull the guns further forward now that the new positions had been achieved. Such had been the speed of the Allied counter-attack that the Germans had abandoned some of their artillery which was in the process of being towed away by the French in the distance. Joe managed to inch both himself and Cherry Blossom across the expanse previously known as no-man's-land which had divided the combatants for so long. Once again he negotiated a series of trenches, German this time. He noted they were very carefully constructed and neat. There were still bodies lying there. The question of whether it was all worth it did cross his mind as this enforced sightseeing tour continued unabated until at last he came upon a huge stretch which was relatively undamaged. This, he concluded, must have been the area behind the previous German trenches which the war hadn't touched. The area was rolling with shallow hills, rising and falling. German artillery had been positioned on the higher ground to the rear of their own original lines where they could fire over the heads of their own troops assisted by spotters in their tethered balloons, yet be protected from attack by being dug in and camouflaged in this undulating landscape. Some had been retrieved and moved back with the retreating troops but the rest had to be ignominiously rendered hors-de-combat and abandoned.

Finally after a further trek Joe could see the new Allied lines in the distance up ahead. He could hear firing, the pop, pop, pop of small arms. It sounded so harmless from this distance but he felt the flush of a sudden sweat. As he drew closer he began to feel exposed up there on the back of Cherry Blossom. Off to the right he could see some buildings surrounded by trees. There were two paths leading to them. One of them went round the back and he gently prodded the horse towards that one with his spurred heel. He had a plan. He would dismount and leave the animal there while he made his way forward, less conspicuously on foot.

As he got closer he was amazed to observe that this place had escaped relatively unscathed. He was walking by now, leading Cherry Blossom by the reins. The place was tranquil, apart from the clucking of hens as he entered what was obviously a farm. It was sheltered by trees and undergrowth. The first building he came to was a barn. It was so devoid of humanity around and about that he assumed the occupants of this dwelling had fled with the Germans before the advancing French and British. There were however ducks and chickens here which were giving vent to their emotions, whether it was hunger or fear, or just communication or alarm, there was a racket of quacking and clucking as the domestic birds, which had the appearance of being abandoned, wandered around near the house. He led the horse into the outbuilding. There was even straw in here and stalls but still no other sign of life. He led his mount inside one of them and closed the gate. At least the beast would be able to rest while he was away. He left the saddle and cloth in place and hoped it wouldn't be too uncomfortable for the horse if it did decide to lie down.

Intent upon his mission he would have a better look round after he had delivered his message. He left the farm the way he had come

taking his Lee Enfield with him slung over his right shoulder with his messenger's bag over the left. Gradually he drew ever closer to the rear of the forward allied position and encountered soldiers, French mainly, some resting, from whom he had to ask directions to the French Field-Command. Joe was aware anyway that the British were subordinate to the French who were in charge of the combined operation in

France. This was why the message was to be delivered straight to them. Joe was relieved to see that it was quite well behind the shallowly dug-in troops as he approached the tent which has been pointed out to him. It was a few hundred yards behind the new positions in fact.

"Oh ho they're not silly either," he thought with a wry smile.

He had already been acquainted on the different ranks within the French Army when he had first come out here but had to undergo a refresher at the chateau. So he asked the first French caporal he saw. He stopped him and asked in French who the most senior officer was, that he had an important message from British Headquarters for him. The caporal informed him that the man in overall command was Le Colonel Hulot. "Would you please tell him I'm here?" "Bien! OK Tommy," the man replied eager to try out his limited English. He made his way smartly to the tent and spoke to the guard then went in. Almost immediately an imposing figure of a man emerged. He was smartly dressed, although how that was possible amidst the recent chaos escaped Joe. He could see that this was le marechal de logis – the French equivalent of a regimental sergeant major.

"Vous est le courier Anglais."

"Oui mon marechal'" responded Joe. The NCO looked visibly pleased and said, "Donnez moi le message,"

"Je regret, ce n'est pas possible mon marechal," explained Joe,

"C'est un message verbale."

"Bien. Suivez moi," he responded catching on quickly.

Joe followed him into the tent and found himself before a distinguished looking French officer in a clean blue uniform and the usual officer's round kepi hat lying on a field table.

" Je suis le Colonel LeBrun,"

Joe drew himself up to his full height and saluted smartly. To his surprise the man began to speak in English. "Le Colonel Hulot has been injured. I am now the officer in charge. What is the message you have for me? What is your name?"

"Driver Joseph Kurtin sir."

"What is a driver doing delivering messages. You should be with the artillery. What are you doing as a messenger?"

Joe hesitated before starting to explain but the officer was holding out his hand for the message, so was clearly not really expecting, nor was he interested in, a reply to his question. Joe opened the dispatch bag and handed the message to the colonel who read it quickly and then turned to Joe and said. "Well? Speak man!"

"I am to tell you sir that there will be no immediate reinforcements nor supplies. Headquarters asks that you hold this position with what forces and strength you have at your disposal. We will do our best to consolidate our supply lines within the next hours and days. In the meantime it's imperative that this position be held and not lost – Sir!"

"Mon Dieu! C'est ne pas possible! Merde!"

Joe roughly followed what was being said. The colonel continued to rave as he paced up and down for a bit before regaining his reserve. He gathered himself together and said. "Bien, driver, it's not your fault. Please return and tell them that they can rely on us. We won't waver." As he spoke though he knew he sounded more confident than he actually was. He called in the marechal de logis again and told him to give Joe something to eat and drink before he returned. "Don't waste time though," he added as he returned the paper message back to Joe impatiently. Joe noted idly that the form it was written on originally must have been hastily torn from the pad after being written, and that there were two pages laminated together. The lower sheet's corner was now detaching itself from the one above.

Joe was quickly taken to another tent where he was given a pie and some water for which he was truly thankful at that point but it didn't go far in alleviating the anxiety he felt at the dubious situation these people, and indeed all of them, might be in if the Germans attacked again in numbers. Once again here he was taking on the cares of the world. However, self-preservation was foremost on his mind and he put as much distance between the French, their forward line, and himself as he possibly could, as quickly as he could. As he retraced his steps he occasionally met soldiers but just shouted, "messenger," in either English or French as he approached and they let him pass by on his way unhindered.

He came back to the farm where he had left Cherry Blossom. The afternoon was drawing to a close and dusk was beginning to fall. Joe decided to spend the night there in the stable with the horse and set out for the chateau again the next morning. The noises from the animals had ceased and they had gone but he could still hear something.

Was it the sound of voices and the soft lowing of a cow? Could he smell smoke? Joe became certain now and unlatched his holster and withdrew the handgun. It was very heavy in his hand. He knocked off the safety catch and held the pistol out in front of him as he gingerly walked towards the sounds with his heart thumping so hard he thought the noise would give him away. The talking he could hear led him towards the door of the main building, which was slightly ajar. Yellow light shone out into the gloom of the yard. There were wisps of smoke coming from between the tiles of the roof. One or two were recently smashed. It looked as if there had been a skirmish here but not an extensive one. He noted a few bullet holes around one of the upstairs windows and the glass was splintered.

As he stood there wondering what to do, the voices started to rise and Joe noted one of them was that of a girl. He slowly edged towards the slightly open door and eased part of his head round the edge of it and was absolutely stunned by what he saw. Two men dressed in field grey uniforms with mud-encrusted black boots seemed to be intimidating a young woman. So these were Germans, live ones, up close. He had never actually seen any alive close up. He had seen prisoners being rounded up from a distance and plenty of them dead. But to see them here speaking and moving was surreal. But his wonderment was soon curtailed when he realised what they were up to. The young woman, about seventeen years of age, was being seriously molested by them. They had obviously made her take her shoes and stockings off and were eyeing her up and down. One of them, whom Joe noted to be a nasty lecherous looking individual with a hideous nervous tic and twisted mouth, quickly moved. Joe couldn't believe what he was looking at. The man had reached over and ripped off her skirt brutally throwing her to the floor straight afterwards. The other man was clearly an uncomfortable spectator to this and seemed to be distancing himself from his companion's activity. The molester started to unbutton his own tunic as the girl lay there helpless. In the corner Joe noticed a small boy of about six crying quietly in the corner. The girl said something to the boy and he went upstairs. The second German still seated made some verbal protest to his comrade but the first man took no notice. Joe could vaguely make out a few words of the German being spoken. What he said were something along the lines of; "You don't know what you'll be missing gefreiter. Don't complain to me tomorrow. We can dispose of her afterwards?"

"She just made dinner for us you damned schweinhund. Leave her be. You're a disgrace to Germany! Scheize! Rosenkrantz! I'm not going to let this happen. I am telling you to stop this right now."

"Don't you tell me what to ...."

Rosenkrantz must have sensed something because the shifty gaze of this grotesquely caricatured man suddenly flicked to the door. With shock, his eyes lit on this enemy soldier framed in the doorway. By this time though he was too far gone in disarray, so intent had he been upon assaulting the girl. His belt and tunic were off and his braces were unfastened. His trousers were falling down. He stood frozen for a moment presenting a ridiculous sight. Joe seized the advantage. He had the gun and he had the element of surprise. He noted the malevolent look on the man's pock-marked face face as events unfolded. Recovering himself remarkably quickly, the German swept a stoneware pitcher off the table in Joe's direction in one fluid movement and lunged clumsily forward at the same time. It was the worst decision he was ever to make in his life. Joe dodged the flying utensil by an automatic reflex action and pulled the trigger. There was a massive bang and the bullet caught the German in the throat. The man Rosenkrantz staggered back with stupidly bulging uncomprehending eyes and lurched forward again towards Joe who stepped smartly aside and the man staggered outside entangled in his own trousers, fell down and swiftly bled out all over the yard and became still. Joe, suddenly thrust into the realm of new experiences couldn't quite take it all in. Once again though his instinct of self preservation quickly came to the fore. He levelled the gun at the other German and motioned with it but this man was already half standing, looking white raising his hands. What to do now? was the question coursing through Joe's brain. But he was no killer. He motioned the walrus-moustached German to stay exactly where he was, putting on a fierce, and what he hoped was a frightening, face while he picked up the items of the dead German's discarded apparel and threw them outside. This other German sat there quite obediently and said nothing. He wasn't armed and wasn't particularly brawny and looked as if he might even be in shock. So Joe expected no trouble from him. but wondered if perhaps the shot had been heard but nobody came running. They were a fair distance from anywhere and it was unlikely that there would be soldiers out here at this time of the evening. He hoped they would all be ensconced in their tents or dugouts. In any case the walls would have deadened the sound of the gunshot.

"Where are your weapons?" Joe demanded of the terrified man in German raising his eyebrows in a question.

The soldier, dumb with fright and contemplating death at any moment, motioned over to a bench near a wall behind a long scrubbed white kitchen table. Up against the wall in the corner stood two Mauser rifles. Walking over to them Joe gathered them up with one arm and put them on the table. Keeping his prisoner covered, and with his own rifle still slung over his shoulder he glanced intermittently at one of the guns and figured out how to remove the bolt. Placing his pistol down on the table pointing towards the German he used both hands to remove the bolt from each rifle whilst continually glancing up at the man opposite. But there was no sign of resistance pending. Still keeping the man covered, Joe went to the door and threw the bolts as far as he could into the duck pond.

"Outside," he ordered the German.

The man looked resigned to his fate. "Raus." Joe shouted.

Once outside Joe indicated to the soldier to drag the body of his dead companion away behind some bushes our of sight of the girl. Then he made his prisoner swill away any traces of blood by pointing to a bucket and the duck pond. The man quickly cottoned on and did as he had been told with alacrity.

Joe now turned his attention to the girl who had modestly left the kitchen through a door into an adjoining room. She reappeared fully dressed. She then went upstairs and returned with the boy. Sitting on a stool with her arm round the little boy who was still sobbing it was clear there was a strong bond between them. Luckily the little lad hadn't witnessed the sudden violence, and finally he stopped his grizzling. It had been a shocking event that the young girl had been forced to endure but she had been fairly well been spared the worst part of the killing which had terminated outside. Joe started a conversation by introducing himself in French and asking how many Germans there were and she indicated two only. He assured the girl and boy that they were quite safe as the French and Americans were now controlling this entire countryside. She seemed relieved to hear that and told Joe that her name was Marie and the child was her brother Georges. "Nice names," commented Joe.

"Yes, traditional in our family. The eldest girl is always called Marie and the eldest boy is always called Georges. It's been like that here for many years.

" Funny that, we seem to have had a lot of Josephs in our family."

Joe turned his attention to the German who was listening with interest to the conversation. "Parlez vous Francais?" asked Joe.

"Un peu," he replied. "Je ne parle pas l'Anglais."

From then on Joe spoke to him in a mixture of French with some of the German the Miesners had helped him with. He discovered that both the soldiers were messengers. This man to whom Joe was speaking considered himself to be the senior over his dead comrade as the other man had been transferred from another unit. They didn't get along. No, it was worse than that, they hated each other. Evidently they had been sent up to the front with messages but such had been the speed of the Allied attack that they had been overwhelmed, abandoned everything except their rifles and satchels and had taken refuge here. Fortunately the battle had passed them by in their hiding place in the loft of the barn. They had heard some firing and had later found a German body upstairs in the farmhouse but had dragged it outside and away from the building later on, during the course of their residence here, while they decided what to do,

Marie and her brother had suddenly appeared to feed the chickens and Rosenkrantz had thought it safer to keep them here in case they gave the two of them away. Now he realised what his comrade's motive had been. They had got her cooking and looking after them and as Joe had rightly assessed, gratitude took a most distorted form in the mind of Rosenkrantz.

Joe started to think ahead. What was the next logical procedure in this chain of events. He had three choices. He could take the man prisoner and get him back to HQ. He might know something of importance. The problem there was that he only had one horse. The man would have to walk behind or in front. Joe didn't want the bother of it. Could he just shoot him? Joe dismissed that out of hand almost before he had even begun to think about it. The third way seemed most attractive. Why not just let him go?

"If I do release him and allow him to go, how do I know he won't be shot by the Americans or the French? How can I guarantee he

will get back to his own lines? After all he seems quite a decent fellow. But would they shoot an unarmed man?" Joe got to thinking about the military situation. Somehow he sensed they were at a critical point in the war. Did this man already have information that could be of use to the Allies? Unlikely," Joe thought, and there were no despatch bags. As he continued to ponder, his lively mind began to formulate something which he thought might work. "Why not let him get away but give him some false information to take with him?"

As the idea took hold he contrived to think of how it could be done. He engaged the man in conversation again asking him what his name was and what he thought of his companion. The German gave his name as Theo Drifall and assured him that although he detested the man Schutz Klaus Rosenkrantz, as a gefreiter he outranked his companion. He didn't particularly blame him for what had happened. It wasn't his fault, he couldn't help it.

Much of the conversation which took place between Drifall and Joe was stilted in some areas as each struggled to find correct translation but were sometimes stymied and so they approached what they wanted to say to each other laterally from a totally different angle. Occasionally a gesture spoke a thousand words, a shrug, a look, a grin or a frown made communication clear.

"You don't blame him? That evil bastard? How can you say that? I don't understand the logic behind that.

The German messenger, after some thought, retorted, "He couldn't help what he was. It's all meant to be. It's predestined, predetermined – everything that will ever happen. You call him evil. What is evil? What is good? Whatever happens, happens and no-one can do a thing about it. Yes, we make decisions – we think, but those decisions were already meant to be taken," He fell silent. Joe realised that the man had become very animated moving his hands around for emphasis. "Blimey! he really cares about all this deeply," thought Joe. "And he is a philosopher as well. Who would have thought it? But I saw for myself earlier he does draw the line at some things"

"So what do you think is meant to happen in this war then."

Theo thought for a moment before answering.

"I think we have been betrayed. I believe we have been let down by left-wing factions in the Government and in industry. We the people have been stabbed in the back. We are just not getting the support. There is a movement at home towards appeasement."

"Do you think Germany will lose the war then because of that?"

"Very possibly, probably – yes I do."

"Well if it's meant to happen according to your views, what is the problem if nothing can be done anyway?"

"There is no problem. It might seem to be a problem to some. It will lead to something much better. A better system will come out of it. But honestly I don't have all the answers. I need to know more facts. When I have them it will all fall into place. By the way, I forgot to ask about you, what were you doing out here?"

"I don't suppose it will do any harm to tell you because my message has already been delivered," said Joe tapping his satchel and I ought to tell you also that I'm taking you in as my prisoner tomorrow morning. Something's happening which will end the war but I can't tell you about it. You are quite right I think. The war is going to be over soon for you anyway. In fact for all of us, and we can all go home."

"Can I ask you, where are you from? What is your family?

"London," replied Joe. "The East End to be exact."

"Ja, I have heard of it, a proper seething mass of migrants isn't it?" Theo asked, looking disgusted.

"Yes I suppose so, and I'm one of them. Lithuanian by descent."

"Me also in a way I suppose," said Theo, I'm Austrian by birth but moved to Germany so that I could join the army and fight."

"If you're an immigrant too then why do you scoff at other migrants just trying to better themselves?"

"I went to volunteer for a cause, not for what I could get out of it."

"What about your personal life," asked Joe. "If you don't mind me saying you look a bit older that most of the Germans I've seen here, although I must say most of those I have seen have been dead." Theo looked downcast when he heard that comment.

The man then opened up a bit about his background. His family it turned out wasn't extensive, mainly distant relatives, he lived with an aunt. The thing which surprised Joe however was Theo's revelation that he had a baby son, Jean Marie, by a French girl he had met. The mother of his son, a girl named Charlotte Lobjoie, lived near San Quentin with her parents. Theo maintained that he didn't know how it had happened really. Joe smiled to himself with amusement. Theo smiled too as he fell in. Even with incomplete language skills it was amazing how humour could be shared.

"No, no not in that way. We had nothing in common really. She spoke no German and I only a little French, but we managed to communicate somehow on a basic level. I used to talk philosophy to her. I doubt she understood much of that. After a little too much wine one afternoon and after I had sketched her in the fields, one thing led to another. A couple of months later it became obvious she was pregnant and I was transferred, but we continued to write."

"So how old is the baby?" Joe asked.

"Three months only."

"So who is going to provide for it when the war's over?"

"I'll make some arrangements I'm sure. The difficult thing is that I don't love her and I don't see a future for us together. I'll show you the picture of her but I will need to open my knapsack. I promise I don't have a gun or a knife." Joe was at ease with this man. He was intelligent and there was a lot to admire in his bearing. Joe thought he was a good judge of character and Theo's piercing blue eyes betrayed a look of genuine intensity. He was quite an impressive character.

"Let me see it then. Why do you carry it around with you?"

"To tell you the truth, I don't always get on well with my comrades. I think they see me as someone different to them. They think I'm aloof or that I think I am better than them. So I used to find that some of my work had been got at while I was away. I found spectacles and moustaches had been drawn on some of my sketches, or teeth blackened out. Some of my work was even stolen. All very infantile, so I took to sending work home before it could be defaced. This one I just keep with me. She's the only girl friend I've ever had."

"What about you? Do you have someone who is dear to you?"

"Yes and no. I took girls out back home but nothing serious came of them. Then there was one girl who I was madly in love with, Charlise, but she suddenly ended it. I don't really know why. I was a different person then but I will never forget her. But since I came out here I was forced to keep up with the other blokes." Joe made an up-and-down balancing motion with both hands to explain his point. "You've got to fit in haven't you? or it's a miserable life. I have had a few rolls in the hay and sometimes been upstairs in one or two drinking dens. Not exactly dens but you know what I mean. Wine shops with extra facilities. French mothers and daughters have to live in these difficult times. Sometimes the queue stretches halfway down the stairs, but we English are good at queuing. I don't think any of this conflicts with my religion. I must say though that sometimes these activities don't leave much for the collection plate on the Sundays when I do manage to get to Mass, and I am developing a taste for French wine. God knows what my sister would think if she knew. She would faint at the very least, but the whole world is turned upside down isn't it. We have been forced to become other people."

"What did you mean by 'roll in the hay?" the German asked.

Joe attempted to explain but ended up making signs and gestures to accompany his words until he thought by the slight smile on Theo's face that he had fallen in.

Theo went to pick up his satchel but Joe told him to stop and took

a look through it first. All that was in there was a scroll like document which he withdrew. It was a folded and rolled up colour sketch which he opened out. It showed a peasant girl with her face shielded in a red patterned scarf. Joe admired it and told Theo it was good. The German tended to be sensitive about his work so he thought Joe was damning him with faint praise. Being patronised depressed him. He was really unsure if he actually had artistic talent or not and for some reason he found he was slightly jealous to hear of the way Joe fitted in with his compatriots whereas he didn't with his. He was well aware he was always on the fringes, alone and lonely. He told Joe that he had found a little dog while he was out here but even that had run away. Joe assured him that he did indeed have talent. Joe was genuine in his praise. Theo possessively refolded and rolled the document and returned the image of the mother of his son to the safety of his bag. Joe turned his attention to the little boy and noticed him looking at his rifle. Joe took up the gun and stood at ease. Georges smiled and Joe went through a few motions of sloping arms and marching up and down. All the time he kept one eye on Theo. The boy was delighted by the fun and tried to march in time with Joe, laughing and giggling as he went. Joe picked up a broom and showed the child how to hold it over his shoulder and then he started to quietly sing the marching song he been taught by Monsieur Martin and had later heard squads of French Poilus singing as they marched along. 'La Madelon':

> Pour le répos le plaisir du militaire.
> Il e là-bas a deux pas de la forêt
> Une maison aux murs tous couverts de lière
> Aux Tourlourous c'est le nom du cabaret

La servante est jeune et gentille
Légère comme un papillon
Comme son vin son oeil petille
Nous l'appelons la Madelon.

Joe sang it as he marched up and down and the little fellow joined in laughing and enjoying himself as he went. Even Theo tapped his fingers until at last Georges became fed up with it and sat down.

Marie ushered the little boy away upstairs to bed amidst a few tired sounding protestations and with a few parting glances from him towards the two soldiers. Joe then made his way over to the other side of the room, strangely saddened by that song but still with the Webley very much in evidence.

Theo was unable to prevent himself feeling a little downhearted too despite his previously expressed pragmatic approach to fate.

He was deep in contemplation about his own future and that of the German people when it suddenly occurred to him that there might be a way of winning the admiration of his unit. Joe's strategy had worked. The thing which had intrigued Theo the most was the hint which Joe had dropped about something big pending. He was sure he had understood correctly even in a mixture of the two languages. He began to think that if he could somehow find out more detail it might go well with him at headquarters. He was fairly certain that his captor was still carrying a copy of the message. He had seen Joe tap the bag when he was speaking of it. What were the chances?

Joe, with his own agenda, wandered over to Marie, drew her aside and very quietly asked if she had a pen and ink he could use, or a pencil. Her whispered reply made his heart quicken with excitement as his plan began to become real in his mind.

He went back to his prisoner and advised him to get some sleep and told him they would be moving in the morning. Theo did as he was told and hunkered down on a sofa while Joe sat there with the pistol very obviously on his knee pointing in the German's direction. Joe doubted if the man would try to go anywhere as long as he thought he might be shot doing it. When Joe heard the breathing pattern of the other man settle into a deep and regular rhythm he quietly picked up his despatch bag and made his way over to a table in a corner on the other side of the room. A candle was burning where Marie had left the pen and ink. Joe found the message form and separated the two pages. Taking the blank form he filled out the details of a message to the French from British headquarters that a hundred and fifty thousand Americans would be combining with the French and British and would be attacking thirty miles to the north of here. These massive American reinforcements would be arriving at their point of rendezvous any day now The combined French and American forces were building up rapidly. There would be two hundred and fifty tanks scheduled for service on that Northern sector alone. The entire war effort was gaining momentum. The big push along all fronts will be commencing in ten days but the main thrust would be at, (here Joe put in the names of all the towns he could think of which were thirty miles to the north of their present location here on this farm). He marked the head of the sheet, 'Top Secret' and signed it with the name of a British major-general. Burning the genuine authorisation message, he placed the concocted version in its place.

Leaving the bag on the floor he fought to stay awake. He didn't want to have his gun stolen and be shot with it, so he had to remain alert. It was a struggle, after all he had been through. He dozed fitfully. Sure enough, as dawn was breaking he heard the prisoner stir and could almost see the wheels of the man's brain turning. Pretending to fall asleep again he watched Theo through a barely opened eye and saw him tentatively start to move. Theo surreptitiously glanced at Joe and noted the pistol loosely gripped in his hand and the rifle with Joe's arm entwined in the sling. Slowly Theo headed for the despatch bag taking slow deliberate steps on tiptoe. Stealthily bending, he grasped the bag, opened it quietly and carefully took out the paper and headed for the door with his own satchel on his back. Joe watched him all the way. He willed Theo to open the door quietly so that he wouldn't have an excuse to wake up. Good! He was out and walking with the message. Joe would have to make this look convincing. He got up, put down the pistol, unslinging the Lee-Enfield at the same moment and walked to the door with it. He peered through the crack of the semi closed door and waited until Theo Drifall was nearly out of sight then Joe threw the door open with a bang and called out "Halt!"

As far as Theo was concerned he was gambling that Joe wouldn't shoot. Despite the killing of Rosenkrantz he had come to realise that Joe was really quite a decent type. And after all Joe couldn't possibly have known that he had the message. There was no real reason for Joe to kill him. And he was partly right, Joe wasn't going to shoot him. Theo paused, turned round, looked at Joe with a half smile on his face, waved, turned on his heel and started running. Joe stood frozen, finger on the trigger. Theo Drifall was perfectly aligned in his sights. One quick shot to the heart would have done it. Joe however knew what he was doing. He raised the rifle slightly above the escaping German's head and pulled the trigger. The recoil would have knocked him back but he had pulled the gun tightly into his shoulder, just as he had been taught.

He worked the bolt clicking up and pulling back ejecting the spent cartridge case. The next spring-loaded bullet popped up from the magazine to a position level with the open breech. Joe rammed it home with the bolt action and took aim to one side of the fleeing figure and fired again just for good measure. Theo had gone. Joe had become a master of life and death. This time it was to be life.

Chapter 32

La Madelon

Joe returned to the farmhouse and sat down with Marie and Georges who had been awakened by the shots. They looked agitated as well they might after all that had happened. Marie had been traumatised the previous day but now she was much calmer. Joe did his best to allay their fears telling them that the worst was now behind them. The dead bodies were gone, out of sight. When he got back to HQ he would explain the situation and they would send a party out here to clean up. But first he wanted to find out the circumstances of the young woman and the child. Marie after a bit of prompting explained that back here they had been well behind the lines until a few days earlier and their lives had been fine under the Germans. They had found them to be just like anyone else. They had not been short of food and often travelled into town. While she was explaining all this Marie was busying herself carving slices from the goose which Rosenkrantz had killed the day before and which she had been made to cook. She still had some bread from the batch of loaves she had baked a few days previously in the big stone oven in the corner. She proceeded to distribute the food onto two plates and a smaller one. She produced three cups and poured milk from a ewer, the twin of the one which Klaus Rosenkrantz had swiped off the table and smashed the day before. Joe noticed that the farmyard noises had returned this morning and apart from the distant rumbling of a few guns the scene was almost normal, the sun was shining, the sky was cloudless and Joe was wondering how far Theo had managed to get. It was out of his hands now, all in the lap of the Gods.

"Where is the rest of the family?" Joe gently asked, thinking that perhaps they might be dead.

"We were separated when all this happened," she replied, gesturing vaguely all around. The Germans took them along as they retreated or at least they tagged along with them. The horse was gone from the stable so they must have taken him. It was all chaotic, There was a lot going on, a lot of panic. The cows were shut up safely in the barn. As it turns out Georges and I were in the cellar. There was a lot to think about and we were all frightened. I think they must have believed we were right behind them but we weren't, because as you saw there was a flurry of action round here when the soldier was killed upstairs and we had to stay hidden. They must be behind the German lines now, probably in town worrying themselves silly about us. But Papa is very bright he will know that we are amongst French people again. But look Joe, not to worry, you can see how we can look after ourselves. We have the chickens and the ducks and the cow in the barn with her calf, so there's plenty of milk. We have the well for water and a cellar with wine." She noticed Joe's quietness as he recalled what had nearly happened but for his own intervention. Then he remembered Theo's discourse on life. You just do what you do and things happen or don't happen.   Was it he, Joe, who had made the difference or was he just an instrument of something higher and more profound? How was he to know?

"You mentioned wine?" Joe asked.

"Yes would you like to try some," came a small voice.

It was Georges, very quietly, who had suddenly offered.

"Oui, s'il te plait." Joe replied softly. Georges jumped up and ran out through the door and returned a short while later with a stone jar which he then proceeded to tip up over a pair of small thick glasses which Marie had produced. "Where's my glass?" the boy said.

"Oh all right, go and get some water to dilute it. Don't think for a minute you are having it neat." Joe sampled the wine and found it very palatable. It was a world away from Whitechapel and it wasn't until he had come out here that he had sampled the many joys of the estaminet. Unlike in England where drinkers of ale and gin rolled out of the pubs roaring drunk and ready to fight anyone, the French seemed more sophisticated. They knew how to savour and appreciate the qualities of good wine rather than as a medium to get sloshed as quickly as possible. As he got to round about his second or third glass Joe felt really good. Alcohol brought out his warm friendly side and he began to hum the French song they had been singing the previous evening. Georges' eyes lit up and he joined in again and Marie also. "I have heard this from a distance before you sang it last night," she mentioned with a faraway sad look. Joe, encouraged, raised his voice an octave smiling and winking at Georges as he sang. The boy was immensely tickled by this and Joe added to the fun by stamping his feet on the spot on the flagstone floor.   Finally Joe got bored with La Madelon and stopped. Georges would have continued but instead asked Joe if he knew any other songs. Joe, now emboldened by the alcohol started to sing in Lithuanian, a comical song taught to him by his mother when he was a small child. It was the one about a hare sitting on a rock contemplating the meaning of life. It was very funny and every now and then Joe broke off with the tears of laughter streaming down his face. Georges interrupted him asking if he was singing in English. "No Georges this is Lithuanian,"

"What's that? What is Lithuanian," the boy asked.

"It's spoken in a country a long way away from here to the east. It's past Germany just before you come to Russia."

Maria said nothing but left the room coming back a bit later carrying an old dusty dog-eared collection of pages once bound together as a book but now just kept together by providence. It had been protected at some stage by a piece of oilcloth which was now fragile. "Look at this Joe," she said. Joe took it and turned it over, carefully opening it and realised that it was a French-Polish dictionary. What it was doing here in this out of the way place had Joe baffled. "Where did this come from?" Joe was intrigued. "This is Polish."

"I don't know, it has always been here. Papa once showed it to me and even he wasn't sure how we came by it. Fascinated, Joe looked through it, read the preface to it and realised that the Polish was a little more archaic than that spoken nowadays. He felt like a modern English person reading Dickens. Something slightly out of date. At a rough guess he thought it might have been about a hundred years old. They went through a few of the pages with Joe trying to explain the pronunciation but the little boy could scarcely read anyway and Marie was unable to pronounce the unfamiliar complex Polish sounds. In fact Joe began to struggle with the pronunciation himself but that could have been because of the wine he had unwisely drunk too early.

"Why don't you just take it?" Marie suddenly suggested on an impulse. Marie reminded him that it would be of more use to him than them and she wanted to give him something as a token of thanks for all he had done for them. Joe was touched but handed it back saying that he couldn't possibly accept such an heirloom. It was about time to be leaving anyway Joe was thinking. He might be accused of going absent-without-leave, although in his heart he was gambling that Sergeant Boddy would probably be fine with it.

"I'm going to be off now," said Joe at last to the two of them and they both looked a bit crestfallen. "But look Georges I'll make you something to play with. Do you have a handkerchief?"

Marie ran upstairs to get one and Joe proceeded to fold the white cloth in a complicated manner. A few ties and pull throughs and lo and behold a long white rabbit with floppy ears appeared. Georges was delighted and stroked his little rabbit cradling it in his arms. For Marie he took from his tunic pocket his precious pack of cards and showed her an unusual trick. Joe split the pack. She had to pick a card off the top of one of them, memorise it and let the corner down again. Cupping the cards in his hands he dashed them in a downward motion blowing suddenly and strongly upon them as he did so. When she turned the same card up again it was different. Joe performed this trick several times but she was still none the wiser. Joe then explained the mechanics of exactly how it was done and she was thrilled. Joe made her try it herself and after several attempts she finally got it. He then presented her with the cards and as he left they were both busily playing with their respective toys. He had barely got as far as the barn when Marie ran after him clutching a wooden crucifix about nine inches high on a stand. I want you to have this Joe to keep you safe. The wine had made him slightly maudlin and he was emotionally touched, he kissed her lightly on the cheek before suppressing a tear as he got Cherry Blossom ready for action again. He looked at the cross. It was made of a light coloured wood with a small metal figure of Christ nailed to it. It was extremely ornate and immediately struck a chord in him. He put it into the empty despatch bag. He rode off in the direction of HQ by the other lane leading away from the farm. As he did so he passed by an ancient signpost carved from a piece of weather beaten, silver coloured oak. The lettering was worn and rounded, barely legible itself to those coming the other way. If one had studied it carefully they might have deciphered 'La Ferme Saunière. Georges Deschamps – proprietère.' But Joe didn't see it. He didn't give it a second glance as he rode upon his way. It would have meant nothing to him anyway.

Chapter 33

A Face from the Past

Joe made his way back the way he had come feeling slightly woozy from the wine he had drunk earlier. Somehow, even with the slight thumping headache which was warning him of impending migraine he navigated his way back to the chateau past the sentry and straight to Sergeant Boddy's hut. The man came out and looked sharply at Joe. "Where have you been? What took you so long?" he said quizzically and waited for an explanation. Joe told him what had happened but omitted the part about the false message. He now felt very sheepish about that and thought it would sound like something from Comic Cuts. Boddy would think him a fool if he related it. They would come down hard on anyone thinking for themselves acting

without orders. In this case, he thought in retrospect, that he might
have caused immense damage by what he had done. He knew they
wouldn't take kindly to his initiative. The sergeant then asked him
exactly who he had spoken to among the French officers, what he had
said and what the reply had been. Joe told him in detail and was dismissed to the quartermaster to hand in his Webley. Leading Cherry
Blossom, he made his way to the stores, and noticed that Boddy was
coming with him. As well as handing in the pistol, he was forced to
account for the ammunition he had used, by the stores NCO. One
round from the Webley and two .303 shells from the Lee Enfield.
The stores quartermaster-sergeant, clearly a man to do things by the
book, needed to know from Joe the circumstances of the action and
why he had missed with both shots from the rifle. "Don't know sergeant," he stuttered in reply, "The prisoner was a fair way off and I
had only just woken up. I suppose I was bleary eyed or something."

The man seemed to sniff the air. "Have you been drinking on duty
Kurtin? You sound slurred."

"No sarn't, the girl I told you about spilled some wine over me last
night at the farmhouse." He lied, but the alcohol had impaired his
judgement and he couldn't prevent an irritated tone creeping into his
voice. He had also spelled out his response slowly, as if speaking to an
idiot. The sergeant noticed this, took offence and looking at Sergeant
Boddy and then back at Joe snapped sharply, "You're on a charge for
insubordination. You're going before the CO. He is going to want to
know more about your so called 'accident' with the alcohol and these
two German messengers you met. Put your horse away then report
back here on the double." Sergeant Boddy nodded his agreement.

Joe was distracted and a bit distraught. Instead of praising him for
what he had done they seemed to be more concerned with three used
bullets and the state of his breath. Injustice was hard to tolerate even
though he had already had plenty of practice already in his young life.

He led Cherry Blossom across to the stable stopping outside to take
off the harness so that he could rub him down.

He went about removing some of the sweat and foam from the horse's flanks with handfuls of straw. The repetitive action came naturally to him and his mind turned over and over at the way he had had been treated by these two NCOs. It was fine for them with their cushy little numbers here behind the lines. He had actually been there and had been forced to act on the spur of the moment and do as he thought fit at the time. Muttering to himself he led the horse by the halter into the stable and towards its stall. Could he get the horse in? Could he Hell! The horse wasn't co-operating. Joe was carelessly not giving this his full attention. The wine, the telling off, the prospect of appearing before the CO, combined to make him lose his concentration. He lurched and tripped over a hay fork which somebody had left on the floor partly hidden by straw. Losing his balance completely he plunged head first towards the horse's rump which resulted in him head-butting the horses rear end. Joe's cap badge dug in. Cherry Blossom reacted in the only way it could. It stood up on its front legs and kicked out at the back. One hoof caught Joe a glancing blow on the side of the head with a searing, shocking intense pain. It was like the end of the world. It was complete confusion. Things happened too quickly for Joe to even begin to comprehend and then he knew no more long before he hit the floor..

He came to briefly and then lapsed again into a sort of semi-aware state as he heard snatches of conversation. Sometimes there was a pounding inside his skull. He felt his head constricted and his hearing was muffled and he couldn't see anything much except from time to time a wooden ceiling. Then later on, sky with clouds which were always changing. He was being jolted along. Every lurch sent a pain through his head. Every now and then the jolting stopped as someone propped him up and he was given a sip of water which sometimes made him choke and retch. He never opened his eyes, he felt too ill. He wanted to die more than anything, he felt so bad.

" 'e might be a goner........ lift 'im up......... turn right 'ere..... 'ow

much furver? Watch your end! Left 'and dahn a bit."

He seemed to be jolting along faster now to the drone of an engine. He could smell petrol. He could hear groaning from somewhere close by. It seemed to be coming from above him and sometimes from the side. There was a whiff of cigarette smoke which made him feel nauseous. Then he felt himself being shaken around and in a moment of lucidity saw a railway carriage. He regained a semblance of consciousness and was aware of several people lifting him up into something. His vision was a blur, he couldn't quite see what was happening but he was still again and fell into a slumber as a gentle motion and rhythmic clicking drew him towards sleep like a lullaby. The throbbing in his head faded away as he slept again.

The next thing he became aware through hazy vision was of what seemed to be an angel in white stooping over him and looking down. "Joseph, can you hear me it uttered?"

"I must be dead," Joe concluded.

"It's alright Joseph you are in hospital at St Martin. You are quite safe." His level of consciousness subsided again.

He felt hands pulling at him, stripping him, washing him. He was propped up and spoon fed with some liquid. At first it made him sick again and he was just allowed to flop back again onto a pillow to sleep. These actions were repeated periodically and he eventually managed to retain his level of awareness for some of the time.

He began to notice his surroundings as he was able to focus his eyes and it gradually became clear that he was in a hospital ward with other people. He was lying in his own bed between white sheets for the first time since he had last been on leave. The angels he saw flitting about were nurses ministering to him and the other patients. Now the noises these others made began to irritate him and sometimes kept him from sleeping. The man in the next bed had a tunnel raising the sheets over his lower half. He noticed the head of the person opposite was swathed in bandages. Once he came round from his semiconscious state and happened to see them changing the man's dressings. He had seen hideous sights before but never on a live person. This man looked like a creature dreamed up by Hieronymus Bosch. Joe was looking at the face of the Devil. A weak scream was issuing from the space where the mouth should have been. The screens were drawn around but the painful noises continued, etching themselves into Joe's brain. He covered his ears to deaden the sound then slept.

When he awoke all was quiet again. He had been moved into a large wooden barrack room type ward with an iron stove in the middle. He saw thin sunlight transmitting weak rays through the windows. The nurse came to him again. "Do you feel like a change of scenery Joesph?"

"I wouldn't mind." he managed with a muttered groan.

"I'll just have a word with the Lieutenant then," she said.

Returning a bit later on with a wickerwork bathchair, she and two other nurses lifted Joe into a sitting position on the edge of his bed and helped him into a dressing gown over the pyjamas he was wearing. His head throbbed. They then tucked him up in a blanket. Joe hadn't felt as pampered as this since he was a child and if he hadn't still had that discomforting aching in his head he would have quite enjoyed it. One of the nurses started to push him outside passing between the two rows of beds which occupied this ward. They wheeled him through a connecting corridor into the main brick building. He took in the other casualties in varying states of recovery and others who looked desperately injured. He glanced into a room in which a man was being made to walk but

who seemed to have no authority over his limbs which were shaking uncontrollably. His head was also jerking upwards in an involuntary tic. Joe had seen that before but nearer to the front line. He felt that this man was lucky to be here. Others he had seen at the Front had not engendered any sympathy at all as far as he was aware. Perhaps they took this phenomenon more seriously these days Joe supposed. They arrived at the entrance to a conservatory. He was wheeled inside and Joe found himself parked in a small group of three other assorted bathchairs and wheelchairs. It was pleasantly warm in there. The man opposite seemed to be missing both legs. At least Joe couldn't see any evidence of them but he seemed cheerful enough and was strapped in and propped up reading a newspaper.

Another man, who was asleep, had an arm missing, his dressing gown sleeve tucked into his pocket, his good hand helping him puff at a pipe and a third individual who just sat staring vacantly into space.

Joe ventured to interrupt the man reading. "What's happening. I've been out of it for a time I think."

"It's all over. It's finished."

"What do you mean? You have everything to live for!"

"The war."

"What about the war?"

"It's over. An armistice has been signed. We've won. We're all going home. What happened to you anyway?"

Joe began to try and collect his thoughts and memories. They came back slowly and then descended upon his overworked brain in a sudden rush. He recalled the events which had befallen him one after the other until he reached the farm and the Germans and the girl and boy. He vaguely remembered a debriefing and then it came to a halt. After that came the fuddled experiences of this present hospital he now found himself in. He wondered what could have happened in between to have brought him to this pass.

Looking outside he could see it was approaching winter. Most of the leaves had fallen from the trees in the parkland which surrounded these buildings and were scattered on the ground. He realised that he must have been coming and going mentally for several months. He could also see from his position within the conservatory that the people outside were well wrapped up and the military personnel were wearing greatcoats. Motorised ambulances were driving in and out. The inward bound ones were speeding along but some of those going in the other direction were travelling much more slowly.

Later that evening back in his bed he asked the nurse who brought him his tea if he could speak to someone from the admissions section who might be able to account for his present situation and advise him on the prospects for his recovery.

The next morning an orderly came with a walking stick for Joe and he was helped to make his way with it slowly through the building until they came to an office. The orderly knocked and a voice bade them enter. Seated at the desk was a Royal Army Medical Corps officer with the rank of Lieutenant. He gave a start when he saw Joe who himself seemed to know the man from somewhere. The officer motioned him to a chair. There was a silence as they looked at each other with a mutually dawning recognition.

"How are your mother, sister and little brother?" the officer asked with a soft Irish burr. Suddenly a more distant memory flashed into Joe's head. It was of a train journey and a huge religious institution in Brentwood a few years ago. This was that young priest Father Drea, but in a different uniform.

"Father, – Sir! I didn't expect to see you here." Discreetly continuing without any further reference to the circumstances which might have brought Father Drea here, Joe continued,

"They are fine but I'm not so sure about me. I'm told I've been sick. Do

363

you know Sir what has happened to me please?"
Lieutenant Drea consulted the notes before him and explained to
Joe that he had been kicked badly by a horse and hadn't been expected to live. He had been transported by field ambulance to the
nearest railhead and from there to this hospital near the coast at St
Martin. He told Joe that he had been in a semi-conscious state for
months. He had been very lucky to survive with that skull fracture.
"Your next move is going to be to England. I'll be recommending
that you be discharged from the army. I think your condition is
something you will have to learn to live with. Clearly you are not
going to be much good to them with the recurring headaches you
are suffering and I am told there is nothing meaningful that can be
done medically about it apart from giving you painkillers."

So there was a complete episode missing from his life.

"What happened to the course of the war? The part of it I seem to
have missed," Joe asked.

"There was a massive allied attack, not far from where you were
actually." Drea replied. "We broke through. Their defences were
weak at that point, there was very little resistance and the enemy's
resolve just crumbled away. It seems they miscalculated and had concentrated their full strength in another area further North. It was
probably faulty intelligence. Our army broke through and encircled
a large part of their front line and they sued for peace. For them it
was probably the last straw. Strange really and rather unexpected."

As Lieutenant Drea's words sunk in, Joe barely dared to wonder.

Joe thought immediately of Planet Street his mother and family
and his friend Antanas. His own killing of a man. He felt inner
turmoil, a surge of mixed emotions, profound sorrow coupled with
such relief that he couldn't prevent the sobs expressing all the pent-up
emotion he had been harbouring for the past few years.

The sympathetic officer immediately noticed Joe's discomfort.

He got up and went outside and Joe heard him say to someone,
"Fetch two cups of tea to my office."

While he was gone Joe found his handerchief and dried the tears which were trickling down his cheeks

"Tell me what happened to you," said Lieutenent Drea when he returned. Joe recounted some of the things which had occurred as if Lieutenant Drea was Father Drea again hearing confession. In the light of the terrible events he had seen and experienced, all the suppressed fears and doubts regarding his faith resurfaced again as Drea listened patiently. There was a knock and an orderly came in bearing two cups of tea, a sugar bowl, milk jug and two spoons on a tray. There was a pause as the two men helped themselves to sugar and milk and took a few sips. After a while Lieutenant Drea spoke.

"Whats on your mind Joe?"

What's it all for Sir?" Joe asked. He felt he could talk freely to Lieutenant Drea him being an ex-priest. He would understand.

"We cannot know the mind of God Joe. He decides and we just help by doing the best we can."

"Father, that's the second time I have heard something similar to that in not so many words. The last time was from the lips of a very earnest enemy soldier I met, one who escaped, who thought we had no control over any of the events which happen."

He told Father Drea about the German messenger and the fatalistic view he had of life. The Priest turned Army Officer went on.

"No, I don't agree with that. We must believe we can influence things in life, or else we may as well all just give up." said the officer. "We must strive to do good to our fellow man."

"That's just it replied Joe. "What is good and what is evil? Are there actually such things?"

"Of course there are," Drea answered.

"Why? These could just be concepts invented by the human mind? Why do we apply these terms to some individual human beings yet not to other animals?"

"It's because man is not an animal. He is above the animals. We have souls and animals don't. Mankind was given dominion over animals by God at the time of the Creation."

Joe felt rather guilty questioning the received wisdom of the Church but those disingenuous thought processes in other people and the twisting of language had been brought firmly into doubt in Joe's mind on his last mission. The question of good and evil and any degree of it was understood by the clergy who had already assumed that Joe, and others were 'bad' and who were intent upon making them 'good'.

" Look!" said Drea. "A perfect example of goodness The Good Samaritan. You know that parable told by Our Lord don't you?"

"Yes I do, but that German might have been right. There could be another way of looking at it. The Good Samaritan stopped to help the man waylaid by thieves. He is termed good because it is accepted that he must be so. After all he put himself out to aid someone he didn't know, someone not even of his own tribe. Was he wrongly known as 'Good', because he lacked the wit to consider the possible repercussions of his actions? The other man who walked past on the other side is not praised for his caution against being waylaid in a possible trap. Did that other man weigh it all up as he approached and decide not to become involved. Was his personal commitment primarily to himself, his own safety, his own

family, and his future ability to provide for them. Perhaps that was paramount in his mind. And he is condemned for it?"

Drea replied, "You could argue that the Samaritan made a conscious act to help his fellow man regardless of the peril he may have been placing himself in and also disregarding the fact that the victim was one of a race which hated Samaritans. He put all that aside and saw only someone in dire need of assistance."

"Yes Sir, you have a point."

Drea continued, "We are all asking ourselves questions about this war. What was it for? Did I do my duty to my country and to God to the best of my ability? If the answer is 'Yes' you should stop questioning yourself and accept it.

"Yes Sir, that is exactly what I am saying or asking. It's what the German said. "Accept what happens, it's going to happen anyway."

"But there is also the case Joe, of not letting things just happen but for doing something you don't really want to because you instinctively know it's the right thing to do."

"So it's instinct again, something you can't do anything about. I'm beginning to think Drifall was right. Sir, I've thought about this. When I was a child I used to go to the library in St George's-in-the-East and read about Nature Study. I found out that many animals aid each other's survival by acting together to achieve the maximum protection or succour for the greatest of their number. Various sea mammals do this and work collectively. So do some birds such as members of the crow family who will help another bird to survive if it's injured. Bees and other insects work for the common benefit. But this doesn't mean they are good and brave. It's just the way things are.

So is this kind of behaviour altruism or instinct? We don't describe the bees who lay down their lives against attackers, for the good of their hive, as good bees and the attackers as evil. I think it's because we know they are all intent upon the survival of their species. We attach no blame or praise to them. In the case of a so called 'evil murderer'. – someone who has killed another human being. Whilst we are fully aware that there are abnormalities of the mind which render people prone to various kinds of mental illness, we refuse to accept that, for example, a child molester, is also outside the parameters of normal behaviour. These sorts of people instead of being pitied are cast out of society, branded as 'evil' and even lynched or executed if the circumstances arise. Why is there a distinction between one kind of evil and another in the minds of all the other so called 'normal' people?" Joe stopped his discourse, embarrassed, realising that he was ranting a little bit.

But Lieutenant Drea was amazed and inspired by this conversation. He had had many discussions with injured soldiers about things but never something quite so abstract as this. He liked to think however that these chats he made a point of having with patients, were really useful and aided in the mental recovery process. He could draw on his education as a priest. This conversation made him think about his own actions in Brentwood and his decision to resign from the priesthood. And strangely, this very soldier had played a part in that.

How unknowable was fate that they should now be together again discussing these points. "Fate! What was it?"

Lieutenant Drea drew as much from this meeting as Joe had. Just talking had crystallised many points for both of them.

The following day Lieutenant Drea sat down and wrote a report about 1008093 Driver Joseph Kurtin, recommending that he be released from the army and repatriated to England. His physical condition was such that he could now travel, but his mental condition meant he would no longer be capable of further useful military service.

One week later Joe caught his first glimpse of the South Coast of England since his last leave period nearly a year ago. In Planet Street, thought Joe, they could have no idea of just what a wonderful sight was the coastline of England.

Chapter 34

The Crucifix – 1919

Joe wasn't right. He still felt ill. His army discharge was only temporary. They told him he would be spending another eleven years in the reserves before it would be final. Back in Planet Street now, and restricted to the room upstairs at the back, shared with his younger brother, everything had changed. The first thing he had been compelled to do was to go round and see Anthony's family. A lot of time had elapsed since confirmation of his friend's death had arrived, 'Killed in Action.' Anthony's sergeant had written a nice letter to them saying that he had died a hero. They replied to it thanking him and asking for more details but another letter came back from someone else saying that the sergeant had since been killed himself. They had all grown used to the war and its shocks now, but Joe knew that the sight of him would bring it all back. Anthony's father still worked at the slippers and offered Joe a temporary job which he gladly accepted. Mr Baukis was also understanding when Joe was laid low by the terrible headaches and nightmares he had to endure and couldn't work. On occasion he woke the whole house in the middle of the night. His cousins the Dugards who all now lived downstairs in the two rooms there, sharing all the facilities with the Kurtins were not best pleased. He screamed and cried in his sleep imitating the noise of shells and explosions. All that separated them all were planks, laths and plaster.

One evening Joe asked if they still had any of his letters from the front. His mother had kept them all and Joe re-read them and picked through the sheets in front of them and explained some of the things which the censor had crossed out while allowing the beautiful pen and ink drawings of various scenes to slip through untouched. Joe found the letter containing the drawings of Cherry Blossom and Boot Polish and told them all about them, how he had loved them and cherished them but that one of them had kicked him while he wasn't paying attention. "What a wicked creature," said Eva.

"No he wasn't, replied Joe, "It was my own fault. I often wonder whatever happened to them. I hope they didn't end up as horsemeat for the French. They were too good for that."

His mother asked about the strict officer whom Joe had mentioned in one of his letters. "I don't remember that," said Joe leafing through.

"Yes, I remember it," chimed in Julie. "That officer who was really hard on you. You said he was a brick."

"Joe laughed his head off and then became serious. "No! No! he was marvellous and understanding after I was injured. You know who it was don't you?" They all looked blank. "It was Father Drea." they still looked perplexed until Joe reminded them of the young priest whom they had met at St Charles in Brentwood before the war. Young Frankie still didn't remember so Joe briefly told him what had happened in two sentences. For some reason Frankie after some thought said, "I hated it there." They all then put the subject behind them and each of them was left with their own thoughts.

"Where's that cross you brought home Joe? asked Eva. "Under the bed in the case," Joe replied. "I'll get it." Julie was thrilled at this, as it fed her all-abiding interest in religion, which included anything written, printed, or any ikon.

Joe dug it out and they stood it on the table and admired it. The style was quite unlike anything they owned themselves or had seen on sale at the church. "It's not as tall as our one is it?" said Julie, managing to impart an air of criticism into her question, with a whine, as if somehow the smaller it was, the less holy. "Look at those carved leaves! what are they supposed to be. Oh I see, it's Ruta. Look at Our Lord suffering!"

Elzbiėta turned it over and peered at the base. She saw that there was an old piece of brownish paper pasted over the bottom and that it was coming undone. "Look at this Julija," she said and Julie took it from her. Julie ever fastidious over cleanliness noted that the paper was greasy and grubby with age. She started to scrape it off with the vegetable knife. "Something's moving, Oo-er maybe we'd better leave it. We don't want to break it."

"Show!" said Joe and she handed it to him. "There's a bit of loose wood underneath," Joe said. "I'll get some glue." He rummaged through a small tray of tools on the shelf and produce a tube of Seccotine fish glue. Continuing where Julie had left off he removed the blackened remnants of the paper revealing a piece of wood spliced into the bottom of the stand. Joe gave it a tap and it fell out.

Inside was a piece of folded paper which he prised out with the tip of the knife. Opening it up he was surprised to see a series of small characters written in black ink. "Blimey! Love a duck! It's Polish he exclaimed. Julie rolled her eyes up to Heaven and muttered, "Don't swear Joe if you don't mind," setting her lip in a clench of disapproval.

"You're getting on my nerves Julie, keep quiet, this is interesting.

Where's your magnifying glass Mama?"

His mother pulled open the table drawer withdrew the small magnifier and proceeded to examine the paper minutely under the glass. "What does it say?" Julie asked. Her mother read the Polish words. "It says, 'God keep you dearest Ni.....' Just a minute, the writing is a bit faded, I can't quite make it out – 'until we are to...her again.' "It's signed 'Marija' 1813, Smalenai." Elzbiéta spoke but had trouble suppressing the catch in her voice. The emotion she felt welling up reading that name almost overwhelmed her. She didn't know why. They looked from one to another in bafflement. All the children had been told about Smalenai.

"Smalenai? Where did you say you got this Joe?"

"From a farm in France he replied innocently. But now I come to think of it they had an old French, Polish dictionary there. Even the people there didn't know the connection. How I came to be there is a long story that I can't tell you now, but this was given to me by someone, a young girl, called Marie in return for a favour I did them all."

Julie looked at him as if he was under cross examination. "How do you explain 'Smalenai' she snapped.

"How do I know?" Joe retorted niggled by her general tone.

"What was the favour?" Julie wanted to know. Joe ignored her.

"It's beautiful," Elzbiéta said. "We'll keep it up there on the mantelpiece from now on. She allowed her fertile, romantic mind to wander but could only guess at the circumstances which had led it from one remote place in Lithuania to another in France and from there to Planet Street in Stepney. She thought about the message and for some reason felt sad and wondered if perhaps there should have been some more, another sentence, perhaps 'in this life or the next,' she thought of Juozas. She felt compelled to make the sign of the cross. She did it with a sigh. Joe refolded the paper and put it back in the cavity replacing the wooden plug. Then he cut out a piece of a thick brown-paper bag and glued it up again with the Seccotine. In a very few years even this little story would be forgotten.

Life took up again roughly where it had been before the War but everything and everybody had changed. There were gaps in the old life everywhere. People were missing, institutions had gone. Nothing was the same. Joe re-kindled his old friendships with some of his former mates but there were several missing. They used to go out to the music halls, but even those were becoming fewer. Cinemas though were coming in to replace them. Girls were on his mind. He was always on the lookout, but those he met never quite measured up to Charlise Melbourne. He never really knew what had happened to her and he was too proud to try and find out for fear of another rebuttal. Now where he should have been brimming with youthful confidence he was shattered and depressed both by what had happened between them and the effect the War had had on him. He felt that circumstances had conspired to do him down wherever they could.

On a Sunday afternoon in Victoria Park his entire life changed. He and Benny Kairis had been to the boating lake and had rowed around the islands and the Chinese pagoda a few times before their boat number was shouted out and they had to row back and return it. They disembarked and sat in the cafeteria for ten minutes with a cup of tea each. Then they started strolling in the direction of the gate leading out to Bethnal Green and the museum. They passed by a line of anglers fishing for roach from the lake with a backdrop of beautiful Georgian houses obviously occupied by people with plenty of money, beyond a canal, when they spied two pretty young girls sitting on a bench. As they walked past the girls coyly glanced up but one in particular seemed to have eyes only for Joe, looking him up and down. Joe spotted this but was strangely embarrassed and self-conscious.

They walked on for a bit until Benny said, "Joe I think that one on the right fancied you why don't you go and ask her out? I think you might be alright there."

Benny was a good mate and understood what Joe had gone through on the Western Front while he himself had been in the Navy based onshore and had had a quiet life with very little action to speak of.

"Can you ask her for me Ben?"

"Yes," replied Benny with a smile. He returned to the bench and one of the girls said something to the other and they both giggled.

"Good afternoon ladies. My friend and I were wondering if you would like to accompany us to the museum."

The girls hummed and hawed and then got up to join Benny and ambled along until they caught up with Joe, talking quietly to each other. So it came about that Joe met the person who was to become the most important figure in his life. She introduced herself as Sarah Tresadern, she lived in Stratford, came from a large family. Her father was also dead. So they had something in common there.

As their friendship developed she was intrigued by this good look-ing, fair haired young man with a hint of exoticism about him. An unusual name, and Lithuanian, he told her, – wherever that may have been! But he was witty and knowledgeable and on his best behaviour. The real trauma in his life was in the background whenever he was with her. He showed her his best side – always.

She met his family and it wasn't so bad. Most of them spoke Eng-lish with Cockney accents except one of them who sounded very posh and finally Joe asked Sarah to marry him.

"Where will we live?" Sarah had asked him but his family had the perfect solution. "You can live here. We'll let you have the room at the back, it will be plenty big enough for the two of you. Joe was quite happy, there was no putting himself out, just slipping seamlessly back into everything he knew and understood.

The wedding at St Mary and St Michael's was an eye-opener for her. First she had to have counselling sessions with a priest where it was explained that any children would have to be brought up in the Catholic faith. As Joe was a Catholic the wedding couldn't be held anywhere else. Every time she ventured round Joe's house she was badgered by Julie about the faith. How wonderful the Catholic faith was. What she was missing by not being a part of it. The solace she would be able to draw from it if only she would become a Catholic.

The incessant exposure to the religious paraphernalia in both house-holds, upstairs and down, made her feel like an outsider trespassing in someone else's domain. The day of the wedding drew ever closer. The nearer it got the more subtle canvassing Sarah was subjected to by Julie. Her evangelical zeal knew no bounds as far as Sarah was concerned. Julie deep down felt herself to be the moral and intel-lectual superior of Sarah and she finally ground her down completely and Sarah was baptised a Catholic at St Mary and St Michael's with Julie standing as her godmother. So all the loose ends were tied up. If however she thought it would make her one of them, as Emilija Dugard downstairs mentioned, "She had another think coming."

Things never quite worked out the way Sarah had hoped. There was a lack of privacy which got her down. The queueing up to use the lavatory or the copper or tap in the backyard. There was the bumping into the person she might have just had a spat with over something to do with the clothes hanging up to dry, or over whose turn it was to sweep the passage. On top of that was the blasted lan-guage. Every time they wanted to talk about her, she suspected, they used Lithuanian. She could tell, because sometimes in mid discourse they glanced in her direction. So she was a Catholic but was unable to become Lithuanian and therefor still felt isolated. She picked up the odd word mainly the old phrase from Joe, "Mano galva scauda." She soon learned what that meant – "I've got a headache." By the time she had her first child it was clear that this was to be the pattern of her life for ever. It was to comprise of looking after their room mind-ing the child Josie, even named after Joe! Shopping, washing – if and when she could gain access to the backyard facilities. She became at first aggressive towards other inhabitants of the house who she un-derstandably resented. This sometimes resulted in passageway physi-cal brawls with pushing and shoving and once she was so distracted she accidentally dropped Josie down the stairs, but the baby bounced quite happily on her head none the worse for wear.

This couldn't go on! She just had to get out of that household of foreigners at all costs. She discovered by gossiping with other English neighbours that a room would be coming up for let opposite and she determined to go for it. All the justification she needed was that it was three feet wider than the one they already occupied. And so began Joe and Sarah's 'progression' up the accommodation ladder.

Thus the Lithuanians began to merge with the English. It had only taken two generations but it was to be more of a culture shock for Sarah than it was for them. She would be the person to pay the heaviest price on the rocky road of integration with a foreign family.

She now took responsibility for this war-torn, shell-shocked, broken man, fortified by her newly embraced Catholic faith.

Joe brought with him to their new room a small votive figure of Christ carved in Lithuania from limewood.

As she gazed upon the tortured figure of Our Lord, Sarah thought she knew exactly how he must have felt.

Chapter 35

Little Nanny – 1930

Josie sat at her grandmother's feet arranging small objects into a miniature altar. There were two upturned thimbles which represented flower pots and a pair of upside-down cufflinks and a brass collar stud which were candlesticks. Two old matchboxes, which had each spent a week in people's pockets, covered with a folded scrap of a linen handkerchief made the altar itself, and a cross from a rosary made up the centre piece.

The apparently elderly woman, intrigued, looked down with pride at her granddaughter and commented in a mixture of Lithuanian and pidgin English how clever the child was. She rejoiced in her heart at the dedication to the faith which was so apparent, represented in Josie's innocent pastime. Apart from the ever present worry about poor Joey, she was happier and more contented than she had ever been since those first optimistic years with Juozas before events had begun to weigh down on her just as things had always done in her childhood. Now, time had dulled those memories. She could rely on her Julie and Frank who saw to everything. Her life on the whole was at last one of contentment. The pleasure she gained from just being around her granddaughter was wonderful.

The woman wore a clean flower print blouse and a long skirt with a headscarf tied in the Lithuanian tradition from which a few locks of soft greying hair bulged slightly at the front framing a careworn lined face in which were deeply set bright, crystal clear, blue eyes.

Her long black coat, still slightly damp from the sleet earlier, hung on the back of the door on a double hook on top of other clothes. Surmounting that was her black trilby hat stuffed with newspaper against this currently cold weather. She had come straight to Joe and Sarah's room from shopping in Watney Street to do this favour. It was a job she never grew tired of. She was planning on going out again shortly. Her feet which were crossed, her legs stretched out, wore strong shiny black leather shoes with straps across the top. When she was out, her dress style harked back to the Edwardian as did that of most of her contemporaries around these streets, all unable to keep up with fashion.

In fact she was still quite young, only fifty six, yet now she looked older. But the effect was not unpleasant. Her face was quite heavily lined, exposure to the wind and rain in early life had left its mark. The weathered effect oddly, was, somewhat nullified by laughter lines around the corners of her eyes and the kindly twinkle in them linked up with her soft smile below her long, slightly bulbously tipped, nose. She had the look of someone who had taken all that life could throw at her and yet had emerged with something positive.

The room they sat in was not more than nine feet six square and eight feet five inches high. Shabbily furnished it may have been but it was spotlessly clean. Elzbiéta approved, – Sarah, her English daughter-in-law had passed Elzbiéta's appraisal as a good housekeeper.

Two tiny armchairs were placed on either side of a small blackleaded iron range which was to the left and slightly set into the opposite wall as one entered the room. The range's chimney rose to the top of the niche and then disappeared into the thickness of the wall. Further to the left under the narrow vertical sash window which looked out over their back yard, and the yard which backed onto it from a house in neighbouring Winterton Street, was a small folding armchair which was designed to be converted into a makeshift bed for a child. In the centre of the room was a tiny table covered with a square of brightly coloured oilcloth and two brown varnished wooden kitchen chairs. The table stood behind a home made rug only slightly bigger than itself which consisted of a backing of sacking turned over into a hem all the way round, through which had been drawn a myriad of different coloured rag strips. First they had been pulled through to the back with a special hook with a handle then tugged back through another hole adjacent to the first. The two free ends had been knotted together and smoothed out and then flattened and trimmed level. The mat consisted of hundreds of these strips. Sarah had made that in a self-sufficient attempt to brighten her home.

The teapot stood on the table. It was encased in a kaleidoscopic double-layered woollen tea cosy knitted by Sarah. The wooden handle protruded from a slot in one side and from the other, through a hole, projected the enamelled spout. On the right of the room was a small bed, barely a double, covered by a worn and threadbare quilt with some unusual stitching which once again though clean, had seen better days, it had been lent to Sarah and Joe and would eventually have to be returned. Pinned to the headboard was a celluloid covered ovate shaped picture of the Virgin Mary. The edges were embroidered in red brocade and together with a cross made from a dried palm leaf, the items were fixed by a nail banged into the varnished wood.

A small cupboard containing food and a shelf with some utensils and a chest of drawers under it completed the complement of furniture. On top of the chest of drawers was an unusual wooden crucifix made in a slightly different way to those on sale at St Mary and St

Michael. It was the one Joe had come back from France with it and the wooden icon seemed to be squarer and wider than it should have been. Behind that, on the wall was the 'Sacred Heart of Jesus', a painting of Our Lord wearing his crown of thorns and his heart visible on the surface of his chest, the archetypal effigy of the son of God with long hair, beard and blue eyes. These images were commonplace in most of the Lithuanian, Irish and Polish households in the area, having been printed in their thousands. In fact there was another one framed in the adjacent room. The only difference between them was that the other one had a modest little oil lamp, with a small glass chimney framing a wick, which was perpetually burning before it. Such was the unquestioning level of devotion here to a higher being and an ultimate goal, despite their poverty or perhaps because of it.

It was clear there wasn't much space here in this room, but what there was seemed to be utilised to its maximum. The hooks on a wooden strip fixed to the wall held hangers draped with a dress and a collarless shirt. Over the back of one of the chairs was a cardigan. Under the bed could just be seen a couple of suitcases of different sizes and at the bottom of it what looked like an accordion in a case. On a stand in one corner was positioned a single gas ring on top of which there stood prominently a plain iron kettle. Near it, hanging on a hook by a loop, was a thick sewn pad for picking it up once it had boiled. A single gas light outlet protruded from one wall surmounted by a metal gauze mantle and glass shade.

Below that was a shelf laden with small coloured glass ornaments. This white narrow painted shelf had a notch cut from the back to allow the passage of the gas pipe which continued down the wall from the lamp and disappeared into the floorboards. Not much thought had gone into the positioning of the gas lamp, if indeed the shelf had been there first, because it threw a shadow in the direction of the floor in the evening when the gas was alight which rendered reading difficult underneath it. However there was the bonus that the ornaments were illuminated fully which together with the shadow gave a degree of atmosphere and homeliness to the room. The whole of the wall below the level of a painted wooden picture rail including the pipe had been papered over at some time in the not too recent past with a floral patterned white wallpaper and the paper had become yellowed and flyblown and was showing its age. The ceiling and the drop down to the rail was whitewashed over the lath and plaster. It would also need redoing soon. Elzbiéta was planning to see about this as soon as Joe, Sarah and Josie moved out. They had a promise of a slightly bigger room in Star Place.

The room promised to Joe and Sarah across the way was roughly of the same dimensions as the one they already occupied except that it would be at the front of the new house and extended over the passageway below, which would make it about thirty inches wider than their present room by nine feet, adding an extra twenty two and a half square feet, which was a considerable amount of extra space. It was going to be coming vacant soon and as Sarah was pregnant again and Elzbiéta wanted this room back it seemed like the perfect solution.

In all fairness Elzbiéta had told Joe and Sarah back in 1923 that the arrangement could only be temporary until Joe managed to get himself a proper job and sort out his life. She was looking forward to the prospect of more space again and yet still being in close proximity to her son and granddaughter.

Star Place was a mere few paces across the street. It consisted of about seven small houses the same size as her own at 59, Planet Street, and a few more round a corner where it finished in a dead end. If Elzbiéta stood at her front door and looked out and slightly to the left there it was. The small row of houses]extended across the back of the end of Planet street and the visual barrier was completed to the left, as was usual with many rows of houses, by the appendage of the 'Star' public house, on the corner of Morris Street. Next door to Elzbiéta and her family was a slightly bigger house occupied by a large Jewish family called Magnus. Their dwelling was on the corner and people passed it to walk past the end of Winterton Street, and through a passage to Watney Street market. The Magnus family was a noisy one but friendly. The head of it, Barnett Magnus, worked at cigar making.

A few minutes away, along the dusty pavements of Morris Street was Golds the grocers where Elzbiéta sometimes passed the time of day with Mrs Gold both speaking in a combination of languages, mainly Polish. At least Elzbiéta was never lonely and people tended to call on her for company as they congregated together in the small enclave off Commercial Road which was Planet Street, Star Place, Winterton Street, Hungerford Street, and Morris Street. there were more Lithuanians in Solander Street, a short walk away.

While she watched Josie from the corner of her eye Elzbiéta had been reading a Polish newspaper. She effortlessly scanned the myriad of complex characters, tutting or commenting to herself enunciating the most excruciating and unpronounceable words as she pondered on the implications of whatever it was she was reading about, as her grandchild played quietly on the linoleum covered floor. She kept her eye on the brown varnished clock standing on the shelf. It had been her wedding present to Joe and to Sarah, his English wife.

Elzbiéta's mind wandered with a degree of concern and turned to thoughts of her brothers and sisters, nieces and nephews. Some were abroad but others has stayed in Lithuania and she worried about them. She had recovered to an extent from the news received from home of the death of her mother, which for a time had filled her with deep melancholy. She had arranged for Masses to be said at St Mary and St Michael's and at St Casimir's.

The situation back home was not good, even though Lithuania now had its independence, she knew that most of those countries particularly Germany had not recovered from the war. Britain was supposed to have won, but if they in England were in such a poor state, then she knew it must have been worse for those she had left behind. Sometimes, if she didn't control it firmly she found herself taking on their cares and even the cares of the world. She had had enough of her own closer to home. Comparing her own history with that of theirs back in Lithuania she thought that even though she had been forced to bear many troubles maybe things now weren't so bad.

She broke off from her reading every now and then to go over in her mind again the events of the past thirty or so years which had brought her to this point in her life in a new land with new family.

The year 1912 seemed for her to have been the pivotal point. That was the year in which everything had changed so dramatically. She and her dear Juozapas had already endured their share of life's hardships. Their interminable struggle to earn a living was interspersed by the heart-warming pregnancies, then the heart-wrenching loss of infants to barely understood ailments and the funerals which followed. Their dreams were beginning to be replaced by everyday leaden practical events and concerns. Day after day as each new morning dawned they recommenced their routines anew. They had been in England now for too long. It was harder to make the break from Stepney and their ambition was beginning to fade. They had put down roots, made friends. They had surviving small children, but some others were buried here. How could they leave them? The pain was always there for Elzbiéta and would never go away. These events seemed destined to root them both to this place. The young couple were enduring their lot stoically, making the best of it. It was becoming too late to make that break from Stepney. They were seventeen years further on in their lives than when they had taken those first decisions to leave their homeland. Yet, they carried on fortified by the mainstays of their community and the Church. How would they have managed without those two cornerstones holding them up, supporting them? It was their consolation for some of those terrible disappointments which had befallen them from time to time. Their future had developed now into a decision they would never take.

Juozas had always suffered from the fog here in the smoky East End. It was a shock to his system adjusting to the smoke-polluted air in the new land. Where every household relied on a coal fire for heating, cooking and washing, winter and summer, his bouts of annual Bronchitis became steadily more virulent year after year until one winter in early 1912 he was too weak to do anything other than lie in bed coughing. By the time it dawned on them just how ill he was, it was too late and it was with a sudden shock that Elzbièta realised that he had sunk into a semi-coma which looked unlikely he would be able to recover from. The doctor when they called him just shook his head and advised continued nursing and departed with half-a-crown but Juozas didn't improve until a point when he was too weak even to cough and just became motionless. Elzbièta continued to mop his brow against the fever which seemed to be gripping his body until there came a time when he no longer even opened his eyes, his skin became clammy and cold and finally there was no more sign of life. The doctor came again into that upstairs back bedroom and pronounced him dead. All four of them cried their eyes out hugging and consoling each other. And little Frankie wailed too, being aware that something terrible had happened and taking his cue from the grown-ups until they managed to control themselves for his sake.

Elzbièta now sat with Josie in that very same room pondering and dwelling on the past happenings with a kind of stolid resoluteness. Some memories were bad, but the events were in the past. They were still a family and things were progressing, even if only slowly.

Elzbièta fretted all the time about Joe. By the time he was six he spoke English like the native he was and he had gradually realised that to fit in, he had to adopt the accent and ways of his contemporaries. Back before the war when he was only ten he had been bright enough to gain a place at that school. They were proud of him. Julie too was bright. Unlike Joe though, she had wasted no time while at school in doing her utmost to raise herself from the poverty of those streets and elevate herself above her own embarrassment concerning her immigrant parents. She had became the translator for her mother, being younger and therefor more often at home than Joe. It was she who handled the reading of official documents and the writing of letters for her parents. Though most Lithuanians were literate in their own language, when it came to official matters in English they were out of their depth. Elzbiėta certainly was, so Julie gradually assumed a kind of authority within that household which was way beyond her years. This young woman now just twenty four, whom everyone but Joe deferred to, became the pivotal person in the household when she wasn't at work in the accounts department of the office in Mile End.

So here they were twelve years after the end of the war. They had all been forced to share Joey's suffering upon his return from France. He was enduring intermittent break downs in his self control. In the period between his return, and meeting Sarah he had fared badly. The things he had seen and experienced continued to resurface in his mind. As thoughts occurred to him at random he fixated upon them as he was forced to relive the terrible events of his war, over and over again. Unable to sleep, his habit of waking them all up in the night with his screaming left everyone debilitated the next day. It was a source of worry, and exhaustion, and created tension between the households downstairs and upstairs.

His air of distraction was clear but Elzbiėta picked up quiet muttering from time to time as he re-lived his experiences in his own mind, and it made her feel helpless. There were one or two things her resourceful mind found to do to be kind to him and sympathise. And she prayed for him and made him tea. Julie was of very little help with Joe and his problems. Her contribution was to go through the rituals of her religion fervently, and appeal to God. She was concerned to see her mother worried. She doted on her mother and dominated her at the same time, and she continued to pray for all of them.

Joe had left Stepney in 1915 as a boy and returned like a broken middle-aged man only three and a half years later. His mother suspected his time at the Front had been indescribable yet she knew that he must have been withholding his experiences from them. She had followed the course of the interminable war with extreme worry, losing count of how often she had been beset by her own endlessly recurring headaches. The newspapers then had generally presented an optimistic glow but she knew the truth. She saw for herself the shattered lives as families in the streets round about had paid the ultimate price in order to protect Britain's place in the world and to help ensure their own continuing prosperity. She looked at their lives and her own and was struck by the irony of it. She knew her father would have had something to say about it had he been here.

Some of that was in the past and time had dulled most of the pain. It was all fading into memory for those other poor people, she hoped.

Elzbiėta, baby-sitting for these few hours optimistically imagined the child's father was out successfully finding work but more than likely, probably unsuccessful, he would be passing the time in a snooker hall fit for heroes. The endless, often fruitless, tactic of lining up on the dockside a few streets away whenever a ship came into port presented a poor prospect. Union cards were almost impossible to get. Dockers operated a closed shop and nepotism was the deciding factor in who got work. So he, along with scores of others pushing and jostling, was only sometimes employed as a casual labourer, if he was lucky.

Very few were chosen each time. The foreman would walk down the line of desperate hopefuls and, it seemed, arbitrarily pick one or two from the crowd of men who strove to catch his eye. Whenever Joe did manage to get picked there might be an additional bonus. If the cargo was tea, after all the chests had been unloaded and hoisted into the warehouse the hands could brush the quayside and take the sweepings home in a bag which would save them having to buy it. Tea, the elixir of life so essential to any occasion. Julie though desisted from drinking tea made from those dusty leaves, complaining about the flavour of it. "It has an aftertaste," she said. "I prefer Lyons."

There were other fiddles going on at the docks too, but if Joe was ever involved he never let anyone within his family know about it.

The foreman wasn't bothered about who he picked, as long as they all knew the rules, worked hard and were not troublemakers. It was said that he creamed off so much per hour from the wages of those he had chosen as casuals. That was *his* bonus. And for Joe he would have to accept the system or there would be no living at all.

Josie's mother had found some part-time work cleaning for the well off Finkeltaubs who had come from Vilnius, and owned a tailors in the Mile End Road. She came into her own at Shabbos when Jews were forbidden to do anything which constituted work. Thus Sarah would get things ready for the family on a Friday night, laying down and lighting their fire and so on. The half a crown a day she would earn would make a valuable contribution, maybe the only contribution, this week, to the budget for the room the small family shared.

'Little Nanny', was what Elzbiėta was called by Josie to distinguish her from 'Nanny in Stratford and 'Nanny Dugard', who lived downstairs. Elzbiėta actually lived in the next room upstairs at the front which faced the street, together with Julija and Pranas, Josie's aunt and uncle. There might have been four others if things had been different. The children who had died in infancy were twins, Veronika and Jonas and another boy, Antanas. Her other beautiful daughter Eva, who had such a wonderful singing voice, born in 1900, had fallen victim to the Spanish Flu ten years ago. It was scarce consolation that so many others had also died in the epidemic.

But this was now1930 and Julija had a good job in an office in Mile End while Pranas, was a typewriter mechanic at Remingtons. So both of them – Julie and Frank to everyone else, had an adequate income which meant that their mother had put behind her those days when she had sewn the linings into trousers for a tailor by candlelight, head throbbing, seated on a tiny wooden stool, late into the night.

Their living arrangements though were as difficult for her and her other two children as they were for Joey and his wife and child. They themselves skilfully improvised in their own single room with mother and daughter sleeping together in a double bed with a thick flock mattress while Frank bedded down every night on the other side of the tiny room behind a makeshift screen.

She was really content at the thought of reclaiming her back room again whilst not having to forego contact with her son and his family.

Suddenly looking up at the clock yet again with a start she said to Josie, "Nagi Juoza, atėjo laikas mums eiti į bažnyčią." Then remembering herself she re-phrased it as, "Come on Juoza, it's time for us to go to church." It was a phrase Julie had made a point of teaching her.

"Alright Nanny," responded Josie eagerly. She always looked forward to these trips with her grandmother.

"Go toilet first Juoza."

Josie doing as her nanny bade her, clattered down the stairs, doubled back at the bottom past Dugard's back room door, which was closed, and opened the door to the yard. Josie saw with childish pleasure that there were a few flurries of snow out there now replacing the sleet. She excitedly made her way across the cobbles of the tiny back yard to the lavatory on the left which was a little sloping-roofed brick built appendage on the side of the house. She emerged a few moments later after having climbed up onto the oblong wooden seat to pull the chain. She automatically went to the cold water tap above the drain which was set in a dip in the cobbles and rinsed her hands. Her aunt Julie had already drummed into the child the importance of cleanliness. As Josie re-entered the house she saw the copper at the back of Dugard's ground floor window where yesterday evening she had overheard an altercation between her aunt Julie and Nanny Dugard's daughter Nellie, concerning some clothes which had mysteriously picked up dirty smudges after Julie had hung them up under cover in the yard to dry. Somehow black smuts from the open fire under the washing copper had found their way onto the arm and shoulder of Julie's white blouse. It was almost as if the blouse had been moved and dropped. Julie quizzed her cousin closely on how it had happened. Under the piercing gaze of the Grand Inquisitor

Nellie vehemently denied any knowledge of it but Julie knew better. Even if she couldn't prove it she was confident she had emerged with superior dignity over her rough and ready cousin who had really had no defence other than flat denials. There was no love lost between the families. They existed upstairs and downstairs in a kind of uneasy incompatibility born out of necessity. Two widows and their families in one tiny terraced house with shared facilities did not do much for either Elzbièta's gentle nature, Julie's superiority nor Nellie's combativeness. The two families with diametrically opposed personalities alternated between bouts of friendliness interspersed with petty domestic disputes, to open hostility, particularly when the Dugards were late with their weekly money to Elzbièta who was still the overall tenant paying the rent on the whole house to Lord Winterton's rent man and then collecting Mrs Dugard's share – in arrears, mostly.

"Put on coat" said Nanny, haltingly, still unable to come to terms fully with English, as she picked her own coat from the hanger and adjusted her trilby at an angle. She lovingly helped her granddaughter put on her coat and together they left the room and went down the winding wooden staircase, along the passage past Dugard's front room. The inside of the front door had a piece of string with the key on it dangling in front of the letterbox, which they all used for entry.

Walking along Planet Street towards Commercial Road the elderly lady noticed that the sleet had now turned to light snow and the wind had got up a bit. She amused her granddaughter as they walked along swinging their joined hands backwards and forwards exaggeratedly, by making up a little rhyme in pidgin English in time to the movement. "Snowin' blowin', Juoza, Nanny to bažnyčią goin'. Previous history forgotten Elzbièta was happy, and so was Josie tripping along and looking back at her footprints in the light snow which was beginning to settle.

Unfortunately for Elzbièta though Julia had other ambitious ideas which would mean for them all a small leap upwards to the next rung on the ladder of social mobility but it came at a price.

A few years after Joe, Sarah and Josie moved away, even though the Kurtins gained their room back, Julie decided they were all moving away from the ghetto to more refined and sunnier climes. She had been to Hackney and seen in the local paper that there was a flat to let at Clapton Common and after taking her mother by bus to see it they both agreed it would be a positive move. It was only a little further from the Lithuanian church than Planet Street was. Anyway, many of their old Lithuanian friends had already moved further out towards the less densely populated parts of London. By the time war came again they were safely ensconced in the lower floor of a Victorian house facing Clapton Common with its ponds and trees, and they had access to a large garden. It would have been even better if Julie had not forced her mother to throw away the old Lithuanian quilt, and with it the last tangible link to her homeland. She agreed to this with a heavy heart, browbeaten by the common sense and non-sentimental outlook of her daughter. She took one last look at it as it was bundled up and consigned to the dustman together with its intricate stitching and Lithuanian designs of long, long ago. Joe's wartime letters too were unceremoniously screwed up and thrown in, along with the wartime drawings, but not before Julie had spotted and rescued one of the Pope which Joe had drawn, and put it safely away among the family papers.

Chapter 36

Solidarity – 1936

It was a Sunday morning in early October and something was afoot. People were running down Planet Street in groups of three or four, their metal heeled shoes clattering on the cobbles. Some were talking and shouting animatedly, and they were carrying sticks and placards, .

Joe, Sarah, young Frank and Josie, visiting the Kurtins upstairs at number 59 wondered what was going on. Lukas Daugirda, Joe's cousin and friend, who still lived downstairs on the ground floor, came along also from the direction of Commercial Road as Joe stood by the front door having come down to see what was happening.

"What the hell's going on?" Joe asked him. "Why are you all coming down here, I thought you were going to Mile End?"

"We're all together! We've come through from Commercial Road.

We went to block Mosley's march but it's been re-routed through Cable Street." replied Lukas.

Joe had read about this march only a few days earlier, and Lukas had told him about it too Mosley was trying to whip them all up, against the Jews and other immigrants in the East End. Apparently amongst their many other sins and vices the Jews were stealing jobs and wouldn't integrate with the rest of us. He was aware that Lukas Daugirda was more politically astute than he was. But Joe just wanted a quiet life. His family's recent move up, to a two roomed attic flat in The Highway was all the trauma he could handle in one go.

"Why don't you come along?" said his friend.

It was the last thing Joe wanted to do on a Sunday afternoon. "Hang on a minute," he replied I'll just find out how long dinner will be."

He fully expected Sarah and Julie to tell him it was almost there but his excuse collapsed and fell flat when Sarah shouted down the stairs, "We won't be having it until tonight, we've not even taken it round the corner to be cooked yet." There was a bakers in Watney Street where, for a couple of pennies you could take your meal to be roasted in a huge oven, still hot after the bread was baked, where it would take its place alongside a multitude of similar meals belonging to other families. It was one of the drawbacks of having an ineffectual range in each room which was too small and no proper kitchen as such.

Denied his excuse, Joe really had no alternative. If he wanted to appear to show willing, he had to go along with Lukas. And he had now had his rug of an excuse pulled out from under him by Sarah.

He stepped out adjusting his flat cap as Frank his seven year old son came down the stairs and appeared on the doorstep.

"Can I come too Daddy?" he whined.

"No! Go back in!" Joe replied somewhat harshly.

"Joe?" a voice shrieked from upstairs, "Take him out, we're busy, 'e's getting under our feet. Josie can stay"

Casting his eyes up to Heaven Joe mentally conceded defeat and the boy trailed along behind them.

"What's up with you Joe?" his friend said to him. "You don't like unions, you're not a Communist and you ain't bothered about a man who models himself on the German Chancellor, and wants to persecute the Jews – and us too I wouldn't be surprised. It's just not going to happen, we can't let it."

Lukas Daugirda or Lukie Dugard, as he sometimes called himself, quoted things heard at various meetings about Mosley trying to get into power on the back of scapegoats, convenient outsiders whom he was trying to turn the British public against. He was on the crest of a wave and it looked like he was succeeding. Some newspapers were certainly for him, and he had sympathy in certain quarters with some of the toffs of the upper echelons.

"Don't worry, he won't turn me!" retorted Joe. He had listened to all this before from Lukie Dugard and he just wantd to keep out of it and not become involved.

"All I want is a quiet life. I'm not interested in politics and I don't want any trouble. Can you imagine if I got arrested? and you too. Supposing you get beaten up?"

"No, no you're wrong, you're too weak, you should get involved. People have to stand up and be counted. If thousands of Jews can, even though their elders have told them not to, then I'm bloody sure I can do my little bit – and you could too." Joe said nothing.

"I know you are my mate Joe," said Dugard, "But there are too many like you. You're happy to let others make all the effort and then you'll reap the rewards. We have people like that in our furniture union. Won't do a thing yet will also enjoy any benefits we might win."

"That's all very well for you Lukie," replied Joe, " You've got a trade to fall back on. There's a difference between what you do – cabinet making, and what I do – labouring. Having a skill makes a massive difference. You're less likely to be sacked than someone unskilled who they could replace at the drop of a hat. That gives you the luxury of protesting. They'd think twice before sacking you."

All the time Frankie was trailing along behind holding his new catapult in his pocket. He was as pleased as Punch with it, imagining himself as an Indian out hunting or as David against Goliath, a story which had been mentioned last week at school. He had bought it with sixpence which Little Nanny had rustled up for him. Almost the second he had brought it home, as soon as she had spotted it, his mother had confiscated it. Sarah wasn't having a lethal weapon in the house and that was that. She hid it away, but Frank had noticed it tucked behind a mirror and quietly got a chair, climbed up and retrieved it when she wasn't looking. Made from a forked piece of wood and with a thick length of square cut rubber supporting a sling it was now safely tucked away in his jacket pocket. He had nothing to fire from it but thought he would get some stones from the Thames foreshore and shoot them over the river at Shadwell.

The three of them continued amidst an increasing throng of other men down the dusty, shabby streets from Morris Street then a dog leg and the right turn into Cable Street. There was turmoil going on here. By this time, Joe had grasped Frankie's hand and he was having serious doubts about the wisdom of coming.

Passing by Dellow Street and Anthony Street on the right as they approached Cannon Street which ran right across, Joe saw with foreboding a huge press of people. All the upstairs windows of the three storey buildings in this dusty shop lined street were open and people were yelling and throwing things down into the roadway up ahead. They were gossiping and laughing and there was a sort of festival atmosphere in the safety of their impregnable positions on the up-

per floors. By this time he was having a struggle to hold onto Frank in the crowd. The boy had nearly been swept away in the melée. There came a point where a tug of war ensued between the nameless mob

394

and himself for the possession of Frankie. With a final jerk of young Frank's arm he turned on his heel and headed back the way they had come. "Come on Frank let's get back home."

Frank was crying and Joe realised that he had made a mistake

in even contemplating coming down here. It had only been Lukie Dugard's persuasion which had brought him this far. As they made their way back now, against the flow of humanity, occasionally knocking shoulders, he couldn't help noticing that the men going in the opposite direction were mainly Jews and hard looking Irishmen, most of the latter probably being dockers.

As he came level with the door of their cousins the Cernauskas family he looked up and saw that Agnes Cernauskas was leaning out of an upstairs window. "Can we come in for a minute?" Joe shouted. The head disappeared and above the hubbub of the crowd he heard someone coming down the stairs. The door opened and the tiny figure of young Marija Cernauskas appeared and stood aside as he and Frankie fell into the passage and the door was shut tight behind them. They went up to the first floor where the Cernauskas's lived over a grocery shop below, which had been closed up and shuttered like all the other shops along the Street. What on earth are you doing here?" Agnes asked him. "I don't know," he muttered. "I really don't." Several other members of her family were there in the front room standing on the lino, leaning out of the two windows. They turned around and after exchanging greetings went on with their spectating. He went over to the window where the curtains had been pulled to one side making a concertina at the end of the string and peeped out and up the road to where the noise and furore was coming from.

"I don't know what's happening or why it's here in Cable Street," Agnes said, bewildered.

She shouted to the woman across the road, a Polish lady, Mrs Mu-vinsky, in that language. A couple of men walking by in the street below looked up uncomprehendingly.

Joe could see from this high vantage point that the number of policemen up there ahead was phenomenal but most of the action seemed to be taking place between them and the near rioting men in the vicinity of a barricade near Christian Street. There were scores of mounted police on the other side of the barricade and many more on foot. It was just a swirling mass of fighting with no sign of any Blackshirts nor any glimpse of Mosley himself. The police seemed to be making baton charges against the disorganised defenders and it looked as if the police were relentlessly making progress.

The barricade itself, it seemed to Joe was formed by an overturned lorry lying on its side with other detritus piled up on either side, things like mattresses, dustbins and bits of furniture. There was also stuff like paving stones and builder's planks. Every now and again someone staggered past the house going in the opposite direction ei-ther limping, holding their head or mopping at a bloody nose. He hoped that Lukie was alright. Thank God he himself had decided to turn back with little Frank. The boy was still crying and one of Agnes' daughters aged about eleven was comforting him with the words, "Don't cry Frankie you're safe up here with us. Would you like a cup of lemonade?" He nodded. Then she asked her mother if it would be alright. The woman got the bottle from the shelf and poured some into a chipped cup. Frankie took the lemonade and sat down on a wooden chair at the oilcloth covered table, drinking it, but still not looking very happy.

Joe could see that people were throwing marbles at and under the horses from large bags full which they had obviously taken along for that specific purpose. This form of attack must have been pre-ar-ranged evidently, and the horses were slithering and skidding all over the place. One of the policemen had been thrown into the air and had fallen with a thump and lain still. A Metropolitan Police two wheeled ambulance trolley pushed by a couple of police orderlies appeared from the rear somewhere and the two men lifted him onto it and wheeled him away. Another one retrieved his horse, which wasn't panicking. It had clearly been trained in the chaos of many a public order and riot exercise. Every so often a pair of policemen would clamber over or around the barricade, plunge into the hostile mob, wielding truncheons, and withdraw, dragging a screaming, struggling protestor along with them to the rear.

"So" Joe thought' "This is a battle with the police and not with the Blackshirts for control of the street. Where are the Blackshirts? I wonder. What's actually going on?"

By now hunger was beginning to get the better of him and it was past four o'clock. "I'm going to chance it!" he said to no-one in particular. "Come on Frankie."

They made their way downstairs and walked through the maelstrom of people pressed in the street, hugging the inside of the pavement as they did so. Frank had ceased crying now and was feeling temporarily more cheerful. "Why were they all fighting Daddy and why did we go there?"

"I don't really know why we went. I once said I would never get involved with the police again."

"What do you mean Daddy – again?"

"When I was about fourteen I was playing over on the other side of Sidney Street on the rooftops collecting the rubber balls that had got caught in the gutters."

"How did you get up there Daddy?"

"By climbing up a drainpipe! I crossed over a roof from the back to the front. I looked over the parapet and there was a huge

crowd of police and soldiers on the other side of the road. Some of them had guns. I was never so frightened as I was then. Suddenly someone saw me and yelled out, 'There he goes.' They started chasing down the street as I crossed back over the other side and scrambled back down the pipe. I was chased by a policemen into Commercial Road. I ran across dodging in and out of the traffic with this policeman in hot pursuit, but he got held up a bit trying to cross the road. I still reckon someone tripped him up deliberately. That gave me a bit of a start."

"So what happened then Daddy?"

"I turned my jacket inside out and carried on legging it as far as Watney Street market. I dodged through there and arrived back home. I rushed in and threw myself into bed and pulled the clothes up over my head almost, but I could just see out. From the corner of my eye I saw a policeman's face appear at the window as he peered in but I just kept very still and eventually he went away. I was very lucky."

"So what was going on then?"

"They were searching for some criminals. Latvian anarchists they called them, and in particular a man called Peter the Painter. But they never did catch him like they never caught me. It turned out that three policemen had been killed earlier. They were determined to get those people. Later on a fire started, I read in the paper. After it had burned out they found some bodies but not the main person. From

that day on I said I wouldn't ever get involved in any trouble again. Ever since it's always been known as, 'The Siege of Sidney Street'."

Finally, dishevelled and harassed, Joe and Frankie were back at Morris Street and the sounds of fury from the battle had died away in the distance and could no longer be heard.

The next day, Monday, Frankie's mother was cleaning the mirror when she noticed that the catapult was gone. Knowing that Frankie was still miserable and assuming that Joe must have found it and thrown it away she didn't give it another thought.

Joe wandered back with a newspaper the next morning after his usual unsuccessful bid at the Docks for labouring work. It was full of reports on the goings-on the day before. It seemed to him that it was all greatly exaggerated especially in the numbers quoted. Evidently Mosley had been denied his original route down Mile End Road by the protestors. Then a tram had broken down which led to a complete build up of other trams unable to get past, which in turn led to a total blockage. Some thought that this had been a deliberate act on the part of one of the drivers. The Blackshirt's march was then re-routed down Cable Street, the Metropolitan Police out in their thousands to ensure the way was kept clear so the march could go ahead.

The demonstrators, getting wind of this had hurried in their hordes to Cable street where they started setting up their barricade egging each other on with the shouted and written slogans, 'They shall not pass', and 'No Fascism here,' Down with Mosley and the Spanish anti- Fascist slogan 'Non passeron."

The battle raged for hours when all at once and inexplicably according to reports, Sir Phillip Game had suddenly given the order to withdraw. No one could understand it as the police had by then started gaining the upper hand.

Sir Oswald Mosley who had been waiting for the Police go-ahead with five thousand supporters near the Tower had been told that the way was closed. The march then had to go in the opposite direction where it effectively fizzled out without making any impact.

The casualty rate though had been very high. Hundreds of people injured, both police and civilians. Over one hundred people had been arrested, but fortunately nobody had been killed.

All Frankie had on his mind though, as he made his way to school was what had happened to the toy which had disappeared out of his pocket the day before, the loss of which was why he had been so upset.

At St Katharine's Dock early that same morning one dock labourer from Roscommon had been talking to another.

"Did yer see what happened there yesterday Paddy?"

"Aye of course. We were all there so we feckin' were. Air, well now wait'n oi'll tell ye. I tought we were losin', even with the feckin' mairbles we were rollin' under the ponies, but then I foinds this feckin' catapult on der flags so I starts foirin' the mairbles at de Gairds. Oi hits the one on the big pony, the one in chairge, right square on the feckin' kneecap and oi seen him'n his face screw up wi' pain. It must have nigh on kilt him! All of a sudden he looks loik he's had enoff and he signals the whoole lot back. Laeves the pony and gets helped back into his limousine cair."

"Soo we lives to foight another day Paddy. Jesus, Mary and Joseph! you saved the bloddy day!"

"Aye but not without that feckin' catapult to be shorr! Yer get the leader an' the rest of 'em collapses." He paused as he thought.

"Air noww" he went on finally, shaking his head and with an intake of breath, "It was loik the bleddy battle of Hairstings."

Chapter 37

The Man in the Newsreel – 1944

John walked down the Narrow-way of Mare Street in Hackney holding his father's hand. John was pleased with his new Cub Scout cap which mum had bought and he had the old scout jersey with the crumpled collar which Frank had outgrown and it was a little too big for him. Mum had un-picked Frank's badges from it, so there were now small patches which were slightly darker than the rest of the worn and faded garment. But John's polished brown shoes were smart and made up for it a bit. Joe had recently bought new leather and had repaired them using his father's last. He was good at that. Those smart shoes though were rather offset by John's socks one of which had a visible darn in the heel of it, done in a slightly different grey to the wool of the sock and they had both slipped down around the ankles so that they resembled two small concertinas. They would be tugged up one after the other before John entered the church when they arrived. However there wasn't much that could be done about the threadbare grey shorts with the baggy seat. They were the only pair he had and they had been everywhere. They had climbed trees, clambered over walls, been buried in the sand pit; and that was when they had belonged to Frank. Now that he had outgrown them the trousers would go through the ordeal all over again. The Kurtons were not much worse off than other families. Basically they had nothing but the bare essentials of life, but at least they had a decent roof over their heads. They were continually being told after all, that times were hard for most people but in 1940 Churchill had promised broad sunlit uplands ahead.

They stopped briefly at the sweet shop in Clarence Road where Joe bought his son two ounces of boiled peardrop sweets in a small white paper bag. John had almost drooled as he watched the woman with the thick-lensed glasses weigh them into the scoop of the scales on the counter, just held in equilibrium by the brass weight on the counterbalance. She held the upended jar with one hand while allowing the sweets to drop through the splayed out fingers of the other, one peardrop at a time. John looked to see if the pointer would go just over the two ounce mark. He always hoped, but once again it didn't. It sometimes did, but not by much. Joe handed over three ha'pence and his ration book and and the woman did something with

it, John didn't know what. Then she handed it back to John's dad.

Aged seven, John was a miniature version of his father , with fair curly hair, bright blue grey eyes and high cheek bones.

It was late Saturday afternoon and they were on their way to Confession at St John the Baptist in King Edward's Road. They often walked, it saved on fare money and it was only a mile and a quarter.

John had been to Confession only once before and he was worried about what he was going to say this time. Since his last confession he had taken a cream cracker without asking his mother. She hadn't been pleased when she found out, but he had been hungry, so he wondered whether it should be mentioned. He had played knock-down-ginger a couple of times, but that wasn't really his fault. An older boy had encouraged him to do it. Apart from those things he couldn't think of anything else he had done wrong. He couldn't even remember what he had eaten at school dinners each day, after he got home when his mother asked him, let alone any grievous sins he may have committed. He wondered if perhaps he should make up something fairly mild just to keep the priest happy. But not too much, as he didn't like the idea of kneeling for a long time doing unnecessarily tedious penance.

He had decided to stick to the cream cracker incident when his train of thought was suddenly interrupted by the tightening of his dad's hand. He looked up at his father and then almost immediately became aware of an ugly mechanical clacking sound from high up and some way off. In the pale blue sky framed between the Victorian upper floors of the shops on either side. John was seeing those upper floors for the first time stretching away towards the flying bomb almost guiding it in. He could just make out the black speck speeding straight towards them about two miles away doing four hundred miles an hour at two thousand feet. He had listened to grown-ups talking about those 'bloody contraptions'. Sometimes he felt compelled to ask a question or make a comment but in mid train-of-thought he was invariably told to "shush, be quiet." Even so he knew quite a bit about them.

There was no air-raid warning this time and no anti-aircraft fire because it was pointless shooting them down over the Metropolis as complete destruction in mid-flight couldn't be guaranteed. Damage to its guidance system or wing would only result in it falling at some different point to the one which fate had already decided.

403

Occasionally they would spot a Typhoon trying to shoot one down. Some were brought down over the open fields of Kent but inevitably many still got through and fell piecemeal. The Germans had found a way of bringing the war to the home front in an entirely unpredictable way. As fast as the RAF bombed the launch sites, the Germans set up others. At least you could hear these V1s coming, but rocket powered V2s travelled too fast and fell without warning and they were fired from mobile launchpads. There was always the hope that these terror weapons would overfly London and fall in the open countryside to the North. Some did, but on the whole, Londoners had to live with this deadly inconvenience twenty four hours a day. The fortified flat on the ground floor of their block or the air raid shelters in the grounds were not proof against a direct hit, also there was little warning and not enough time to get there.

Milsted House had already had some near misses. Joe had once seen a V1 through the living room window headed straight for their block and the same turmoil had ensued in his head as now. He had herded his family into the passage at the back of the third floor flat in a panic-stricken frenzy which communicated itself to the rest of the family. The bomb cut out and dropped a hundred yards short destroying the top end of Amhurst Road. Another fell on Birchington House on the other side of Pembury Road, killing seventeen people.

The promised land his parents had so optimistically arrived in, for Joe, had become hell on earth for the second time.

"Doodlebug!" Joe screamed clenching John's hand in a grip of iron. As it drew nearer, the people in the crowded shopping street ran about looking for cover. Joe dragged John by the arm bundling him into the safety of a shop doorway. But it was done with such over-protective force as he was jerked away from the view that John gulped and the peardrop which he had been sucking slid down his gullet. It was a tight fit and John felt momentary panic as a deep pain passed from his throat slowly and steadily down his chest. The V1 now about a mile away had reached the end of its journey as its pulse motor spluttered and cut out. From experience Joe and the people around them knew that at least they were safe now.

Joe, peering round the doorway saw it drop in the distance near London Fields as it plummeted to earth in a vertical dive. The sound reached them long after it had disappeared from view as a huge pall of smoke arose from the ground behind the built up conglomeration of houses, factories, trees and shops he could see in the distance.

Given the circumstances, people were naturally worried and disorientated by the events of the past five years, but Joe had an anxiety neurosis. He was panic stricken. He translated every event outside the norm into extra worry. Where was Sarah and young Frankie? and his mother, and his brother Frank, and Julie. Was Josie alright?

This was happening to him all the time, his nerves were shredded. He needed somebody to talk to and had thought about unburdening his worries to the priest but he couldn't bring himself to do it.

The responsibility he felt to his family, and to everyone else was enormous and yet there was now an unusual additional guilt bearing down on him. The image which haunted him came back again and again, and the thought of what he might have done but hadn't.

This most recent burden had been thrust upon him, without warning, in the cinema in Lower Clapton Road, a few weeks ago. He had seen a face and recognised it. During the Newsreel at the Kenninghall the stark realisation had hit him like a bombshell. He had seen that person before in newspapers but broken down into coarse black dots of varying size but the images were static and blurred and he had never made any connection.

But the face flickering on the screen was lifelike, older than the first time he had studied it, more self assured and in a totally different setting. It was moving speaking turning, front face, profile, mannerisms. The black hair was slightly different, the moustache more clipped but there was no mistaking the shape of the nose and chin and the cheekbones too, and above all, the piercing eyes. Somehow

the colour came through even on the black and white screen in front, which held him spellbound. Blue eyes, capable of delving into one's soul. The artist in Joe looked at that face on the screen, and imagined it as he had first seen it with a fuller walrus moustache, with a round cap and high buttoned tunic in field grey covered in mud. It was the same man. There was no mistaking the face of the German soldier he had first encountered at the farm in France. It was Theo Drifall, the humble messenger.

His stomach turned over and he felt sick. It was dark in the cinema. He closed his eyes and slowly recovered his composure as he took some more drags on his roll-up. Sarah, sat beside him puffing away on her Woodbine adding to the general fug in the auditorium forming an indicator of the passage of the flickering beams overhead cascading onto the screen in front. Sarah had absolutely no idea whatsoever of Joe's tumultuous feelings, her eyes were fixed on the screen.

During the intervening time between that evening in the pictures and now, he had bottled up this latest revelation alongside all the other thoughts and anxieties which he could never divulge. He realised then, almost with a sense of wonder, that he had once made decisions which may have directly led to subsequent earth-shattering events and to those which millions of people were living through right now.

On this Saturday afternoon, walking with his son, in his mind's eye Joe clearly recalled the fateful events that day. Theo Drifall, the man he saw last week on the screen had lied about his name. But why? Joe's anagrammatical mind made the deduction. What a mug he had been to fall under the sway of someone who had now been revealed to be ruthless, without scruple, and who excused his actions by blaming everything on fate. Joe had been no different to many others, taken in by the personality rather than the argument, by the earnestness, the rhetoric and magnetism rather than the content.

Even in the conversation he had later with Lieutenant Drea, he had espoused one of the German's theories. The quirky name the man had chosen must have been just a way of gaining some advantage, in his own mind, some measure of control over others.

Joe looked down Mare Street at the skyline and over London with its masses of tethered barrage balloons, the column of black smoke rising up into the atmosphere and the people timidly reappearing from their refuges. He had been given an opportunity in his lifetime to make a difference and change history and he hadn't been fated to take it. The tide had rolled upon its way unchallenged. Had he unwittingly helped all this to become a reality? But the false despatch – sparing Drifall's life – had it helped to end the Great War? and if so, had it made this war possible in some way. What if? – He would never know? Slight changes in life's actions had dramatic consequences.

So it was possible Theo Drifall had even been right, things do just happen. But then, would Joe have really killed him to prevent this? Could he have overcome his own scruples had he known he could affect the future? Too lazy to take the man prisoner at the time, he could have simply shot him and none of this would have happened.

Joe's self-recrimination as a confused failure was now complete. Too old to fight, no job and now a new mental burden weighing upon him. There were very few vestiges of his self respect left. He had been broken by the Great War and the nightmare continued, just one more weight in his burden of self loathing which he could never speak to anyone about. He couldn't even earn a living. Sarah was the family's breadwinner working in Barlow's metal box factory mind-numbingly examining the finished tins for sharp edges passing by on a conveyer belt. One of her job's redeeming factors was the camaraderie between the women there chatting and gossiping to the sound of 'Worker's Playtime' bellowing out from the Tannoy above the clattering machinery. She experienced a feeling of belonging in that atmosphere within the company structure. In these dangerous days management was still paternalistically concerned about the welfare of the people they had working for them. Before the war, fringe benefits including clubs, outings, annual company dinners and a subsidised canteen offset the tedium of the workers' tasks. Those benefits had been disrupted by the war, but nevertheless Sarah still gained most of her security from this communal atmosphere. All the employees lived locally. With her wages she supported four people, herself and Joe, Frank, fifteen and John, seven. Josie was by now away in the Land Army. When Sarah returned home at night she was very quiet.

To make up for his lack of status Joe worked hard around the flat. He was up at dawn raking out the ashes from the cast-iron range in the living room and rekindling the fire. If there was no wood to light it with, he folded old newspapers into tight strips plaiting them into substitute sticks. He knew exactly how to go about kindling the flames which started to fire the small pieces of coal he had placed on top. He adjusted the ventilation to its maximum until it took, then piled on more coal placing a folded newspaper in front of the ten or so open vertical slots in the front. This 'drew' the fire up the chimney as it promoted a rush of air, and then it was set for the day. His lateral thinking and resourcefulness had always been good. He got breakfast ready and washed up afterwards. He made endless cups of tea. But his routine was interrupted by feelings of panic. He kept looking anxiously out of the window. This morning he had gone with Sarah to carry the shopping bags for her, waiting patiently while she went to all the different counters in Sainsbury's. First the meat and bacon counter where they queued up, then the butter counter where the girls whacked and banged the raw butter into manageable portions, then to another counter for some pies. Young John loved those square meat pies, Sainsbury's was renowned for them. All the people in the different queues had their ration books to hand making sure they didn't exceed the small quantities of essential foodstuffs in short supply, which were officially allocated to each family, and person. Joe sometimes pumped the bellows for the organ at St Scholastica's. He often chatted to the Polish priest there in his own language. In that way Joe retained a small measure of individuality for those who could perceive it. While he did that, Sarah took part in the Mass. She embraced the Faith to the letter.

Long ago had been the time when Joe and Sarah first stopped discussing anything above the level of the mundane. Problems with John's birth had resulted in a doctor's advice to conceive no more children and thus avoid further difficulties. On Church advice therefor they had to sleep apart too as there was no other alternative. The influence of celibate Rome reached even into the bedroom. But more than that, Sarah seemed happy to embrace this new arrangement. Very gradually Joe noticed there were fewer and fewer spontaneous demonstrations of affection. She never kissed him when she went to work. She never touched him, she never praised him. He began to suspect she no longer loved him in the same eager way of youth. It had become more like the inanimate love between sister and brother. Whilst she may have been satisfied with a platonic relationship, he was not. But Joe had never been a person to force himself on anyone when he knew he wasn't wanted so he began to imagine that he himself was at fault. He naively wondered if perhaps he had lost some of his masculine appeal. So he made sure he shaved every day and did everything he could to please her and keep in her good books. But it made no difference. Once those basic, earthy feelings she used to have, which overrode some of his faults, had diminished, she was clearly irritated by him from time to time and there were no mitigating circumstances nor opportunities to put things right. While he saw her no differently to when he had first spotted her on that park bench, something had changed inside her. With his guilt-ridden religious background, and poor self-esteem he suffered further. She found an acceptable alternative also, in her religion.

He thought back to happier times before the Great War when he had been carefree and had met and loved a young woman passionately

with all his soul. Then war became imminent and it had gone wrong.
She had suddenly ended it. He never saw it coming but knew now
that she hadn't given him a chance but also that he must have been
wanting in some way. He had been brash in those days. Was that
the reason? He had had years to figure it out. If only he had done
this, if only he hadn't done that! The love of his life was looking for
something he was unable to give her. She may have believed she had
come to know his personality without allowing for the development
of his character which would only come with time. He himself had
been less calculating. He had just loved her unconditionally and could
see no flaws in her. But he had taken her for granted and something
hadn't worked, some little thing, some twist of fate. He knew her
father hadn't liked him, had taunted him once on his Polish ancestry.
The man hated all Poles, describing them as lazy – all twenty million
of them! Had he influenced his daughter? Was she just a materialist
who thought he was never going to make good? He was convinced
there must have been an aberration of fate, some sort of imperfection,
a cruel blip in the universal mechanics of how things were meant to
be. Why else would he still feel this way after years and years?

Joe's mind often came back to Sarah's previous sweetheart who had
been killed on the Somme. He had accidentally found the man's
love letters years later, and her replies, returned to her by his parents,
which Sarah had kept hidden away, and knew straight away that
Sarah had really loved that man. She had never expressed anything
like those same feelings towards him. All her grief gushed out when
he had confronted her. His war-shattered nerves couldn't cope and
any generosity of spirit he may have had deserted him. It merely
confirmed what he had always suspected, and then he couldn't find
in himself anything but frustrated rage. She threw in his face the name
Charlise Melbourne who he had been foolish enough to mention to
her once, thinking that she might understand, but she hadn't. So
what followed were ugly scenes of grief, comparisons and anger. The
marriage had come within a whisker of ending there and then. Sarah

blamed Joe for the drudgery of her existence when she had expected something more. There was yearning in Sarah for what might have been? She blamed Joe in a way for the repeated pregnancies which led to miscarriages, and Michael's infant death at two weeks. The death of baby Mary at eighteen months old had all but destroyed her, turning her in upon herself. His nerves erupted every time one of the children did something unexpected or naughty or made a sudden noise. He became heavy handed, if not brutal with them as he vented his frustrations and took it all out on them. So they had both married partners who were not their first choice. Who could know or understood the deeper workings of their subconscious minds? But the fact remained that now with the physical relationship gone there was not much left. Some instinct in Sarah, a psychological diminishing of the need for that feeling of closeness, now made it impossible for her to countenance any marital contact with Joe and he was reluctantly compelled to accept that. They were both into early middle age. So the arrangement now was that she had her own bedroom which she shared with Josie. Joe slept in one of the three single beds which occupied the other bedroom shared with his sons. This practical but hopeless situation left each of them with a fathomless void inside, but for different reasons, which they both knew would always be there. But this was how the marriage had worked out. Joe did his best to look after Sarah and help her as much as he could, whilst she became the breadwinner. When this man, shattered by his life and experiences, left an emotional and physical wreck, was unable to face the prospect of work even when it was available, the roles of husband and wife became reversed. Joe with his frequent debilitating headaches and the halting limp and shaking hand he had developed as a result of his war injury, didn't engender much sympathy in her. It was an attitude towards him which the children picked up on and copied. Except by John, it was his Dad whom he looked up to. John, who had grown up under the protection of his sister, knew nothing of any of this save to observe Sarah's sharp comments to her husband.

Joe's mind turned to his imminent visit to the confessional. Like John, he would quote a few minor misdemeanours to Father Patrick. He would be told to recite the Rosary and that would be about it.

Joe took off his cap which he wore winter and summer, He was conscious of his thinning hair. He was sweating. He unbuttoned his crumpled white shirt at the collar, just the one top button as he took out his white handkerchief from his pocket and wiped his forehead. He took off his jacket, revealing maroon braces, and held it folded over his left arm as they continued on their way. They had bought a paper yesterday and read that the Germans were steadily being pushed back and that victory was within sight. It sounded good but it did nothing to alleviate Joe's overwhelming anxiety and his low sense of self-worth. The mental burden he now carried, and the indifference of Sarah towards him, Josie's sudden coming of age and rebellious defiance and his eldest son Frank's contempt, had cowed him. The order of things had changed. He was no longer able to express his war-torn brutalised personality on Josie and Frank. They weren't having any more of it. He now found himself adjusting to a new sense of reality. It was another milestone, a new turning point in his life. The only two people in the world who treated him still with unconditional love and respect were his mother and John.

Weighing up the events which had happened all those years ago during the Great War, his part in them, and their consequences had left him questioning everything he had ever been taught. His Catholic faith was so ingrained that it led to an almost irreconcilable conflict in his mind about the very nature of things. Being forced to reassess everything made him feel worse than ever. He had striven, like his mother and grandfather before her to improve himself to make a better life for his family, to make sure they did not undergo the privations he had. But no matter how he had tried, whatever he had done, he never felt that he had succeeded. The best he had managed was to get better and better accommodation over the years. Starting off sharing with his mother, progressing into better and better rooms. The pinnacle of his success had been the attic in the Highway. But the roof had leaked and no amount of entreaties to the landlord brought much more than temporary remedies until at last it was Sarah who had prevailed upon the London County Council to rehouse them in one of their flats. In view of the size of their family the L.C.C had been happy to oblige. So the third floor end-of-balcony flat in Milsted House in Hackney it was to be then. He had been pleased. Hackney Downs was nearby and a Catholic church. He could have done with a job. But he had taken the first step in leaving the familiar streets of his parents and entering the vast unknown diaspora which existed outside that world.

How was one to measure success? Were material things necessary to the process of improvement? What was freedom? Never having been actually deprived of it made the answer difficult for Joe to figure out.

His parents' generation had all been engaged directly in a struggle for identity, for racial tolerance and for freedom of speech. Then they had come here, but those they had left behind continued to suffer.

The chilling facts were beginning to emerge from across the channel. He began to understand for the first time, based on tales of hardship which had been passed down the generations, the difference between discipline and obedience within society and indeed within the army, and oppression, servitude, and persecution in life. The first may have been necessary and tolerable the latter were neither. He owed much to his ancestors' refusal to accept the status quo, their bravery in taking the decisions they had and the humble aspirations he had inherited and passed on unwittingly.

Arriving with John for confession he had been on the verge of mentioning the Saunières farm incident to the priest but concluded that there was no point. Thus it would have been two of them burdened with it instead of one, even if the priest had believed him. Joe knew that given the same options again as he had faced in 1918 he would probably have made his choice no differently. It had been the right thing to do. So was it all pre-ordained by God? As he limped along with his son he went over the conversation he had had with that

German messenger in the war, years ago, and the one with Captain Drea at St Martin just after the end of the conflict. Had he stopped one war and started another? What passer-by would have imagined that thoughts such as these were going through the mind of this shabby inconspicuous man with the scruffy little boy? They walked on, Joe immersed in his thoughts. He wondered what would happen to the leaders on the losing side in this war if they were ever caught and held to account. Would they be treated as mentally ill and cured, or as evil and punished? He doubted they would simply be treated as irrelevant cogs in the mechanics of life. Is good and evil all in our own heads? Is there no such thing, just people who do things and things which happen? These were the arguments that had been put to him by the man with the moustache. He had listened with interest but realised now that thinking of that kind had been used as a justification for what was to follow. The abrogation of any personal responsibility. The war was nearly over and he and Sarah had taken their family away from the docks and so far they had come through the war safely. It had been a case of the ingrained survival instinct passed on through the generations. Joe knew he just had to come to terms with his rotten life. In a way he felt better.

The next day John went over to London Fields to where the bomb had made a huge crater in the grass. Joining some kids there, who had climbed into the fenced-off hole when nobody was looking, he found out that no-one had been hurt. John delved around until he found a small piece of jagged iron shrapnel and took it home in his pocket. He was thinking of swapping it for some cigarette cards he needed which his friend Steve had. It was a bit of a long shot. All the boys had shrapnel.

Chapter 38

Journey's End – 1957

Elzbiėta lay on her back in bed gazing up at the ceiling bewildered and apprehensive as she clutched at the floppy white sheet which came up to her chin. Its all enveloping folds tucked up to her neck were reassuring, despite the pain in her head, and she clutched it up around her neck with both fists clenched. She felt safer now. It seemed to her that this was her home and she could hear faint familiar voices but as she fought to make sense of her surroundings, the flickering shadows which came and went and the murmuring which rose and fell, a jumble of dream-like thoughts and images filled her head. In brief interludes of clarity, which lapsed more often than not into obscurity, she sensed fleeting impressions of other events in other times in far distant places.

She felt the thin white hospital sheet which they had covered her with. She had been there for some time it seemed to her but her memory was blurred and she didn't know quite why she was here and not in Clapton Common or should she have been in Smalenai? From time to time she heard other people cry out in delirium but she could understand nothing of what was going on.

As she lay there, day turned into night as the darkness slowly came and then seemed to last for a lifetime of memories before a faint glimmer of light appeared on the ceiling and the brightness increased with the sounds of activity and voices. She felt herself pulled about and seemed to remember accepting sips of water, trying to eat then having to refuse soft food. She wondered whether she was perhaps back home in Lithuania. Was it her mother who was tending her? She had no idea as she slipped from sleep into semi-consciousness and then back to the threshold of reality before it became night again. Then the same cycle was repeated. There was no pain, only confusion.

A hazy face appeared and a warm hand was placed on her forehead followed by a hot compressed cloth. Someone had come to soothe and wash her brow. She tried to tell her mother she was cold and to bring the quilt but her thoughts would not translate into words. She had done this before during the day from time to time but the crisply starched staff could not understand what she was saying. So she continued to lie there helpless. Often she didn't know they were there as they came and went on their rubber-soled shoes. Sometimes she could hear footsteps and somewhere in the depths of her mind she knew the sounds would mean a doctor or a visitor. A cacophony of steps moving along the ward always heralded visitors, always including her children.

Julija was here she sensed, and she could hear Pranas. "Julie do you think she is warm enough with just this sheet?" Was it he who dabbed her brow kindly and gently with the warming water soaked flannel? She wondered what had happened to her quilt with the intricate patterns that she had brought with her all the way from Smalenai. Then came a hazy thought of Planet Street and an image of Julija came into focus, coming home from the office with her first pay packet intent on buying new bed linen. "No Julija," she wailed, " I want to keep it." She had prevailed that time but later she hadn't. She pictured her precious quilt stuffed into a dustbin covered in ashes from the fireplace. Julija was running everything, and she wouldn't be swayed. Elzbiėta's comforting link with the past was gone and she was cold.

Her tears of sadness turned to those of joy as she began to make out her mother's voice now and she was happy. All was clear to her as she came to her senses. Her headache was gone and her mother was speaking again. Elzbiėta repeated the words as they were spoken and Julija's voice said. "She doesn't know what she's saying poor dear." "Of course she does Julija." she mumbled springing to her mother's defence. "Can you hear that?" Her mother's beautiful voice singing softly to her in Lithuanian filled the air, as only a mother could sing to a child. Feelings of peace and security washed over her in waves as she was overwhelmed by indescribable happiness. Once again, as ever, her mother was here at the right moment just when she needed her. She opened her eyes and suddenly there she was with arms out-stretched to welcome her into that familiar embrace.

There with her also was her father, and her brothers, sisters, her granny and grandpa. There were children there too. They had all come to see her, to make sure she was alright. She must have been sicker than she thought.

"Mama," she cried.

"I think she's gone," she heard someone say.

"No! I'm here, I'm here! She turned again and made her way to the people who now appeared with ever increasing clarity and close-ness. All else had been waiting, marking time. She was home, she was happy. It had all been for this moment. Now she understood it all.

Julie blinked back her tears and looked up at the stark ceiling of the hospital ward. When her eyes had cleared they had spotted the peeling paint and the windows in need of cleaning. From the first moment she had walked in here with her stick just about a week previously she had appraised the cleanliness and general condition of the hospital. She was irritated by it and made a comment to Frank in a whisper. Fastidiously she had always shunned dirt as if it reminded her somehow of her connection with a past life of deprivation.

The truth was that they had been given no choice when they first noticed their mother's erratic behaviour. A doctor's visit, and their mother's dementia was diagnosed. Then there was committal to this Mental Hospital in Epsom. It was the only option available at such short notice. It had all spiralled rapidly downhill from there and after a week had finally come to this moment.

A vital stage of her own existence was now coming to a close. The opportunities of normal life, which had presented themselves from time to time over the years, and been rejected, had already passed her by. Hers had been a life of devotion caring for her mother and brother within a compact three point family triangle. On another, higher, level there was a devotional trinity, It had been the object of her spiritual life, an almost evangelical obsession which spilled over into her relationship with the wider family.

Those had been the orbits of her two trinities revolving closely together in syncronicity. One of them was about to be broken.

"I'll get the nurse," muttered Frank, blinking back tears, as he walked down the ward.

Julie looked at her mother and rested the back of her hand gently against the care lined cheek. It was still warm but was becoming paler she imagined. She brushed back a wayward tress of Elzbiėta's hair and spoke lovingly in Lithuanian, beseeching the blessings of Mary and Jesus on her dear mother's head.

At the funeral Mass in St Casimir's the rites of the Holy Catholic church were administered according to religious custom by Father Jonas Sackevičius. The middle-aged priest, was an exile himself from his own country. He had lived in his apartment at the church since the end of the Second world War, administering to the needs of his ex-patriot flock swelled by a wave of new arrivals fleeing the Russians. And there were the English Lithuanians, first second and third generations. But even here, in this shabby, grimy corner of post war London, painted on the columns on either side of the altar were folk designs in the Lithuanian rural style, reminders of the home country. Nobody really knew what they represented exactly but they were uniquely ethnic, a little flavour of Lithuania in a faraway place.

After the Funeral Mass, as the coffin was carried down the aisle to the waiting hearse, a song began to be heard from an unseen singer in the gallery delivered in a beautiful Lithuanian Baritone voice. All the pathos of the Baltic Catholic faith was encapsulated there in that heartachingly moving lament.

The cortège; the hearse and the following black cars containing relatives and friends, made its way eastwards through the streets at a respectful walking pace preceded by a man on foot in black tailed coat and a top hat, until it reached the main road when it paused briefly to allow the walker to climb into the hearse's passenger seat. It then sped on its way along Cambridge Heath Road and Mare Street, through Hackney and out across the marshes, taking the coffin with its precious occupant on its final journey to St Patrick's cemetery.

At the interment in Leytonstone and despite Josie's continuous grief, Frank, ever dry and pragmatic said, as they were getting back into the funeral car afterwards, "No point in going home really, we've all got to come back here again."

That comment was a spontaneous, light-hearted but deep-rooted piece of inescapable philosophical logic.

The unexpected remark drew a subdued wry laugh from the mourners amidst the solemnity.

They were indeed eventually, all to be together again.

The burial plot was named 'Trinity.'

Chapter 39

Legacy

More than seventy five years after the so-called 'Battle of Cable Street,' Joe's grandson Matt was in an Essex dentist's waiting room. Idly picking up a dog-eared Sunday supplement, he leafed through it looking with a critical eye at the design of the advertisements and the quality of printing. He went through the prelim pages to see who had done the origination. A lifetime spent in the privileged world of the Reprographics industry made it automatic. He continued to flip through looking at headlines and cartoons; most were no longer topical. Skimming past an article on Africa's vanishing wildlife, which he couldn't bear to read, he stopped briefly at the crossword. Cryptic crosswords were a tradition in their family for some unknown reason. He glanced at the first clue; *1 across, Break mach three and smash the beggars cry, audible, at a town pub. 3,7,4.* He looked at it, from different angles but he had no pen. Just holding one helped in the thinking process as well as for unravelling the letters in the blank margin. You had to get into the mind of the compiler and tune in to the same wavelength. It must mean something to someone, but he was struggling. The answers were always achievable. There was a list of winners from the previous week below. He was never quite as good as his grandad had been so he sometimes took as long as a couple of hours to do something like the Daily Telegraph. The thought of the impending treatment was putting him off. He allowed himself one more go; *16 down, Fail school subject – but be remembered. 2, 4, 2, 7.* It was easy and he got it right away. Matt then quit while he was ahead. Flicking on through the magazine, an article caught his attention. It was about a civil disturbance in London before the War. A byline to the piece showed that it was written by a Jewish Communist who had been there in the East End, in Cable Street on Sunday 4th October 1936. The article set out;

'*How important the event had been and how it had remained ever since inescapably in the psyche of all who had taken part. The importance of thwarting Fascism wasn't lost on the Jews and the Irish and indeed the English people who had made a stand against Sir Oswald Mosley and his Fascist Blackshirts. Had he secured some sort of foothold in the East End then the whole train of events on the world stage could have been so very different. It could have even led to an alliance with Hitler against Communist Russia had Mosley prevailed. The Jews alone would never have succeeded in stopping him had it not been for the working class solidarity shown by the entire population of the East End, with the might of parts of the Establishment and certainly the Police, ranged against them*'.

Matt recalled there was now a mural near the site commemorating the event. He wondered what that writer made of it all later on, once Nazism had been defeated and even Communism itself had collapsed.

This family, with one exception, had never been left-leaning but Matt would always remember with clarity one afternoon in his youth, when visiting his grandmother's flat on his way home from the College of Printing with a copy of the Daily Worker under his arm. She was incensed out of all proportion and had insisted in no uncertain terms that he immediately remove it from her house, or she would destroy it. She meant it too. At the time, it was intriguing, almost amusing, how anti-Left she was. Matt could still picture his uncle's smirk but John hadn't said a word, after all, he had to live there.

Remembering that the family had, all of them, once lived around the scene of that action near Cable Street he wondered if and why they were reluctant to get involved? What had Grandad made of it? he wondered. He couldn't remember ever hearing him mention it. It was an important event which hadn't gone down in history as far as this family was concerned. And yet they had been there, on the spot! Why were they so passive? He threw the magazine down as he was called in to the adjacent torture chamber by a nurse.

A bit later he left the Shenfield dentist's surgery, sixty pounds lighter, teeth cleaned and polished by the jolly Afro Caribbean hygienist. In talking to her, when he had been able to, he had found out that she came from Romford, which was becoming more and more like an uprooted old East End, full of ex-patriot, mainly white, Cockneys and their children. Her family, unlike Matt's which had taken three generations to move upmarket, had done it in only two.

His main concern today was the TV he was going to buy. Driving in the direction of Romford he pulled into the retail park at Gallows Corner and parked his car in a vacant space near a giant caravan selling drinks and food. He walked towards the massive aircraft hangar which was Comet. The large snacks wagon would provide the land mark which would guide him back when he came out. That was its only use as far as he was concerned – as a point of reference. The unhealthy grub they served up there was hashed up by girls in white hygienic overalls. The thought of the food being laughed, shouted and sung over during its preparation was enough to make him cringe. When the sun shone, their verbal comments could be seen descending over it all through the sunbeams.

He knew he tended towards snobbishness, acquired gradually over the years. The air of mild superiority he had always seemed to have was inherited. He knew it, but justified it by calling to mind the quotation from his one-time work colleague Harry Levitt, at the Curwen Press years before, when Matt accused him of being a snob,

"What's wrong with a bit of snobbery?" Harry had retorted, to which Matt had ever since been unable to find an adequate reply. So he fully embraced it and came round to Harry's way of thinking, that snobbery did indeed help to keep standards up.

The glass doors of the store opened as he approached them welcoming him inside to a vast Aladdin's cave of electrical equipment.

He was pounced on quickly by an Asian assistant.

"Are you alright there?"

This salesman was one of many young Asians who were hovering, dressed in suits. Matt noticed they seemed to be in the majority here. They meant to get on, but he felt vaguely threatened by these new arrivals to his country, although he couldn't fault their work ethic, running garages, newsagents or other enterprises and working in the National Health Service. Asians had strong family ties, were bright, knew their stuff and worked hard and prospered. But present day reality conflicted with the rose-tinted memories of those halcyon, safe days of his childhood spent amidst the white working class of 1950s Hackney. Anyone with a dark skin then was a novelty which drew a great deal of attention, and was discussed excitedly at school. Social change had developed into a challenge to his sense of security.

There was little choice but to accept it. All of these Asian assistants were at least second generation. They spoke as he did, with the same Thames-Estuary intonation, a milder form of Cockney.

People like Matt had never had any choice in these matters. All the political parties had given this open-door policy their blessing with very few dissenting voices. It appeared that none of it had been thought through. There were checks and balances built into the system but some were overridden by membership of the EU and the safeguards which survived became more and more hazy with each successive government. The displaced persons from war-ravaged 1946 Europe, including those who fled from the Baltic States annexed again by Russia, and the Jews who had survived the Holocaust, were not an issue. Their numbers were proportionate. The odd Russian ballet dancer claiming asylum, or the victims of the Hungarian uprising who managed to flee here were not going to present social problems. Within a few generations they would be assimilated. In the future their origins would only be betrayed by their strange names. Their culture was broadly the same as ours. The 21st century was another matter entirely. Large areas of British cities had been taken over by an alien way of life which demanded more and more concessions.

The perception which emerged into the public domain from the ghettos, was that the onus was on Britain to adapt to them. Added to this now was the influx of Poles, Lithuanians and others from the European Community in large numbers, about which we could do nothing. None of them was fleeing political oppression. They were economic migrants. Matt pondered on whether there really was such a pressing need for more Big Issue sellers or car-wash operatives, camped in Sainsbury's car park, bringing their skills all the way from Africa, here to the UK. Given his own origins, of which he was aware, Matt had never thought of himself as bigoted but he sensed that lines should be drawn, convinced that the sudden increase of population couldn't be good. There was a powerful viewpoint among liberal activists, and in the news media, against any form of criticism of ethnic minorities. It was never to be discussed. It became incorrect even to imply questioning of the accepted view. However, there was most definitely a groundswell of subterranean public opinion which took the opposite view. Yes, this attitude was definitely there among the benevolent, welcoming, reasonable British public, and in particular among older people who saw the fabric of their districts changing.

Both views were easily understandable. On the one hand there was a strong case reasoning that even if the slightest thought of dissent, or a culture of racial jokes, was allowed to flourish it could evolve into something more serious – what had occurred in Nazi Germany happening again was unthinkable. But conversely, the swamping of an indigenous culture by an alien one without proper well thought -out integration and limits on numbers, would be disastrous.

The politically correct were not justified in smartly nipping everything they perceived to be racist in the bud. The spin-off from political correctness was stifled debate and more resentment. Accepting establishment political expediency uncritically, well meaning though it may have been, was hard.

No left-leaning legislation nor education would ever really sway Matt from his gut feeling. His Lithuanian ancestors had kept a very low profile and blended in. Why wouldn't the current wave of migrants do the same, instead of being so militant? It was to be hoped that it might very well be different for later generations who would grow up never having known anything else. But in reality he doubted it. The ideal melting pot didn't exist, but racial factionalisation did. The cultural differences were too great when it came to people from the middle-east or the Asian sub-continent. When walking in London, the large numbers of foreigners who occupied the pavement, or those with whom he rubbed shoulders, and shared space in an underground carriage, produced a sense of unease in Matt. Being genuinely interested though he did look at the different racial types, and tried to guess where they came from. Did this make him a racist? Of course he didn't believe so. Almost every foreigner he had ever met he had liked. In his younger days he socialised with friends from the Caribbean, went to parties where he had been the only white person. His friend Errol from Jamaica had come on holiday with his circle in the Sixties. He had had two Asian girlfriends back then. His idealistic younger self had strongly supported the principle of immigration and defended it from all attacks by those he regarded as ignorant people. He was pilloried for it by his elders, and others, earning himself, from the people at work, the nickname 'The White Knight.'

Ever so gradually however, bit by bit over many years, he had come to the viewpoint that if we allowed our own way of life to be swamped, by another, it could be a mistake which would backfire on future generations. Perhaps all this was caused by a shift of world population brought about by global warming which had been predicted for years? The problem ultimately seemed to lie in the State's propensity for being welcoming to every refugee who wanted to come here. With each additional wave, wages were driven down, most obviously for the underclass at the bottom of the social scale. – who tended to be also those with limited opportunities of self expression.

That could well have been a deliberate policy employed by the Establishment to depress wage levels without fear of a coherent response, assisted by something in the British psyche which made us so accommodating? The tradition that we must live up to our stereotypical image of tolerance perhaps wasn't such a cliché.

The seeds of destruction, one main voice had claimed early on, were being sown. But there was by now a large immigrant electorate involved, so public words had to be chosen carefully and that lone voice had to be silenced – it was a vote-loser.

Matt considered it was the final irony to now see the descendants of black people interviewed in the media proclaiming that immigration should be curtailed? The expression of their view was somehow more allowable than his, which was the same. It was the matter of their colour which allowed them to speak. Added to that was a certain irony at the thought of Polish craftsmen migrating here and effectively building their own accommodation.

"Can I help you?"

Shocked away from his reverie, Matt was at least pleased he hadn't been addressed as 'Mate' when 'Sir' was a form of address of the past.

"Yeah, please! I'm looking for a TV"

"Any particular one?"

"One not made in Japan?"

In response to the assistant's quizzical look, Matt went on to explain,

"If I have a choice I try not to buy anything Japanese. Whaling and Sushi bars! They're trawling sealife to extinction without any thought for the world's ecology. E mailing the Japanese Ambassador draws no response. So this is my form of protest."

Suddenly he knew he was sounding intense. He ceased his monologue. The salesman just looked at Matt with bemusement as he glanced around the vast floorspace filled with electrical goods of every description mostly made in Japan and China.

"You've got some hopes, it's a global economy," he might have replied if he'd been prepared to possibly lose his company a sale.

The tag on the front of his shirt showed him to be 'Naseem Khan – Sales advisor.' and although he was aware he was dealing with a boring old codger he guessed he was probably one with some disposable income. He came into contact with all types in this store. He couldn't give a toss about whales. On this old bloke's point of principle Naseem's looked at Matt with blank incomprehension. It was a subject he had never bothered to consider. "What's he talking about, the silly old fool?" He thought.

"What's the difference between Plasma and LCD? Can you talk me through it – I will be needing some other stuff too."

They walked around together and Naseem showed him the different choices. During the course of their discussion the assistant explained how high-definition worked as Matt tried to get his head around it.

He had meant to do all the stores first before he bought – Currys Digital, Richer Sounds, Stellisons, John Lewis. Comet was the first shop he'd come to. He wasn't really looking forward to trailing around though and then he would have had to go back again to the cheapest shop and the extra petrol he would have to use might offset any savings he might make. He could have checked it all out online but at that stage he didn't know which TV he wanted in the first place.

"Can you beat, internet prices?" he asked. It turned out that the prices across the internet varied, but the thought of such a big purchase arriving at the door faulty in some way and the aggravation in sending it back was another sales factor which Naseem made sure he used. He was mentally rubbing his hands together. This was what he was good at. It was his day-to-day job and he was easily capable of making this old guy feel he was getting some sort of deal.

Forty five minutes later Matt walked away with his TV in a cardboard box on a trolley. It had been assembled in Holland with electronic parts mostly made in the Far East, many in Japan. Stacked on top of that was another box containing a smoked glass stand reduced by £20 and two free DVDs containing films which he wouldn't normally have bought. They had hundreds of them out the back gathering dust. The stand was old stock they were getting rid of anyway.

Matt was happy with his bargain. He considered that he wasn't so peasant-like that he would be bothered to go to the other shops just to save a couple of quid. He didn't really need to. He wouldn't be going without anything as a result, whatever the cost of it was.

Naseem wasn't too bothered. He wasn't on commission. He just wanted to keep his job at the very least and at best progress to manager. The more sales he clocked up, the better, but the loss of one sale wouldn't dent his percentage much.

As Matt came out he saw a car being loaded with a washing machine by two East End types. They had got it in as far as they could then discovered they couldn't close the boot lid. They stood there staring at it, one munching a beefburger and the other tentatively sipping at

 a polystyrene cup, as if somehow they could make the machine fit into the car by willpower alone. Or perhaps they waited for inspiration. But they looked blank as they ate and drank their refreshments.

Matt, still basking in that glow of superiority that came with getting the deal, butted in, offering his advice together with some string which he went over and got from his car. He helped them lower  their boot lid as far as it would go and tie it to the bumper.

"Top of the range?" Matt commented somewhat cheekily, looking at their gleaming washing machine.

"Yeah, the missus got fed up wiv the colour of the old one and sent us dahn 'ere fer anuvver one."

"This one's a different shade o' white," his mate added, smiling. Matt laughed. Amazing how the Cockney sense of humour carried over from one generation to the next.

"Got far to go?" Matt asked. "Nah, 'arold 'ill," came the reply. "Not far then, better take it easy over the potholes, Bloody Councils – useless! Dunno how strong that string is. How long have you been there – in 'arold 'ill," Matt asked, dropping the aitches the same as them and addressing his question to the elder of the two in his effort to maintain the rapport.

"Me mum an' dad came there in the seventies."

"Where were you before you moved?" Matt enquired.

"Lea Bridge Road, – Dja know it mate? Long straight road, runs across the marshes between 'ackney 'n Leyton."

"Know it? I was done for speeding down it, twice! – years ago in a Triumph Spitfire. Once by two coppers on Thunderbirds and then again by a pair of them – up for a race, not wearing their hats in their unmarked Daimler Dart."  Matt recounted the story of the perceived Police duplicity and then followed up with,

"Don't you ever fancy going back? Some of it's becoming quite gentrified round there, but get in quick, prices are going up fast."

"You must be effin' joking," responded the other one. "Not that bit. I lock me bleedin' car doors driving frough there naah. There's an effin' mosque at eiver end of it. Used to be factories. It's like a bleedin' foreign country. We should've gone to Australia when we 'ad the chance. Some of us fought of goin', but in the end we didn't."

Matt in his turn empathised and quoted muggings and robberies that he knew about and the crime that was now the norm around his old Hackney stamping ground. But then he added, "England ain't such a bad place, even now, still a green and pleasant land if you know where to go, and if you can keep away from those 'areas' that've gone downhill." He made speech marks in the air with the first finger of each hand. "I don't think I could stand the wrench of leaving it, even for Australia. Imagine your heartbroken parents, your family and everything you've known. It doesn't bear thinking about. Anyway, apart from, ' *Them,*' it all came good here." Then, what with the anxiety of getting home with their goods and the subject pretty well exhausted, the conversation fizzled out as they had nothing much more in common that they were aware of, except for those topics. The two men slung the detritus from their recent snack under the nearest car and went off on their way with farewells born of the friendliness of a common cause. So clearly it wasn't just Matt then who felt the need to talk and bemoan current trends. In a perverse way he enjoyed these conversations with older ex-East-enders. It often came back to that same old topic. They were like kindred spirits meeting in a mutually hostile environment and banding together with talk about things they held in common Those meetings often developed in the same way. They all needed this link with the past. Something to do with understanding and celebrating where they'd come from, and what and who they identified with. It was simply tribalism. They shared, so they thought, common origins.

It was reassuring to travel back to the past even if only verbally and in memory. There was a comfortable nostalgic pleasure in it. Matt thought for a minute and wondered what his wife would say, or his daughters if they could have heard him spouting off like that. They would probably have called him a racist. But he knew in his heart of hearts he wasn't that at all – just an objector to the way things had become, someone who wanted things back as they were before. Selectively anyway! But the next generation was already moving on.

As he heaved his new TV into the back of his car Matt couldn't help pondering on how shallow that guy's wife must be who changed her kitchen stuff on a whim. Matt, brought up in austerity, hated waste. So this was how far they had all come. Even the lower stratum of society. They departed from the ghetto and another different lot moved in. Now, with their own houses, loans for essentials which had once been luxuries, credit and debit cards, frequent dining out, shopping trips to Lakeside or Bluewater and holidays abroad, they seemed to want for nothing. This new material security had made worthwhile the previous sacrifices of others. Matt often wondered where it would end but he was a part of it himself. The whole thing fuelled itself, and revolved around consumption. The cards that Matt had been dealt had been good. He had done well at his trade and that had laid the foundations for his childrens' upbringing. He and his wife had encouraged them all down the road of education, art, music, sport, respect for the environment and they had emerged as people with the right values. Even so, their views did vary slightly from his, as did their experiences. They had never known disruptive events nor sudden change. Never endured wars, and had suffered no deprivation, neither had they ever been hungry.

So of course they *could* be more liberal in their outlook on life, not having known anything different. For them, the terms 'peasants,' 'working class,' and 'unions' were anachronisms from another age.

The ancestors were now shades and shadows of the past but their humble aspirations had finally been achieved. This was freedom.

If those who had come before could see now these material benefits, enjoyed by their descendants, the results of their own vision and aspirations, maybe they would think it had all been worth the struggle. Their histories; the persecution, the ceaseless toil, the hardship and sacrifice, the infant mortality and making ends meet, the heartache and the fighting and dying wouldn't only be justified or symbolised by this six hundred quid television would it? Weren't there indeed other benefits too? Human benefits?

Now, all of those actions and deeds and the old way of life were mostly deleted from present-day family memory. The passed-on legacy still lingered vaguely, but was faded and heavily obscured in the collective consciousness, in this magical place which those who came before had always thought of as the Promised Land.

The End

Text & Cover Design, Typography & Graphics – by SDP Shenfield, UK

WS - #0014 - 080720 - C0 - 216/138/24 - PB - 9781784563912